THE FIRST STRAND IS DRAWN

THE TEST O' FIRE

The Red Guards lifted their claymores and began to run towards them. The witches were in very real danger, for if they were taken, they would be burnt to death.

Meghan gripped Isabeau's arm. "Use the flame as a weapon," she said. "Now, Isabeau!"

Instinctively Isabeau threw a great ball of flame and was shocked to the core when soldiers fell screaming. Shaking with an inner chill, she threw another and another. Jorge huddled by her side, not even trying to protect herself as arrows rained towards them from the crossbowmen.

Isabeau spun to see the soldiers very close now, the Mesmerd hovering right behind them. Rearing up against the billowing clouds, it was more than seven feet tall, with a face of inhuman beauty, and huge gauze wings. Its clusters of eyes shimmered with iridescent light. Isabeau found her gaze being drawn irresistibly to those huge glittering eyes, and her fire faltered and dropped.

"Do no' look at it!" Meghan shouted. "Do no' let it breathe on ye."

With a shriek Isabeau scrambled backwards, slipping and falling. . . .

The Witches of Eileanan

KATE FORSYTH

RoC
A ROC BOOK

ROC
Published by New American Library, a division of
Penguin Group (USA) Inc., 375 Hudson Street,
New York, New York 10014, USA
Penguin Group (Canada), 90 Eglinton Avenue East, Suite 700, Toronto,
Ontario M4P 2Y3, Canada (a division of Pearson Penguin Canada Inc.)
Penguin Books Ltd., 80 Strand, London WC2R 0RL, England
Penguin Ireland, 25 St. Stephen's Green, Dublin 2,
Ireland (a division of Penguin Books Ltd.)
Penguin Group (Australia), 250 Camberwell Road, Camberwell, Victoria 3124,
Australia (a division of Pearson Australia Group Pty. Ltd.)
Penguin Books India Pvt. Ltd., 11 Community Centre, Panchsheel Park,
New Delhi - 110 017, India
Penguin Group (NZ), cnr Airborne and Rosedale Roads, Albany,
Auckland 1310, New Zealand (a division of Pearson New Zealand Ltd.)
Penguin Books (South Africa) (Pty.) Ltd., 24 Sturdee Avenue,
Rosebank, Johannesburg 2196, South Africa

Penguin Books Ltd., Registered Offices:
80 Strand, London WC2R 0RL, England

Published by Roc, an imprint of New American Library, a division of Penguin Group (USA) Inc. Previously published in an Arrow Book edition by Random House Australia Pty. Ltd.

First Roc Printing, July 1998
20 19 18 17 16 15 14 13

Printed in the United States of America

Isabeau the Foundling

Isabeau swung her pack over her shoulder and strode down the track, her eyes roaming over the ground as she searched for the first unfurling of leaf and flower through the muddy snow. It was only a few days till Candlemas and the beginning of spring, and since it was the first fine day in months, Isabeau had spent all day digging and cutting, filling her herb bag with roots, leaves and early flowers.

Although the sun on her neck was warm, snow still glittered on the jagged peaks above her and lay piled in the shadows below the massive trees. It had been a bitter winter and Isabeau was glad to be out in the meadows again, breathing deeply of the sweet air and calling the creatures of the valley to her. Animals of all kinds were stirring as the sap flowed again in the stem, and they gamboled about her feet or twittered to her from the bushes, tempting her to lay down her spade and knife and play with them. She smiled and spoke to them in their own language, but did not stop, knowing she was tired and the light already fading. She must be home before nightfall. Although the hidden valley was almost impossible to find by chance, these mountains were dangerous, the valley's teeming life temptation to hungry hunters, whether human, beast or fairy.

The path led down through the trunks of ancient, towering trees. Through the entwined branches came glimpses of the rocky finger of Dragonclaw, rearing above the lesser mountains around it, its narrow tip dusted with snow. Isabeau paused at the crest of the hill, stretching her aching back and enjoying the spectacular view. The loch below her stretched toward the eastern rim of the valley bowl, coiled over the edge and fell hundreds of feet to the valleys below. Above the far distant hills, the two moons were rising. Magnysson bronze in the sunset sky, Gladrielle lavender. There was a faint tang of smoke to the air and Isabeau stepped forward eagerly, realizing her guardian must have returned while she was out in the meadows. Meghan had been away for several weeks now, and Isabeau had begun to wonder whether she would return in time for her sixteenth birthday, only two days away.

Reaching the base of one of the massive trees that stood around the loch, Isabeau tucked her spade more securely into her belt and began to climb swiftly and easily. Soon she was forty feet off the ground and reaching out for the gossamer ropes that hung between the branches, almost invisible in the twilight air. She swung out of the tree's branches and into the next, hands clinging to the ropes that formed a bridge from trunk to trunk. As always, she cursed her guardian's obsession with secrecy, which was what made the entry in and out of their home so difficult. "It does no' take long for paths to appear, Isabeau, ye ken that. We must leave no sign that anyone bides here, for that could be our undoing." If Isabeau left even a bent twig behind her, she was scolded thoroughly and made to scrub out the evil-smelling pot in which Meghan made her potions.

With a twist of her body she swung into the branches of the biggest tree in the forest, which grew on a small rocky outcrop above the loch. Its roots were protected by thorns, starred now with white buds. Clinging to one of its thick branches, Isabeau paused to look around her. It was almost dark, and the waters of the loch below were black. In the east, the moons were fully risen, and in their trail a red comet had appeared, pulsing with life and rising steadily across the sky. Isabeau stared at the Red Wanderer with mixed awe and anxiety, for the comet had appeared six days earlier and there had been no one to ask what it meant. She knew there were rites to be performed at the rising of the comet, but for the life of her she could not remember what they were. It could not be important, though, for if it had been Meghan would have told her what to do before she left. Meghan would never forget a date in the witches' calendar, no matter how rarely it occurred.

Balanced precariously some sixty feet off the ground, Isabeau found the secret catch with her fingers and swung open a door in the huge trunk. She threw her pack in before maneuvering her own long body through the narrow entrance.

"It's grand for Meghan," she muttered, as she had ever since she had grown to her full height, "but if I get any fatter, I will no' be able to squeeze through this bloody door anymore."

Isabeau was standing in a small, round room, its rough walls lined with uneven shelves fitted in wherever the knots of wood allowed. These shelves were filled with jars and bottles, while dried plants and the shriveled bodies of bats, chameleons and drakes hung from the low ceiling. The room was so small that Isabeau could touch both walls with her hands. In the center of the floor was a small hole with a ladder that lead to a lower story. Again Isabeau had to drop her pack through before squeezing through herself.

Each successive room was slightly larger than the one above and each had a hole in the floor with a ladder that lead to the next. By the fourth floor, the rooms were hung with tapestried curtains and their shelves lined with books and curious objects—a crystal ball on clawed feet, a yellow skull, a globe of the world, a piece of twisted driftwood. The fifth floor was Isabeau's bedroom, and most of the space was taken up by a narrow bunk hung with blue velvet curtains with golden tassels, another remnant of her guardian's mysterious past. The sixth floor was Meghan's bedroom; thick books were piled on all the shelves and on the floor, and a carved wooden chest stood against one curved wall. Isabeau wondered yet again how her frail guardian had ever managed to get the massive chest into the tree, not to mention all the other furniture.

As she bent to swing down into the lowest floor, where the kitchen and storerooms were, she heard a murmur of voices. Instantly she froze; then as silently as she knew how, lay flat on the floor so she could peer through the hatchway to see who was within.

The ground floor was much larger than the rooms above, since the tree had grown up against a natural outcrop of stone that held within a small cavern, concealed by the trunk and roots. Subsequently, living wood providing the northern walls, hand-smoothed rock the rest, with the fireplace built into a crack which provided a natural chimney. The roots of the tree provided a tangled ceiling, with every nook and cranny serving as a shelf or hidey-hole. Hidden ingeniously behind two of the shelved walls were the entrances to secret passages, one leading to a hidden cave by the loch, the other into the forest.

Craning to see beyond the hanging bunches of herbs and onions, Isabeau saw Meghan sitting in her curious high-backed chair in front of the fire. In her lap was a blue book, its pages filled with her thin, spidery writing and drawings, and in one hand she held a jewel that glittered with golden fire.

"So do ye recognize my mystery emblem? I am sure I have seen it before somewhere, but I canna find it in any o' the books I have here . . ." Suddenly she stopped, and drew back her hand, tucking it under her plaid. "Come down, Isabeau. I've been expecting ye back for an hour or more. Did ye find any trefoil?"

Relieved to see it was only her guardian, Isabeau swung herself down lightly. "Aye, two lots," she responded.

"I hope ye did no' pull it out by the roots," the wood witch said irritably, as she closed the book and tucked it down the side of her chair. A diminutive woman, her iron-gray hair was bound into a long plait that hung over the edge of the chair, pooling onto the floor below. A white streak began at her left brow and could be seen twisting through her plait all the way to its end. Her familiar, a donbeag called Gitâ, perched on the low rafters above her head, nibbling daintily on a nut he held in his paws.

"O' course no'! Ye taught me better than that," Isabeau replied, dumping her pack on the handmade wooden table.

"Ye must be hungry. We were just having some tea—pour yourself a cup."

We? Isabeau jerked upright in surprise, and only then saw the other woman sitting in the chair on the other side of the fire, half obscured by the flickering shadows. It had not occurred to Isabeau that Meghan had been speaking to anyone but Gitâ, for in all the sixteen years that Isabeau had lived in this valley, no one had ever visited them before. The valley was far away from any town or village, and lay right below Dragonclaw, home of the dragons. No one trespassed lightly on land over which the shadows of dragons passed.

The woman was staring back at her and Isabeau felt uncomfortable under her intent gaze. She was pale-skinned with black hair and green eyes, and was wearing a brown dress with a wooly plaid wrapped over her shoulders and across her chest. Her hair was very long and very untidy. It flowed over her shoulder and hung toward the floor, tied here and there with leather thongs.

"So this is your wee lassie," the woman said. Her voice had a pronounced accent, drawn out and very thick. "What a scarecrow!"

Isabeau was immediately aware of her stained breeches, the twigs and leaves in her matted hair, the dirt under her fingernails. She scowled. "I've been out hunting herbs all day. It's hot and dirty work!"

"That it be," the woman said calmly. "Come here. I want to see ye."

Isabeau did not move, only glared at the stranger suspiciously. Meghan rose stiffly to her feet and lit the candles on the mantelpiece and table with her finger. Warm light flickered up, and after a moment Isabeau moved reluctantly closer.

"Come sit here, lassie," the woman said, and Isabeau kneeled on the floor by her feet, frowning a little but compelled by the serene authority in the strange woman's voice.

At first, because of the blackness of her hair and the smoothness of her face, Isabeau had thought the woman was young. Now she was not so sure. Although few lines marred the pale skin, there was an undeniable maturity in her gaze and under her eyes were dark circles. There was a sense of weariness about her, of long roads traveled and long years endured. It was hard to keep her gaze steady under those calm, searching eyes, but Isabeau stubbornly refused to look away.

"I am glad indeed to meet ye, Isabeau," the woman said at last. "My name is Seychella and I'm an auld friend o' your guardian's. I traveled long and hard to get here—it's been a tiring few months."

Isabeau wondered why the woman would make such a journey just to visit their hidden valley. Although beautiful, there was not much here except trees and rocks, and she would have had to find her way through the deep ravines and gorges that made the Sithiche Mountains so impenetrable. Isabeau realized that Meghan's unexpected absence the last few weeks must have been due to the expected arrival of Seychella. Meghan must have gone to meet the stranger-witch and guide her back through the labyrinth of caves that was the only entrance to the valley. So why was Seychella here? One did not undertake such a long and difficult journey to make a social call.

Isabeau's interest quickened, for her birthday was only a couple of days away. In the days when the Coven was a power in the land, acolytes were Tested on their sixteenth birthdays for acceptance into the Coven as apprentices. Most acolytes would have spent the previous eight years at the Theurgia being taught many of the basic principles of magic after undertaking the First Test of Power at the age of eight. Isabeau knew that acolytes won their first ring and the witch's ceremonial dagger after the Second Test of Power, to indicate their status as apprentice-witches. Eight years later, after passing the Third Test of Power, apprentices won their witch's staff as a full member of the Coven.

Many witches never gained more than their moonstone ring, but if they had power and ambition, they could go on and try for their rings of elements. If a witch passed the first, second and third Tests in any one element, they were counted a sorcerer or sorceress, and could wear the appropriate precious stone on their left hands. Of course, no one dared wear rings of any kind anymore. Still, Isabeau had often dreamed of winning her moonstone ring and becoming an apprentice. Could Meghan be meaning to Test Isabeau, even though the Coven was disbanded and witchcraft outlawed? Isabeau's heart began to race, for her burning ambition was to learn more of the art of magic.

Although she knew witchcraft was forbidden, and that anyone found practicing it was put to death or exiled, Isabeau was fascinated by the subject. She loved the feel of drawing on the One Power, the gradual heightening of all the senses, the feeling of power and grandeur that filled her. Why, their whole history was spun from magic threads, though this was a history no one would admit to now. And although Meghan would talk little about the uses and practices of the One Power, Isabeau had gradually been working through her guardian's hundreds of books. Most of them were fairy stories, vague prophecies and simple spells, that anyone could do, but in one, a very ancient magical book, Isabeau had read of witches who could command the weather, make themselves invisible, tell the future, and even fly.

"The tea," Meghan said, and Isabeau felt herself flush as she stumbled to the fire where the old clay teapot hung above the flames. It was not like her to lose her composure; she wondered at it, even as she poured the fragrant brew into the cups and got the honeycakes out of the tin on the mantelpiece.

"Made with honey from our own bees," Meghan said.

"And where have ye hidden the hives?" Seychella asked with amusement in her voice.

"Now that's a secret," Meghan smiled, drinking the tea and nodding at Isabeau, who was perched on a stool by the fire, her usual seat taken by the stranger. "Why no' have your bath, Isabeau? Ye're filthy!"

"But I want to listen," Isabeau protested.

"Ye can still listen," Seychella soothed. "I will talk while ye bathe."

A little shy at the idea of bathing before a stranger, Isabeau nonetheless pulled out the hip-high tub from the corner beside the fire and poured in hot water from the kettle. She mixed it with cold water from the barrel on the other side and tested the temperature with her finger. It was only just lukewarm, so Isabeau stirred the water with her finger and concentrated. Slowly she felt the water around her finger begin to heat until steam billowed up from the rippling surface. She felt rather than saw the exchange of glances by the two women, and flushed.

"So the lassie heats her own water," Seychella murmured, and Isabeau clearly heard the amusement in her voice. "Well, certainly quicker than boiling the kettle over and over!"

Slowly Isabeau unbraided her hair, conscious of the dark-haired woman's gaze. Fiery red and very curly, Isabeau's hair reached below her knees and, released from its tight braids, stuck out in a frizzy halo all round her face and body.

"So she has no' cut it like so many lassies do now," Seychella said in satisfaction.

"O' course no'," Meghan responded grumpily. "I'm no' yet that far removed from the Coven!"

"No, ye be an auld-fashioned one, that be for sure!"

Ignoring them, Isabeau tossed a bundle of fragrant rose leaves into the water and a few drops of oil scented with starwood, before stripping off her grimy breeches, the woolen jerkin and her sweat-stained shirt.

"Does she ken *ahdayeh*?" Seychella asked as the girl stepped into the water, studiously ignoring the older women's gaze.

"The rudiments," Meghan responded. "Only what I could teach her, and ye ken I canna move around as much as I once did. She knows all the stances though, and I've been as critical as I could."

Isabeau concentrated on scrubbing her back with the long-handled brush. She had always been more interested in swimming in the loch or exploring the valley with her animal friends than in *ahdayeh,* the art of fighting. She just could not imagine needing to fight or use a weapon.

"What else can she do?" Seychella asked, rather contemptuously.

"She does have a way with animals," Meghan admitted grudgingly. "She was talking to the birds when she first toddled, and she can charm any coney, deer or snake."

"I spoke to a saber-leopard one time," Isabeau said, trying very hard to keep her pride out of her voice. "It was frightening, his words were so fierce, but it was exciting too."

"And what did the saber-leopard say?" Seychella raised an eyebrow.

From Isabeau's mouth came a deep purr that rose into a snarl at the end.

"Sweet sweet the wind rich in smell the step o' horned one the taste the smell the sweet chase the pound o' blood the chase the dance the smell the taste o' flesh the sound o' muscles tearing oh die beloved oh die!" Meghan translated, and smiled. Seychella snorted.

Isabeau lathered her hair with rose soap, and winked at

Gitâ the donbeag. The soap smelled delicious. She and Meghan made it every year, some with rose petals for their calming properties, some with lavender and some with murkwoad and trefoil for their healing properties. The murkwoad was a luxury, since it was one of the precious essences that Meghan had brought to their forest home from the outside world.

Although Seychella had promised Isabeau could listen as she and Meghan talked, Isabeau could hear only snatches of their murmured conversation. What little she did hear only inflamed her suspicions that somehow Seychella's visit was to do with her.

"So what are ye going to do with the lass?" Seychella said quite clearly as she poured herself some more tea. Meghan's answer was inaudible, but the black-haired witch then said, "If she really does have some ability, we must do what we can to help her."

Excitement filled her. Perhaps, at last, Meghan would begin to teach her the secrets of the One Power. A wood witch, Meghan had always thought it more important for Isabeau to learn how to heal, and to nurture plants, and speak the languages of the woodland creatures. So that is what Isabeau had learned, at least until a few years ago when the coming of her menses had brought her a surge of power that saw her red hair crackle and her blue eyes glow. Isabeau had always been able to exercise her will in small ways and, simply by watching Meghan, had learned how to start a fire or move small objects. The week her blood began to flow, she inadvertently started a fire by snapping her fingers, when all she meant to do was light a candle.

Remembering, Isabeau grinned, and lay back in the bath, looking up at the scorch marks on the wooden ceiling. "That is no' the thing to do when ye live in a tree," was all Meghan had said when she came limping down the ladder to find Isabeau, frightened and in tears, desperately trying to put out the fire. After that, the wood witch had agreed to give Isabeau occasional lessons, for she could see her ward would keep on trying things in secret and the sooner she learned control, the better.

After her bath, in her soft shirt and leggings, Isabeau sat on the stool, combing her damp hair. She was longing to ask questions, but knew that if she had something to do with Seychella's mysterious appearance, she would soon find out. So she helped Meghan serve the thick vegetable stew that was their normal evening meal and sat back in her corner to eat in silence.

The two witches kept up a light conversation all through the meal, talking of people Isabeau had never heard of and places she had only seen on the map upstairs. Gitâ came down out of the rafters and curled up in Meghan's lap, his eyes bright. Isabeau listened in interest, her curiosity about her guardian's former life growing with every story. For many years she had taken the house in the giant tree and her life here with Meghan for granted. It was only recently that she had begun to wonder how they came to live here, and why Meghan took so many pains to keep their life secret. Meghan rarely answered her questions, only occasionally letting drop a tantalizing scrap of information that only made Isabeau more curious. Listening now to the women's conversation, she realized with greater force than ever that Meghan had not always lived in the Sithiche Mountains, collecting herbs and knitting by the fire. They spoke of journeys on the sea, flirtations in great castles, spells cast and foundered, and news of other witches, in exile or in hiding.

"I have news o' Arkening," Seychella said in a low voice. Meghan lifted her eyes from her knitting. "She has been hiding in the Sgàilean Mountains, near the Rurach border. I saw her as I came through the mountains from Siantan."

"I have no' heard from Arkening since the Day o' Betrayal," Meghan said quietly. "I have only been able to find a few o' the sisters, and then only those who are no' too frightened to answer my messages."

"I'll no' tell ye a lie, I barely recognized her, she were so auld and ragged. She was begging in a village square. She would no' talk to me, she be that terrified o' being called a witch; the witch-hunts in Rurach have been savage the past five years, ye ken."

"Aye, I heard."

"Ye would." Seychella's voice was ironic. "What else have ye heard? It amazes me how ye can live so deep in these misbegotten mountains and still hear more news than I!"

"Aye, but ye never really mastered the Skill of scrying through water and fire, did ye? Your abilities lie elsewhere."

Seychella shrugged her shoulders irritably.

Meghan continued knitting placidly, saying, "I have news from Rhyssmadill, at any rate. Our auld friend Latifa sends me regular dispatches, though I worry for her safety. She says things are getting worse every day. The Rìgh does no' go out anymore, he does no' even seem interested in eating, let alone the affairs o' the country. The forests are infested with bandits, and the merchants are bitter about the standstill o' trade with the other islands—without the songs o' the sea witches, they say the sea serpents are getting very bold and no ships dare go out, even though the winter tides are receding. Then there is great dissatisfaction amongst the lairds, especially the MacSeinn clan, who were driven out o' Carraig by the Fairgean four or five years ago, with the Rìgh doing nothing to help them regain their land."

"There be dissatisfaction out in the countryside as well," Seychella said. "The peasants in Siantan have been hiding weapons in the thatch, and there be much talk o' a man they call the Cripple. They say he rescues witches from the fire and champions the poor. For the first time in many years I have heard talk against the crown . . . and I hear yon Banrìgh grows more careless each day. One day soon she'll take a stumble, and then who kens what could happen."

"I do no' believe it," Meghan said flatly. "More arrogant, aye, that I'll believe. But Maya is cunning as a snake; if she seems careless, it'll be because she hopes someone will make a move against her."

"Rebellion be in the air, Meghan, I smell it."

"Maybe so, maybe no'," Meghan responded.

"It's true our attempt at rebellion in Rurach was no' at all successful. I had gathered together many with Talent, and we made contact with the rebels there, as you directed. It was from them that I first heard o' the Cripple—the stories they tell! Did ye ken he rescued a whole cartload o' witches from under the Banrìgh's very nose? The rebels all worship him, though no one kens who he is. Sometimes I think he's only a myth and all the stories fabrications . . . though some o' the orders that came through for the rebels were nothing short o' brilliant, and they had to come from somewhere. With our help, the rebels rescued many a skeelie and cunning man from persecution by the Red Guards, and we even managed to save some Tower witches from the fire, no' that it did us much good in the end. I do no' ken how she found out about us—I'm sure the local crofters did no' betray us, for the people o' Rurach have never forgiven the Rìgh for the banishment o' Tabithas, and they helped us hide Skeelies many a time. I hope it were no' the MacRuraich who lead the Awl to us, though he certainly hunted us all down afterward. I find it so hard to believe Tabithas' own brother would betray us. The Banrìgh must have laid a spell on him."

"There are other compulsions." Meghan's voice was sad.

"Ten years I spent building up the resistance in Rurach, and a couple of hours was all it took for the Red Guards to destroy it all. The MacRuraich hunted each and every one o' us down . . ."

"Ye were no' hunted down," Meghan observed.

"I am the only one who escaped. The only one!"

"Still, ye ken the MacRuraich would have found ye if he had so wished. The MacRuraich clan find anything they search for. That is their Talent."

"Aye, we had no hope once the Banrìgh set Anghus MacRuraich on our trail. I do no' ken what sort o' spell she could have laid on him, to turn him against us like that. The MacRuraichs have always been loyal to the Coven."

"I'm no' sure I understand," Isabeau said, unable to keep silent any longer. "Ye speak o' the Banrìgh as if she is a witch herself, yet how can she be? I thought she was supposed to hate witches and magic."

"All magic but her own," Seychella growled.

Meghan turned to her charge. "Isabeau, how many times have I tried to teach ye about the Day o' Betrayal, only to have ye sneak out to go swimming or playing in the meadows as soon as I turned my back?" Isabeau had the grace to blush. In fact the only lessons she had really concentrated on were those in magic or woodcraft. "It's important ye understand this, Isabeau. I want ye to listen and remember what I tell ye now, for the shadow o' the Day o' Betrayal still falls upon us and we're all fighting to be free o' it. If witchcraft is ever to be a power in the land again, all witches must understand what it is Maya has done." Isabeau nodded, awed by the tone in her guardian's voice. "Can ye remember the story o' the Third Fairgean Wars, Beau?"

"Well, I ken the Fairgean invaded us—I do no' ken why . . . it was years ago, afore I was born. They came in stealth, filling up the lochan and rivers so that it was dangerous to even water the herds . . . The Rìgh called together the first army in centuries . . . since the Second Fairgean Wars. They drove away the Fairgean . . . He died, I think . . ." Isabeau's voice faltered.

"Listen to me well, Isabeau, a witch needs to learn as much as she can—only with knowledge and understanding can she gain the High Magic. Ye are no' a bairn anymore. If the rumors be true, there may be civil war across the land and that will affect us all, even ye and me in this wee valley o' ours. Now listen well," Meghan said. "Twenty years ago Parteta the Brave was killed, fighting off the invasion o' the Fairgean, who had come with the rising tide to try and win back the coast o' Clachan and Ravenshaw. That same day his eldest son Jaspar was crowned the new Rìgh, kneeling amongst the blood and fire o' the battlefield, the Lodestar blazing in his fist. Although he was still a boy, without hair on his chin or chest, Jaspar drove the Fairgean from the shores o' Clachan, and they fled back into the sea."

Isabeau nodded, though she could not see much difference between what she and Meghan had said.

"The Rìgh Jaspar returned to Lucescere as a hero, to be greeted there in joy and sorrow by his mother Lavinya, and his three younger brothers, Feargus, Donncan, and Lachlan. For three years peace and prosperity reigned, till Lavinya followed her husband into death. Again the castle mourned, for Lavinya had been both kind and wise, and she would be sorely missed. The Rìgh was now standing on the threshold o' manhood, strong and bonny like a sapling tree, and all Eileanan had reason to believe he would be a rìgh as his father had been and his father afore him—just but merciful, strong but compassionate, brave but wise. However, by his eighteenth birthday, the Rìgh was filled with a restlessness he did no' understand, and was growing impatient with affairs o' state. When a bonny stranger came to the castle dressed in red velvet with a hawk on her wrist, the

Rìgh was struck with love for her as if by lightning. They were married that week, with much rejoicing in the city, and so it was that Maya the Unknown became Banrìgh o' Eileanan." The musical lilt of Meghan's voice hardened with rage, and Isabeau thought that she spoke the name of the Banrìgh with hatred.

"Now we come to the events which more closely involve us. No' everyone was pleased with the marriage o' the Rìgh. There were many who spoke against Maya, those who distrusted her because she was a stranger, and those who were perturbed by her growing power over the Rìgh. It seemed as if a spell had been laid upon him: he no longer rode out among the people nor sat in judgings nor helped plant the summer crops. He spent his days with Maya in her boudoir, and when he emerged, his eyes were glazed like that o' a man who had drunk o' moonbane. He seemed barely to recognize his brothers, or his faithful auld servants.

"He began to disdain the Coven o' Witches, who had helped his father govern the land for so many years and who had studied much o' wisdom and knowledge. Maya used her power to sway the Rìgh—she said that the magical creatures were *uile-bheistean* and must be destroyed. So it became a great feat to kill the dragons and nyx and winged horses and all the other magical creatures that were once great allies o' the Clan o' MacCuinn. She spoke against the Coven o' Witches, and infiltrated it with acolytes o' her own that twisted the Creed and made it serve Maya. Tabithas, who led the Coven, fell from the Rìgh's favor and he would no longer heed her advice. Eventually he raised the Lodestar against the witches, who had always served him faithfully, and allowed the Red Guards to storm the Towers. That was, o' course, the Day o' Betrayal. It was then Tabithas the Keybearer disappeared and the Towers were brought down."

Isabeau listened, but most of this story she had heard before and paid little attention to. "I still do no' understand," she said. "What about the Banrìgh?"

"It seems she must be a powerful and subtle sorceress, to win the Rìgh's heart so easily and then to turn him against the Coven so quickly. Jaspar had always loved the Coven and he has Talent himself—he canna have been made to act so without a very strong compulsion. Then, when the Red Guards stormed the Tower o' Two Moons, Maya was there, giving the orders and making sure they were carried out. Tabithas went to confront her, and ye must remember, Tabithas was Keybearer, the strongest witch in the land."

"So what happened?"

"We do no' ken. Tabithas disappeared. We never saw her again, though I searched everywhere for her, and called to her with my mind, but to no avail. Later the Rìgh said she had been banished, but Tabithas was never one to do what others said she should. She was as proud as her wolf, and as slow to forgive an insult. She would never have accepted such a sentence meekly. Somehow Maya must have overcome her, though whether it was by craft or cunning, I do no' know."

"She overcame ye, too, did she no'?" Seychella said, with an ironic inflection in her voice.

"Did she? Really?" Isabeau asked.

"We could not withstand so many soldiers," Meghan responded obliquely. "I had to get Ishbel away, and Maya and that servant o' hers thought to try and stop me. I opened the earth at their feet and watched them plunge into the abyss, yet only moments later both were at my heels again. That is no ordinary power."

"And she bends others to her will," Seychella said. "That is her real crime. It's more than just compulsion, too, for she does it to crowds o' people at a time."

"But why? If she is a witch, why does she want to destroy other witches?"

"And no' just witches," Meghan said. "She is destroying all the magical creatures as well."

"Nobody kens why." Seychella said. "The black-hearted witch seems to ken all our secrets and all our movements, but we ken nothing about her. She says she was born in Carraig, but all our questions have not found out where or when, nor who her parents are. She truly is the Unknown."

"And so did she . . . cast a spell on the Rìgh?" Isabeau asked stumblingly, not sure she understood.

"Whether it is the working o' enchantment or merely the spell o' love, all we ken is the Rìgh grows daily more weary, and Maya now openly sits in council and judgment, and orders the soldiers," Meghan replied. She looked tired, her thin body slumping in the chair.

"And by Eà's green blood, she had something to do with the disappearance o' the three prionnsachan or I be no witch!" Seychella exclaimed.

Isabeau's eyes rounded. She had been a young girl, around four, when the three young prionnsachan had disappeared one night, apparently stolen from their beds. She and Meghan had been traveling through the highlands when they heard the news, selling herbs, healing sicknesses in return for supplies, and listening to gossip. Once or twice a year they made these journeys to the villages, always dressed in their roughest clothes. The disappearance of the Rìgh's three brothers had caused widespread consternation and anxiety. Many rumors had circulated through the marketplaces and inns, and Meghan, mixing medicines and potions or selling her little wooden boxes of herbs, heard them all. Most seemed to think they had sailed away to distant lands, seeking adventure. It was still common practice for young men and women of high courage to set out on a quest, of which there were many—to look for the fabled gardens of the Celestine where all illnesses could be cured; to find the black winged horse of Ravenshaw, often seen but never tamed; to find the Lost Horn of Elayna or the Ring of Serpetra. "But the youngest prionnsa was only twelve years auld," Meghan had said softly. "Surely too young to be thinking o' quests?" The villagers had shifted uneasily, one muttering, "Never too young to want adventure, eh?" As the years passed and Isabeau grew older, they occasionally heard rumors of sightings, but the Lost Prionnsachan of Eileanan never returned home.

"Maya herself ordered the search, for the Rìgh was beside himself with grief, we heard. But nowhere was there sound nor sight o' the lost prionnsachan. After the three bairns had disappeared, feeling rose up against Maya and there were rumors she'd something to do with their going. They called her a witch herself, and this was, ye ken, only five years after the Day o' Betrayal when an accused witch still faced death by burning. Maya faced them down, though, cutting off all o' her hair as proof she was no' a witch, for even then few witches would let their hair be cut . . . In the end, she won them all over, as she always did. I fain think she used compulsion on them, though I've never heard o' compulsion being used on more than one or two people at a time, and this was literally thousands!"

"She seems to be a powerful sorceress, Isabeau, and we can only guess at her motives but I personally have seen her order the deaths o' two hundred witches and apprentices. Once the Coven o' Witches was a power in this land, its Towers the center o' all learning and study, its witches among the finest healers and thinkers. Once witches were respected and feared, now they are hated and reviled. All o' Eileanan carries Maya's yoke across its shoulders—she is no' to be underestimated!"

"Have ye heard the other big news? Apparently the Redcloaks have been sent into the mountains to hunt out *uilebheistean* again. They say the Fairy Decree is no' working fast enough, and that the peasants fain be stubborn." The scorn in Seychella's voice was very clear. "I heard in the highland villages that a force was being sent against the dragons, to wipe them out for good."

"She's sent a force against the dragons?" Meghan said incredulously, her brow furrowed deeply. "She must be very confident . . . the dragons do no' take trespassing lightly, and will no' hesitate to defend their land . . . She must have dragonbane," Meghan mused, more to herself than to the others. "There's nothing else that'll fell a dragon, though I wonder where she found it. A very rare plant, and dangerous to distill ”

"The villagers are all nervous. They say the dragons will come and burn the houses in revenge."

"If Maya breaks Aedan's Pact, that's exactly what they'll do."

"Well, I heard it was because the dragons had broken the Pact that she sent the Guards against them in the first place."

"I do no' believe that for a moment. Where did ye hear that?"

"In the Whitelock Mountains, on my way through. The dragons have been raiding the herds; I heard men were taken as well. They certainly killed soldiers, for I saw the bodies on my way, and it could be nothing but dragons with those wounds."

There was an expression of intense interest on Meghan's

face. "Indeed? So the dragons are violating the Pact. That is interesting. I wonder we have no' seen them."

"I thought I saw a dragon the other day," Isabeau said, excitement filling her. "It was just a shadow passing across the moons. I thought I was imagining."

"I have no' heard o' the dragons raiding herds syne Aedan's Pact, four hundred and more years ago." Meghan looked as if she was making swift calculations, and a small smile had sprung up on her face. "Maya will find she has bitten off more than she can chew if she challenges the dragons on their own ground. Fancy sending a group o' Red Guards against Dragonclaw!"

"There has been talk o' creatures o' all kind. One thing is interesting—they've been killing wolves, particularly in Rurach. I heard that from a pedlar in Whitelock too. Apparently the wolves have been attacking regiments o' the Red Guards, and they've suffered heavy losses; also, I heard, the wolves have been raiding the herds o' the Banrìgh's supporters, which is interesting."

"They're killing wolves?" Meghan said slowly. "But . . . surely no'. She canna believe . . ."

"I saw the wolves myself. It was when I was on my way, in one o' those villages near the source o' the Wulfram. They had six o' them, strung up on poles. They were crowing like a bunch o' farmyard roosters: "Aye, will my lady no' be happy with us! Aye, will we no' be heroes when we get back!" It made me sick to my stomach."

"But I thought Tabithas was gone. I have had no word o' her since she disappeared after the Burning."

"No one has," Seychella said softly.

The mention of Tabithas the Wolf-Runner made Isabeau sit upright. Like many of her clan, Tabithas NicRuraich had had a wolf as her familiar, a great gray beast that, like his mistress, had been more comfortable in the forests and mountains of Rurach than in the gardens and courtyards of the Tower of Two Moons. Meghan often smiled when telling how the sight of Tabithas' wolf lounging near her foot had caused many a recalcitrant prionnsa to blanch and tremble, when moments before they had been proud and cold as a glacier.

"That's no' all o' it. The villagers be talking about some strange new horror that seems to work in Maya's favor. It can hardly be seen but it's gray and has wings and its gaze casts a spell on people so they canna shout or run. It steals bairns from their beds, particularly those with Talented bloodlines, and in Bléssem they say anyone who mutters against the Banrìgh is found dead, a smile o' ecstasy on their face."

"A Mesmerd? Surely no' . . ."

"What is a Mesmerd?" Seychella spat the syllables out like bitter fruit.

"The Mesmerdean are creatures o' mists and mud. They come from the Murkmyre, and are perhaps the most dangerous o' all the fairy, for they do not think or feel as we do. What one sees, all see, and what one hears, all hear, and ye canna lie to them for they do no' listen to your words but only to the intent behind. They never forget, never, and are utterly ruthless. I have never heard o' a Mesmerd out o' Arran before—I wonder if the NicFóghnan is meddling in our affairs again? That clan has always been an enemy o' the MacCuinns . . ."

"They sound most blaygird, though no one I spoke to had actually seen one, only . . . found the bodies they left behind."

"I wonder . . ." Meghan looked as though she was about to say more, but then her eye fell upon Isabeau, noting her shining eyes and eager face, and she stopped herself, picking up her knitting instead.

"What kind o' witch are ye?" Isabeau asked Seychella, gazing intently at the woman whose untidy hair snaked around the seat of her chair and fell to the floor.

"What makes ye think I am a witch?" Seychella asked in a voice of deadly calm. Isabeau said nothing. After a moment Seychella laughed. "I appear out o' nowhere, I speak o' power and Talent; I ken Tabithas. Silly question." After another pause, she said quietly, "I am a wind witch, Isabeau."

"Can ye teach me to fly?" Isabeau asked eagerly. That had always been her secret desire. Once she had broken her ankle, trying to take flight from the bough of a tree after reading of the antics of Ishbel the Winged, a witch who flew as effortlessly as any bird. Meghan set her ankle and bound it with herbs and mud, and fed her bone-strengthening teas, scolding and mocking all the while. Isabeau had only tossed her red head and ignored her, sure she would one day crack the secrets of flight, as Ishbel the Winged had done.

The two witches looked at each other, and Seychella curled her lip. "The bairn canna even walk yet and she wants to fly! Only the most powerful learn to fly, my dear, I doubt ye have the capacity."

Isabeau flushed again, and blurted out. "Well, do ye? Can ye fly?" With her red hair falling out of its braids into twists and tangles around her face and her red cheeks, Isabeau looked as though sparks would literally burst from her head.

Meghan had to laugh, murmuring, "Ye see why I think she will take to fire!"

The other witch looked quite taken aback, then angry at Isabeau's question. Then she gave a harsh laugh. "No, lassie, I canna. At least, no' the way ye mean it. I can jump a twelve-foot fence and I'll never fall out o' a tree, but I canna fly."

"I've read about a witch who could fly from one end o' the country to another in a week, and who could do somersaults and backflips in the air."

"Ishbel! Well, a Talent like Ishbel's does no' come along too often." Seychella sighed, "I fear we'll no' see a Talent like it again in our lifetime. Damn and blast the Banrìgh! So many witches killed, so much ability lost."

"I've also read about witches who folded the fabric of the universe and sailed across space. Is that true?"

"Where did ye read that! It's forbidden, ye ken, to talk about the Great Crossing. Ye'd be put to the Question if ye were heard! What sort o' book did ye read that in, lassie?"

Meghan cleared her throat. "I've always had a passion for books."

"But that's a story she could only be reading about in the Book of Shadows, which was destroyed by the Banrìgh on the Day o' Betrayal!" Seychella was sitting bolt upright, her cheeks crimson. "She would be burned by the Awl if they heard her saying such things—they deny all stories o' the Great Crossing now, ye must ken that?"

"I wrote down what I could remember, from all the books. So many books were burned, so much knowledge lost. I was afraid it would never be found again if someone did no' try to remember."

Isabeau said nothing, thoughtfully choosing another honeycake from the plate on the unsteady table by the fire. She knew as well as Meghan did that although many of the books piled on every table and shelf were written in Meghan's spidery handwriting, this particular book was an enormous, ancient affair, bound in red leather, with a tarnished silver key as long as Isabeau's longest finger. Each page was filled with handwriting different from the page that had gone before; many were ornately illustrated with brightly colored pictures of dragons and winged horses, or the tracks of stars and moons, or the shape of unfamiliar lands. Like many of Meghan's books, the last page was empty, untouched, yet Isabeau knew by experience that if you should write on that page and turn the leaf, there would be another blank page there waiting for your pen. She was never able to work out how it got there or when, but the magic never failed.

As Isabeau wondered why Meghan had denied the book's existence, Seychella, apparently accepting Meghan's explanation, went on to talk about how difficult it was to get the right ingredients for spells and medicines when the merchants' ships no longer dared face the sea serpents. "I am almost out o' rhinfrew," the witch said testily, "and the Power ken, I havena much murkwoad left either."

"Aye, it may be time for a journey to the ports," Meghan said dreamily.

Isabeau's heart jumped with excitement. They had never ventured further away from the mountains than the highlands of Rionnagan. Isabeau had heard of the dangerous beauty of the sea, but she had never seen any water greater than Tuathan Loch at Caeryla. She hoped Meghan meant what she said. What an adventure! It would take months to reach the sea from their home, and they would have to travel half the country. She might see fairy creatures, or sea serpents, or even visit the Rìgh's palace.

"Bedtime, Isabeau," Meghan said, getting stiffly to her feet and gathering up the dirty dishes.

"But it's only early—"

"Ye've been out on the mountain all day, remember. Ye can hardly keep your eyes open!" her guardian retorted, limping around the room.

"But—"

"No excuses, Beau. Bedtime."

Reluctantly Isabeau bade the two witches goodnight and climbed up the ladder to her room, which was cold and dark. Faint light flickered up the stairs, but she did not bother to light a candle for her night vision was exceptionally good. She was able to see in the dark room almost as easily as she had out in the meadows that afternoon. Meghan had always said she could see like an elven cat.

In her cold little bed, Isabeau slowly stretched her legs, enjoying the chill of the sheets against her skin, and wondering about the unexpected appearance of the stranger-witch. She smiled, imagining how she would impress the supercilious Seychella by passing the Test of Power with ease. She would make the black-haired witch's eyes pop out. She was still planning her triumph when Meghan clambered up the ladder and came and sat on the edge of her bed, as she always did.

"Asleep, Beau?"

"Mmm-mmm. Meghan, did ye mean what ye said about traveling down to the sea?"

"Indeed, I did. Things are afoot, and much as I am loath to leave our wee valley, if things are to go the way I wish, I must take a hand in the weaving. Now, go to sleep, Isabeau. It'll be a long day tomorrow." With that cryptic remark, the old witch bent and kissed Isabeau on the forehead, between the eyes, as she did every night.

When she was gone, Isabeau gave a wriggle of excitement and fell into a reverie of adventures and explorations, palaces and fairies. She had been feeling restless ever since the snow had begun to thaw and life again quickened all around her. She was often bored with their sedate life in the secret valley, where every animal was a friend and there was no one to talk to except Meghan. Every season she looked forward to their forays into the mountains for herbs and semiprecious stones; even greater was her excitement when the two of them journeyed down into the villages to sell their potions and love spells. Isabeau had never been further south than the highland town of Caeryla, which they had visited eight years earlier.

It had been festival time, the time of the red comet, a season of fertility and strong magic. The streets of Caeryla were strung with colored ribbons and flags, pots of flowers decorated every doorstep and the townsfolk were dressed in their finest clothes. Minstrels strummed their guitars and sang of love, and jongleurs juggled colored balls and did backflips, while performing bears nursed their sad heads. Isabeau had never seen anything like the jongleurs, who entertained the crowd with jokes and magic tricks, fire-eating, sword-swallowing and juggling, their bright cloaks covering tattered clothes. One was a young boy, thin and quick, who could turn along the road as quickly as a wheel. Isabeau was openly envious, hanging back against Meghan's hand to watch him. She thought she would like traveling from town to town in the gaudy little caravan, juggling oranges for a living. Meghan's hand was firm, though, and Isabeau was gently pulled away from the square with its bright swinging lamps and the flickering shadows.

It was dangerous for them in the towns. This Isabeau understood. The Red Guards were everywhere, suspicious of strangers, and brutal in their dealings with suspected witches. Isabeau knew she must not play with the One Power or speak of it. She knew she must always be quiet and unobtrusive and never draw attention to them. When they entered a town, Meghan's limp became more noticeable, her body somehow more frail. She draped her plaid about her head so her thick braid was concealed, her face half in shadow. In the towns, Isabeau discarded her breeches and dressed in gray wool, her hair covered by a linen cap—a model girl-child.

Isabeau was only eight, however. She had not yet learned how to melt into a crowd so cannily that afterward no one could be sure whether or not she had been there. And with her unruly red hair and her bright blue eyes, it was not easy for Isabeau to pass unnoticed. But it was not Isabeau's striking coloring which was her downfall. It was her playing with the One Power. She and Meghan were staying at an inn in the center of town. Because it was Candlemas, the streets were full of travelers come to dance the fire with other young people, and visit relatives and trade with the pedlars. Meghan said she was there to try to buy powdered foolsbalm, shepherd's spikenard, black hellebore, and maybe some murkwoad if by some chance a pedlar had some. Isabeau knew, though, that she also came to gather information, whether it be market gossip, the stories the jongleurs and minstrels told, or old books and manuscripts.

The inn was full of people. Meghan was hunched in a chair by the fire, nodding over her knitting as bawdy jokes and tales of sightings of the lost prionnsachan rivaled the mournful tales of the highland crofters. At first Isabeau was tired from the long journey and the heat of the fire made her sleepy. However, after obediently eating a bowl of watery stew and resting her aching legs, Isabeau grew restless. Slowly she eased her body off the bench and began to creep away, only to receive a stern glance from Meghan that proved the witch was not really asleep. Isabeau pretended not to see it, of course, and knew the talk of trouble between the Rìgh and Banrìgh was too riveting for Meghan to leave. However, the glance was enough to keep Isabeau quiet and unobtrusive for a time. She wandered around the common room, listening to the minstrel strum his guitar as he sung of quests and magic swords, watching the maids flirt with the customers.

After a while she slipped out through the big doors into the courtyard behind the inn, where grooms and stable-hands rushed around unloading bags and boxes from coaches and carts, brushing down horses and carrying heavy buckets, water sloshing onto the bricks. In the center of the courtyard a big stallion was causing an uproar, rearing and dancing about, grooms ducking to avoid hooves as big as dinner plates. Black as coal, Isabeau could see the red rims of his eyes and the red roof of his mouth as he whinnied. She was not frightened. She liked horses, and often rode some of the wild horses that lived in the mountains around the secret valley. She had never tamed one, though, since the herds that inhabited the mountains were proud and wary of humans, no matter how well they spoke the language. Isabeau had learned to speak with horses almost as soon as she learned the language of the birds, for as Meghan said, horses often knew as much as their masters, if not more, and were usually happy to chat. This horse was angry, Isabeau could hear that, and also frightened. Her ready sympathy was stirred and she crept forward, looking up at the horse as he reared and plunged about. What she planned to do, she hardly knew, but before she had a chance even to reach up a hand to the horse's snarling muzzle, a strong arm whipped around her waist and she was swung out of the way.

"Stable yards be no place for bonny lasses," a laughing voice said in her ear, and she was thrown up into the air and caught. Isabeau squealed with pleasure. "Here, catch," the man said and threw her over to one of his companions who caught her easily and set her down on the ground.

Rather rumpled and on her dignity, Isabeau turned back to see her rescuer moving forward easily to catch the stallion's halter, seizing one ear in his big hand. He was tall and very dark, and dressed in tight black breeches, a torn crimson shirt, and a leather waistcoat, his long black hair tied back from his face. Isabeau recognized him—he was one of the jongleurs that Meghan had not allowed her to watch earlier in the evening. The stallion had quietened at his first touch, but his eyes were still rolling and his hooves danced across the bricked floor. Stroking the stallion's sweaty neck, the jongleur whispered a few words into the ear that he still held and gradually the stallion calmed.

"He's guid wi' horses, my da," someone said with pride. Looking round, Isabeau saw the boy who could turn cartwheels as easily as she could run. His dark face was dirty and his clothes—a sky-blue embroidered jerkin over a frilly shirt that had once been white—were ragged. His thin legs were like sticks below the short, torn trousers, stuck into boots obviously far too large. Isabeau did not mind his ragged appearance—he had a mischievous face and black eyes that sparkled with interest as he looked at her in her demure gray dress and white cap.

"What did he say to the horse?" Isabeau asked.

The boy's face clouded a little. "Och, just nonsense," he said. "The words do no' mean much—it's the tone o' voice that matters."

Isabeau was about to press the point, when she felt herself caught around the waist and swung up into the air again. She looked down into the jongleur's handsome face and laughed with delight as he tossed her up into the air. "Has your mumma no' told ye wee lassies shouldna try and play with big bad horses?"

"I like horses," Isabeau protested.

"Aye, but maybe no' all horses are nice horses," he said.

"He was a nice horse, he just did no' want to be here," Isabeau explained. "His new master is horrible."

"Is that so, lass?" the jongleur exclaimed. "And how would ye ken that?"

Isabeau immediately flushed with confusion. "I just ken," she said lamely. "He looked like a nice horse."

For some reason the jongleur found that funny, throwing back his head and laughing. "Well, my bonny lass, next time maybe try no' to play right under a horse's hooves, no matter how nice the horse may be."

He set her down on the ground and from somewhere about his clothes found some colored balls which he juggled smoothly from hand to hand as he talked. "Run back to your mumma, now, lassie, she'll be missing ye. Come on, Dide, ye'd better be runnin' home too. I'm going to find out what entertainment this sleazy inn can offer." The balls disappeared as if by magic, and he strode off into the inn, followed by his companions.

The two children looked at each other, and with squeals of laughter began to play a scrambling game of chase and hide through the bales of straw and barrels and boxes which lined the courtyard and stables. It was the most fun Isabeau had had since she left the valley two months earlier. In fact, Isabeau felt it was the most fun she had ever had, since she had never had a playmate other than the beasts of the forest. Dide was quick and agile; he could walk on his hands and turn cartwheels without a moment's thought, and he knew so many funny stories that he had Isabeau helpless with laughter. Eventually they were chased out of the stables by the headgroom and, flushed and excited, ran back into the inn.

Tumbling through the door, Isabeau was immediately pierced by Meghan's black gaze, though the old woman seemed for all the world asleep in her chair by the fire. Isabeau skidded to a halt, suddenly conscious of her gray dress covered in dust and straw, her lost cap, her red curls tumbling out of their braids, the laughter and comments from the customers. Mortified, she crept back into a dim corner, tidying herself and trying to melt into the walls. That she was reasonably successful was shown by the return of the room's attention to the jongleurs, who were at a table in the corner playing dice with some of the customers—a fat man in a furred cloak, a tall, saturnine man with a squint, and a quiet man who hardly spoke. The minstrel had put away his guitar and was tucking into a big plate of stew, one hand around the waist of one of the maids, holding her securely in his lap.

The jongleurs' bright clothes and loud talk dominated the room, and Isabeau was able to compose herself without any more comment. Dide had crept into her corner with her, and she knew he did not want his father to realize he had not gone home as commanded. The two of them whispered and giggled together for a while, Isabeau careful to stay out of Meghan's sight.

It soon became clear the jongleur was winning, as he scraped piles of coins toward him with a laugh and a jest. "We'll eat tonight," Dide whispered, and Isabeau turned to him in shock. Despite their isolation from the rest of the world, Isabeau had always had enough to eat. She looked at Dide's thin arms and legs, and the shadow of a bruise on his temple. Maybe traveling from town to town, juggling and telling stories, was not such an exciting way to live after all.

As the night wore on, Isabeau grew sleepy again, and she and Dide curled up together by the fire, watching the gamblers and listening to the minstrel as he softly began to play again. The jongleur's run of luck did not continue—soon he was losing again, and Isabeau watched in concern as the pile of coins slowly sank.

"Well, that's enough for me," the fat man in the furred cloak said, yawning and pushing back his chair.

"Ye canna leave yet, man," the jongleur laughed. "I still have some coins to lose."

Isabeau was conscious of Dide's sigh, and was glad when the fat man shook his head and stood up.

"C'mon, man, one more throw. I'll stake everything I have left against all o' yours." The jongleur pushed forward his small pile of coins, idly flipping one up and down so it spun in the light.

The fat man was tempted. He watched the coin flash as it spun in the air, then nodded and sat back down again.

"Only one throw, mind ye," he warned, and the jongleur smiled and nodded, and tossed the coin onto the table.

The tension in the room mounted as the fat man emptied out his pouch so coins rolled across the table. He threw first and smiled with satisfaction at the dice came up with double banrìghs. For the first time the jongleur's face was shadowed. He cupped the dice in his hands for a moment, frowning; then, with a flick of his wrist, he threw. The dice spun in the air and fell, and leaning forward Isabeau watched them roll over the table and slow. It seemed as if the jongleur would lose so, without thinking, Isabeau pointed her finger and the dice rolled over one more time and settled on double rìghs. There was a sigh from all round the room. The jongleur laughed and swept up all the coins, and after a moment the fat man shrugged and walked away from the table. Isabeau settled back in her chair, conscious of Dide's puzzled gaze and the strong steady look of her guardian.

"How did ye do that?" Dide whispered. Isabeau said nothing, just tried to look as if she did not know what he meant. The jongleur too was staring at her with a calculating look on his face, and with dismay she realized that the other player, the quiet man with gray eyes, was also leaning forward over the table to watch her. In confusion, she slipped back to Meghan's side and was caught close to her, tucked up in her plaid so no one could see her.

"Foolish lass," Meghan whispered. "Let us hope ye've done no harm."

Peeping out from the shelter of Meghan's arm, Isabeau saw that the jongleurs were picking up their cloaks and preparing to leave, still talking and laughing, with Dide high on his father's back. The quiet man was standing in the shadows, his face thoughtful, while the minstrel tried to kiss the maid and the innkeeper clattered pewter mugs together as he cleared the table. As the jongleurs crowded out the door, Dide's father looked over to her and winked, and Dide himself waved a tentative goodbye, a puzzled expression still on his face.

Meghan waited until the inn was empty before getting to her feet, pushing Isabeau before her. "We must go," she said. "Get your things."

"Leaving, mistress?" a voice said from the shadows.

"It's late to be taking the wee lass out into the town. Do ye no' have a bed?"

Meghan turned slowly, her back bent almost double. "Och, thankee, kind sir," she said in a cracked whine. "But I mun take the wee lass home to her ma. I shouldna stayed so late but the fire be so warm . . ."

"But surely ye do no' bide in these parts. I've never seen ye afore," the voice said, and the man moved forward a little so the dim light of the fire flickered across his face.

"Aye, sir," Meghan said in her cracked voice. "The Collene family has bided in these here parts for aye long year."

"But surely that red hair is no' what you'd expect to find in these parts," the man said smoothly, and Isabeau was conscious of a sudden fear.

"Och, the reds be from her granda," Meghan cackled. "He didna bide here. He came from the west to jump the fire; a good man he be, if a wee hasty. But ye mun excuse us, sir, the lassie's ma will be fraitchin'." And without waiting for an answer, she hobbled out of the door into the dark night beyond, then immediately picked up her skirts and ran nimbly across the courtyard and into the stable. "Hush, Beau," she cautioned. "Say nothing. Do no' move."

Obediently Isabeau crouched by her side; as the man came out the door in a hurry and paused, peering down the street as if to look for them. They watched in silence until at last he shrugged and went back inside; then Meghan shook at her skirts and dragged Isabeau to her feet. "Ye'll be fetching water and cutting wood for a month after this, lassie!"

Meghan then hustled Isabeau out of the town as quickly and unobtrusively as she could. Since Caeryla had only three gates set in its high stone walls, each guarded closely, this had involved slithering down a sewer and into the loch below. The misty loch of Caeryla was famous for its *uile-bheist,* a mysterious serpentlike creature which often snatched those unwary enough to stand on its shores or swim in its waters. They had therefore slipped into the loch with a fair amount of trepidation, even though Meghan's charm worked on most beasts, fairy or otherwise.

That night they walked until dawn, at last finding cover

in the forests to the east. Meghan had still not allowed Isabeau to rest, even though it was Candlemas, and so Isabeau's eighth birthday. In the fresh dawn, she lit a fire, and the two of them performed the Candlemas rites as Isabeau had done every year since she was born. This year was different, though, for once the rites were completed, Meghan did not douse the fire and allow them to rest, but tested Isabeau on her witchcraft skills and knowledge. The tests went on for hours, despite Isabeau's exhaustion, and the little girl knew she was being punished for her demonstration of power in the inn. At last Meghan was satisfied, and allowed her to sleep, but Isabeau's dreams were filled with nightmares.

When she woke that afternoon, she found to her delight that the caravan of jongleurs had chosen the copse of trees to camp in as well. Dide was there, impatient for Isabeau to wake so they could play again, with his little sister Nina tumbling about the copse without a stitch of clothing on, her hair almost as red as Isabeau's. For seven days they stayed in the shelter of the forest, Isabeau having the time of her life with so many playmates. Meghan seemed to have made friends, too, with Dide's grandmother Enit, a frail woman with a hunched back and hands like claws, and a sweet, melodious voice. The two old women spent a great deal of time huddled over the fire, reading manuscripts and arguing about spells, or else disappearing into the woods with the grandmother's familiar, a blackbird with one white feather above his left eye.

Isabeau was surprised to discover Meghan and Enit knew each other from old days, before the Day of Betrayal, since the wood witch had not demonstrated any sign of recognition when they saw the jongleurs in Caeryla. Isabeau was used to Meghan's mysteries, though, and so she took advantage of her preoccupation to have the best fun she had ever had. At the end of the seven days, they made the long journey back to the secret valley, this time avoiding the Pass and its guard of soldiers, making the long detour along the Great Divide instead. Isabeau was heartbroken to leave Dide, and Meghan seemed sad to leave Enit, her face as grim and shadowed as Isabeau had ever seen it. So silent and unhappy was Meghan on the long journey back that Isabeau was afraid she was still angry at her. When Isabeau stammered out another apology, Meghan merely looked at her absently, and said, "Och, that's right. I'd forgotten," which merely alarmed Isabeau more, for Meghan never forgot a trespass.

It had been another year before she and Meghan again ventured out of the Sithiche Mountains, and never again had they gone any further south than the highlands.

With such happy memories of their last long journey, it was no wonder Isabeau was excited at the prospect of another. She had always hoped for another meeting with Dide, though all she could remember were bright black eyes and silly jokes. She smiled at the memory, then tried to compose herself to sleep. The last thought to cross her mind was that no doubt she would find out about her future in Meghan's own sweet time, and not a second before. Meghan had a way of keeping secrets that infuriated Isabeau, but no amount of wheedling or sulking would ever convince her to tell before she was ready.

When Isabeau woke, she lay still for a moment, wondering why she should have such a feeling of delightful anticipation. Then she remembered and her toes curled with pleasure. Bounding out of bed, she threw on her clothes and clattered down the stairs calling, "Time for a swim afore breakfast?"

Meghan, who hardly ever seemed to sleep, was stirring the porridge while Seychella leaned against the wall, chatting. "If ye're quick," her guardian replied. "Take Seychella, I'm sure she'd fain freshen up. And would ye mind taking the folding up with ye when ye go?"

Isabeau opened her mouth to protest, since she had intended just to slip out by the secret passage, by far the quickest way out to the loch. However, one glance from Meghan's black eyes was enough, and she said nothing.

Seychella gave a look of dismay. "Swimming!" she exclaimed. "Dinna ye hear the Fairgean be returning to the lochan?"

"I hardly think we need worry," Meghan said with a dryness in her voice that Isabeau knew well. "The Fairgean need salt water, no' fresh. Besides, no Fairge could leap that waterfall, and there's no other way in for them."

"Well, if ye be sure . . ." The black-haired witch sounded

doubtful, but she followed Isabeau up the ladder, helping to carry the load of clean washing Meghan passed them.

They squeezed out of the tiny trapdoor at the highest level and, hand over hand, crossed the rope-bridge that hung between the trees, Seychella laughing and joking about Meghan's obsession with secrecy. Isabeau only smiled. She was used to her guardian's idiosyncrasies and, though she often groaned at the inaccessibility of the tree house, knew it was a matter of safety. Even one of Meghan's books was enough to condemn them both to death, not to mention the crystal balls, the jars of herbs and powders, the ancient maps and precious oils. Magic was dangerous, the Rìgh said. Witches were evil, and use of the One Power strictly forbidden. Isabeau had herself seen the Rìgh's Decree Against Witchcraft painted on the front door of the mayor's house in Caeryla. She had heard how the Red Guards were still having witch-hunts through the countryside, dragging out any woman or man who was suspected of witchcraft and taking them back to Dùn Gorm for trial. Meghan was full of pity for those taken. "They could have no power, or only a wee, if they were taken so easily," she would say as they climbed the steep paths home. "A true witch would escape those bullies without even lifting a finger."

Isabeau had her first demonstration of the wind witch's power when Seychella lightly bounded to the ground from a branch of the tree, rather than clambering down the great length of the trunk as Isabeau had done. Isabeau, who had always thought herself as agile as a squirrel, had let herself down easily enough, even putting in a quick somersault to show off her strength and flexibility, but Seychella simply leaped off the branch, landing lightly some forty feet below.

"How did ye do that?" Isabeau demanded, but the witch only amused herself by calling the wind so it whipped Isabeau's long hair around her face and into her mouth.

The water of the loch was, as always, icy cold. Seychella floated on her back, staring up at Dragonclaw, her hair floating out behind her like a mass of weeds. "Meghan really has found herself a magic valley, has she no'?"

Isabeau was not quite sure what the witch meant, but she nodded, "It is bonny."

The witch looked over at her, and idly turned and swam a few strokes. "And ye were born here, were ye no'?"

"I think so," Isabeau replied uncertainly. "I ken I was found here. I was only a few weeks auld, so I suppose I must have been born here."

"Some shepherd's babe, I ken. There be no one else crazy enough to spend much time on these slopes, bonny though they be."

Isabeau said nothing. She supposed it was true that her parents must have been shepherds or herders, yet she preferred her own highly colored imaginings. Her red hair was so unusual, and the mystery of her birth so intriguing, Isabeau had woven several complicated tales to explain her abandonment. Her favorite was that she was heiress to a great estate, abandoned by a wicked uncle who wished to inherit in her stead. It explained everything quite satisfactorily, and completely discounted the possibility that her parents may not have wanted her.

"Can ye show me some more o' your magic?" she asked. "Something really amazing."

Seychella lay back dreamily, moving her hands lightly in the chilly water. She said nothing, but Isabeau felt the temperature drop as the witch drew upon the One Power. At first the placid surface of the loch began to quiver, the reflection of the mountains breaking apart and dissolving. Cats' paws of wind rippled toward them and the branches of trees began to sway. Faster and faster the wind rose, until clouds were scudding madly overhead and the branches thrashed wildly. Petals swirled from the flowered bushes, scattering in the wind like snowflakes. It became colder and colder, and Isabeau shivered and sunk lower in the water. Suddenly a giant thunderclap sounded, and lightning flashed down, splitting one of the ancient giants in the forest so it fell with a roar, dragging other trees down and making the ground shake. Isabeau was overawed. She had never seen such a powerful display of magic. All the tricks and games she played with the One Power were nothing in comparison to this. Even Meghan's occasional demonstrations were insignificant compared to those of Seychella.

"Teach me," Isabeau begged. "How do ye do that?"

"Playing with the weather is dangerous," Seychella said wearily. "No' for lassies."

Indignation filled Isabeau. "I'm no' a bairn anymore!"

"Ye need to understand how the weather works," Seychella said. "Bringing a storm is particularly hard—ye have to reach deep into the winds o' the world and change their shape and direction. Making lightning be the hardest o' all, particularly for a woman, for it involves the Power o' Fire as well, and fire is more a male force. I find it quite exhausting. Can ye listen to the wind?"

Isabeau swam closer. "I do no' ken . . . I'm no' sure . . ."

"Do ye ken when it be going to snow?" Seychella asked.

Isabeau nodded. Sixteen years in the Sithiche Mountains was enough to teach anyone the weather's signs. She could tell when rain or snow were coming, or when the wind was rising.

"Good. That be the start. Once ye can listen to the wind it be only a few wee steps from there. Ye must exert your will on the wind. Tell it when to come and when to go. Ride it in your mind. Ye'll begin to see how it flows."

Isabeau was beside herself with excitement. Meghan never told her things like this. She only ever said "listen" and "watch" as if those words held all the mysteries of magic.

"Ye may no' be able to do it, though," Seychella said dismissively. "Few witches ever do. Ye must ken that each individual's Talent is different. I can do things no other witch I ken can do, while Meghan . . . well, all witches must find their own limitations. Often ye find things out by accident. I knew air to be my element, since I always learned those things faster and more easily than any other, back when the Theurgia still existed. I did no' realize I could whistle up the wind though, till I was much older than ye. I was in a boat on a loch when a big storm blew up. We all would've died if I hadna told the wind to go away."

Isabeau, listening raptly, was suddenly aware of Meghan's bent figure waiting on the shoreline. Her guardian's face was grim and angry. Isabeau swam for shore, wondering anxiously what she had done wrong this time. It was not her, though, but Seychella that Meghan glared at.

"Seychella, did ye summon up that lightning?" she asked.

Isabeau was surprised at the wind witch's chagrined look. "Aye, Meghan," she responded. "I was just demonstrating a wee power—"

"Seychella, ye were the one who told me the mountains

are filled with Red Guards. How could ye take such a risk? That lightning would have been seen many miles away . . . lightning out o' a blue sky! Any Red Guard worth his shillings would come and investigate that."

"Do no' fraitch, Meghan, ye ken there's only the one pass into this valley and that's so well concealed ye'd have to ken where it is to find it. Besides, these mountains are a complete maze! Any Red Guard trying to find us would spend months backtracking out o' all the deadend valleys. And the lightning could have struck anywhere, how are they meant t'ken?"

Meghan pointed to the jagged spire of Dragonclaw cutting into the sky. "All they need to ken is that it occurred near Dragonclaw," she said wryly. "No matter where they are that bloody mountain will lead them straight to us!"

Seychella was not abashed for long. Isabeau spent most of the day with her, listening to her stories of the grand days of the Coven, when witches helped rule the land and were respected by lords and courtiers. Seychella talked a lot about the Theurgia at the Tower of Two Moons. Isabeau would have been sent there as a child, Seychella said, as soon as she had demonstrated any power. She would have learned the basic laws of desire and will, and been taught many useful skills.

"I would have had lessons in magic?"

"Ye would have been taught mathematics, history, alchemy, and the auld languages," Seychella replied briskly. "Also astronomy and anatomy."

Isabeau began to think the Theurgia would not have been much fun after all. "But what about magic?"

"Ye need to understand the laws o' nature and the universe before ye can start comprehending the One Power," the witch answered sternly, before smiling with unexpected charm. "Do no' look so downcast, my bairn. Ye would have learned to call on your Power and been taught various different ways o' using it, but indeed, I feel ye've learned as much, if no' more, from Meghan anyway. We o' the Coven believe in a long apprenticeship—it is no' until after the Second Test of Power and acceptance into the Coven as an apprentice that the real lessons in witchcraft begin."

It was true that Isabeau had learned many Skills from

just watching Meghan. The One Power was not easy to master. Meghan said many people lived all their life without realizing they had any power at all, while sometimes a Skill remained undiscovered, merely because no one had ever thought of applying the One Power in such a way.

All day Isabeau tried to call the wind, but could not even manage to lift a leaf off the ground or flutter the anemones on their long stalks. At last she gave up in anger and frustration, vowing to ask Seychella to call up the wind again so she could divine the trick of it. In the meantime, she let Seychella instruct her in the art of *ahdayeh,* and found the black-haired witch a much more exacting teacher than Meghan.

Later that day Isabeau was digging for roots and vegetables for their evening meal when she suddenly became aware that she was being watched. Again she was filthy and covered in sweat, since Meghan would never allow her to plant the seeds in a neat, orderly row like other gardens Isabeau had seen. All of their food was grown scattered through the forest so that no sign of cultivation would indicate to any stray intruder that people lived nearby. Isabeau had therefore been scrounging around in the forest undergrowth for the better part of an hour, trying desperately to remember where she had planted the potatoes.

The feeling began as an irritable prickling on the back of her neck. Isabeau rubbed at it with her grubby hand, and continued digging with her small wooden spade. The sensation intensified, and Isabeau suddenly swung around. An old man sat on a log behind her. A stray beam of sunlight fell through the branches and he sat in its light, so at first he was almost invisible in its dazzle. Everything about him was old and frail. His face was a mass of wrinkles; his pale scalp showed clearly through the thin, white hair, and the hand holding a carved staff was gnarled as a bird's claw. His straggly beard was so long it flowed over his knees, trailing in the leaves of the forest floor. In the trees above him a raven sat, regarding Isabeau with bright eyes.

"So this is the bairn Meghan discovered on the mountain," the old man said. Isabeau wanted badly to protest her maturity, but something held her silent. She was glad a moment later when the man continued in his faded voice, "A bairn no longer, it seems. How auld are ye, lassie?"

"Sixteen tomorrow," Isabeau replied gravely.

"Time then to take your Test," the old man said.

Isabeau's heart leaped, but still she said nothing, sitting back on her heels and gazing at the old man as he gazed at her. With a shock, Isabeau realized the old man was blind, his eyes glazed over with a white film.

"I am Jorge the Seer," the old man said. "I have come a long way for ye, Isabeau the Foundling. Come kneel afore me."

Isabeau's surprise and wonder were so great she could not say a word. Obediently she crossed the clearing and knelt in the dust before the white-haired man. She felt bony fingers on her hair, then Jorge was holding her head, his thumbs together in the middle of Isabeau's forehead. She felt a strange burring in her mind, and shook it off irritably.

"Odd . . ." Jorge murmured.

"What can unlock a dream o' a thousand years?" It was Meghan's voice. Isabeau could not turn to look at her guardian because the old man still held her head firmly in his bony hands, but she heard her cross the clearing.

"Ah," the old man said, and leaned forward to kiss Isabeau on the forehead, between her eyes. At once Isabeau's head was filled with a thrumming and drumming like the sound of horses' hooves on hard ground. His knobbly fingers dug into the skin of her temples and she had to resist the impulse to pull her head away

"It is true, ye do have power," the old warlock said at last, sitting back and resting his hands on his staff once more. "Ye are ignorant, though, ignorant and arrogant. How can ye be so ignorant after living all your life with Meghan o' the Beasts?"

"She was always a wilful bairn," Meghan said softly. "It is glad I am to see you, Jorge. I could only hope that ye would come. I was afraid . . ."

"I have been away a long time," Jorge said. "It must be seven years or more. There are omens in the sky, Meghan, I can feel them tugging me."

"Aye, the Red Wanderer is here again. I wish I knew what it meant for us. Ye have heard the tales o' witch-hunts and executions?"

"Aye, my child. It was very hard for me to come here—passage through the land is growing daily more difficult."

"Ye had no trouble finding the way?"

The old warlock chuckled. "Dragonclaw was easy enough to find with Jesyah to show me the way. Finding the entrance was a lot harder. Jesyah must have flown into hundreds o' cave mouths on that bloody mountainside. Thank ye for your mind-message yesterday. Are all the witches gathered?"

"Ye are only the second, Jorge. I have hopes, though. I've been expecting the lad for weeks now, and I sent out messages to all the witches I ken, and still I scry for more."

"Aye, but we are so few now and we are all afraid. I have made myself a wee snug home in the Sithiche Mountains so I did no' have to cross the land to get here, or come through the Pass, which is guarded."

"What news, Jorge?"

"Only bad, Meghan. The seas are full o' Fairgean—happen they smell the Rìgh's weakness. I have heard they have penetrated the Wulfram River as high as the third loch."

"That is fearful news indeed." Meghan got stiffly to her feet. "Come back to the house, Jorge, ye must be weary."

The old warlock got to his feet, the raven fluttering down to sit on his bony shoulder. Jorge stroked the black glossy feathers and said, "Will Gitâ mind a visitor?"

"He willna like it," Meghan laughed, "but he'll be hospitable." They began to walk back through the forest, Isabeau trailing close behind, consumed with curiosity.

"Meghan, I did a sighting afore I came. It was very odd. The vision kept changing, though I tried to hold it steady. I feel we are at a junction o' events. The Spinners are weaving new colors into the cloth and what this will mean for us only time can tell."

"What did ye see, Jorge?"

"I saw a babe being born that straddled the world with its feet—one foot upon the land, the other upon the oceans. It carried the Lodestar in its hand. I tried to see deeper into the vision, but it changed and I saw two faces that were the same, as if in a mirror, yet different. Everything I see in my dreams is in pairs, it seems—the double-fruited pomegranate, cherries, a coney with two kittens, two moons that reach out to each other, sometimes to kiss, sometimes to bite. There was one dream which brought me to tears and so woke me. I dreamt I was in Lucescere again. I ran into the auld throne-room, gladness in my heart, and saw there on the throne a winged man who had the Lodestar shining in his hand. Such a strange and bonny sight! And then the dream turned, and again I was running into the throne-room, and all I could hear was the wailing o' a clarsach. And there, on the throne, I saw a woman, with the Lodestar blazing in her fist. At first I am glad, and I see she has the white lock, all the way to her feet as only a true NicCuinn can have. But, Meghan, here is the worst o' it. I come closer, and she is Fairge! No doubt about it, I see her scales shining, and her fins and tail, and her mouth is no mouth o' a woman!"

"That is a strange sighting indeed," Meghan said slowly.

"Indeed, by my beard and the beard o' the Centaur. There is something else . . . I ken it means something important but yet I canna tell what. Every night I dream o' Magnysson and Gladrielle. I see them in my dreams, rising and setting, and I see one being consumed by the other . . . Magnysson takes Gladrielle in his arms, as the auld tales always told, but he swallows her, Meghan! He eats her! I think this can only mean war is coming, war as we have no' seen for many centuries."

"*When Magnysson shall at last hold Gladrielle in his arms, all will be healed or broken, saved or surrendered,*" Meghan murmured.

"What is that?" the blind seer asked, leaning closer. "What did ye say?"

"Just an auld rhyme I remember from my childhood. I have no' thought o' it for many years . . . Aye, this year is the year for us, I ken it. I wish the Stargazers were still alive. I would give much to ken if my readings o' the skies be correct."

"First let us Test this young witch and see if all that promise o' power is to be fulfilled," Jorge said. "What is your Talent, lassie?"

"I do no' ken," Isabeau said, confused. This was a secret source of sorrow to her, although Meghan reassured her by saying witches were often quite old before they found their special vocation.

Jorge now did the same. "Och well, never mind. I was over forty when I found I had the gift o' seeing into the future, and I had to lose my everyday sight first." He then turned to Meghan and said, "We need the right spot, ye ken, one near water, earth, air and fire."

"I have been making ready," Meghan said. "Tonight is Candlemas, the end o' winter and the beginning o' the season o' flowers. We'll begin the Ordeal at sunset, and perform the Candlemas rites at dawn. Let us hope the circle will be complete."

THE TEST OF POWER

Isabeau crouched beneath a thorny bush, trying to warm herself by rubbing her bare arms and shoulders with her hands. It was just before dawn on the first day of spring, and bitterly cold. She was tired, having not slept all night, and hungry, not having eaten. As Meghan had directed, she had tried to empty herself, tried to become part of the dark, silent night, the great trees soaring into starry distances, the mingled light of the two moons shining on the snowy peaks. But all she had felt was cold and afraid.

Soon the mountaintops could be seen silhouetted against a pale green sky. Isabeau scrambled to her feet and began to lope down the hillside, her arms crossed over her naked chest. Gradually she began to warm up, and she ran faster, for she was stiff after the long Ordeal, and she thought she might need every advantage in the upcoming Test. Somehow she knew it was important that she do her best this morning, that it would help define her future. Isabeau had no intention of living her life quietly among the trees and the mountains, gathering herbs and making medicines to sell each year at the village festivals. Isabeau wanted adventure.

Through the trees she could see the loch, shining faintly in the dawn light. The loch filled most of the bottom of the valley, trickling over the eastern rim to pour in thin ribbons to the plains far below. By the waterfall, a small fire had been lit and Isabeau headed that way.

As she ran, she repeated to herself the rhyme she had been taught as a child.

> "If Candlemas be fair and bright,
> Winter will have another flight.
> If Candlemas be shower and rain,
> Winter is gone and shall no' come again."

Unless it rains afore nightfall, it looks as though winter shall have another flight, Isabeau thought, and remembered how many birthdays had dawned fine, only to have her birthday picnic ruined by storm. Weather in the Sithiche Mountains was dangerously changeable.

On an open patch of earth near the edge of the cliff, the tremulous surface of the waterfall's edge only a few feet away, a large circle had been scratched deeply into the dirt. Within the circle, a five-pointed star had been traced, its shape barely discernible in the dim light.

At four of the five points of the star sat a witch; their staffs stood upright in the soil behind them, marking the point where star and circle met. The witches were naked, their hair unbound, and they sat cross-legged, their eyes closed. They had sat that way all night, each enduring the Ordeal in silence. Isabeau bowed to all four witches, then sat at the fifth point of the pentagram. To her right was Meghan of the Beasts; to her left Seychella, whose powers were strongest in the elements of air. Opposite sat Jorge the Seer, who saw what others could not. At the fourth point sat a witch Isabeau had never seen before. Like Jorge, she was very frail, and she sat wreathed in pale hair that floated about her, long as a banrìgh's wedding train. As Isabeau stared at her wonderingly, she opened her eyes and they were a bright and brilliant blue, and wet with tears.

"Let us celebrate the rites o' Candlemas," she said, in a melancholy voice, very soft.

Isabeau bowed her head, and fell into the familiar chant, the rites which she and Meghan had performed at the dawn of the Season of Flowers every year of her life. "In the name o' Eà, our mother and our father, thee who is Spinner and Weaver and Cutter o' the Thread; thee who sows the seed, nurtures the crop, and reaps the harvest; by the virtue o' the four elements, wind, stone, flame and rain; by virtue o' clear skies and storm, rainbows and hailstones . . ."

Deprived of food and rest for a full night, and shivering in her nakedness, Isabeau fell into a light trance, so that the sound of the chanting, the thick scent of the incense and woodsmoke, the gleam of light on water, came and went in rushing billows. When they rose to dance, she felt as though her body was twisting and stamping her feet into the earth without any prompting or control from her—she was apart, separate, away.

Afterward Seychella said, "Isabeau the Foundling, ye come to the junction o' earth, air, water and fire, do ye bring the spirit?"

"May my heart be kind, my mind fierce, my spirit brave."

"Isabeau, ye come to the pentagram and circle with a request. What is your request?"

"To learn to wield the One Power in wisdom and in strength. To ask for admittance to the Coven o' Witches so I may learn from them the laws and responsibilities o' the magic. May my heart be kind enough, my mind fierce enough, my spirit brave enough."

All four witches made a circle with the fingers of their left hand and crossed it with one finger of their right. "Meghan, your guide and guardian, says ye have passed the First Test o' Power." Isabeau looked at Meghan in surprise. "She tested ye on your eighth birthday, as the auld laws decree."

Isabeau remembered her eighth birthday, clearly. Meghan had tested her all morning on her witchcraft skills, but she had thought those tests had been to punish her for carelessness, not the First Test of Power.

"As the Second Test o' Power decrees, ye must first pass the First Test again." Isabeau looked to Meghan for reassurance but there was none in her grim face. Suddenly a stone was thrown at her by Jorge, a hard throw and directly at her face. Automatically Isabeau deflected the pebble and it spun into the stones.

"Isabeau the Foundling has passed the Trial o' Air—to move that which is already moving," the unknown witch said. Her voice was very faint. "Breathe deeply o' the good air, my bairn, and goodwish the winds o' the world, for without air we should die." On the last words, her voice was tremulous with tears.

Obediently Isabeau breathed deeply of the forest-scented air and felt exhilaration fill her. She had passed the first Trial, and it had been easy!

Seychella then got to her feet and, carrying a deep bowl of water between her two hands, crossed the pentagram to where Isabeau sat, careful not to step outside the lines. She placed the bowl on the ground before her. Isabeau was surprised to see the witch's hands were now laden with rings. It was always possible to judge a witch's strengths by the number of rings, and the order in which they were worn, Meghan had once explained. On the middle finger of Seychella's right hand was the moonstone that was the reward for passing the Second Test of Power. On her heart finger was the blue topaz, showing her strongest element was air, and on her second finger a garnet, showing she had also mastered the element of Fire. On her left hand, Seychella wore a sapphire on her heart finger, indicating she had passed the Sorceress Test of Air. Seychella was therefore a powerful sorceress—many witches never earned more than one or two rings. Only rarely was a witch powerful enough to earn all ten rings, and even Tabithas had only won seven.

Meghan and the silver-haired witch also rose and came to where they could see the bucket of water. Isabeau had time to notice their hands were also laden with rings before Seychella intoned, "The Trial o' Water. Immediately Isabeau focused all her energies on the bowl, trying not to move a finger. It was somehow easier to use the One Power if you could use gestures, but Meghan said that was the sign of a novice: real witches could exert the One Power even if their hands and feet were bound. Isabeau had never found the element of water very easy, and though she strained, there was no response from the bowl. Exerting every ounce of her strength she willed the water to move. At last it began to lurch about in the bowl, slopping from side to side, splashing over the rim.

"Control," Meghan said, and gradually the water quietened until it was gently lapping the sides of the bowl.

"Isabeau the Foundling has passed the Trial o' Water—the ebb and flow o' water contained," Seychella said. "Drink deeply o' the good water, lassie, and goodwish the rivers and seas o' the world, for without water we should die."

Isabeau gratefully drank from the bowl before her, for she was very thirsty. The water tasted clear and fresh and rushed through her like rain through the dry bed of a burn. Meghan went back to her position where she picked up a pot of soil and three twists of bark. Isabeau sat back confidently, and when her guardian brought over the clay pot, looked carefully at her hands. She could hardly contain a gasp when she saw that Meghan wore seven rings—a moonstone, garnet, jade, turquoise and blue topaz on her right hand that proclaimed her as master of all five of the elements, and on her left hand, an emerald, the highest level in the Element of Earth, and an opal, sorceress ring of the Element of Spirit.

"Meghan, are ye . . . ye must be . . . Meghan, are ye a sorceress?"

"How can ye no' ken!" Seychella scolded. "Ye live for sixteen years with a Sorceress o' the first order, and ye do no' guess?"

"Peace, Seychella. The lass has known no witch but me, how was she to ken? All her learning has come from books and from mimicking me—she has never seen the rings afore, they are too precious for bairns to play with and too dangerous for me to wear. How was she to ken?"

"But—" Isabeau began.

"No' now, lass. I will answer your questions later. Now I want ye to undertake the Trial o' Earth."

With shaking hands, Isabeau undid the first twist of bark. She could hardly believe Meghan was a sorceress—and of seven rings! Her dear old grumbly guardian, who limped about the steep meadows as nimbly as Isabeau herself, and knew more about the creatures of the field and forest than anyone Isabeau had ever met. It made everything Isabeau knew suddenly shift out of place, and she shivered a little.

Inside the twist of bark was a collection of seeds, all different shapes and sizes. One by one she held the seeds aloft and named them. "Nightshade, madder, sweet balm, hound's tongue, periwinkle, ragwort," she chanted, while her mind continued to grapple with the revelation that her guardian was no common wood witch. "Elder, silverweed, juniper, hazelnut, bryony, lady's smock, loosestrife, blackberry, bellfruit, apple . . ."

When she had finished, the four witches did not indicate by word or gesture whether she was correct, but merely told her to choose three of the seeds and plant them in the pot. This was difficult. Isabeau was given no clue as to what the witches wanted from her and each of the seeds had different properties, some healing, some nourishing, some poisonous. After giving the matter due consideration, Isabeau carefully selected three seeds—angelica, oats and hazel—and planted them in the soil. Angelica was sometimes called heart's ease, for its healing and strengthening properties. Every part of the plant from the root to the flower to the seed could be utilized, and it could reduce any fever or inflammation, whether internal or external. Oats was an obvious choice—if food was scarce, a body could live on porridge alone for months. The third seed had been harder, but Isabeau at last settled on hazel, for like angelica it had strong medicinal powers but, like oats, it could also be eaten and was rich in protein and other vital minerals. Most importantly, it was one of the sacred woods, the timber from which witches' staffs were often made, the handles of witch daggers. After she had planted the seeds, she watered them and passed her hand over the soil, concentrating, as she had often seen her guardian do.

Inside the next twist were pieces of fragrant bark, leafy twigs, dried flowers and berries. Again Isabeau named each one and its properties, and again there was no reaction from the witches. With a sigh, Isabeau opened the third twist. It was now fully light, which helped her in naming the powdered ores and minerals contained within. Isabeau had a little more trouble here, for the powders were not ones she came across in her daily life, as the seeds and herbs had been. As she named them, Isabeau scattered some into the pot of soil and watered the minerals in carefully. Next she was asked to recite the first seven languages of beasts, the common speech of birds, fish, insects, reptiles, amphibians, mammals and those other myriad creatures, named by some fairy and by others *uile-bheistean*. Isabeau not only knew the common languages, but many of the dialects, particularly the languages of the birds and mammals, so this was an easy challenge for her. Out of a sudden sense of mischief, she recited a full fourteen, but the witches did not seem to notice.

All the while Isabeau had been talking, she continued to concentrate on the seeds in the pot, warming them with her mind, feeding them with her own energy. As she recited the last few languages, she saw the soil begin to stir and blessed the many times she had seen Meghan perform this trick.

A hiss of satisfaction escaped Jorge for his blind eyes had seen what the witches had not. Seychella was on her feet in an instant, and when she saw the first seedlings feeling for the sun she called, "Bravo!"

"Isabeau the Foundling has passed the Trial o' Earth—the challenge o' knowing," Meghan said, and there was satisfaction in her voice. She brought Isabeau a plate of bread and cheese and apples and a cup of mint tea. "Eat deeply o' the good earth, my bairn, and goodwish the fruits and beasts o' the world, for without them we should die."

Isabeau, who liked her tea hot, heated it with her finger before drinking, and ate some of the bread and cheese. She felt strength returning to her, and jubilation, for she had passed the first three Trials.

The blind warlock now rose to his feet and carried a candle over to Isabeau, who smiled at him and lit the wick without even a twitch. Bored, she decided to give them a demonstration of what she really could do. She lifted her hand so the flame leaped from the candle to the tip of her finger, and then played with the flame, until she was juggling three tiny balls of fire. Before she could do anything more, Meghan said sternly, "Ye have shown us the flame, now show us the void."

Obediently, Isabeau winked the candle flame out, feeling a little resentful. *The challenge o' the flame and the void's an elementary exercise—any novice could do it,* she thought. Nonetheless she waited for the praise she thought inevitable.

"Humility and self-control are necessary attributes o' any witch," the Sorceress Seychella said sternly. "If a witch misuses the One Power, or grows to enjoy the use o' it too much, only evil can follow." Isabeau felt her heart sink.

She had heard the same words many times from Meghan, but had never paid much heed, being too eager to exercise her will upon the One Power. "Nonetheless, she has succeeded in the challenge o' the flame and the void and so passes the Trial o' Fire. Draw close to the good fire, lassie, warm yourself and bask in its light. Goodwish the fire o' the world, for without warmth and light in the darkness we should die."

Isabeau crouched by the fire until her cheeks were red and her limbs warm, before returning expectantly to her spot.

"Now for the final challenge, the Trial o' Spirit," Jorge said.

Isabeau waited but nothing happened, no one moved or spoke. She glanced at them all, meeting the silver-haired witch's sad blue gaze, Jorge's glazed eyeballs, Seychella's impatient glance. Only Meghan did not meet her eyes, staring sullenly at the ground.

"Tell us what ye see," Seychella said, and Isabeau looked about in some perplexity. She saw nothing that she had not seen for the past four hours—loch, waterfall, forest, sky.

"In your mind's eye, lassie," the unknown witch prompted.

In desperation Isabeau shut her eyes but saw nothing but fizzling darkness. She thought back to the morning of her eighth birthday, when she had been tested in this way before. She remembered how Meghan had drawn something on a piece of paper and had made her guess. "A star in a circle," Isabeau said, and heard them sigh in relief. Involuntarily she looked at Meghan and saw her guardian was staring at her with her piercing black eyes. The stare made her blush and stammer, "I remember the game. I see nothing now."

"Odd," Seychella said. "Do we pass her or fail her? She has given the right response."

"Surely she must see it. It is the challenge o' clear seeing," the stranger said. Isabeau looked appealingly at Meghan but it was Jorge who answered, saying, "She gave the right answer. Who are we to understand the ways o' the Power? How she came to the right answer is surely a matter for Eà."

Relief flooded her. She tried to remember if she and Meghan had ever played that game again, but she did not think they had. Surely her teacher should have prepared her for that Trial? And why had she not seen anything, when they all expected she would?

"Isabeau has given the right answer to the Trial o' Spirit," Jorge intoned. "Feel the blood pumping through your veins, my bairn, feel the forces o' life animate ye. Give thanks to Eà, mother and father o' us all, for the eternal spark, and goodwish the forces o' Spirit which guide and teach us, and give us life."

Isabeau was not allowed to rest for long, though they gave her more water and congratulated her on her Passing. Seychella was openly puzzled about the final Trial, but bowed to Jorge's judgment. Isabeau crouched by the fire again, for the sun was obscured by rising clouds and the wind was sharp, then rose and found a flat patch of rock to do her *ahdayeh* exercises.

"Snow Lion Goes to Drink," Seychella snapped, and immediately Isabeau felt her body swing into the loose, arrogant walk that she had been taught.

"Snow Lion Sniffs the Air," and Isabeau turned to face the witches, every nerve alert, her back straight and her head raised.

"Snow Lion Leaps the Rock."

Isabeau lightly bounded into the air, her arms close to her body, landing a good six feet away, her feet together, knees bent. For the next hour, the commands flew and Isabeau was made to show every one of the thirty-three *ahdayeh* stances. As her body grew tired and the commands more difficult, she felt her muscles beginning to ache and her legs tremble. Only once did she stumble badly though, and that was toward the end, performing Dragon Dives for the Kill, an exercise that involved a complicated somersault and tumbling run. Although Isabeau made the somersault as tight as she could, the rock was uneven and she stumbled as she landed. The witches said nothing, just sat at the points of the pentagram on either side of the fire, and waited for her to recover herself.

Isabeau had hurt her ankle in the fall, but she knew better than to complain or show any sign of pain. She finished the final three steps, landing neatly back in her position before thankfully sinking to the ground. Her whole body ached and she felt tears prickling her eyes, but she said nothing, only looked down at her hands clenched in her lap.

Then the Second Test of Power began. Isabeau felt her confidence returning as she easily passed the Trials of Air, Water and Earth. The first exercise involved lifting a stone from one spot to another—the challenge of moving an unmoving object. For the second, she poured water from one jug to another without moving either receptacle—the challenge of the ebb and flow uncontained. For the Trial of Earth, she called beasts to her—an otter from the loch, a coney from the forest, a crested falcon from the sky, a salamander from the sun-baked rocks, a spider from its web. This was easy for Isabeau, living as she did with Meghan of the Beasts, for all the animals in the valley were her friends. After coming to Isabeau's hand, the animals clustered around Meghan, and she spoke to them kindly, petting the coney's soft fur, stroking the falcon's bright head.

Isabeau should have found the Trial of Fire the easiest of them all, for all she had to do was use fire as a tool. She had forged many knives and spades before, and had sometimes been allowed to make simple jewelry to sell in the village markets. But her task today was to make a moonstone ring, and her hands trembled as she twisted the heat-softened silver. She had never made a ring before, and this ring would be worn by Meghan if she passed the Second Test, while she would wear her guardian's. She wanted the ring to be perfect, so Meghan could accept it with pride. It was a serious statement of trust, to give something forged by your own hand—as serious as giving away something that had been long worn and used by you, since such things could be used against you if they fell into the wrong hands. Yet this was the custom of the Coven, and so the ring she would win if she passed was the ring given to Meghan by her previous apprentice, Ishbel the Winged. Isabeau knew this ring would be one of her greatest treasures, yet one day she too would give it away, in return for a newly forged ring from the hand of her own apprentice.

It was while she was waiting for the silver to soften again that she noticed Meghan talking with a long-eared hare. Hares were not easy to talk to if you had no hindleg or white tail, but Isabeau noticed Meghan beating her hand rhythmically against the ground and wondered what had happened to alarm her. When next she glanced up, Gitâ was scurrying away from the wood witch at a great pace, even taking flight every few steps, unfolding the sails of skin between his legs.

Some other donbeag must be invading his nest, Isabeau thought idly, before turning her attention to setting the moonstone. She recognized the jewel—she had found it one day several years before while exploring in the mountains, and had given it to Meghan, expecting it would be made into a pretty belt buckle or brooch to sell. It was the only moonstone she had ever found, a slightly misshapen circle that glowed with lambent light.

She set the moonstone between silver single-petaled roses, as Meghan had instructed her the previous night, before Isabeau had been sent out to face her Ordeal alone in the forest. The other witches had left her alone with Meghan, who had spent some hours teaching her the rituals of the Testing. Once Isabeau had her responses word-perfect, and understood what was expected of her in the dawn, her guardian had taken down a narrow book with a blue cover. This was, she learned, her acolyte book, and Meghan had written in it nearly every day of her life. Meghan would not let her read it, but showed her several pages which described her conduct and progress at the lessons Meghan chose to teach her, usually in censorious tones.

The wood witch had then turned to a page very early in the book, and showed Isabeau a design drawn there. It was of a ring, the jewel set between two roses, the single-petaled variety that grew wild, in the mountains. Engraved on the band were delicate lines of thorns. Meghan made Isabeau practice her visualization Skills on the drawing, until Isabeau could draw the design again perfectly. "Remember," the witch had said, "for when ye make your first ring tomorrow."

She wondered why Meghan had insisted that she use such a design, for usually witches set their jewels in the emblem or crest of their family, or designed new shapes and patterns for themselves, according to their history. She had asked Meghan, but the old witch had just scowled and snapped, "Why must ye be always asking questions? Ye will understand when the time is right."

Isabeau had known better than to ask again, but as she carefully engraved the band of the ring with the waving lines of thorns, she wondered again. It was not an easy design to re-create in silver, but at last she finished and set the ring to cool with mingled hope and anxiety.

After each challenge, Isabeau was told to breathe, drink, eat, and warm herself and each time she goodwished the element as instructed. The sun was sinking into a bank of dark clouds, and the wind was rising, and Isabeau was so tired she could barely sit upright. She had no doubt the witches would not let her rest until the end, despite the threatened storm. However, she knew she had only one more Trial to pass, so she took several deep breaths and began to gather in her will.

Meghan passed her a piece of broken pottery. Isabeau ran her fingers over it and concentrated. She felt nothing. She had seen Meghan do this before—hold an object and tell its past—but had never tried it herself. With all her strength she stared at the shard of pottery, willing it to speak to her, but she heard nothing. In despair she passed it back to Meghan, whose face was shuttered.

Her failure astounded Seychella. Under the Creed, a witch did not have to pass the Trials in all four of the Elemental Powers but must succeed in the Trial of Spirit to be permitted entry into the Coven. As far as she could remember a novice had never passed all four elemental challenges but not the final one. Despair rocked over Isabeau and, despite herself, she began to cry.

"Stop your greetin', lassie," Seychella said. "Greetin' shall no' do any o' us any good."

Again Jorge spoke in her defense. "Her face is veiled. She canna open her third eye. I can sense the spirit in her, but she canna see. This happened to me when I was a novice, before I lost my sight. My guide allowed me to try a higher challenge in another element and when I succeeded, I was allowed to pass the Second Test o' Power."

Reluctantly Seychella agreed to allow Isabeau this loophole. Although the sun was still above the horizon, it was darkening quickly as storm clouds poured into the valley. Dragonclaw was completely hidden, and the wind was blowing the witches' long hair about wildly. Isabeau looked apprehensively at the greenish clouds, lit with lightning.

"Did ye call up this storm?" Meghan asked the black-haired witch, who shook her head indignantly. "This is no' the shape or direction storms take around here in spring." Meghan muttered and looked accusingly at Isabeau.

Isabeau found the higher Trial of Fire ridiculously easy, for all she had to do was handle the flames, which she had already done. She laughed when they told her, and conjured a ball of flame that she tossed from one hand to another. She was juggling seven balls when Seychella said with a barely suppressed smile, "Enough! I think we can say ye can handle fire!"

"I did this before, why make me do it again?" Isabeau asked, smug curiosity in every line of her body.

"Everything in its rightful time and order," the unknown witch said with a faint smile. "I think we can say ye have passed all the Trials, my bairn. Now ye must show us how ye use all o' the elemental powers. Make yourself your witch's dagger, and make it with care, for ye shall carry it for a very long time. Take the silver of the earth's begetting, forge it with fire and air, and cool it with water. Fit it into a handle of sacred hazel that ye have smoothed with your own hands. Speak over it the words of the Creed and pour your own energies into it. Only then shall ye be admitted into the Coven."

Unaccustomedly nervous, Isabeau forged herself a dagger, using the tools they gave her with dexterity and skill, and fitting it carefully to a handle of hazelwood. Her voice a little shaky, she spoke Eà's blessing over the narrow blade, then looked across at Meghan, a tired grin breaking across her face.

She had passed her Second Test! Isabeau was too tired to feel much excitement, but a certain self-satisfaction seeped through her.

Seychella spoke first. "I am concerned that Isabeau has too much pride and self-will to be admitted into the Coven o' Witches, even though she demonstrates the necessary power. I feel she is too immature. In other times, I'd say that she should spend an extra year as a novice in the Theurgia, with extra duties scrubbing floors and beating rugs, to teach her humility. However, the Theurgia is no more, and she canna have even one year there to learn the order and discipline that she needs."

The sorceress Seychella paused, and the witches fixed

their wilting acolyte with a fierce eye. The tears were very near the surface again, and Isabeau's shoulders were slumped, her cheeks crimson. She was sure that Seychella was going to say she should not be accepted into the Coven, despite her success in the Tests.

Seychella waited for a moment before letting her voice ring out strongly again. "However, the number o' lassies who can pass even the most elementary challenges is dwindling fast, and Isabeau has clearly passed the Tests with flying colors, despite her conceit. I therefore recommend that she be allowed to wear her mentor's moonstone, showing she has passed the Second Test!"

Isabeau's head jerked up, her eyes glowing blue. A deep thrill ran through her, and she gazed at the four witches with excitement.

"Come here, Beau," Meghan said, and Isabeau heard the pride in her voice. She ran and knelt in front of her guardian, burying her crimson face against her lap. "How many times do I have to tell ye to do only what ye are told to do and no more!" the wood witch scolded. "Ye must learn obedience, humility and self-control!"

"Aye," Isabeau said humbly, too happy to even think of a canny comeback.

"Hold out your hand."

Isabeau complied, tears stinging her eyes as the sorceress Meghan slowly slid the moonstone off the middle finger of her right hand and slipped it onto Isabeau's. The moonstone was small and perfectly round, and set in silver smelted to resemble two protecting hands.

"Isabeau, with this ring ye are admitted into the Coven o' Witches. Ken that ye are bound to seek knowledge, and use the One Power wisely and sparely. Ken that ye have taken but the first step on a path that may be fraught with dangers and loneliness. Ken that ye are to use the One Power only to teach, to heal, to help, but never to hurt or harm, except in the defense o' yourself and others. Ken that the use o' the One Power is in itself dangerous, filled as it is with the glamour o' power. Swear to me that ye ken and will remember these things!"

"I swear," Isabeau said, and looked down at the moonstone glimmering on her right hand. As the Coven decreed, she then handed her guardian the ring she had made and smiled at her, surprised at the trace of tears in the usually sardonic black eyes.

Meghan smiled back and thanked her, then said, "By the Creed o' the Coven o' Witches, ye must swear to speak only what is true in your heart, for ye must have courage in your beliefs; ye must swear no' to use the Power to ensorcel others, remembering all people must choose their own path. Ye must use the One Power in wisdom and thoughtfulness, with a kind heart, a fierce and canny mind, and steadfast courage. Do ye swear these things?"

"I swear. May my heart be kind, my mind fierce, my spirit brave."

"Ken this, though, Isabeau, in times o' trouble and dissent, such as we ourselves are now living, choose how and when ye tell your truth. Too many witches have died or been banished or maimed for too candid a courage. Ye were always a chatterbox and a mischiefmaker—well I remember the time ye almost had us pointed out as witches in Caeryla! Watch and listen, and be wary."

Seychella leaned forward and looked into Isabeau's eyes intently. "Isabeau, these times be difficult. The Coven o' Witches is broken, its members scattered or dead, much o' its knowledge lost. Ye are now an acknowledged witch, though merely an apprentice. Ye must learn as much as ye can. Ye show some power, though your will is unbridled. Ye must do what ye can to gather knowledge and skill, for the time will soon come when every witch in the land will be needed. Do ye understand?"

"Aye, Sorceress Seychella."

Jorge leaned forward to take Isabeau's hand in his frail birdlike claw. "Do no' fret, my dear, that ye were unable to see clearly. The veils will fall when it is time, and ye shall see and hear what is now hidden to ye. Keep faith, and may Eà's blessing be upon you."

"And on you," Isabeau answered and he squeezed her hand gently before leaning back to allow the silver-haired stranger to pass. She knelt by Isabeau's side, her eyes a vivid blue in her pale face, and embraced the newly admitted apprentice witch fiercely, much to Isabeau's surprise.

"Ye have done well, very well. I am prouder of ye than I can express. Ye fulfilled all o' the challenges, and it is a rare witch that can do that." For a moment she glanced at

Meghan and murmured, "It is more than I was ever able to do." Then she hugged Isabeau again, and tangled her fingers in her unruly red-gold curls. "It is glad I am indeed to see you so strong and bonny. Welcome to the Coven, even in these dark and dangerous times, and keep yourself safe. I could no' bear . . . There has been enough death and pain. Be careful, Isabeau, and guard your spirit carefully."

"I will," Isabeau responded, a little surprised by the emotion in the witch's voice.

"Let us go back and celebrate!" Seychella said. "It has been a long time since we've given the Test! I do no' ken about Isabeau, but I am exhausted!"

"No' yet," Meghan said.

Isabeau looked up from contemplation of her gently glowing moonstone. She recognized that note in her guardian's voice. Something was wrong. Meghan stood by their fire, and said, "I would fain give Isabeau one more Trial."

"Be ye mad? It's pouring down!" Seychella said, and indeed the rain had begun, first as a splatter of great drops, but increasing in speed and ferocity as the wind whipped the surface of the loch into whitecaps. Meghan nodded, her face so grim Isabeau began to feel afraid. "A wee while ago the wards to the valley were breached. I could no' stop the Trials after waiting so long and working so hard to make sure Isabeau was given her chance. In all the twenty years I've lived here no one has ever breached the wards. This is no stray shepherd! The animals have reported a large contingent o' Red Guards . . . and something else—a winged figure—the hare calls it a ghost."

Seychella and Jorge were on their feet in alarm. "We must flee," Seychella shouted. "We canna withstand a Mesmerd!"

"They are already searching the valley," Meghan said grimly. "The beasts tell me where they are. It is too late, they will have seen the fire by now. We will have to distract them, and meet back at the tree house. Do no' let them follow ye, and seek shelter in the trees if ye must for the Red Guards will no' find ye there."

"What about the Mesmerd?" Seychella said angrily. "It has wings, it can fly?"

"Avoid the Mesmerd at all costs," Meghan said, just as Isabeau gave a cry of dismay. Through the trees she could see a line of red as soldiers ran down toward them. There were about sixty of them, and by the expression on their faces, they had seen the five witches.

"I want to give Isabeau the Sorceress Test o' Fire," Meghan said.

The stranger-witch looked at Isabeau with her very blue eyes. "Sorceress level? Is she ready?"

"In the name o' the Spinners, hurry!" Seychella shouted.

"What is it?" Isabeau cried, as the Red Guards lifted their claymores and began to run toward them. There was no doubt that they were in very real danger, for the signs of witchcraft were all about them: the circle and the pentagram scratched in the dust, the bowl of water and the pot of soil, the unbound hair and beringed fingers of the witches. If they were taken, they would be burned to death.

Meghan gripped Isabeau's arm. "The Sorceress Test o' Fire—to use flame as a weapon," she said. "Now, Isabeau!"

Instinctively Isabeau threw a great ball of flame and was shocked to her core when soldiers fell screaming, one desperately trying to beat out the flames that engulfed him. Shaking with an inner chill, she threw another and another, but the soldiers just kept coming. Jorge huddled by her side, not even trying to protect himself as arrows rained toward them from the crossbowmen. Without even thinking, Isabeau deflected the arrows and brought up a great sheet of flame between them and the soldiers. Jorge's raven dropped suddenly out of the sky, beating at the soldiers' heads with his wings. Seychella shouted into the wind, bringing the whole force of the storm whirling upon the Red Guard. As the five witches huddled in the calm eye of the storm, the soldiers fought to advance against the wind and the rain.

The unknown witch took Isabeau's hands. "It is time for me to go. Ye have done well, my daughter. Be no' afraid o' your Power. It is true it does terrible things, but ye can also use it for good. Remember that, and do no' lose your way."

Isabeau tried not to sob. The use of fire as a weapon had indeed shocked her—she had never harmed another living thing, except by accident. However, she did not regret using the fire, the alternative could well be imprisonment and death. "Remember what Meghan has taught ye; she has been a better mother to ye than anyone could have been." The blue-eyed witch kissed Isabeau and then hugged Meghan.

"Go in love, Ishbel," Meghan said, a look of great sadness on her face. "Shall I see you again?"

"I do no' ken," the blue-eyed witch responded, and there was such melancholy in her voice that Isabeau felt sorrow piercing her in sympathy. "If the Spinners wish it, our threads will cross again. But now I must go."

Before Isabeau could exclaim in surprise at her identity, the stranger-witch was gone, her masses of hair billowing out behind her. She simply rose into the air and flew away, like a feather dragged by the wind. Isabeau cried out and even put out a hand as if to catch her, but it was too late, Ishbel had gone over the cliff.

"Will she be safe?"

"I hope so," Meghan responded grimly. "But let us look out for ourselves at the moment."

Isabeau spun to see the soldiers very close now, the Mesmerd hovering right behind them, its arms stretching forward as if to embrace her. Rearing up against the billowing clouds, it was more than seven feet tall, with a face of inhuman beauty, huge gauze wings and a double set of multijointed arms. Around its body fluttered gray draperies, and its clusters of eyes shimmered with iridescent light. Isabeau found her gaze being drawn irresistibly to those huge glittering eyes, and her fire faltered and dropped.

"Do no' look at it!" Meghan shouted. "Do no' let it breathe on ye!"

Wrenching her gaze away, Isabeau tried to engulf the Mesmerd in fire, but in a sudden and gut-wrenching move it darted sideways and forward, avoiding her fire and was suddenly so close Isabeau could smell its marshy muddy odor. With a shriek she scrambled backward, slipping and falling, then a great woolly bear lunged at the Mesmerd, drawing its hypnotic gaze so Isabeau could crawl away. Before the bear's wicked claws could do more than rake the air between them, the Gray Ghost had enfolded the bear in its arms, pressing its hooked mouth against the bear's snout. With a shudder, Isabeau saw the woolly bear droop and fall to the ground in a shaggy heap, then the

Mesmerd again darted forward, nimbly avoiding the strike of lightning that Seychella called down against it.

The great stag, king of the valley, tossed its horns and stampeded the Mesmerd, but the creature darted away, its translucent wings whirring. Bellowing hoarsely, the stag turned and stampeded the soldiers, wounding one severely in the shoulder and knocking another to the ground. Suddenly there was a blood-chilling snarl, and a saber-leopard leaped from a rock onto the back of a soldier. Moments later it raised its fierce head, its tusks stained with blood, then with a graceful bound, leaped for the throat of another.

All the animals of the forest were there, fighting by the witches' side, called to their aid by Meghan of the Beasts. Donbeags flew from the trees, their sharp little claws raking at the soldiers' faces; coneys and hares lolloped around their feet, causing them to stumble; birds shrieked their defiance, attacking their heads and shoulders with beaks and claws; even a pack of wolves came slinking through the undergrowth, harassing the soldiers from behind. For a moment, Isabeau was exultant, thinking they must win, then she saw the Mesmerd hypnotize the saber-leopard with its myriad glittering gaze, grasp it with its four arms, and kiss the great cat's life away. The stag fell beneath an arrow, struggled to its feet, only to fall again as a soldier's claymore sliced into its neck, and the crossbowmen turned and shot down the wolves with their arrows, one gray body after another falling in mid-stride.

In anger Isabeau threw another ball of fire, and the soldier that had killed the stag fell screaming, engulfed in flames, so that Isabeau began to retch with horror.

"Do no' falter now, Isabeau!" Meghan commanded, and threw up her hand so that the ground beneath the soldiers' feet split wide open with a horrible grinding noise, swallowing the foremost soldiers.

"Quick, run! Go now. Take Jorge, look after him," Meghan commanded.

Isabeau grabbed the blind seer by the hand and dived into the loch under the shelter of the pelting rain. She swam under the water, dragging the old man behind her. At first he kicked feebly but soon he was a dead weight and she had to struggle to make any headway at all. She surfaced on the other side of the loch and looked at him cautiously, but he was barely conscious, his face as white as milk. There was nothing she could do. Isabeau dived again, and by easy stages brought him to the other end of the loch. Several times she hid in the rushes at the edge of the water to see if anyone was following them, but all she could see was the battle still raging near the waterfall: great flashes of lightning, the roar of earth moving.

Isabeau saw Seychella bring the wind whirling upon the remaining soldiers so they staggered, their cloaks whipping over their heads or tangling in their legs. The Mesmerd suddenly flashed forward and Isabeau saw Seychella suddenly pause, motionless, staring at the winged creature with bemusement on her face. The Mesmerd caught her in its arms, then turned, as if sensing Isabeau's gaze upon it. With a rapidly beating heart she dived again, her fist clenched in Jorge's hair.

At last she swam under the overhang of rock that concealed the water-cave under the tree house. As soon as she had dragged Jorge up onto the sandy floor of the cave, Isabeau squeezed the water out of him until he was coughing and wheezing, then half carried him through the secret passage into the kitchen.

She was surprised to find Gitâ there, busily rummaging through the pantry, piles of supplies gathered together on the table. He chittered excitedly when he saw her, and dropped the bag to bound up her body, patting her cheek with one paw before taking flight from her shoulder.

"Quickly, quickly," he chittered, and leaped back onto the table, where Meghan's pack lay half filled.

Isabeau pushed Jorge into a chair, and looked around her in panicked bewilderment. The long ordeal of her Test, followed by the sudden onslaught of soldiery, had shattered all her defenses and she found herself scurrying about uselessly as a coney, tears rolling down her cheeks. She forced herself to be calm, to think, but the sight of the Mesmerd seemed like an omen and she was terribly afraid.

Gitâ gave an admonishing chitter, and Isabeau pulled herself together, kneeling to light a fire in the grate. She was worried in case the smoke might lead their enemies right to them, but the chimney was cunningly designed, and the storm still raged outside, so any smoke would be blown into tatters in seconds. It took her a few moments to light the fire, she was so tired and drained of energy. However, at last it flickered into life and she towelled herself dry and threw on some warm clothes.

Then she turned her attention to Jorge, rubbing his arms and legs vigorously, then making him hot tea. She wished she dared make him a hot bath to ease the shivering which racked his body, but she knew how intense their danger was. The tree house might be discovered at any moment—she had no idea how much the Red Guards knew. They must be ready to move out at a moment's notice.

As Jorge ate a hastily thrown together meal, Isabeau began refilling her belt pouches. Thank the Spinners she had spent that day in the mountain meadows! They were fully stocked with herbs, nuts and vegetables, and still had some dried fruit left over from the winter. Gitâ had already gathered many useful supplies, including his own winter store of nuts, and was now busily cramming them into Meghan's satchel.

Suddenly he gave a squeak of excitement and bounded toward the secret passage. Isabeau tensed and picked up her knife, knowing she was too exhausted to fight anymore with fire. It was Meghan, though, dripping wet, her gray hair in rat's tails to her knees.

"Well done," she said. "Get yourself ready as quick as ye can. They must have a witch-sniffer—all that magic you've been expending today drew them to us like a bear to honey."

Isabeau flew to obey as Meghan tried to climb the ladder, swaying as she gripped the handrail. "Seychella?" Isabeau asked anxiously, but Meghan only shook her head grimly.

A few minutes later, when Isabeau bolted up the stairs to get her boots and a change of clothing, she found Meghan, still wet and naked, kneeling on the ground before her chest. She was hurriedly throwing things into a tiny pouch. Isabeau was amazed to see the great book disappear inside it, although the pouch was no bigger than her hand and the book so massive she could barely lift it.

"You're shivering, Meghan, get dressed!" Isabeau cried.

"This is more important," Meghan said abstractedly. "I canna allow them to get their hands on my treasures."

Isabeau's eyes widened as Meghan threw more into the pouch than could ever have fitted naturally. Meghan saw her look. "Magic bag," she said briefly. "One o' the treasures o' the Towers. I used it when I first came here. Everything we own came out o' this bag! Do no' dawdle, Isabeau, they'll be here any minute!"

Isabeau ran up the ladder to her own room as fast as she could, pulling on her boots and dragging her knapsack toward her. She stuffed a spare pair of breeches, a soft shirt, a dress, a woolen vest Meghan had knitted, and her sewing kit into her sturdy pack. She ran downstairs again, and in the kitchen finished packing her and Meghan's knapsacks with provisions. From each she slung a bottle filled with water from the barrel. She stuffed two light kettles with cotton bags of various sizes, all filled with tea, flour, salt, oats, and other essentials. Her belt was hung with leather purses containing dried herbs and spices, for cooking and for magic spells. She packed her witch knife, and a small saucepan, some pewter bowls, some of Meghan's healing potions and grabbed her plaid and tam-o'-shanter from where they hung on a hook by the fire. All the time, her head whirled with everything she had seen and learned that day, and with the knowledge they had to leave the valley. She had always imagined setting out on adventures, but never like this.

Jorge was much recovered after his hastily swallowed meal and had wrapped himself in an old plaid while his clothes steamed before the fire. Isabeau took his tattered robe in her hands and tried to hasten the drying, but her powers were drained and she was as weak as any novice. She was plaiting her damp hair and trying to think what she had forgotten when there was a loud hammering on the trapdoor upstairs. Isabeau jerked to her feet and ran up the ladder. Meghan was in the top room, clearing out the shelves with ruthless abandon, Gitâ helping enthusiastically. Isabeau could hear, faintly, the sound of Seychella's voice, pleading with her to open the door.

"It's Seychella," she cried. "Should I open it?"

"Do no' be a fool," Meghan said, rummaging through the shelves in search of something.

"But what if she is trying to escape the Red Guards? They'll catch her."

"I would say they have caught her already," Meghan said. "Canna ye sense the Mesmerd? It's probably holding her."

The idea that the Mesmerd was right outside made Isabeau recoil in horror. Meghan stood calmly before the trapdoor and made a series of signs with her fingers. An intricate symbol of green fire flared up for a moment, and then was gone. Meghan repeated the gestures at each of the doors on the way down the ladder, after Isabeau had carefully bolted them closed. "That should hold them for a while," Meghan said in satisfaction.

"Should we no' be going? If the Mesmerd knows we're in here . . ." Isabeau shuddered. Her guardian kept placidly transferring the contents of the kitchen drawers into the magic pouch. "Meghan!"

"Patience, my bairn," her guardian said. "They will no' get through those wards in a hurry, and Seychella never ken about the secret passages, remember?"

"But what about Seychella?"

"There is nothing we can do for Seychella now. We must look to our own safety," the old witch responded implacably.

At last Meghan was ready. She looked about her sadly and laid her hand on the living wall of the tree. "Thank ye, my friend," she said. Only then did she let Isabeau pull open the hidden entrance to the secret passage concealed behind the pantry shelves.

As she waited, Meghan absentmindedly went through the knapsack, checking what Isabeau and Gita had packed. Seeing the full bags of provisions, the change of clothing, the knife and pan, she made a grunt of approval. "You've done well, Beau," Meghan said. "At everything. I'm very proud." She thrust her hand into the pocket of her damp gown and pulled out another ring, whose stone glittered topaz yellow in the dying firelight. This jewel was curiously set, with a tiny gold rose on either side, surrounded by an etching of thorns. Isabeau recognized the design immediately, for it was the same as the one Meghan had shown her the previous night, and which now adorned the moonstone ring Meghan wore on her middle finger. She also recognized the unusual yellow glitter of the jewel as the one Meghan had hidden from her the night of Seychella's arrival.

"This stone was found with ye," Meghan said. "It is yours now, ye've earned it today."

Isabeau stared at it in amazement. A sorceress ring! It had her name inscribed on the inside. She wondered if it held a clue to her mysterious heritage.

"I did no' name ye," Meghan explained. "Ye came with the ring. I have kept it all these years for ye. I knew it was a sorceress ring, though where it came from or what the device means, I do no' ken. The jewel is called 'dragoneye' and is very rare. Come, let us go."

Leading the blind seer by the hand, they hurried down the secret passage, Isabeau's heart thumping so loud she was afraid the soldiers would hear it. The passage came out under a giant thorny bush, so they were badly scratched struggling out. They were out of sight of the tree, but nonetheless went carefully through the thick undergrowth, wary of sentries. Jorge went with them, his blind head turning anxiously from side to side.

"Do no' use your magic," Meghan warned. "They have a seeker with them." In single file, walking softly and looking about them, they made their way through the forest. Both Isabeau and Meghan knew every track in this valley, and they encountered no trouble. The storm was already passing, so that between the thinning clouds they saw the red comet rising into the sky. It seemed a bad omen.

There was only one way in and out of the valley, and that was through a system of caves that riddled the mountain wall to the west. Some were only shallow, and others gave the promise of a way through, only to lead to a dead end. There was even a loch, far below the surface, an eerie place where stalagmites and stalactites touched fingers and the ceiling rose into an intricate cathedral of stone. The caves were a maze, and a natural defense; Isabeau could still hardly believe the Red Guards had been able to find their way through. They must have employed magic. Isabeau, remembering the Mesmerd, shuddered.

Without doubt the seanalair of the Red Guards would have left a guard, and so they regrouped in the shelter of the trees, and had a conference. "It'll be best if they do no' ken we have gone," Meghan said. "When they canna break in they will try fire, and eventually the tree shall burn. It'll be best if they think we burn with her."

"They may find one o' the openings to the secret passage."

"They may. It will still be best if they do no' ken how or when we left. I think I ken a way . . ." Meghan lead them to a cave even Isabeau did not know, a hole under an overhang of brambles. They were badly scratched getting in, but felt safe they were unobserved. "Jorge, we will need light, unless ye can lead us?"

"I can see many things, but no' my way through this riddle," the seer answered, crouching by Isabeau's side in the darkness. "Meghan, dare we risk a sighting?"

Meghan shook her head. "I too would give much to use your Talent, my friend," she said. "But it is too dangerous. When we are free of the caves, perhaps we can risk it, though I'd rather no' use magic if we can help it. It's far too dangerous."

"The spirits are talking to me. We must get out o' here fast, Meghan!"

"Give us a trickle o' light, then, and I will have us away safely. Only a trickle. We must no' draw attention to ourselves."

Jorge complied, and by the faint flicker Meghan examined the tiny cave. She laid her hands on the stone and Isabeau could feel her concentrating. "Very well," she murmured and began to lead them upward, through a narrow chimney that at times had to be climbed with the help of knees and elbows. It was exhausting work, but soon they were in a larger cave and able to move more quickly. At intervals Meghan laid her hands upon one wall or another. Isabeau followed suit, trying to see what her guardian was doing.

Meghan smiled at her. "Listen," she said, and Isabeau concentrated. Soon she discerned a faint difference in the quality of the stone—one seemed colder, darker. "No' that way," Meghan said.

They wandered the stone maze for over an hour, until Isabeau was stumbling with tiredness and beginning to wonder whether Meghan knew where she was going. Once or twice they heard voices, and once they passed through the cave that looked out onto the other side of the mountain. Its rough floor was littered with the small, black bodies of the elven cats who normally guarded the entrance. A Red Guard stood uneasily in the entrance, peering out into the darkness. They flitted silently through and into an antechamber without him suspecting a thing. A few minutes later they were free of the mountain, Meghan leading them out through a crack in its flank. Outside the ground was thick with snow. Isabeau pulled her tam-o'-shanter down over her stinging ears, and huddled her mittened hands under her plaid. "Havers it's cold!" she cried.

"Quietly, now. Try no' to leave a trail. Remember the Mesmerd," and Meghan lead them through the night, Jesyah the raven flying ahead on midnight wings. By the time they finally stopped to rest, Isabeau was virtually sleepwalking. She huddled into her plaid and was asleep in a moment, but she slept badly, becoming more and more restless. She woke with a jerk and the conviction that something had happened. It was pitch-black, though overhead the comet slowly passed, huge and red, a long trail blooming behind it. Both Jorge and Meghan were on their feet, staring at the comet. Birds screeched everywhere in the forest, and somewhere a snow lion was roaring.

Dark shapes flew around the jagged peak of Dragonclaw, and the resonating bugle of their call made Isabeau's blood run cold. Dragons!

"What's happened?" she asked.

"I do no' ken," Meghan replied.

"A great act o' magic," Jorge said. "Something strange and magnificent. Someone has mastered the comet magic. Comets are no' lightly bridled." He shivered. "I am frightened, Meghan."

"So am I." They stood and watched the comet for a long while, until the flowing tail at last faded and the comet sank. "Today was the eighth day," Meghan said. "Come, Isabeau, we must speak."

She wrapped her ward back up in her blanket and sat beside her, clutching her own plaid tightly around her. "Today is your birthday, Isabeau. Ye were a few weeks auld when I found ye, wrapped in a torn cloth and placed in the roots o' my tree, where I could no' help but fall over ye. Ye had the dragoneye ring in your fist, and around your neck, a tablet o' ivory with your astrological details. This tablet I will keep, for such precise knowledge o' your place and hour o' birth can be dangerous." She paused for a moment.

"Isabeau, this is your birth-hour and this is your birth-place now."

At Isabeau's expression she chuckled a little, and said, "Really, I do mean it that way as well, for ye are now re-born a witch, no longer Isabeau the Foundling, but Isabeau the Apprentice Witch. But I mean that this hour—midnight on the eighth day o' the comet—is when ye were born, six-teen years ago. Ye were born here too, if no' quite on this precise spot. Your astrological tablet says quite clearly ye were born at Dragonclaw."

"So I wasna brought here, I was actually born here?" That demolished Isabeau's theory of a wicked uncle.

"According to the tablet," Meghan replied. She paused, her face bent. "Ye were given to me partly because o' who I am, but mainly, I would say, because I was the closest person. No one bides in these mountains, they're consid-ered too dangerous. I have no doubt that our valley was discovered today by mischance. The Guards were here to hunt dragons, and were lead to us by that pretty trick Sey-chella showed ye the other day, and by the other various demonstrations o' power that we've been throwing around. You see, Isabeau, you must no' play with weather until ye understand a wee more about it. Although that storm ye conjured up yesterday may well have saved all our lives, it was certainly luck rather than good management."

Isabeau gaped. Meghan smiled at her expression but nodded. "Aye, ye certainly brought that one up, lassie. Ye are the only one with enough power who'd be silly enough to do it." Isabeau still gaped. Meghan explained a little gruffly. "Yesterday was your sixteenth birthday. Ye ken what a key day that is for a witch, particularly ye who was born at the time o' the comet. Which is what I'm trying to explain to ye. The comet is brimful o' magic; to be born at the zenith o' its power is a very strong sign. That was why I ken ye could manage the Sorceress Test o' Fire, for I had always suspected fire would be your element. The thing is, your power is a sign I canna ignore. There is a battle going on here, Beau, and I suspect ye are going to be one o' our hidden weapons. Ye have to take on a charge for me." She paused and looked at her ward, but Isabeau was still gap-ing. "Listen, please. I want ye to take something to a friend o' mine. This is very important. Matters are coming to a head in Eileanan, and the whole future o' the country and the Coven may depend on ye seeing this charge safely through."

"A quest?" Isabeau breathed.

"Aye, a quest, if ye like. Listen to me carefully, we haven't much time and I have a lot to say. Ye must go to the Rìgh's palace—the new palace, by the sea. Ye must give this to my friend, Latifa. She will know what to do." Meghan pulled a soft black pouch out of her pocket and opened it slightly to show a magic talisman nestled inside. Fitting easily inside Isabeau's hand, it was shaped like a tilted triangle, each of the three sides about half an inch wide and inscribed with magical symbols.

"Where do I have to go? I do no' even ken where the palace is!"

"You'll find it. First ye must get out o' the highlands, and believe me that's enough to worry about at this stage," Meghan said. "The land is wild, Beau, and this time I will no' be there to watch over ye. Ye must be careful. Remember the news Seychella brought—some o' the magical creatures are growing restless and hatred o' humans runs high ever syne the Fairy Decree. Then the forests themselves can be dangerous; there are rivers and waterfalls and cliffs, wolves, snow lions and woolly bears too, Isabeau. Do no' rely on talking your way out o' problems either. Woolly bears are no' the brightest o' creatures and will no' wait for ye to say hello."

"I've lived in the forests all my life," Isabeau said indignantly. "I ken about wolves and woolly bears."

"Aye, but ye do no' understand. I've lived here for many years. The creatures o' these hills ken me, and ye are under my protection. When ye leave ye leave my protection."

Isabeau was a little sobered, both by the unknown before her and by the knowledge the valley was magically protected and she had never known. Those scary nights stumbling home after playing truant, imagining snow lions lurking behind bushes, saber-leopards behind rocks, the shadows of dragons passing over the moons! She need not have worried.

"More dangerous, though, are the people ye will meet," Meghan continued, leaning forward. Her eyes were black and piercing in her wrinkled face. "Isabeau, ye must learn to listen, no' speak; to watch, no' seek the center o' attention. Ye have received the moonstone and the dragoneye. Hide them with the talisman in this black pouch, do no' wear them. They will reveal ye as a witch to those who ken and, Isabeau, ye do no' want to be discovered. Maya's servants are strong, ye could no' fight them. Ye are only a fledgling witch, ye ken nothing! Do no' let your arrogant youth mislead ye. The ways o' the One Power are very strange and very difficult. Do no' force your learning and do no' overestimate it. Hide yourself in mediocrity."

"But—"

"Ye are no' close to being ready to wear your sorceress ring, Isabeau," Meghan said gently. "Ye understand the magic instinctively; ye need to understand it with your mind as well. Ye need to study much harder. One does no' win a Sorceress ring so easily. Ye have much to learn and many more trials to undergo."

"But I whizzed through most o' the Trials. It was only the spirit . . ." She fell silent.

"Ye were crackling with the power o' the comet, Isabeau. It was your sixteenth birthday, a very significant date. And it was only my training that got ye through the earth Trials."

"But they were easy . . ."

"Only because I taught ye. Earth is my medium, I would ken if ye were strong in it. Ye ken nothing o' the deeper secrets o' the earth and how to harness them, and I wish I had time to teach ye. Already we have started, though ye would no' listen to the silence as I bade ye. Ye canna ken the earth until ye hear her song and her daily grumbles, but ye would always chatter, despite what I said."

"I did no' ken!" Isabeau protested, startled. "Ye never said it was a lesson."

"I always said 'listen,' but ye were never good at listening," Meghan sighed, half mocking, half serious. "I hope ye have been listening tonight, Isabeau, for it may be a while afore I see ye again. The Spinners are spinning their wheel and weaving cloth o' our lives, and who kens when our threads will next cross."

"Why? Where are ye going? Why canna ye come with me?"

"In normal times I would," Meghan replied seriously.

"No matter how much I'd rather stay here in the peace o' Dragonclaw's shadow or go traveling with ye down to the sea. But I canna. I too must venture out. It is too hard to see the pattern tucked away in this wee valley. I must go and gather news and meet auld friends—the future o' all that we ken and care about may be in the balance."

"So how do I find the palace? What do I do when I get there?"

"Ye must head down through the southern pass, and travel roughly south and east through the forests and valleys till ye leave the highlands. Try and avoid the villages there, the people are surly and suspicious and may remember ye visiting with me. If all portents are true, now is no' the time to be remembered as the companion to a witch."

"But no one ever ken ye were a witch," Isabeau protested, remembering the disguises they had adopted.

"Och, some ken. With some it does no' matter; there are still witch-friends in Rionnagan. But it is better no one knows. No one must suspect ye."

"Is that only for my own safety or will it affect some plan o' yours if I'm discovered to be a witch?" An undefined disappointment filled Isabeau and made her voice sulky.

"Ye are no' a witch yet, my bairn," Meghan responded coldly. "An apprentice, merely. But ye are right, it will no' give the Coven any joy to have one o' its apprentices caught and tried, particularly one that knows the hiding place o' Meghan o' the Beasts. It would make Maya very happy to squeeze that information out o' ye!"

Isabeau was frightened. "Who are ye?" she whispered.

"I am who I am, Isabeau. The same person you've always known. Meghan o' the Beasts, wood witch, Keybearer o' the Coven."

"But I dinna ken . . ."

"There are many things ye do no' ken about me, Isabeau. My nature and character do no' depend upon your knowledge for their existence. Ye had plenty o' opportunity for observance."

Isabeau did not know what to say. How could Meghan be the leader of the Coven of Witches, the most powerful witch in the land since Tabithas the Wolf-Runner had been exiled?

Meghan read her thoughts. "I was the Keybearer for

many a long year; far too many. It has always been the custom to hold the position unto death, but what is one to do when your body refuses to die? So I retired, found this valley and the tree, and went back to the Tower more and more rarely. I was proud indeed when Tabithas was asked to become Keybearer. She held the Key only a short time, the poor lassie. When the soldiers came and the Tower was burning, she gave the Key into my hand and told me to guard it well. So here I am again, carrying a burden I thought I was free of, while Tabithas the Wolf-Runner is dead or banished. I ken no' where. But enough o' all this talk. All ye need to ken is that I am again the Keybearer, leader o' the Coven and the Thirteen Towers, and ye are an apprentice witch and must do my bidding.

"Once past Caeryla, ye must catch the ferry across Tuathan Loch to Dunceleste, then head north again until ye reach the edge o' the forest. Ye canna mistake it—it's an ancient forest and none o' the local people will go near it for it is thought to be haunted. A friend o' mine will be there to meet ye and guide ye through to Tulachna Celeste, a high green hill with standing stones in a ring. Do no' be afraid, my friend will look after ye. It is safe there, it is one o' the last places o' safety. It is a magical place, though, Isabeau. Be careful."

"I do no' understand . . ." Isabeau faltered.

"Tulachna Celeste was built by the Celestine, Isabeau, built by magical creatures from magic stone and bound about with spells so difficult they have never been unwound. Even Maya, with all her powers, could no' break down Tulachna Celeste."

"Ye keep talking about the Banrìgh as if she was some great sorceress . . ."

"Listen to me carefully, Isabeau. Maya is the strongest and most subtle Talent in the land. Only a very powerful sorceress can have done what she did on the Day o' Betrayal. But she is tainted with the corruption o' magic—she loves the Power for its own sake. She uses it for her own ends, she uses it t' hurt and harm. This is against the Witches' Creed, which ye swore to uphold tonight. Ye break your oaths, ye are in danger o' becoming another Maya—cruel, tyrannical, hated," Meghan waited until she was sure her apprentice had understood what she was saying. "Stay in

Tulachna Celeste, Isabeau, till my friend Cloudshadow says it is safe to leave again. Put yourself in her hands. I do no' want ye traveling through Rionnagan by yourself. There are bandits and outlaws everywhere, and the way is tortuous. She will no' be able to go with ye, but she will find ye the safest way down to the blue palace, or find someone to go with ye."

After a moment, Isabeau nodded. Rebelliously she wanted to protest her ability to get herself anywhere, but only a moment's reflection made her feel this might be a good time to practice listening, not speaking.

"Follow the Rhyllster for now. Stay out o' the villages if you can. Strangers are long remembered among these lonely hills. When ye get to the base o' the hills, then start worrying about crossing the river. Do no' use the ferries once you've passed Dunceleste—the ferrymen are paid well to report any suspicious strangers to Maya. Once across the river do no' follow it, syne it winds about like a sleepy snake. Head due east, toward the sea. It'll take ye a long time to reach the palace; ye should be there afore May Day, though."

Isabeau's heart sank. She could not imagine a land so large it took months to cross it.

"Maybe less." Meghan smiled at the look on her face. "The idea is to get there safely, no' quickly. The closer ye get to the palace, the safer ye'll be, strangely enough. The larger cities are used to strangers passing through and the people are less observant than the country folk. Keep the talisman in its bag; that'll muffle its force. Do no' use the Power where anyone can see ye or hear ye or smell ye . . . Aye, remember, a trained witch can smell the One Power, will be able to hear ye and smell ye using it! Take flint with ye and get in the habit o' using it. Even wee actions, like repairing your hem, can be detected if another witch is nearby."

Real apprehension stole over Isabeau. She used the One Power as naturally as breathing, in a hundred little ways, always discovering more. How was she to stop using the One Power when she was in the habit of using it so often and so usefully?

"It will do ye good," Meghan said. "Ye do no' understand what it is that ye do. Ye have real potential, Beau;

I've only ken one other apprentice to learn so quickly when they're so undisciplined and noisy."

"Who was that?" Isabeau asked with interest.

"Never mind who. Just remember, if ye are to progress beyond childish tricks and common spell-making, ye must learn control and judgment and insight. That is one reason why I am sending ye to Latifa. She is a very auld witch, very wise, though sharp-tongued. She will no' stand impudence from ye like I do."

"When am I impudent?" Isabeau exclaimed indignantly. "As if you'd ever let me . . ." Seeing her guardian's black eyes twinkle, she sat back rather ashamed.

"Latifa knows more than any other witch what is happening in the castle. And she can play tricks with fire that ye could no' imagine."

Isabeau's eyes gleamed blue with excitement. She liked the Element of Fire, it was the most challenging, sometimes arching into her hand like an affectionate cat, other times burning her with a spiteful whiplash of sparks. Earth was obdurate, Air rather frightening and Water pleasant, if rather difficult. Only with the Element of Spirit did Isabeau have no experience. She had no real conception of what it meant.

She knew it was the Element of Spirit that made great acts of magic possible, like the spell enacted by the witches' ancestors when they made the Great Crossing from their world to this one. According to the Book of Shadows, the First Coven had pooled their considerable powers and folded the fabric of the universe so they could sail their ship across the vast distances between the worlds. Meghan had often demonstrated the principle to Isabeau by pinching the cloth of her skirt between the fingers of each hand and bringing the folds together. Isabeau had always been very impressed with that story, thinking what a strange and marvelous spell it must be, to cross the universe like that.

"Will she teach me?"

"If she likes ye. Either way ye will work with her, learning what she does, and listening to all the news in the castle. I will send messengers to ye at regular intervals and ye must tell them all ye have heard. Isabeau, nothing will be too small or unimportant to tell me, I canna stress that enough. Anything which seems odd, anything at all. If portents be true, the affairs o' Eileanan are at last coming to a head."

"How will I ken your messengers?"

"I will send an animal of some kind. Beware hawks. If ye are good and study hard, ye might even be able to scry me, though not until Latifa allows ye. It is very dangerous to scry when a seeker may be watching."

"What is Latifa's work? What shall I be learning?"

"Latifa is Maya's cook," Meghan replied.

"Cook!" Isabeau cried. "I hate cooking!"

Meghan raised her eyebrows in disapproval and continued, "Cloudshadow will do her best to deliver ye safely into Latifa's hands. Ye may trust them both. Stay in Rhyssmadill till I send word. Latifa shall take good care o' ye, and teach ye much that I cannot. She is a fine witch and a loyal member o' the Coven."

"Meghan, how could ye no' tell me who ye were?"

"Who I am? I am who I have always been," the sorceress snapped. "And ye have just grown out o' childhood, Isabeau, in dangerous times. Discretion has never been your greatest strength. So I am Keybearer o' the Coven now Tabithas is gone. How would ye have profited by knowing that? Would ye have listened more to my teachings? I doubt that. I wish ye did no' ken now, since it may slip ye anytime and the last thing I want is Maya's attention. Ye must be prepared to look after yourself. Jorge canna travel with ye either for he must go to warn the rest o' the witches in the Whitelock Mountains. We can mind-talk to the ones we ken, but that is often too risky."

"What about Seychella?" Isabeau asked.

Meghan's old face twitched a little, but she said, "If they take her down to the city for trial, we should be able to help her, or she will escape herself. She is a very strong witch. If they have killed her, there is nothing we can do."

Isabeau tried to swallow the tight knot in her throat, and wondered at the wood witch's lack of grief. Surely she must be sorry? But the thin, wrinkled face was set hard with determination and the black eyes were fierce.

"Isabeau, I have taught ye as much as I can, now ye ust learn by yourself. Wherever ye go, listen and watch, ye must find many o' your teachers yourself. The jour- itself will be your first lesson. Just remember, the penalty for witchery is exile or death, and the power o' Maya grows ever stronger."

"Where are ye going?" Isabeau asked petulantly, not so sure now she wanted to leave the serenity of the mountain loch, with its flowery meadows, massive trees and the sharp fang of Dragonclaw always rearing above.

Meghan looked behind them, where the peak loomed. "I go in search o' the dragon," she said.

THE SPINNING WHEEL TURNS

Maya the Unknown

Maya rode through the woods, her shirt damp and sticky, her short hair dripping water down her neck. Despite the warm sun, the singing birds, and a general sense of health and well-being engendered by her swim, the Banrìgh was frowning. She wished she did not have to return to the castle, its corridors filled with spying servants, suspicious courtiers and zealous acolytes, her pallid husband waiting in the royal suite. For a moment her mouth curved, and she thought about her husband. He could not bear her to be away from his side for more than twenty minutes, and he would be fretting now.

He's addicted to me, she thought, *like any fool to moonbane.* Even that thought had its sting, though, for her hold over him had weakened again with the first smudge of red on the night horizon. She thought of the comet with a feeling oddly akin to fear. For sixteen years her hold on the Rìgh had been without question, so much so that she had let him drift away a little these past five years. She had known she could reel him back anytime, and she had been busy cementing her rule over the country, searching out and eradicating those thrice-cursed witches and fighting the resistance movement that had inexplicably begun to erode her power. Slowly, her enemies had been nibbling away at her security, undermining her strength.

Maybe it had been a mistake to confront them that manic day so long ago. It had seemed too good an opportunity to be missed: Jaspar in the first rage of his love, her unsure of its lasting power, and the witches unsuspecting and arrogant. The Day of Reckoning had taught her much about the range and subtlety of her own power, and had set them all on the path she had chosen. *It was the worth the risk,* she decided, *though my path is tangled now.*

Far overhead, a hawk flew through the sky, bright ribbons dangling from its talons. As its shadow passed over her, Maya shivered. The trees were thinning and she could see the gleam of water. Soon the high blue towers of Rhyssmadill would appear through the branches, built on a great spur of rock that thrust out into the loch so the castle was surrounded on three sides by water. In a way Rhyssmadill was a symbol both of Maya's triumph on the Day of Reckoning, and of her failure. She had convinced the Rìgh to build her a new palace, far away from the old castle and its Tower, with its ghosts and magics, its mysteries and secrets. For the first time in more than a thousand years the Clan of MacCuinn had moved its court from Lucescere. That was her victory and a sign to the whole land that a new order had been ushered in.

However, Maya had wanted the palace to be built on the shores of the sea, in constant sight and hearing of the waves, with the sun rising on their faces. Instead, Rhyssmadill was built on the shores of the Berhtfane, where the salt of the sea was already thinned by the rush of the Rhyllster. That was the only time the Rìgh's will did not bend to hers, for he was superstitious of the sea, like many of his people. Only the sea witches of Carraig had truly understood the sea, and they were all gone now.

Maya smiled again, and raised her gauntleted wrist for the hawk, which dropped silently and with deadly grace. It was heavy on her wrist but she carried it with customary ease. It turned its head to regard Maya through the slits in the leather of its hood, and gave a dry hiss of displeasure. With its beak it tugged sharply at a strand of her dripping hair, hurting her.

Maya pulled her head away, and stared straight ahead, her mouth sulky. As she rode over the rise of a hill, she saw Rhyssmadill ahead, its towers more ethereal than ever in the twilight. Behind the highest tower she saw the red throb of the comet, and her frown deepened. After a moment, she threw the hawk in the air so that she could scrub at her hair with the linen towel she carried in her saddle-bag. She then wiped her face free of salt, and tucked the towel out sight. The hawk gave a loud shriek and dived toward her, its claws raking through her wildly tossed locks before it again rose. With a grimace, Maya slicked back her hair with her fingers, trying not to show her irritation.

Work in shadows, she reminded herself. *Have patience.*

Her hair decorously tucked behind her ears, the hawk perched on her wrist again, she cantered up the hill by the lake. She crossed the narrow stone bridge, nodding and smiling at the guards who stiffened at her approach, their chins raised high. She passed through the great gates and, rather than crossing the formal gardens to the massive front doorway, turned down the narrow pathway that lead to the kitchens and stables. A boy ran out to take her horse, and she dismounted gracefully, stroking her mare's nose in thanks, and giving the hawk into the care of the falcon master.

As soon as Maya had reached the gardens and courtyards near the kitchen, a small, fat woman appeared in front of her with a quick curtsy.

"The Rìgh be asking for ye, m'lady. He's a wee . . . restless."

"Thank ye, Latifa," Maya said and smiled at her. "Should I wash up first, or would it be best to see him straight away?"

"A wee wash and brush wouldna hurt, m'lady," the old woman said, and trotted away, the keys at her waist jangling loudly.

Maya sighed. She was sure the old cook knew where she went when she went walking in the woods. Those shrewd old eyes did not miss much. The question was, did she share the Rìgh's superstitious fear of the sea? What would she think of Maya's love of swimming? So far the old cook had said nothing that could raise Maya's suspicions but she decided to keep a close eye on the old woman anyway.

Having climbed the many stairs to her rooms, Maya stripped off then dived into the long green pool in the center of her bedroom. Her servant Sani knelt stiffly by the pool's edge and, pouring scented oils into the water, washed her mistress' short hair thoroughly. Maya was tempted to linger, the water was so cool and sweet, but she knew how dangerous the temptation was. Sani dressed her in the Rìgh's favorite gown—a red velvet similar in style to the one she had been wearing when they first meet—and combed her hair sleek against her head.

"It is almost time," the old woman murmured, her strange pale eyes bright. "Ye must no' fail tonight, lassie, this be our last chance."

Maya nodded, and slipped through the door into her husband's suite. The Rìgh was sitting listlessly on the padded seat of the eastern bower, staring out at the comet. She smiled and sat next to him, slipping her arm about his emaciated form.

Jaspar turned his head, only then noticing her. His face lit up. "Och, my darling, ye've come back. Ye've been gone so long, I was worried. Where've ye been?"

Maya laid her head on his shoulder. "Hunting, darling. It was such a fine, crisp day."

"Aye . . ." he said, and frowned, his eyes vacant. Then his face brightened. "Hunting? I remember once—"

"Och, do no' tease me anymore about that!" Maya interjected quickly. "Ye ken it's not usual for me to be such a wet goose! I have no' fallen off a horse in years!" Jaspar laughed dutifully, but his eyes were vacant again. Maya sighed gratefully—it was not always so easy to deflect him from some memory of the past, a past that did not include her. So many of his memories were dangerous to her that she tried hard to keep him from remembering at all.

That night they ate alone in the Rìgh's quarters, served only by her own servant, Sani. The old woman said nothing the whole time, slipping silently away after the last course was served. The Rìgh was quiet during the meal, his eyes often straying to the eastern window where the casements had been left open. The comet was rising through the sky, red as life's blood, and unsettling to look at. Maya let her husband be, getting her clarsach and strumming softly so that music drifted through the gloomy room, filling the corners with melancholy. The Rìgh leaned his head on his hand, and listened. When she had finished, he said fretfully, "Sit with me," and so she came and sat next to him, idly running her fingers over the clarsach's strings. "Maya, are ye sure?"

"What, darling?"

"Are ye sure the Lodestar's gone?"

"Jaspar, it's been twenty years, surely ye still canna be mourning the loss o' that . . . stone?"

"Maya, I can hear it. . . ."

"Jaspar, ye ken the witches destroyed it. It was part o' their treachery to take the Inheritance and demolish it. I'm sorry, I wish I could bring it back to ye but it's gone."

The Rìgh sighed and rubbed at his forehead irritably. "But I can hear it."

"It's only a memory." Maya began to play again, a more lively tune this time, one that made the feet want to skip. The expression on her husband's face lightened a little, and she began to sing, a bawdy song normally heard in the lowest of taverns, not in the Rìgh's palace. That made Jaspar laugh, and soon he had forgotten the Lodestar, though occasionally a vague expression of disquiet crossed his face.

Maya sliced a bellfruit for him and poured him more wine, and as he ate, she dragged back the curtains and opened all the casements so the fresh sea breeze flowed through the room. A few of the candles blew out and the fire leaped higher, but the Rìgh hardly noticed, staring into the ruby depths of his wine. Maya gathered the silken cushions off the hard-backed couch and heaped them on the floor just below the door out onto the balcony. Casting a quick glance out at the night sky, she saw by the position of the stars that it still wanted a few hours to midnight.

Jaspar startled her by speaking. "I still canna believe that she would take the Lodestar from me like that. She must've known I would no' hurt her. It was all those other witches, they were the traitors, they were the ones who worked against me."

"All witches' loyalty goes first to the Coven," Maya said, filling his goblet with wine again. "Ye ken that."

"But she was my cousin!" Jaspar cried, and there were tears in his voice. "Everyone turned against me—the Coven, Meghan, even my brothers—they all turned against me! Everyone!"

"No' me, darling," Maya said, and kissed the side of his neck. He reached for her at once, greedily, but she slipped out of his arms, kissing the crown of his head in passing.

"No, no' ye, my darling. Ye have never betrayed me," the Rìgh said, and caught at her skirts, kissing her hand.

She had trouble freeing herself, but managed it with a smile, crossing the room to sit on the pile of cushions in the moonlight. As she expected, Jaspar followed her at once, grasping her waist and kissing her throat. She played a soft, gentle melody on her clarsach. "Talk to me some more, my Rìgh. It's been a long time syne ye have spoken like this."

"How can I be Rìgh without the Lodestar? It's a mockery!"

"Ye are Rìgh, by birthright," Maya said. "The Lodestar does no' matter. Already the people are forgetting . . ." Jaspar sighed, and began to talk of his childhood, while the comet rose steadily overhead and the light of the two moons crept further into the room. Maya played her clarsach and watched and listened, filling her husband's glass as it grew steadily emptier. Inevitably his talk came back to the Lodestar, as it so often did, but this time Maya did not distract him, just played her instrument and kept an eye on the time.

"It sings to me still. Happen it is true what they say, that it changes your blood, enters your soul . . . Its greetin', I can hear it . . . I remember Dada used to let us play with it when we were bairns. He said the more we handled it, the closer the bond; it was always our right and our burden, he said, it could never harm or be harmed by us . . ." A thought seemed to cross his mind. "Maya, how could she have destroyed it? She's a NicCuinn, she could never have destroyed it."

Maya's fingers moved more nimbly over the strings. He sighed, and listened for a moment, sipping his wine. "I remember one time Lachlan dropped the Lodestar over the battlements. It came back to his hand when he called it, though he was only a babe." Tears flowed down his face, and Maya gritted her teeth. She could not bear the way his face clouded whenever a memory of one of his brothers came to him. It was twelve years since that fateful day, yet still he grieved. He should think only of her, dream only of her, love no one but her.

Again her hand quickened on the strings and she began to sing to him, a crooning lullaby that soon deepened into a more insistent beat. The Rìgh's breath came more quickly, and he caressed her breast through the velvet. Maya slipped away from his grasp and sat on the floor at his feet, playing faster and faster. He tried to kiss her, and she got to her feet, and began to dance as she played, the heavy skirts swaying about her pale legs. Faster and faster she danced, the skirts whirling higher and higher. The Rìgh lay back on his cushions and stared at her over the top of his goblet, his breath uneven. At last the song reached its final wild crescendo and she threw the clarsach from her, dancing without music, her fingers unlacing her bodice. The mad tempo her feet was stamping out slowed, the skirt dropped away from her, and she was on the cushions beside him, his hands caressing her greedily.

As they kissed and stroked each other, Jaspar groaning in pleasure, Maya began to chant, very softly under her breath, an ancient spell. The rhythm of the words seemed to mingle with the rhythm of their bodies, quickening together, and then the tower bells were striking the hour. Triumph and gladness filled her, and she rolled on top of him so his breath caught and his back arched. As the twelfth bell sounded, she ran her tongue inside his ear and whispered, "I love ye."

Jaspar's body jerked upward in instantaneous response, and she shouted the last words of the spell, the binding incantation. Immediately the comet overhead flared brightly and behind it sprung a long tail of fire. Maya closed her eyes, savoring her triumph, sure the spell had worked, as Jaspar clutched her to him, half sobbing, half panting into her neck.

MEGHAN OF THE BEASTS

Meghan waited for a long time in the shadow of the trees, watching her blind friend and her ward struggle down the snowy slope, the raven flapping lazily overhead. Her gaze lingered on Isabeau's bright head. Knowing the child was soon to be left alone to travel these dangerous roads, Meghan's heart misgave her. Maybe she had been wrong to protect her so much. Maybe she had been wrong to let the child wind herself around her heart.

She sighed and began to climb the mountain, the donbeag cuddling under her plaid. She too had a dangerous and difficult journey ahead of her, and she must make headway while the sun still remained. Meghan feared none of the animals of the forests or hills, but these were wild mountains and there were many magical creatures who cared nothing for the sorceress Meghan. Even she had to sleep sometimes and it was then that the danger was greatest. It was then her body and spirit were unprotected. She must sleep as little as possible.

Even though Meghan's magic allowed her to glide lightly over the snow, it was still a difficult journey. She stumbled now and then; the wind was very sharp, and the higher she climbed the colder it became. Soon she had left the trees behind, and was struggling through ice and snow, her breath sharp in her side. The sun had already set behind the mountains so although the snow on the mountains to the west glowed red and gold and orange, all around her were shadows.

Gitâ gave an exasperated chitter and laid his paw on her shoulder. *You should rest, my beloved,* he said, deep in her mind.

Meghan shook her head. *No, there's so little time,* she answered. *That comet spell last night, I think it means nothing but evil for us.*

You are tired. You have not slept for several nights. You must save your strength, Gitâ scolded.

What is my strength compared to the dragon? she replied. *The dragon is more powerful than any other creature. Its strength would easily overwhelm mine.*

It is power of the spirit you need with the old one, Gitâ said, patting her earlobe. *Strength of body too, so it does not weary you. It has many tricks, the old one.*

Time is o' the essence, Meghan said.

As are you, my beloved, the donbeag said. *Sleep awhile and I will watch over you. No harm will come to you when Gitâ watches.*

Meghan shook her head. She felt clear-headed and filled with a strange strength. Her witch senses told her the Red Guards were on her trail, and she knew she had to move quickly. Her whole body ached, and reminded her of the many years she carried, the long, wearying life that dragged at her strength. When Gitâ protested again, though, she felt an aching hunger in her belly and remembered the long hours since she had last eaten. *I will stop for a while, and eat. Find me a holt,* she said, and Gitâ bounded ahead, almost invisible in the darkening air.

He found her a narrow cave in the side of the hill. Meghan sat and chewed some potato bread half-heartedly, thinking about Isabeau. Did she understand what a trust Meghan had placed in her hands? What would happen if she failed? Dread washed through her, and once again she wished she had been harder on the girl, driven her more fiercely, hammered knowledge into that stubborn, wayward head. Still, Isabeau had passed her Test, and as an apprentice witch, it was fitting she traveled her road alone. She was canny and she had power, and the journey in its way was as necessary a test as the Trials themselves.

Thinking this made Meghan rise to her feet again and begin the climb. The path was narrow now, and the fall steep. Although the moons shone brightly, each turn showed a section of path deep in shadow that could hide pits or enemies. She stumbled a little, but kept on walking, the great peak of Dragonclaw looming above her. As she walked, Meghan pondered the meaning of the comet spell, and the mysterious appearance of Ishbel the Winged. She had thought Ishbel dead. For sixteen years she had searched for any trace of her young apprentice, who had disappeared on the Day of Betrayal. She had rescued Ishbel from the Red Guards herself, and had drawn fire so Ishbel could escape. Then the girl had vanished. Meghan had sent out dream messages and carrier pigeons, asked pedlars and skeelies, tried to scry through water and fire—all to no avail. For sixteen years there had been no word or sign of Ishbel; then suddenly she had reappeared at the Test-fire for the night-long Ordeal, naked as the other witches were, hair unbound as theirs was, and as long as a banrìgh's mantle. Her blue eyes had met Meghan's in one charged look before they had closed their eyes as the Ordeal ordained, but the silence between them all the long bitter night rang with questions, accusations, pleadings and a fierce joy. It had been hard for Meghan to empty herself, to become a vessel of quietness and solitude as the Ordeal demanded. She knew it had been even harder for Ishbel for she heard the stifled breath and gasp of her weeping several times during the night.

Meghan's teeth ground in frustration. To have found Ishbel sixteen years after losing her, and be bound to silence and ritual proclamations! To have her disappear again, swept off the cliff like a white feather spinning into the storm! Where had she come from so unexpectedly, and where had she gone? Meghan's mind was busy with calculations, a burning ember of hope in her chest.

Years ago, she had been weighed down by an aching sadness that came from having outlived most of her friends and family. It was then she first wondered why her old body lived on, and began to wish for release. Then a young fair-haired girl from Blèssem had arrived for training at the Tower of Two Moons, as so many nobly born girls did in those days. The Tower of Blessed Fields in Blèssem was more of an agricultural college than an initiator into arcane mysteries, and the other neighboring Towers had either fallen into ruin or were dedicated to a single Talent or school of thought. Only at Two Moons was there training in all different facets of witchcraft, and research into magic's many manifestations. Even those with minor abilities found themselves a place at Two Moons, and there an increasing diversity of Talents was explored and celebrated.

Meghan had first seen Ishbel waiting in the courtyard of the Keybearer's quarters, her bags at her feet, a dove perched on her shoulder. The wood witch had come down to the Tower of Two Moons from her secret valley to visit Tabithas, the newly elected Keybearer, who had once been her apprentice. Such a chill of premonition crept over her when she noticed Ishbel that she had asked to be present when the girl took the First Test of Power which all novices had to pass to be allowed admittance to the Theurgia. Eight-year-old Ishbel had failed the Test, and so rightly should have been turned away. Strangely though, the old nurse who had brought her had wept and insisted Ishbel be taken in. Her father and brother had died in the Second Fairgean Wars, the old nurse told them, and a cousin had inherited the estate.

"We are no' an orphanage," Tabithas had said impatiently. "Surely the lass has some other relatives who will take her in."

The old nurse shook her head. "They all be frightened o' her."

Tabithas and Meghan looked at the nurse in bewilderment. Fair-haired, blue-eyed, the girl was the very epitome of angelic beauty.

"She can fly," the nurse said, and began to weep. "She does it all the time. In the middle o' the summer fair or when the men are bringing in the harvest; when her cousin is trying to judge the cases o' thieves an' murderers or when she is meant to be in bed. She do no' walk anywhere anymore, an' it's just no' guid for the people."

Keybearer Tabithas and her one-time teacher exchanged a meaningful look, and instructed the young girl be brought in again. Sure enough, the child floated a good foot off the ground, her fair hair shining in the light through the window, the dove flapping its white wings beside her. She drifted up and began to examine the paintings on the ceiling with an absorbed expression on her face, and would not come down or answer them. At last the old nurse climbed up on a chair and after a few futile leaps and jumps, managed to grasp Ishbel by the ankle and pull her down. All this time Ishbel had not said a word.

On impulse Meghan decided to stay at Two Moons, taking the child on as her acolyte. She had both taught her what she could and studied her closely for some clue to her magic. Nowhere in the library were there any records of flying witches, except those who somehow conquered or connected with dragons, flying horses or other magical flying beasts. There was one story of a pair of magical boots that enabled the wearer to make great leaps across the ground, covering vast distances in only a few seconds, but nowhere could Meghan find any reference to someone who could fly as easily and effortlessly as Ishbel. She seemed more at home in the air than she did on the ground, and sometimes unnerved Meghan by floating a foot or so off the bed while she slept. The mystery of Ishbel's Talent gave Meghan back a sense of mission in her life. Much as she loved the serene beauty of her secret valley, Meghan had missed the company of other witches and the challenge of exploring a new Talent gave her a new interest in life. For the first time since giving up the Key, Meghan moved back to the Tower, and for the next ten years, had enjoyed its staid routine more than ever before.

The beautiful, fair-haired fledgling witch had changed into a frail woman with such an air of other-worldliness that Meghan had been afraid. Why had she appeared just in time for the Testing of Meghan's apprentice? How had she known she would be needed? All through the long night, Meghan pondered these questions, suspicions she had harbored for years crystallizing into certainty.

Meghan was still stumbling along as the sun began to rise, her body stiff and sore, frantically trying to remember what she could of the language of dragons. She had had to learn all of the higher languages in order to pass her Sorceress Test of Earth, but that had been many, many years before, and she had never had to use it since. The energy which had carried her the long, weary miles had faded away, and Meghan was sorely troubled in mind and spirit by the exertion and events of the past three days. All she could remember of the dragons' language were stray phrases and words, and she began to fear she had made a very bad mistake.

She ate a scanty breakfast, then continued the difficult ascent toward the peak, leaving Gitâ to sleep in the darkness of her pocket. Even in the dimness before dawn, she could now see the narrow line of the Great Stairway cutting across the sheer face of Dragonclaw in an ever-rising zigzag. Soon she was at the wide platform that marked its beginning, and ready to cross under the massive arch, guided on either side by a much-damaged stone dragon, its weathered wings spread wide.

Meghan looked up uneasily, the fang of the peak jagged against the lightening sky, the first rays striking the arch so it sprung out against the dark backdrop. After a moment she sat down under its perfect curve towering far above her head, her back to the great stone dragons. She drank some water and fumbled for a handful of dried fruit. Every joint in her body ached, and she wished she could heat some tea. As sometimes happened to her lately, she slipped off into a light doze. What seemed like only a few moments later she jerked her eyes open, her witch senses warning her of danger. At first she saw nothing, but then with a chill and a sharp lurch of her heart, she realized the dragon perched above her was not another statue, as she had thought in the first confusion of waking, but living flesh.

The dragon was much smaller than Meghan expected, as high as two men but slender and surprisingly lissom. His angular head, silhouetted against the dawn-streaked sky, was crowned with a serrated crest that ran down the rippling length of his neck and back. He was perched on a high crag of rock, his tail wrapped several times around the stone, and he regarded Meghan with narrow eyes of gleaming topaz.

Despite herself, Meghan's heart pounded and her legs trembled. She lowered her eyes and said in the oldest of languages, *Greetings, Great One.*

There was a silence, then the dragon slowly moved, rising up on his powerful wings and spreading his great wings with a leathery rustle. With heart-stopping quickness and grace, he flew down to the steps, light scintillating off his shining scales. Sweat broke out on Meghan's face and hands and she had to fight the urge to scramble backward. The dragon spoke in a surprisingly melodious mind-voice. *What brings thee here, foolish human?*

I wish to speak with ye and would beg the favor o' an audience, Meghan said carefully, trying to remember the many complicated courtesies of the dragon language.

The dragon smiled unpleasantly, and settled his wings along his smooth back. *I have no wish to converse with thee. Humans hold no interest for me, except as a tasty morsel to add variety to my diet.* He yawned. *Tis been a while since I tasted human flesh, but thou dost not look very tasty to me, all skin and bone and hair. Thou mayst leave.*

Meghan did not know what to do. *But I—* she began, and heard a low growl begin in the dragon's throat. His eyes were slitted dangerously, and he was smiling unpleasantly, showing rows of sharp teeth. *Thou mayst leave,* the dragon repeated, whipping his tail back and forth.

Meghan bowed her head. *I would ask ye a question, my laird dragon.*

The dragon stared at Meghan malevolently. *Thou mayst ask, but I warn thee, I am becoming bored with thy presence.*

Why did ye bring me Isabeau? Meghan asked.

I? I brought thee nothing. I like humans not.

The dragons. Why did the dragons bring me Isabeau?

Isabeau? The dragon mind-spoke the word with a twinge of distaste. *What is . . . Isabeau?*

She is . . . or was . . . a babe. She was left on my doorstep by a dragon. In her earnestness, Meghan looked directly into the dragon's topaz eyes for the first time. She was unable to look away. She had a sensation of time rolling away, vast vistas of years, the swing of planets and stars. Sunsets bloomed above her head, clouds raced away, the world spun on its axis and the dragon's eyes glittered cold. She was conscious of sorrows greater than she could ever have imagined, of a consuming hunger, of knowledge jealously guarded, the dragon's eyes glittering cold.

Suddenly there was a scrabble of claws up her body and

Gitâ screeched in her ear. Meghan blinked, and was immediately able to look away. With horror she realized she was only inches away from the dragon, standing right in the shadow of his claws. He loomed above her, and she could tell he was smiling.

So the human witch has friends, has it? he said sardonically and sent a sudden spurt of flame toward Gitâ, causing the donbeag to scamper back in dismay.

I wish to understand why the dragons, in their wisdom and their perceptiveness, decided to leave the babe Isabeau in my care? Meghan asked again carefully, not moving away from the dragon's shadow but addressing his sinewy leg, which was all she could see without raising her head.

Why would the Circle of Seven interest themselves in the affairs of puny humans? the dragon said disdainfully, sending out a small puff of smoke and coiling away.

Meghan's eyes gleamed. At last, a break in the standoff. She had gained some information, and would hopefully be able to use it to her advantage. *Sixteen years ago, returning to my secret hideaway in fear o' my life, I found a squalling babe on my doorstep, with a dragoneye ring in her hand. It was no' hard to guess whose babe she was, but how and why did she arrive on my doorstep? I can see only one possible answer to the "how"—I ken the dragons chose me to bring up Isabeau. What I do no' ken is why.*

The dragon yawned again, though a little less convincingly than before, and rustled his wings. *And if thy pretty fairy story be true, what makes thou think we would explain ourselves to thee?* A world of scorn was contained in the last word.

The Circle o' Seven must've had a strong reason for involving themselves in the affairs o' the land, Meghan said, and tried not to look the dragon in the eye. *I was chosen to undertake this task; if I am to fulfill the charge successfully, I must understand what I am meant to do.*

The dragon smiled and stretched out his great yellow wings, hooked and clawed, so his shadow blotted out the sun and the dragon-fear washed over Meghan in a choking wave. *Thou knowest nothing.*

I knew enough to come and find ye.

And still thou knowest nothing.

That is why I beg an audience with the Circle o' Seven.

The dragon stared at her until Meghan's legs trembled and her hands were damp with nervous sweat, the impulse to stare again into his eyes almost overwhelming. *The Circle of Seven do not wish to speak with thee.*

But—

Rage against thy kind is hot in our breasts. Go, afore, I blast thy puny bones to ashes!

There was silence for a moment as Meghan desperately tried to think of another argument.

Thou no longer interest me, witch. Leave. The dragon's mind-voice was silky with menace, and tendrils of steam were rolling from his nostrils. *Leave!*

Meghan had no choice. She knew her life was of no account to the dragon. Reluctantly she bowed and began the descent again, the skin between her shoulderblades prickling, her senses stretched to their limits. As she climbed back down the steep steps, a sense of defeat welled up and overwhelmed her. She felt tired and very, very old. A haze obscured her vision, and she stumbled and fell, jarring herself badly, knocking her forehead and scraping her elbow. She swore and blinked away the tears that had involuntarily sprung to her eyes. It was many years since she had last felt so helpless and weak.

The memory of the Day of Betrayal always brought a sense of horror and pain to Meghan. That day her whole life had crumbled; her best friends had died or disappeared, and she had barely escaped with her life. The Witches of Eileanan had been a power in the land for hundreds of years before that fateful day. It had never occurred to any of them that a slip of a lass could swing the nation against them. Maybe they had become arrogant. But surely death by fire was no just punishment for a little arrogance. For that was how so many of the Coven had died, while the smoke from the Coven's ancient Towers had spiralled black and greasy into the sky.

Determination filled Meghan again. She would not allow the Coven to be crushed because the Banrìgh feared rival power. Although her own body ached and a trickle of blood was running down the side of her head, Meghan heaved herself to her feet. Slowly she began to limp back down the path, deep in thought.

She had escaped the Day of Betrayal, helped by the small animals of the field and forest who had warned her of danger and shown her their hidden paths and refuges through the countryside. She had retreated to her secret valley, working from there to rescue those of her kindred still imprisoned, and to build up a network of spies. Within days there had been a price on her head, and Meghan found it more and more difficult to move freely. She only ventured out to gather news or to buy any relics of the Towers that made their way into pedlars' carts. Soon after retreating to the valley, she had found Isabeau, and bringing her up had inevitably curtailed her movements too. So sixteen years had passed, and Meghan had worked all that time to undermine the power of the Banrìgh. She was not going to give up now.

Meghan set up camp on the bare field, well out of sight of the wide platform where she had met the dragon. This time she lit a fire and made herself a hot meal, knowing that she had been disorientated by tiredness and hunger. It had been a mistake to push herself so hard that she was exhausted when she met the dragon. Gitâ had warned her, but a sense of urgency had overridden Meghan's caution and so she had let the dragon intimidate her. She heard the donbeag chuckle as she mentally admitted her mistake, but she ignored him, making plans. Gitâ was anxious at her preoccupation, curling up on her shoulder with a cold paw tucked inside her neckline, but Meghan knew she had made an error of judgment, and she was determined it would not happen again.

At dawn the next day she made her way back to the stage at the foot of the stairs, and this time crossed under the arch resolutely.

The cobbled road lead upward at a steep angle, with a sharp step upward every twenty or thirty paces. Meghan's eyes widened with dismay when she saw how high each step was—an awkward scramble for someone of her small stature. The walls on either side of the stairway were taller than her head, and decorated with partially obscured shapes and symbols—moons and stars and circles and wavy lines, depictions of battles and crownings, magic acts and magic creatures, all surrounded by intricate knots of stone and a border of double roses etched in thorns. As Meghan could only occasionally see the view through a gap in the wall where the stones had crumbled, she found herself becoming absorbed in the everchanging scrollwork as she climbed. It seemed stories were being told, but she lacked the knowledge to decipher the scenes and so enjoyed them merely for their strange and sensuous beauty.

The higher she climbed, the thinner and colder the air became, and the more Gitâ wished for his snug little nest in a hole in the tree house's trunk. Meghan was glad of his chatter, no matter how complaining, for the further she climbed the more her apprehension grew. Once the shadow of a dragon passed over her and she found herself crouched against the wall in a paroxysm of terror, the instinctive response of humans to dragon-fear.

Once the sun was gone, Meghan had to rest for the night because the darkness hid gaps in the roadway where an unwary traveler could easily fall to their death. Even though the night was bitterly cold, she dared not light a fire, for it would act as a beacon to dragon and witch-hunter alike. She ate some bread and dried fruit, warmed some tea with her finger, as Isabeau did, and tilted back her head so she could see the stars. They seemed closer and brighter than she had ever seen before, and she studied them with a now familiar sense of unease.

Directly over her head, the Kingfisher spread his wings, while to the south the Centaur strode away, the great waterfall of stars they called his Beard glittering brightly. Just above the eastern horizon the Child with the Urn poured industriously, while to the west flamed the Fire-Eater. It was these constellations in particular which caused Meghan unease, for she had never seen them together in the sky. Normally the Child with the Urn had swung below the horizon by the time the Fire-Eater was rising. Even more strangely, the two moons seemed to have reversed position, so Magnysson the Red was lower than the delicate Gladrielle, rather than pursuing her as he always did. She wished she knew more about the night sky; she wished the Stargazers had not all met their deaths at the hands of the Banrìgh's Awl; she wished she knew what the sky foretold.

Meghan did not fall asleep until a few hours before dawn,

and woke to find a bird on her knee and a marmot in her lap, which comforted her greatly.

During the climb of the second day, she managed to scale the outer wall so she could examine the view. Despite the beauty of the panorama spread before her, Meghan's anxiety was not relieved. The lower slopes of Dragonclaw were dotted with the tents of Red Guards, and more soldiers were coming, the sun glinting off the narrow line of their spears as they climbed the steep paths. The size of the army sent against the dragons disturbed her and for the first time she wondered what other magic they commanded to be so confident. The presence of a Mesmerd with the Red Guards that had invaded her valley had been a shock, showing both the hypocrisy of the Awl's fight against magic and its ruthlessness. They must have made agreements with other magical creatures, some of which were very dangerous. Meghan tried to see what had become of her home, but the secret valley was hidden from view by a high spur of land.

As she climbed, the road became very steep, and was badly damaged by weather and time. Often she had to pick her way cautiously, testing the cobblestones before her with her staff and staying as close to the shoulder of the cliff as she could. At one point, the road entirely crumbled away, leaving a gap of nine feet or more that showed a dizzying fall of stone.

Gitâ bounded up Meghan's body to her shoulder, sending her a wry mind-message: *It's times like this I wager you wished you had Ishbel the Winged's Talent.*

Meghan had to smile at the truth of this, and stroked the donbeag's silky fur. She looked about her carefully, and noticed a small plant clinging tenaciously to life in a crevice in the sheer rock face, about three feet above her head. About the size of her fist, the herb dropped a tangle of leaves and tiny blue flowers below its exposed root. Meghan raised her hand and slowly the tendrils thickened and grew, the roots giving a visible heave as they wound tighter into the crack. A shower of stones and gravel rattled down on their heads, and Gitâ retreated under Meghan's plaid. The witch had to sit down, clenching her fists on her lap, as the tangle of branches and flowers—now the size of dinner plates—spread across the cliff face. The donbeag nestled under her hand, and she took a deep breath, feeling her age.

When the stones and boulders at last stopped crashing down, some measure of strength had returned to Meghan and she stood, surveying her handiwork. The bunch of wild thyme had blossomed into a great waterfall of vines completely covering the wall along the dangerous gap. Gitâ gave an approving chirrup, and bounded from Meghan's shoulder to the wiry branches and in a few swift movements was on the other side, his tail high over his head. "I wish it were that easy for me," Meghan sighed, and secured her staff to her pack with a rope. It took her almost twenty minutes to make the crossing, sometimes stepping on the broken remnants of the road, sometimes having to trust the vines with her full weight. Once a stone crumbled and fell away under the testing pressure of her foot, and Meghan lurched forward, her hands slipping on the vine. She was able to regain her footing after an undignified moment swinging helplessly while the roots strained at her weight. The rest of the crossing was accomplished safely, though, and she sat with her head bowed and her chest heaving for quite some time afterward.

Although the magically enhanced plant would be of assistance to the Red Guards behind her, she left it be. It had struggled hard to survive and had helped her valiantly, and she could not bear to destroy it now.

It will help us make the crossing when we come back, Gitâ said practically, and Meghan realized with a sudden chill that she had not been expecting to return.

It rained that night, a steady persistent drizzle that soaked through her clothes and left her shivering and weak. Before dawn the rain had turned to sleet, and the puddles turned to ice. Meghan crouched against the stones, rubbing her numb hands together and stamping her frozen feet. Gitâ ran back and forth, chittering loudly in his high voice. *Settle down, Gitâ,* Meghan mind-said.

Can we not go back to our nice, safe valley? Dragons should not be meddled with. Dragons are very old and strange, beloved, they do not like human beings, they do not like donbeags. Why are we here? One does not question what the dragons choose to do, one is just grateful not to be fried to a crisp. Oh, my beloved, I do not like this cold mountain with its hard stones, I want my nice snug nest in the tree. I should be cleaning out my nest now that spring is here. What if some other donbeag finds my nest and takes it for his own? Gitâ's mind-voice was shrill with anxiety.

No one will take your nest, Gitâ, but if ye wish to return ye may, though I will sorely miss your company.

Gitâ leaped onto her knee, rubbing himself against her neck. His fur was damp and cold to the touch. *How can I leave my beloved?* he said. *Already I have saved you once from the dangerous lizard, and you may need me again. No, no, Gitâ will stay, Gitâ will look after his witch.*

Thank ye, Gitâ, Meghan replied, and returned her attention to her lap, where her sorceress rings gleamed fitfully. She played with them absently, knowing that tomorrow she would reach the heights and begin the journey down the other side of Dragonclaw into the valley of the dragons. The very thought made her bowels loosen with terror. Her fingers closed around the rings so that their hardness hurt her; then, with a shiver, she carefully wrapped them up again, and stowed them safely in her pocket where she could reach them easily. She kept out only the garnet, her Ring of Fire, which she pushed onto her gnarled finger with some difficulty.

It was almost dawn now and the sky was streaky with pink and gold. Overhead a crested falcon flew, and after a moment Meghan called it down to her. The news was not good. The force of Red Guards gathering at the very foot of the Great Stairway had reached over two hundred and fifty men, and more were coming. Meghan groaned a little, then laughed harshly. There was no going back.

When she had eaten some cold porridge and drunk some revitalizing tea, Meghan rose stiffly to her feet and began the now tiresome journey to the upper platform, which marked the height of Dragonclaw. As she walked, she performed centering exercises so that she was as strong and calm as she could possibly be, knowing the dragons would not let her pass easily.

By the time she had reached the platform the shadows were lengthening and Meghan was very tired. She stepped onto the wide stone dais with some trepidation, but it was deserted, only the great statues spreading their weathered wings against the sky. She went over to the eastern corner and looked down, at last able to have a clear view to her secret valley. Meghan felt her heart shrink at the sight of great patches of burned-out forest and what could only be the corpses of animals lying here and there. The great tree which was her home was badly damaged by fire and axe, but still stood, which gave Meghan some hope.

She paused for a long moment, studying the lie of the land and memorizing where the Red Guards had set up their camps. She wondered again how Isabeau was managing, traveling through the land with so many soldiers abroad, but pushed the thought away, knowing she had no way of finding out. Grimly she shouldered her pack again and picked up her staff, but before she could take a step a shadow dropped over her, blotting out the sun.

She looked up to find a great bronze dragon diving toward her with a strident bugle, his golden wings translucent against the sun. Although she was trembling with the power and beauty of him, Meghan stood calmly on the ledge, calling greetings to him with her mind. Despite her cordiality, the dragon folded his wings and nose-dived toward her at a perilous rate.

Meghan, trying not to cringe back, yanked off her ring and held it up so the stone glittered red in the light. *Great One, I bring a gift for ye,* she mind-spoke.

With a twist of his lissom body the dragon broke from his attacking dive, settling instead on one of the crags that reared sharply upward. This one was much bigger than the dragon Meghan had spoken with before, and he had a malevolent glint in his eye. He stared at her like a cat at a mouse, and said, *What gift dost thou offer that would interest me?*

It was hard not to gaze back, but Meghan knew better than to meet his cold topaz eyes. She stared at his glittering hide instead and opened her fingers to show him the ring that lay concealed within.

A witch ring, the dragon yawned, flickering a thin blue tongue. *A pretty trinket.*

She stepped forward and laid the ring on the ground. Before she could take even a step back, the dragon had moved, as quick and deadly as a snake, seizing the jewel with the tip of his tail and tossing it into the air, catching it in his clawed foot with ease. *I thank thee for thy kind gift, witch,* the dragon said mockingly. *Thou mayst leave now.*

She stood before it and bowed low. *I beg an audience with the Circle o' Seven.*

Humans seem to have grown very bold and foolhardy in the centuries since I last spoke with one, the dragon said in Meghan's mind. *A witch who will not go away when we request it, and a gaggle of soldiers camping at our doorstep. This does not please us.*

Please forgive me for my intrusion, Meghan said. *It is only in the most extreme o' circumstances that I would no' gladly fulfill any request o' the great dragons.*

Nicely spoken, witch, the dragon replied. *Yet we have asked thee to leave our domain and thou hast returned. Why is this so?*

I am in desperate need, my laird dragon.

Why should thy need concern the dragons?

I wish to consult the dragons' acclaimed wisdom.

And are these men in red cloaks also in need of our wisdom that they bring such a force to our mountain?

I do no' ken, my laird. I am no' connected with these soldiers. I do no' ken their purpose here, though I believe they wish me ill and, I suspect, the dragons also.

The dragon regarded her with a spurious kindness. *I do not think it is thy place to tell the dragons who are their friends and who are not.*

No, my laird.

The great topaz eyes regarded her, and the long tail—longer than three horses—began to sway back and forth. Meghan waited. The dragon yawned, showing a blue-roofed mouth and many sharp, pointed teeth. *I grow weary of thee, witch. Tell me why thou hast come. Surely it is not to warn us of the coming of soldiers?*

No, my laird, I ken ye have no need o' my help. I come to seek yours.

Unexpectedly the dragon laughed. *Bold but honest. Unusual for a witch.*

Witches take an oath to speak nothing but the truth.

Aye, but how many witches keep thine oath?

I do no' break my vows.

Do witches not also take an oath to respect the lives of others?

Meghan clenched her fists. *Except in the defense o' life. Not in anger? Not for revenge?*

Carefully the wood witch relaxed her grip. *They are certainly strong motivations,* she said dryly, and she heard the dragon laugh again, unpleasantly.

Come, sorceress, I am tired of playing with thee, clever as thou art. Why dost thou bother our peace?

I wish to address the Circle o' Seven, my laird, if they will spare the time.

The Circle of Seven has greater concerns than the petty wishes of a mere human. What is the subject of thy concern? The dragon's tail swayed back and forth.

There is great trouble and unrest in the land, and evil forces at work. I ken the dragons see both ways along the thread o' time, and I am hoping their knowledge and wisdom will help me understand the right course o' action. As Meghan spoke, her mind-voice grew more confident, the strange phrasings of the dragons' language returning to her.

The Circle of Seven are not interested in the muddles and messes of humankind, no more than thou art interested in the battles of ants or the jousting of caterpillars. Those of thy kind are always fighting and killing each other, why should we take notice?

Because the civil war spreading across Eileanan is affecting the dragons also, Meghan responded bluntly. *Maya the Unknown has issued proclamations against the* uilebheistean *and already dragons are being killed. I know the dragons have taken interest in the affairs o' humans in the past, for why else would they save the life o' a human child? Isabeau's fate must be o' interest to the Circle o' Seven, else they would no' have given the babe into my care. Dragons do no' act without due consideration.*

True, witch, but neither do we give audience without the offering of appropriate gifts. I cannot let thee pass, for thou art empty-handed.

I have brought gifts, the sorceress said, and spread her fingers to show the dragon the jade, turquoise and blue topaz rings she had kept concealed till now.

A petty gift, one hardly suitable for the Great Circle, and unlikely to capture their attention.

True, my laird, and indeed I am ashamed to present myself afore the Circle o' Seven with so pitiful an offering. If

I could, I would fain brought the Crown Jewels o' Cuinn and the Ring o' Serpetra, but I am just an auld wood witch, with no treasures to my name but my rings.

The dragon flickered his blue tongue. *And the blood and meat of thy body.*

Mainly gristle and bone, Meghan said ruefully. *Indeed, I think the Great Ones would spit me out in distaste, my laird.*

To her surprise the dragon laughed, and the sound chilled her to the core. *True speaking, witch, true speaking indeed. Very well. I will allow thee to pass but know that the Great Ones will hold thy puny life in their talons. Do not displease them.*

Thank ye, my laird. Meghan bowed again, and the dragon spread his wings and raised his tail so all the sky was filled with the brightness and danger of his presence.

I will see thee again when thy funny little legs carry thee down the Stairway. Do not take too long or the Circle may forget thou art coming.

Meghan bowed, though her heart sank at the thought of the three days' journey ahead of her. She was heartily sick of the Great Stairway and its rotting stones.

The dragon looked at her slyly. *So thou wishes thou hadst wings to soar like the dragon, old witch. Dost thou wish to ride on my back?*

Terror and desire filled her like the hot rush of moonbane, but she lowered her head, and said, *That is an honor I would never dare imagine.*

The dragon rose on his hind legs and bugled, so that Meghan cowered down against the stones, her hands over her ears, the dragon-fear turning her blood to ice. *No human has crossed their leg over my back,* he hissed, *and no human ever will.* With a swirl of his wings and tail, the bronze dragon leaped from the stone arch and was gone. Meghan picked herself up from the stones, sighed, straightened her skirt, and began the descent.

The roadway was in much better repair on this side of the mountain, and the carvings in the walls much clearer. The old witch studied them carefully, noting the panels were now depicting a tall man with a crown of antlers, standing beneath a flowering tree. The frieze was edged with symbols of power, in particular an emblem of two dragons twisted together, and divided by the device of two roses etched in thorns.

Gitâ perched on Meghan's shoulder. *The Summer Tree,* he said, indicating the carving of the antlered man. Meghan wondered what he meant, but when she questioned the donbeag, he merely gave a chirrup and ran down her back.

Soon Meghan found a section of wall which had crumbled enough to allow her to clamber up. She sat on the top of the wall and stared with amazement at the northern mountains, which stretched as far as she could see. They were far higher than the Sithiche Mountains, and covered in snow despite the warm spring weather. Below her was a wide crater shaped like an uneven bowl, with the sharp point of Dragonclaw mimicked in miniature on the opposite side. In the center of the crater was a loch, curiously green and wreathed with steam. Meghan squinted her old eyes, and stared at the loch for some moments before realizing with a little shock that what she had thought were rocky outcrops in the water were in fact dragons. She had to stop for a moment, her heart was pounding so, and she lay down flat so her silhouette would not betray her presence. She could see three dragons in the loch, steam rising from their nostrils, and another sunbaking on a rock, its pale belly exposed. It rolled luxuriously, its muscular tail thrashing the water, and she saw that it was much larger than the dragons she had already spoken to. Trepidation filled her, and she went over her plan in her mind. She had never expected to find so many dragons, but one dragon or five meant little difference in the end and so, after a moment, she went on.

Meghan found it much easier to swing herself down the tall steps than it had been to clamber up them, and so she was in good heart by the time she reached the bottom. The statues that guarded the arch were also in much better condition, sheltered by the high walls of the crater, and so she took the opportunity to study them carefully. They were superb works of sculpture, showing every rib and claw of the dragons' wings. She could almost believe they were real dragons, turned to stone by some great act of magic.

The cobbled road continued on past the wide, green loch and led to an identical archway at the foot of the opposite cliff. Meghan realized that there must also be a Great Stairway leading to the lands of the north, where the wild snow-dwelling tribes lived. She knew of the savage tribes, one having traveled to the Towers to study a few years before the Burning. He had flown to Lucescere on the back of a dragon, causing a sensation among the witches since dragons were notoriously hostile to humans and did not take kindly to being ridden. Before the dragon-lord had arrived, the witches had thought the stories of the snow-dwellers were merely tales of the imagination, for Tìrlethan—as the land on the other side of Dragonclaw was named—was so inhospitable no one lived there except frost giants and blizzard owls.

Taking a deep breath, Meghan stepped out between the statues and onto the road. The smallest and youngest of the dragons slithered out of the loch, water streaming off his golden hide. He said nothing, but paced along beside her, dwarfing her with his sinuous length. One by one the other dragons followed suit, until Meghan's tiny form was surrounded on all sides by the great bronze bodies, their wings folded along their sides. Meghan, trying without success to control the fear their silent presence inspired in her, gripped her staff tightly and concentrated on examining the crater. Its walls rose high and sheer around the loch, zigzagged by the Great Stairway at the northern and southern ends. The loch filled most of the valley floor, with steam writhing above it, pale and ghostlike. In one side of the crater yawned seven great caverns, but unlike the caves which lined the walls of Meghan's valley, these were not natural. Shaped in a perfect arch and surrounded by intricate carvings, they were obviously built by whomever had made the Great Stairway.

The road led past the seven caverns, with wide, circular steps leading up to the greatest of the caves, the one in the center. The smallest of the dragons lead her up the steps, stepping daintily and apparently not noticing how awkward the high steps were for Meghan. Within the carved cave entrance was a wide roadway, curving down in a steep spiral so that Meghan could not see the end, and lit only at the entrance so that the heavily carved walls sank into gloom. Another dragon crouched within the shadows, his hide glimmering. Meghan bowed to it but said nothing, her breath coming fast in her throat.

Greetings again, witch, the older dragon said in contemptuous tones. *I see thou hast returned despite my warning.*

Greetings, lordly one. May your bed always be warm, your skies always blue.

May thou live to see another dawn, he replied urbanely, twitching his tail. He then led the way, pacing like a war-charger, his great head raised proudly.

Meghan followed, looking about her with amazement. The roof of the cavern was many hundreds of feet above her, smoothed into an arch and painted into the semblance of the sky, with moons and stars, comets and planets all gilded and jeweled so they glittered. The curving walls were carved like the trees of a great forest, the leaves and branches filled with the peering faces of animals and fairies, some as beautiful as a dream, others grinning wickedly. Soon it became so dark Meghan could not see, so she lit a witch light and set it at the head of her staff so she could see her way. Lit only by the faint blue light the faces seemed alive, winking at her as she passed.

The procession of dragons slowly descended into the mountain, the old witch in their midst, the taste of fear like steel in her throat. Gitâ, curled tightly into a ball, shivered in her pocket. Lost in shadows, the dragons were mere shape and sound—claws clicking on stone, wing and scale rustling, the hum of their breathing that seemed to swell and deepen the lower they descended. At last Meghan approached the end of the downward spiraling ramp and peered through the gloom, apprehension beginning to overwhelm her. The air smelled of smoke and sulphur, and the great cavern was filled with a sound like the sea, except the sea was many weeks' journey away. The sound came and went in billows like waves on a pebbly beach.

Meghan edged her way forward, hearing the dragons spreading out behind her. Beneath her feet were great flagstones, hollowed by centuries of dragons pacing, and massive round pillars supported the vaulted ceiling. Suddenly light sprang up in torches attached high to the wall in ornate brackets. The shadows shrank and fled, and the dragons' bright hides glowed. Their silhouettes, thrown against the walls, looked like a host of even greater dragons, lifting hooked wings and writhing tails in harmony with the dragons pacing forward below.

At the far end of the cavern was a set of shallow stairs that lead up to a wide dais piled high with treasures of all kinds—swords and cups and rings and statues—jeweled clasps and strings of pearls, all covered in dust and tarnished so that only here and there did gold gleam in the dancing light. The rhythmic roar grew louder, and Meghan's heart beat erratically, her fingers clenched on the staff. Between the mounds of treasure, she saw a great clawed foot, as high as her head. She lifted her staff and spread the witch light out higher and higher, at last seeing the great mound of the shoulder, taller than any tree. At her first sight of the great queen-dragon, Meghan felt her knees tremble and she fell to the ground, shaking with awe and terror. The queen was a dark bronze-green, and far larger than the others, the arch of her back hidden in shadows. Her great eyes were shut, her massive angular head resting between her front claws, her tail writhing out over the steps and along the wall. It was the sound of her breathing that filled the hall with the sonorous roar that came and went in great rushing billows. Meghan's skirt undulated behind her, the tendrils of hair that escaped from her plait blowing in the warm, sulphurous breeze of the dragon's breath.

At last Meghan gained the courage to look up, trying to control the clenching of her bowels and the trembling of her limbs. Looming through the flickering light were five other dragons, their hides a burnished green, their heads alone as large as a crofter's cottage. They were curled around mounds of treasure, in a loose half circle around the queen, their great unblinking eyes shining in the dim light. Dragon-fear washed over her in waves. If she could have moved, she would have run, but her body refused to respond to her panicked thoughts, and so for a long time the witch crouched, her arms crossed over her head.

At last Meghan's trembling eased a little, and she glanced up again, realizing as she did so that the male dragons had gathered at her back, and that they too knelt, their wings folded along their sides. There was a long silence, and then slowly the wrinkled lid rolled back and the queen-dragon looked at Meghan.

There was no looking away. The bright eye caught and

held Meghan's, and she felt a great rushing, as if the world was falling away. Again time seemed to unravel, so that she saw stars wheeling in their heavens, the passing of seasons as forests bloomed and shriveled, the race of disintegrating clouds over skies that darkened and grew bright in moments. Flesh fell away from bones, the bones decayed into dust, grass sprung through, and all the while overhead the wheeling sun chased clouds across a flaming sky. She saw her own life, saw it in the space of a heartbeat—all the long years, her triumphs, sorrows and contentments sliding past and disappearing—felt herself unravel and blow away.

Thin and bright as a burning wire, she was floating somewhere beyond time. A voice spoke in her mind, and at the sound her whole being thrummed as if she was the string of a clarsach stroked by a minstrel's fingers.

Meghan of the Beasts, I am surprised indeed to see thee, the voice said. *I had thought thou were wise for a human. What folly is it that brings thee here?*

Meghan felt like weeping. *I am . . . sorry.*

Twice thou hast crossed our command. We do not like our will to be crossed.

Meghan tried to remember why she had come, what it was she wanted, but all she could do was stare into the mother-dragon's blazing eye and watch cities be built and destroyed, seas rise and disappear into abysses, mountains spout fire and crumble into dust.

My son tells me thou hast brought gifts. Show me.

Obediently Meghan brought out her rings and laid them on the ground before the dragon, though she was unable to tear her gaze away.

I do not think this is all, the dragon said, and Meghan felt her hand slip into her pocket and bring out her great emerald, flashing with green fire, and the opal, sorceress ring of spirit. With a pang of loss she laid her sorceress rings on the ground with the others.

Where is thy moonstone, sorceress?

I gave it to my apprentice, Isabeau, when she passed her Test, as is fitting.

Ah, so little Isabeau is now a fledgling witch. The dragon seemed to sigh in satisfaction. *Her mother would be pleased.*

I believe she was, Meghan said boldly. *She seemed pleased.*

The dragon's eye widened, and Meghan felt the world spin and topple. Time rushed past in a burst of sparks, and for an instant she saw the pattern the Spinners were weaving and found it terrible. Then the insight was lost and the world steadied. She still stared into the dragon's eye, but saw now only its vast rough color and the flare of torches and vault of pillar reflected back to her, and her own tiny dark form. With the steadying of the visions came a steadying of her resolve.

Indeed, thou art not only wise for a human but clever, the dragon said. *So thou hast guessed the secret of Isabeau's birth. Did she not give thee a ring in return, as is the custom of witches?*

Meghan felt sorrow pierce her. Reluctantly she slipped her hand into her pouch and took out the simple moonstone ring that Isabeau had made for her. The loss of this ring hurt even more than that of her sorceress rings for it had been made and given with love.

The massive old dragon smiled, flickering a forked blue tongue as long as Meghan herself, though slender and supple as a snake. *It is the gifts which come hard that we appreciate the most,* she purred.

With a pain around her heart Meghan watched her rings as they were gathered up in the dragon's great claw and flicked away into the mound of treasure. Each of those tiny rings had been worked and longed for, won with years of patience and study, and worn with pride. It was hard to see them disappear into a dusty corner of a dragon's hall, just part of a pile of the treasures of ages.

So I was right? Meghan asked, determined now to extract information to the equal weight of those hard-won witch rings. *Isabeau is Ishbel's bairn?*

Indeed, she is. Well puzzled out, sorceress. There was a trace of amusement in the mother-dragon's mind-voice.

Ye forget Ishbel was my apprentice at the time o' the Day o' Betrayal, Meghan said coldly. *I ken she was with babe and I ken she escaped the Burning for I made sure she did.*

And so, my clever little witch, dost thou know who her father was?

I remember her lover, the red-haired warrior from Tìrlethan. Khaghard was his name.

And what dost thou know of Khan'gharad, Dragon-Lord, Scarred Warrior of the Fire-Dragon Pride?

Meghan spoke slowly, picking her words carefully and making sure she now pronounced his name correctly. *Khan'gharad came to the Tower o' Two Moons many years ago, when the Coven o' Witches was at the height o' its power. He said he came to learn from us, saying he had mastered all that his country's wise ones could teach him and he wanted more. He was, I remember, particularly interested in dragon lore, and so I arranged for him to be apprenticed to a warlock named Feld, a witch who had devoted much time to this study. My former apprentice Tabithas the Keybearer having long outgrown me, I had taken on Ishbel as my apprentice. She and Khan'gharad met and became lovers, despite my concern over the disruption to both their studies. Yet young people are young people, even witches, and so soon I was both pleased and dismayed to learn Ishbel was with babe.*

For a moment memories threatened to overwhelm her and as if in mockery of her pain, she saw again in the queen-dragon's eye the burning of the Tower, the execution of the witches there, the escape of Ishbel and herself. Overcome with weeping, she dropped her face into her hands. Still the visions continued, though, and she saw the final confrontation with Maya the Ensorcellor, and the death of Khan'gharad at her own hands.

I had to, Meghan sobbed. *I had no choice, it was our lives or theirs. I did no' mean to kill him, I did no' ken . . .* Then she stopped, for even in her grief she could not lie, and she had known Khan'gharad was held by the Banrìgh, even as she ordered the earth to break open beneath their feet and swallow them. She had killed Khan'gharad, her apprentice's lover, in her blood-lust to destroy the Banrìgh, and she had never forgiven herself.

And dost thou know who Khan'gharad was? the dragon asked, and Meghan heard anger in her voice. She shook her head, raising her head again and voluntarily looking the dragon in her massive golden eye. This time she seemed to fly, the earth dropping behind her and the wind rushing past her, hair billowing. She swooped and spun and soared, and the dragon's eye was the sun, drawing her ever higher.

Khan'gharad was the First Warrior of the Fire-Dragon Pride and so precious to his people. He was also the Dragon-Lord, the only man permitted to cross his leg over our backs since Aedan himself. Dost thou know why he was so favored? He saved the life of my daughter, the only female left of my line and heiress to the Circle of Seven.

Meghan's head swam and she felt faint. Her vision spun. She felt herself falling. *Then why did ye leave his daughter in my care? In the care o' the one who killed him?* she called into the sun-blazing void.

Khan'gharad is not dead, Meghan of the Beasts, Sorceress of the Earth. He still lives, though not in the form in which thou knewst him. Thou mayst rest easy in thy conscience if the thought of his death troubled thee. Besides, what care I? He was only a man, after all.

Somehow Meghan's head had cleared again, and she no longer felt time buckling around her or saw visions of terror and beauty. She reoriented herself, clutching the solid stone beneath her crouched body, and stared steadily into the dragon's blazing eye. *Wise One,* she said, *I do no' understand. Ye say Khan'gharad Dragon-laird is alive, though I saw him swallowed by the earth at my very feet. I now ken that Ishbel is no' dead either, though I thought she must be. Ye have confirmed that Isabeau is their daughter. Will ye tell me: did ye bring her to me?*

Yes, I instructed my seventh son to take the baby between his claws and fly to the valley where thou wast living. I have often observed thee there over the years and knew Isabeau would be safe with thee.

Great One, I braved the journey to your land in order to understand what role it is that Isabeau is meant to play. I have taught her and protected her as best as I could but now my hand is forced. I have been driven from my valley, the beasts o' the forest slaughtered, my own life threatened. Why did ye give me Isabeau?

There was a long silence and Meghan was aware of the other dragons still lying behind her, listening intently, though she sensed their presence rather than saw them. Her eyes were still fixed on the eye of the greatest dragon of them all, the mother-dragon, Queen of the Circle.

At last the queen-dragon answered, though reluctantly.

It is simple, sorceress. He saved my daughter, I thought I would save his. I do not interest myself in the petty squabbling of thy kind. So many wars, so many lives and deaths, what are they to me?

Then, Wise One, why have ye broken the Pact o' Aedan Whitelock and killed men and beasts in Eileanan?

Meghan was conscious of the dragons lashing their tails behind her, and the great bulk of the mother-dragon shifted, her breath hissing, so that Meghan scurried backward in instinctive terror.

For four hundred years we have not dabbled our claws in the blood of thy land, beast or human, the mother-dragon said, and her mind-voice was resonant with an ancient anger. *We honored thine forebear, the great MacCuinn, who brought us many lordly gifts. But the skies are ours and shall always be ours. Four of our kith have been killed in the last sixteen years. Four!*

All the dragons rose on their hind legs and began to bugle, a high haunting sound that echoed round and round the vast hall and must have been heard many miles away. Meghan fell to the floor, her hands covering her ears, but the sound penetrated deep into her brain, almost bursting her eardrums. At last the keening stopped, and cautiously Meghan lowered her hands. The great topaz eye regarded her sternly.

Meghan of the Beasts, Keybearer of the Coven of Witches, I know thou art not party to the hunting of dragons that seems to have become a national sport for thy people. The first dragon to die was but a kitten, and foolish to boot. He flew close to a herd and caused it to run. So when the lord of the castle rode out with his men and thy red-robed witches and shot him down, we grieved but understood it may be thy barbaric justice. Indeed, by running the herd to its death, the kitten had broken the finer points of Aedan's Pact. However, the other dragons were killed in their own land, in our traditional hunting grounds in the Sithiche and Whitelock ranges. They had done nothing to court the ire of thy people.

Dost thou understand? Humans rode into their land and hunted them down, using trickery, guile, and deceit. One of those dragons was a female, and with child! The Circle of Seven has been reduced to six! Never before have the dragons not had the full seven in the Great Circle, and to have a queen die without female issue is the worst of tragedies for us. We did not retaliate after the murder of our sons, in memory of thy ancestor, Meghan of the Beasts, but the butchering of our daughter and her unborn kitten, that we will not forgive!

The other dragons roared in approval, and Meghan felt the five other queen dragons rustle their wings, their sinuous necks bending and rubbing together. The mother-dragon continued. *It was then I called in the Circle of Seven to debate this cowardice and injustice, and a course of action decided upon. From all over the island, dragons have flown in, and the anger against thy people has been great. Still I advised caution. There are many omens surrounding us and I wished to wait until their message became clearer. Now, though, the forces of thy Rìgh are climbing the Stairway and gathering at our gate, and I cannot think they mean us well. They must know all the dragons of the land are now here, in this one place. They shot down our daughter with a poisoned spear! If they come against us in force, I fear more of my children will be killed.*

Again the keening filled the hall, rising and falling so that Meghan thought her head and heart would burst. She was horrified by what the mother-dragon had told her, and knew the dragons would lay waste to Eileanan in revenge for the death of the she-dragon. For dragons were slow to breed, and females rare among the offspring, so that the loss of a pregnant she-dragon could mean the dying out of the entire race. Meghan tried to express her shame and consternation, but the dragons were lashing their tails and twisting back and forth, so that waves of dragon-fear washed over her, choking her throat. *We shall have restitution! We shall have revenge!* the dragons began to chant, and suddenly Meghan realized there were eighteen dragons in the room with her now, some almost as big as the mother-dragon, their skins dark with age.

These are all the dragons left in the land, the mother-dragon said sadly. *Once our hordes darkened the sky, once the sound of our wings was like the beating of a god's gong. Now there are only six left of the sacred Circle of Seven, and nothing to succeed us but children.*

The keening and wailing went on for a very long time, and Meghan bowed her head and thought furiously as she waited. At last the grieving dragons quietened, and Meghan spoke again. *Great Mother, I grieve with ye that the great and honorable dragons should be hunted and destroyed in this way. It is dark times indeed that have fallen upon us, and I swear by Eà, mother and father o' us all, that I shall seek out the black-hearted witch who set her servants against ye. I think I understand now. The sorceress Maya who calls herself Banrìgh has long been jealous o' other magics. She knows the dragons have long been friends and allies o' the great Clan o' MacCuinn—.* Meghan heard hissing behind her and felt rather than heard the protest of the younger dragons, who had not known Aedan, direct descendant of Cuinn himself, the greatest sorcerer in the history of Eileanan.

Quickly she went on, *Indeed, the Clan o' MacCuinn has had many occasions to bless the goodwill o' the dragons, who have so generously and indulgently allowed us to run our herds and build our villages on the land o' Eileanan. I beg the kindness and mercy o' the Great Dragons once more . . .* Again she had to wait for the dragons to calm down, and felt deep sorrow that the dragons' distrust of humans was now running so high.

When she could, she continued. *All I beg is that ye do no' punish the good people o' Eileanan, who rightfully fear and respect ye. I ken your grief and rage consumes ye, and rightly so. So too does mine, who has always revered the wisdom and greatness o' the dragons. I ken ye could lay the land to waste, killing the stock who are our livelihood and the men who herd them, destroying our cities and towns, and fouling our rivers and lochan. I know this is within your rights under the Pact o' Aedan. It is no' the good people of Eileanan who are your enemy, though. It is the evil-hearted unknown, who has ensorcelled our Rìgh, the descendant o' the great Aedan Whitelock who was your friend and ally. I will ride out against her myself, and swear to ye I will waste my lifeblood to avenge the death o' your brothers and sister!*

This time there was a roar of approval from the dragons, though Meghan was conscious the great queen was regarding her closely. She forced herself to meet her eye again, that great golden eye slitted like a cat's and bigger than Meghan's entire body. This close to the dragon she could see how rough was the texture, and how deep the blackness of the slitted pupil, and fear was tight in her throat.

And why, Meghan of the Beasts, wouldst thou take on the dragons' debt of honor?

Because it is mine also, Meghan answered honestly. *For sixteen years I have scrabbled around like a mouse in the dark, trying to fight Maya the Ensorcellor from my valley. Slowly I have made contact with the witches who survived and they have been my eyes and ears; slowly I have helped build a resistance movement that shall be my sword; at last things are stirring! I hear reports that Maya's hold on the Rìgh is weakening, and I know he must hear the song o' the Lodestar in his ears, for I too hear it. Every day I hear it more strongly, and it sings o' battle and blood! And I too, Great One, see the omens written in the sky and in the waters, though unlike ye I canna tell all that they mean. All I ken is that the Spinners are weaving the cloth o' our lives and a new thread has been strung.*

I see. So thou dost not ride against the Banrìgh of your land because of the great evil she has done my sons and daughters, but because she does evil to yours?

Aye, Great One, Meghan admitted, though she feared the dragon's anger at her truthfulness.

Strangely, however, the mother-dragon seemed pleased, and Meghan realized her oath of truth-telling had just been tested. *So in all these schemes of thine, thou must have some plan for the dragons?*

Meghan was conscious of the dragons behind her stiffening, and again chose her words carefully. *No' at all, Great One. Who am I to make plans for the dragons who are the lords o' the sky and the smoking mountain, and the greatest o' all magical beasts? I merely beg your clemency toward the people o' Eileanan, at least until I have tried and failed in my endeavor against the Banrìgh. That way ye have still honored the Pact o' Aedan, and it is only that foul murdering witch who has broken it!* Meghan's voice broke as she spoke, years of grief and anger roughening her voice, and she could tell she had moved the queen-dragon.

Suddenly another dragon spoke, and Meghan recognized the mind-voice of the big bronze, whom she had meet on the mountainside. *And what of our anger and rightful thirst for revenge?*

Meghan took a breath and said casually, *There is still a legion o' Red Guards camping on your doorstep and dreaming o' the glory o' butchering dragons. What are they but the sword o' the so-called Banrìgh?*

There was a rustle of wings and a collective hiss as the dragons grouped in the hall moved about eagerly. The mother-dragon fixed her great eye on the wood witch and stared her down till Meghan thought her knees would buckle beneath her. *Enough,* the mother-dragon said. *I have sent my seventh son to speak with the soldiers who have dared to cross under the Arches of Dragons without permission. We will deal with the soldiers as we see fit. Leave us now. I am tired of thy meddling.*

Meghan bowed, though her heart sank in her. There were still questions she wanted to ask, but she dared not risk the dragons' anger. Suddenly a thought came to her, so crystal clear and perfect that she had to take the risk. *Certainly, oh wisest and greatest o' all creatures. May I visit with my friend Ishbel afore I leave ye?*

There was a long, deadly silence, and Meghan's head sank lower and lower until it was again resting on the floor before the dragon, her back curved. Suddenly, though, the old mother-dragon began to laugh, and the sound of the deep, rich chuckle resonated around the hall. For a long time the echoes lasted, then the great green-bronze dragon lowered her head to the floor and closed her eyes.

I have indeed underestimated thee, old witch, her mind-voice said. *Visit with the scrawny little witch if thou so desirest. It is another four or five days' journey for a witch with little legs and no wings, maybe more.* Suddenly the mother-dragon laughed again, a terrifying sound, and said, *I will call someone to fetch thee. I think thou shalt have several surprises, Meghan of the Beasts, whom dares to make demands of dragons.*

Meghan bowed as far as her stiff old body would allow her, and then began the long walk back down the hall with trembling legs. Gitâ's sleek brown head popped out of her pocket and she could feel him shivering against her side.

Boldly played, my witch. I don't know how you dared. Meghan hardly knew herself.

She was almost at the ramp when there was a great roaring as the dragons lifted their voices in anger and pain. Meghan's heart filled with dread. What had happened? She saw the mother-dragon rise on her legs so that her head brushed the roof of the cavern, a hundred feet above. *My son!* she called, and the sound of her bugle knocked Meghan over as if she were a straw doll tossed by a storm wind. She rolled over and over, and slammed into the wall of the cavern, the breath knocked out of her.

Most of the dragons had taken flight and had flown down the shadowy hall and up the spiraling ramp like fiery arrows. Only the queens were left, pacing up and down on the dais, treasure scattering under their claws. The mother of them all was still bugling in distress, and Meghan covered her ears with her hands to try to block out the noise that was louder than a hundred cymbals.

After a long while, the male dragons flew back through the great carved entrance, bearing between them the body of the youngest and smallest of the dragons—the one Meghan had met at the start of the Great Stairway. He was thrashing from side to side, his long crested tail beating against the pillars and dislodging rocks that thundered down onto the floor.

They laid him on the ground, and he cried aloud in pain, a painful sound that made Meghan's heart swell. A short spear protruded from his side, but it seemed strange that such a small weapon could be causing such a large beast so much pain. One of the dragons seized the spear shaft between his teeth and made as if to pull it out.

Stop! Meghan called. *The spearhead will be barbed. That's no way to get it out. Besides, I think it must be poisoned . . . Gitâ! Get my herbs, and hurry!*

The old witch worked on the dragon all night, trying to stop the slow spread of dragonbane through his system. As she worked she questioned the moaning dragon until she found out what had happened. The Red Guards had climbed the Great Stairway just as Meghan had done and, despite the dragons asking them to turn back, they had continued on, just as Meghan had. At the final arch they had again asked permission to speak with the Great Circle, and despite many gifts and glib words, the mother-queen had refused. The youngest of her sons, sent with the message, had been first cajoled, then threatened, and finally, wounded as he spoke with them.

At first feeling nothing more than a sting, he had delivered another warning to the leader and flown home, but the higher he flew the dizzier he became and the more pain the wound caused him. By the time he struggled back into the valley, the young dragon was in agony.

As the poison spread, the dragon became fevered and almost killed Meghan by thrashing from side to side. She called upon the other dragons to help her, and they spoke to him with their minds and held him upright with their great bulk. The mother-dragon, too large now to move far from her dais, lumbered down the stairs so she could check her son's progress herself. At last the fever began to abate, and the ugly discoloring and swelling around the wound began to die down. Exhausted, Meghan slumped back, sitting with her back to a pillar and drinking some of her healing *mithuan,* a fiery liquid that would restart almost any heart, no matter how old and tired.

Thou hast saved my son, Meghan of the Beasts, Keybearer of the Coven, Sorceress of the Earth, and for that I thank thee. The mother-dragon's mind-voice penetrated the mists of exhaustion clouding Meghan's mind. *In gratitude, I shall tell thee our name. Call it and one of my blood shall come, and give thee whatever aid is needed. Do not call it unless in great need, though, Meghan Keybearer, for even with my decree the dragon does not come lightly to any whistle.*

Then, deep in her mind, Meghan heard a name of such power that it seemed to wrench away some veil, and again she had the sensation of time unrolling away, the great joy and sorrow of a living life.

Caillec Aillen Airi Telloch Cas, the dragon intoned.

Meghan was overcome. She stared into the dragon's huge golden eye and said quietly, *Thank ye, my Banrìgh. I ken the honor done to me,* and felt a part of her drown in that rough fire.

Thou mayest choose anything thou desirest from our treasures, the dragon said.

Meghan got to her feet and stumbled forward to kneel before the mother-dragon, who regarded her with a bright topaz eye that seemed suspiciously moist. *My thanks, Your Greatness, and indeed I want nothing but the safety o' my people and your help in defeating Maya the Ensorcellor.*

So be it, the mother-dragon said, and she lifted one great claw and threw something across the room to Meghan in a scatter of bright sparks. Meghan threw up her hand automatically and when she opened her fingers, found within all seven of her rings, including the moonstone Isabeau had made her. There was also a dragoneye stone, blazing with red-golden fire. *My thanks,* she stammered and with a bound of her heart slipped her rings back into her pocket.

Now, my sons, it is time to wreak our revenge on those misbegotten soldiers! the mother-dragon cried and there was a great whirring of wings and lashing of tails as the dragons sprang into the air and flew out of the great hall. Meghan felt her breath catch for never had she seen a sight of such perilous grandeur as those great creatures on the wing.

Now, sorceress, I would like thee to meet my daughter, the mother-dragon said and heaved herself back onto the pile of treasures, where she turned round and round before settling her great bulk down again. *She will fly thee down to where thy friend is kept. Be thou careful, Meghan Dragon-Lord, and do not stay long.*

Meghan bowed her head in thanks, then rose as straight as her old back would allow, and looked the queen-dragon directly in the eye. The bright blaze opened all around her and she flew into its dark heart confidently. *My Banrìgh, there is one more thing I would fain ask ye. A few nights ago, at the height o' the Red Wanderer . . . something happened. A spell was enacted. We felt it and I ken ye did too, for we heard the bugling o' your sons. I would fain understand what it was.*

The queen-dragon shifted her great bulk, and treasure scattered under her claws, a massive chalice rolling down the stairs and coming to rest at Meghan's feet, a string of lambent pearls tangled in its handle. When she spoke there was unease in her mind-voice. *It was a Spell of Begetting,* she answered. *A very ancient spell, and one that requires great power and careful timing.*

Was the spell successful?

Indeed it was. The babe born of that spell shall have great powers indeed. Conceived at the height of the comet, it shall be born with winter and the tides of darkness. It is then that the veil between the world of the living and the world of the dead is at its thinnest. This will be no ordinary babe.

Meghan nodded, ice gripping her entrails. The queen-dragon blew gently on her, the steamy, sulphurous breath lifting her hair and warming her through. *Be of good heart, Meghan Dragon-Lord. I have known thy family for a very long time. Aedan's blood is strong in thee. Thou art his daughter indeed. Remember our name and when thou callest, I shall send my sons to thee. That I pledge for the centuries of friendship between our families.*

Meghan thanked her again, though she was still shivering with a cold the dragon's warm breath and words could not dispel. A Spell of Begetting . . . and a child born at Samhain, night of the dead. A new thread had indeed been strung.

Slowly Meghan began the long ascent out of the dragon's hall, first checking her patient, who now lay still, his hide dull and gray tinged. His skin was cooler, however, and his breathing steady. She felt great satisfaction in having been able to save his life, particularly since it had resulted in the dragons pledging their support, a result she had hardly dared dream of. The climb up the spiral ramp left her legs trembling and her heart shaking, and she cursed her old body, wishing for the resilience and vigor she had once known. Of all the challenges Meghan had faced and bested in her long and challenging life, this had to be the most difficult, the one in which she would most need all her resources of strength, cunning and wit.

Meghan reached the blessed safety and light of the valley at last, and there found a tall youngster clad all in white fur. Dazzled by the contrast between the dark hall and the brightness of the rising sun, Meghan strained her eyes to see the person's features, wondering what he or she was doing here in the valley of the dragons. Then a shock like a knife blade went through her, for the shadowed face looked just like Isabeau's. She staggered and would have fallen except for the saving arm of the stranger with Isabeau's face.

Propped against the high step, Meghan groped into her pouch and came out with a small flask. The stranger helped her unscrew its lid, and she drank a few mouthfuls of the heady liquid.

"The dragons be indeed fearful, auld mother," the stranger said, by her voice a young woman.

Meghan said nothing, only scrutinized her face and body closely, realizing the resemblance had not been the wishful thinking of a fond old woman or the aftereffects of her terrifying day and exhausting night. This young woman was indeed identical to Isabeau, except perhaps a trifle thinner in the face. She was as tall as Isabeau, and as slender. Her hair was concealed by a fur hat and ruff, but by the color of her brows and lashes Meghan could tell she would be as red-haired.

"What is your name?" she finally managed to ask.

The girl's brows rose with a certain hauteur, but she answered readily, with a halting accent as if the language was foreign to her. "I am Khan'derin, ad-Khan'gharad gessep-Khan'lysa o' the Fire-Dragon Pride, Scarred Warrior and heir to the Firemaker."

"Khan'gharad. I ken that name . . . Is he your father? Who is your mother? Ye could be Isabeau's twin, ye look so alike!" She scanned Khan'derin's face carefully, and the girl lifted her head and stared back at Meghan coldly, her face austere beneath the white fur cap.

"My mother has always been unknown to me," Khan'derin said with no sign of sorrow. "But I am daughter to the son o' the Firemaker, he who is called Khan'gharad."

"Who is the Firemaker?"

Khan'derin's answer was extremely reluctant and Meghan thought it was only the girl's respect for her age that made her answer at all. "The Firemaker is Auld Mother o' the Fire-Dragon Pride. The Firemakers are children o' the Red, given to the People in reward for their long exile, to bring warmth and darkness to the howling night, and protection from the enemies o' the prides. I am her granddaughter and heir, so it does no' really matter who my mother was. However, I am bonded to the service o' the sleeping sorceress, and I have wondered if that was done because she is my mother. Asrohc says she thinks this is so, though no one tells her anything either."

"Who is Asrohc?" To Meghan's amazement a wave of burning color swept up over the girl's face and her eyes fell for the first time. Against the crimson of her sunken cheeks Meghan saw two thin scars that ran across either cheekbone and remembered Khan'derin's strange way of introducing herself. Meghan repeated her question, but Khan'derin looked up coldly, saying, "Please come with me. I have been informed ye wish to travel down to see the sleeping sorceress. I will take ye there."

"Where are we going?"

"To the Cursed Valley, o' course," the girl replied scornfully.

Feeling very tired and very puzzled, Meghan leaned heavily on her staff, clutching her plaid about her. "I am tired. I need to rest and eat afore I can begin a journey."

"We may no' sleep in the dragons' valley, auld mother," Khan'derin said in a respectful voice that still seemed somehow mocking.

"I see," Meghan said. "Then we must go slowly, for indeed I am feeling my age this morning."

"We need no' go far, auld mother," the girl said in her cold voice. "I have been informed ye have been given the Queen's name. That means ye may cross your leg over the dragon's back. We shall fly down on dragonback."

Meghan had lived a very long time, so long she sometimes wondered why her body had not died long ago, letting her escape the prison of her body. Sometimes she longed for that release; other times she was afraid she would die before her tasks were complete. Still, she often wondered what more life could bring, she who had been born a banprionnsa but was likely to die outlawed and reviled. The moment she heard she was to fly by dragonback, she knew, and great joy welled up in her. To think she was to fly, at last, after so many years reading of it, so many years longingly watching Ishbel's aerial acrobatics! To think she, Meghan of the Beasts, was to cross her leg over the back of a dragon, that most mysterious and frightening of fairy creatures.

Khan'derin lead Meghan toward the loch where steam billowed up from the warm waters that lapped at the sides of a small dragon. Only her head was fully visible, the eyes shut, the nostrils floating just above the water.

"The dragons love the water. It is cold for them up here and the water is bonny and warm," Khan'derin said, the first thing she had said without prompting.

"Why is that?" Meghan asked, as always insatiably curious.

"The belly o' the mountain is hot. Long ago he ate all o' his enemies at a banquet in revenge for the rape o' his daughter, but the gods were displeased, for he had broken bread with them then betrayed the law o' the prides by killing his guests. So his enemies lie uneasily in his stomach and sometimes he belches. Once, long ago, he tried to rid his stomach o' them by vomiting, but all that came out were his own fiery entrails."

"Is that why the palace o' the dragons is at Dragonclaw, because the mountain is warm?"

"The dragons live deep down in the belly o' the mountain where the stone walls and floor are warm. The palace is where they come to meet their guests. No human or fairy is allowed past the surface halls. Even I have never done more than try to peep past the gate."

The baby dragon slithered out of the loch, steam rising from her gilded back and water streaming everywhere. She was a bright green-gold and smaller even than the injured dragon, only twenty feet long from nose to tail-tip. Her eyes gleamed topaz, and she bounded along rather like a colt, her sinuous body undulating gracefully.

Meghan made the dragon a deep bow, but the youngest and smallest of all the dragons merely yawned and sent a few childish-sounding thoughts to Meghan's mind. *I will take thou wherever thou wishes,* she said. *My wings need a good stretch and I can fit both Khan'derin and thou on my back. Mother says thou saved my brother from the evil soldiers, and for that I thank thee, though he be so rude most of the time. My name is Caillec Asrohc Airi Telloch Cas.*

Asrohc! Khan'derin exclaimed.

It is permitted, Khan'derin. Mother said I could. Besides, thou hast already said it so thou canst hardly lecture me!

Khan'derin again flushed red, and Meghan stared at her scars in silent curiosity. Suddenly she was so tired she thought the ground was moving faintly beneath her feet.

"Come, eat some food to fill your stomach afore we go,"

Khan'derin said. "The first time on dragonback can be truly fearful."

As Khan'derin spoke she harnessed the dragon princess with a complicated method of straps and padding that would give the humans something to hold on to and keep them from falling. Once the harness was strapped on to her approval, she laid out on a cloth some freshly baked bread and soft cheese, dried bellfruit and a flask of herbed water. Meghan ate thankfully, conscious of the steady gazes of girl and dragon alike, and trying to nerve herself for the flight. The tall girl eyed Meghan's woolen dress and plaid, then stripped off her furs. Underneath she was wearing breeches and a jerkin, both made from soft, white leather.

"It is very cold on dragonback, auld mother. Ye must wear my furs."

Meghan eyed the white skins in horror, and shook her head. Although her handwoven plaid had strands of white *geal'teas* fur entwined through the fabric, the fur had been gathered from where it had caught on thorntrees on the mountainside. Meghan could no more wear the skin of a dead animal than she could that of a dead human. Her stomach roiled at the very thought, and she continued to shake her head, despite Khan'derin's repeated offer. The girl looked at her in surprise then shrugged, and put the furs back on. She then strapped a short crossbow to her back, slung a quiver of arrows over one shoulder, and pulled on a pair of leather gloves lined with white fur. Against the gray of the stone and the blue of the morning sky, she was a dazzling figure.

As soon as Meghan had eaten, Khan'derin vaulted onto Asrohc's back. She held down a hand for Meghan, who clambered up, using the dragon's knee as a step. She only had time to tie the strap around her waist and take a deep breath, before being jerked forward as Asrohc launched off. Suddenly all the world was tilting below her, vaster than Meghan could ever have imagined, and far too far below for any degree of comfort. Behind them snowy peaks curved into a wide blue haze; over Asrohc's crested head she could see the green valleys of the Sithiche Mountains and, far far away, a glitter that could only be the Rhyllster winding its way to the sea. The cold pierced her like a dagger, and she huddled her woolen plaid closer around her head and shoulders, and tried to keep her skirts from swirling up in the wind. Gitâ, huddled deep in her pocket as always, gave a protesting squeak, his sharp claws digging through her clothes.

Asrohc turned and dived, and Meghan's heart plummeted into her boots as the horizon blurred. For one awful moment she was afraid she would lose her breakfast. Then Asrohc's dive steadied, and she circled the peak several times before again plunging at a rate that had Meghan's cheeks wobbling and her long iron-gray plait streaming behind like another dragon tail.

Let us go and see what my brothers have been up to, Asrohc said exuberantly, and raced around a jagged corner of Dragonclaw as if wanting to see how close her wing tips could go to the mountain.

The sight around the corner sickened Meghan. The wide, snowy meadow that she had labored up that moonlit night a week ago was now strewn with the dead and dying bodies of the Red Guards. More than three hundred bodies lay there, their cloaks no redder than the bloodied snow, their bodies torn and charred beyond recognition. Three of the great bronze males were snacking on some of the corpses, a sight which made Meghan sick to her stomach. She leaned over Asrohc's shoulder and vomited into the air, causing the dragon to screech and whip her wing away.

"I thought they were your enemies," Khan'derin shouted into the wind.

"They were," Meghan said, trying to wipe her mouth without loosening her grip on the dragon.

"Then why do ye weep and sigh and empty your stomach at their death? Is this no' what ye wanted?"

"Aye," Meghan said grimly. "This is what I wanted. Now I am sure that blaygird times are with us!"

A little taken aback that Meghan did not find the full-scale slaughter as interesting and exciting as she did, Asrohc turned away from the sight and flew steadily over the shoulder of Dragonclaw, heading due north. Meghan had a brief glimpse of her secret valley, its loch shining green in the morning light, then they were over the high range and swooping down the other side of the mountain. Meghan peered down, seeing a wide snow-covered valley split by a river which wound away to the north. All around was peak after glittering peak of snowy mountains, where the slopes would stay white all year. In the center of the valley was a thorny forest.

"That is the Cursed Valley below. From here ye can just see the tops o' the Towers. Can ye see them?" Khan'derin said.

Wondering at her words, Meghan strained to see but her eyes were old, and all she could see were trees. They began the descent, both shivering in the cold wind that blew straight off the ice plains to the north. "What is the Cursed Valley?"

"Do ye no' ken? Are ye no' a Tower witch?"

"Indeed, I was when there were Towers," Meghan replied. "But they are all gone now."

"No' all," Khan'derin replied.

The small dragon dropped them at the foot of the northern Great Stairway, explaining that she could not fly closer because of the thickness of the forest, which would tear her fragile wings. *Besides, I am forbidden to fly very far from the Circle yet, and we have a pact with the prides not to frighten their herds.*

Meghan wondered how old the dragon was. The princess answered her unspoken thought, saying *I am only a kitten, almost a hundred years old. I am the last of the dragons to be born, and mother says I must be careful, for all the other females are now getting too old to breed and so it is up to me to have many eggs.*

How auld must ye be to breed? Meghan asked, and the dragon answered, *I am almost old enough now, though I mislike most of the young males, who do not treat me with the respect I deserve.*

As the dragon launched her sinuous green body in the air again, Khan'derin went behind a bush and dragged out a long, curved sled. Longer than her body, curved at either end and painted with the design of a ferocious red dragon, the wooden board must have been heavy, but she handled it with ease and dexterity. In the sled was a satchel of the same supple white leather as her breeches, and she rummaged inside, pulling out a variety of oddly shaped weapons and tools that she strapped tightly in place on her belt.

Meghan, feeling as finely drawn as a newly spun thread, sat down with her back to the great arch. She stared at the scrolled carving decorating the stone walls. Between every triptych was a device she recognized from her climb up the Stairway—two roses etched in waving lines of thorns. She studied these closely, wondering yet again what their significance was. "Do ye ken what the pictures in the stone mean?" she asked the girl.

"Some," Khan'derin answered. "They were carved by the Red, o' course."

"Why o' course?"

"Why, the roses and thorns," Khan'derin said in surprise, and Meghan nodded slowly. She remembered being taught the early history of Eileanan as a child, and how the Thirteen Towers had been established. There had been one, she recollected vaguely, or rather two, called the Towers of Roses and Thorns. They had been ruined long, long ago. There had been some tragedy, she remembered, and the Towers were lost. "The Red? Who is the Red?"

"The Red Sorcerer," Khan'derin replied.

Meghan had learned her history more than four hundred years ago, and much of it had been rewritten since the Day of Betrayal, so that it was hard to remember what was real and what was not. "There were brother and sister sorcerers, were there no'? Who came up into the Spine o' the World and built their Towers there. Was one o' those the Red?"

"They were both the Red," Khan'derin said. "Or so I've been taught."

"Tìrlethan!" Meghan said, and Khan'derin flashed her a strange, hostile look. "Of course. This place is Tìrlethan, now, is it no'? Dragonclaw marks the boundary on the map. Land o' the Twins. They were twins, and red-haired too!"

"Twins are forbidden," Khan'derin said in a stifled voice. Meghan looked at her aghast. "One is always left in sacrifice to the White Gods. That is another reason why the Firemaker was so troubled by my finding. What if I was in *geas* to the White Gods? But the dream told her to take me and so she did."

"But why are twins forbidden?"

"There can only be one Firemaker."

"So the . . . Firemaker . . . is one o' a set o' twins?"

"My grandmother says twins are always born to the Firemakers, and they are always red-headed. They are usually a boy and a girl; I have only ever heard o' two female twins being born once before. But then, twins are no' thought a polite subject to discuss. They are considered bad luck among the prides."

Seeing the hard planes of her facc and the thin lines of the scars, Meghan realized she would have to tread gently with this strange girl, who looked so like Isabeau but was not like her at all. "Please tell me your story," she said. "I ken I am a stranger to ye and nothing but an auld woman, but ye see, I have raised a lass who looks exactly like ye. I think your story will fill many holes in my understanding."

Khan'derin looked her over and slowly nodded. "Indeed, it is a strange story. Ye must rest a little while I speak, for your cheeks are white, auld mother." She sat down on the stone platform, crossed her legs, and turned her palms upward in her lap. She took a few deep breaths, visibly calming and composing herself. When she spoke, it was not in her natural tone of voice, but in an oddly singsong manner. "Many years ago, at the height o' the Dragon-Star, I was found on the slopes o' the Cursed Peaks by the Firemaker o' the Fire-Dragon Pride—" she began.

"I'm sorry, but I am no' sure what all these terms mean," Meghan interrupted. Khan'derin explained that the Dragon-Star was the comet that had been flaming in their skies in recent days, and that the Cursed Peaks were the mountains on whose back they were now sitting.

As Meghan nodded, Khan'derin said, "May I recommence?" Meghan smiled and Khan'derin began her story again. "Many years ago, at the height o' the Dragon-Star, I was found on the slopes o' the Cursed Peaks by the Firemaker, who had been sent a dream. In her dream she was told to come to the Cursed Peaks, and she saw there two roses, white and red as they are in the Cursed Valley, threaded through a magic talisman that was sometimes a triangle and sometimes a star. Waking the next morning she remembered the dream and so she set out alone to travel the high roads to the Cursed Valley. There she found me, half dead from exposure, and with me were my dragoneye jewel and my *sheyeta*. The Firemaker realized then that I was the babe o' her grandson, he who was long lost in the land o' sorcerers."

"How did she ken that?" Meghan asked, and saw anger cross Khan'derin's thin face. For a moment she would not answer then said reluctantly, "Because o' the red, o' course."

Meghan was puzzled, but Khan'derin had already moved on. "And I had the dragoneye." She pulled off her white leather glove to show the wood witch the ring she wore there. "The dragons had given my father, Khan'gharad the Dragon-Laird, the stones long ago, and he had taken them with him when he left the pride. Such stones are very rare in my land and highly prized, as they are known as a mark o' favor from the dragons."

Meghan nodded to show her understanding. Khan'derin recomposed herself, and continued in the curious singsong voice: "The Firemaker realized that I was the child o' her grandson, he who was long lost in the land o' sorcerers, and so she took me back with her to the pride and there I was nurtured and taught the way o' the People. This brought much consternation to the Pride o' the Fighting Cat, who had long expected the daughter o' Khan'fella to inherit—"

"Who was she?"

Khan'derin paused for a long moment, eyes downcast, fingers clenched, then said, in a normal tone of voice, "She was my grandmother's sister, rescued from the Gods o' White by our enemy the Fighting Cats. She challenged for the godhead when the Firemaker, my grandmother's mother, died. My grandmother defeated her in tests o' power and the pretender died, showing the Gods o' White had accepted her as sacrifice. Her death should have ended the question, but she had had twin daughters, while my grandmother's daughter died in birth, and she had only a son, my father. One of Khan'fella's daughters was given to the Gods o' White, of course, but one still lives."

"So your aunt—the daughter o' the one who died—she claims the . . . inheritance, because she is descended from a straight line o' daughters?" Meghan asked.

Khan'derin flashed her a glance. "Aye."

"But ye are the direct descendant o' the existing Firemaker, and so ye think ye are the heir?"

"Aye."

"And so the Firemaker is like our banrìgh?"

"I do no' ken. The Firemaker leads and protects the prides, and settles disputes between them. She can bring fire when there is darkness, and she can command the birds and beasts o' the Spine. She can even speak with dragons and, as ye ken, sometimes fly them, as I do, and my father afore me. Her word is law, her decision final. The Auld Mothers and the Scarred Warriors may speak to her, but they may no' cross her or thwart her wish. That is why I am the heir, because the Firemaker wills it so."

"So she is a witch?" Meghan asked, and saw a strange look cross the girl's face.

"I do no' ken much o' ye witches," she responded. "I ken anyone who has power can be taught but that is no' the case with the Firemaker. The Firemaker's daughter will in time become the next Firemaker, and so will her daughter. If there is no daughter to carry on the line, then the eldest daughter o' a son, though that is considered very sad, and has happened only once. There has never been two o' the Red afore; at least, no' since the Red Sorcerers themselves."

"I think I see," Meghan said thoughtfully. "So when your grandmother found ye, it meant there were two contenders for the throne."

"The discovery o' the child o' Khan'gharad brought much consternation to the Pride o' the Fighting Cat—"

"Aye, I got that bit," Meghan said impatiently. "Ye were saying they did no' believe ye were really Khan'gharad's daughter and thought your grandmother was trying to foist an imposter on the prides so the Fighting Cat one would no' inherit. What happened then?"

This time the look of reproach was closer to anger. "The Firemaker showed the prides the dragoneye ring, and as I grew I had to show I could summon fire, for that is something no one but the Firemaker's get can do." Meghan pursed her lips thoughtfully. "On the eve o' my eighth birthday, when the Dragon-Star was again crossing our skies, another dream was given to the Firemaker, and though she shook with fear she obeyed the dream and brought me to the foot o' the ancient road between our land and that o' the dragons. I was instructed to climb the stairway, and so came into the land o' the dragons. At first a fear and a trembling possessed me, for the dragons spoke to me and told me I was to go to the Cursed Valley and live there in the Towers for one half o' every year, to tend the sleeping sorceress and to study in the libraries. I was very afraid, for it was well known that the Towers o' Roses and Thorns are evil, filled with ghosts and wailings. I was also sad because in the spring o' the Dragon-Star the People do travel to the Skull o' the World for the Gathering, to barter and trade, and to organize weddings. There is much feasting and festivities, and I had heard much but never been, for the previous Gathering had been the year I was born. However, the Firemaker said I had a *geas* laid upon me, and that I must accept it, as is fitting. So for the past eight years I have spent the spring and summer months at the Towers of Roses and Thorns, studying and learning."

"And are there ghosts?"

"Indeed, aye, and sometimes very terrible they are too."

"What sort o' ghosts?"

"The ghosts o' rage and grief," Khan'derin replied. "Come, auld mother, it is still a long way to the Towers and we must be there afore sunset."

Meghan sat on the sled, as directed by her companion, who tied her on with long leather straps. Gitâ burrowed deep into Meghan's pocket and stayed there, complaining again about the cold. Khan'derin began to pull the sled, floundering through the thick snow until it began to move. She then jumped onto the front, moving the board down the slope with only the weight of her own body. The snowy horizon flew past, Meghan lost in surprise and admiration.

"This is a long board and no' what I usually use," Khan'derin explained. "We really only use these boards in the spring, when we begin moving down to the summer pastures. It is a good thing ye are only a wee bit, like my grandmother."

"Isabeau would have loved to have known she had a grandmother," Meghan said as the dark mass of the forest sped toward them.

Soon they had to dismount and walk through the slushy

snow, but they had descended the mountain in a matter of minutes rather than the day it would have taken them by foot. Khan'derin hid the sled under some bushes and led the way through the patchy snow at great speed. Looking back at Dragonclaw, Meghan was surprised to see that from this direction, she could see two sharp peaks, identical in size and shape. She realized that it must be the perspective which made the smaller peak—hidden behind the bulk of Dragonclaw from the south—appear the same size.

"Legend says that the Red Sorcerers decided to settle in this valley because o' the twin peaks," Khan'derin said over her shoulder. "That is another reason why you call this land Tìrlethan, o' course."

"Are twins common among your people?"

Khan'derin hesitated. "No, they're very rare," she answered at last. "It is only the Firemaker who bears twins."

"Among my people, the birth o' twin witches is considered the very best o' luck," Meghan said. "It is so rare for those with true power to be born. Witches rarely marry and rarely have bairns. I believe use o' the One Power makes ye infertile, and certainly your sexual impulses are sublimated into other forces. So for me, the discovery o' another Isabeau is certainly wonderful news."

"I am no' another Is'a'beau," Khan'derin said, pronouncing her twin's name with an odd intonation. "My life has been very different."

"That's true," Meghan said, as the dark branches of the forest closed over their heads. "I would fain Test ye though, if ye do no' mind. I sense power in ye, though I canna tell its nature."

"We will soon be at the Towers," the girl answered, striding ahead, her white-clad form ghostlike in the gloom under the overhanging branches.

The forest was an almost impenetrable barrier of tangled trees and riotous thorn bushes, with no clear path through at all. Meghan doubted she would have been able to find her way through without Khan'derin, despite her woodcraft. Khan'derin lead her under branches and through thickets, clearing a way with the dexterous use of her curved knife and sharp-edged ax. "This forest sprung up after the Towers were deserted. Once they looked directly over the loch to the Cursed Peaks, but now all ye can see from most of the windows is the barrier o' thorns," Khan'derin said. "If ye did no' ken the Towers were here, ye could pass right by without noticing a thing."

Meghan noticed that many of the thorny branches were budding. "Are they roses?"

Khan'derin nodded. "Later on this whole forest will be a mass o' roses, white and red. When spring comes it is always bonny. It is hard then to remember this is the Cursed Valley."

The thorny briars were now so thick that Khan'derin covered her face with a scarf and put her gloves back on. With only her blue eyes showing through a narrow slit between the fur of her cap and the scarf, she looked strangely sinister. Meghan followed her example, wrapping her gray plaid tighter about her and pulling it up over her head to try to protect her face from the vicious branches. It was futile; the thorns dug through the thick material of her clothes and seemed to wind around her ankles and wrists, as if preventing her from going any further.

"The forest does no' recognize ye," Khan'derin said, slashing at the entwining branches with her knife.

Meghan sent out her mind, calming and reassuring, and saw the long tendrils slither away. After that her passage was easier, and she concentrated on sending out encouraging thoughts.

When they finally arrived at the Towers, Meghan did not realize they were there. Khan'derin came to a halt and gestured with her hand. Meghan looked about but all she saw was a great mossy cliff, criss-crossed with thorny briars. Khan'derin laid her hand on the rock and, looking up, Meghan saw it towering above them, the forest pressed up close to its side. Suddenly she realized what seemed like weathering on the rock was in fact elaborate carvings of roses and thorns around a massive stone door. Khan'derin pulled a large, beautifully worked key out of an inner pocket, inserted it into what appeared a mere crevice in a rock wall, and turned it with a visible effort. There was a loud click, then Khan'derin put her shoulder to the door and pushed with all her weight, until at last the door began slowly to groan open.

Within was a great hall, as intricately decorated as the Hall of the Dragons had been. Dust lay thick on the floor, and cobwebs draped in spectacular forms from the towering ceiling. There were a few broken pieces of furniture, but otherwise the hall was empty, showing only echoing spaces between the carved pillars. It was very dark, and Meghan lit a witchlight at the end of her staff so she could see.

At one end of the hall was a spiral staircase, wide enough for seven people to walk abreast, and beautifully decorated with the now familiar device of roses and thorns. Khan'derin lead the way upward, as silent as ever, and Meghan followed, eyes darting this way and that as she tried to take in as much as she could. The Tower was obviously round, the staircase spiraling up its center. They passed two landings, which showed short corridors leading off in four directions. Each corridor had two doors on either side and ended at a tall window that once would have showed views to the north, south, east and west. She recognized the design, since the Tower where she had lived most her life had been built to a similar design—the crossed circle, a symbol of great power.

On the third floor, Khan'derin left the staircase. Here, rather than the four short corridors identical in length and design that Meghan was used to, there were only three, with the one to the east a great hall set with high windows on either side. Looking out of the northern windows, Meghan realized with a start that the hall was built across the river, leading to another seemingly identical Tower. The water glimmered darkly beneath them, clogged with branches.

"Look out the other side," Khan'derin said, and Meghan complied. She saw that the river flowed north from a small loch, rather like the one in her secret valley home. Once the Towers would have been reflected in its waters, but the loch was now overshadowed by the forest, the sunset sky barely visible through the overarching branches.

"Which Tower is this?" she asked, as they came to another spiral staircase and began climbing upward.

"I do no' really ken," Khan'derin replied, frowning. "I do no' think one is o' Roses and one o' Thorns. I think they are both, but I'm no' really sure."

At last they reached the top floor, and Khan'derin opened a door on the eastern passage, standing back so Meghan could see inside. At first glance the room seemed full of strands of silver silk, shifting and glinting in the light from her staff. Closer examination showed a nest in the center of the room, spun from the silken strands.

"She sleeps," Khan'derin said, and slipped into the room, gathering the strands in her hands and patting them in place against the soft sides of the nest. "Do no' worry, ye will no' wake her."

Meghan gathered her courage and stepped into the room. She had to push her way through the great swathes of silk, but soon was able to see into the large nest. Ishbel was sleeping within. Her frail face and form were gently cocooned in the great lengths of what Meghan now recognized as her hair, grown to impossible lengths and as silver as a cobweb shining in the sun. Tears started to her eyes, and she felt Khan'derin take her hand and lead her out to the hall.

"Come visit my quarters and I will make ye tea," Isabeau's twin said in her cool voice, and led Meghan to another room like the one Ishbel had been sleeping in, though furnished roughly with a bed, a chest and a chair. With a wave of her hand Khan'derin lit the candles, as thick as Meghan's forearm, and they each studied the other by its light.

"The sleeping sorceress is someone close to ye?" Khan'derin asked at last. It was the first question she had asked.

"She was like a daughter to me, many years ago," Meghan said. "She was my apprentice. Until a few days ago I had no' seen her for nigh on twenty years. I had thought her dead."

This one is a solemn little owl, Gitâ said, sitting up on his hind legs and observing the girl as he nibbled on a piece of bread.

Meghan ignored him, saying, "She is your mother, ye ken."

"Aye, I had thought as much. But why does she sleep? Eight seasons I have looked after her here, and only once has she woken."

"I do no' ken why she sleeps. Ishbel's magic was always strange and unknowable. I can only guess that her mind and body needed the healing spell o' sleep. It was terrible, y'ken, the Day o' Betrayal, the burning o' all we loved. It came so unexpectedly."

"Did ye no' have dreams to tell o' its coming?"

"I do no' have the gift o' prophecy," Meghan sighed. "I wish that I did, much might have been saved that is now lost. All the Towers were attacked, ye see, or at least the ones that were still standing after all this time."

"The Towers o' Roses and Thorns were no' attacked."

"No, but then we all thought they had disappeared long ago. And they are so deep in the mountains, so difficult to get to."

"Aye, Feld said it took him almost a year to get here."

"Feld?" Meghan exclaimed. "There is a sorcerer here called Feld?"

"Indeed. It is he who taught me to speak your language, and to read, and to use the One Power." Khan'derin waved her hand so the flame of the candle leaped higher, but Meghan was on her feet.

"My auld friend Feld is here! Thank the Spinners! May I see him? Take me to him!"

They found the old sorcerer in the library on the sixth floor, a pair of glasses perched on the end of his beaky nose as he turned the pages of a book almost as large as himself. He looked up when Meghan came in, and began to laugh, a dusty-sounding chuckle that ended in dry coughs. "So, the rumors I heard are true! Ye did survive the Burning."

"Och, I'm a tough auld thing," Meghan said. "I canna believe my eyes! What are ye doing here?"

It took many hours to tell the story, for Feld was noted for his ability to get sidetracked, particularly when boasting about the great library of the Towers of Roses and Thorns, but at last Meghan had the details from him. Feld had barely managed to escape the Day of Betrayal—a sudden impulse to visit the flea markets in search of old manuscripts had meant he was away from the Tower of Two Moons when the Red Guards struck, and had seen the smoke and heard the screams on his way back. Always wily, the warlock had slipped away, cursing the Banrìgh, and frantic about his apprentice Khan'gharad and his other friends and colleagues. By stint of clever disguise and the help of some witch-friends he had escaped into the Whitelock Mountains where he wandered a long time, racked with grief and horror at the burning of his precious library and the execution of so many witches. At last some semblance of reason returned to him, and he remembered the tales of his apprentice, who had appeared at the Tower of Two Moons on the back of a dragon, the first human since Aedan Whitelock to cross his leg over a dragon's back. Khan'gharad Dragon-Laird had told him the tale of how he had rescued the young dragon princess from a certain death and so earned the gratitude of the great queen-dragon. So Feld, who had devoted his life to dragon lore, had made the long and difficult journey through the mountains to Dragonclaw and there asked the dragons for sanctuary. He had lived at the Towers of Roses and Thorns for fifteen years, tending Ishbel as she slept and studying to his heart's content.

"I do no' ken if they would have let me stay if they had no' thought I could look after Ishbel, who turned up here in the days following the Burning. The twins were born at the Hall o' Dragons, ye ken, and a strange birth it must have been, their mother out o' her mind with grief and horror and the only attendants dragons."

"So she must have flown straight there. What a journey that must have been, heavily laden with unborn twins as she was. I wonder she could stay in the air!"

"I think it was only the spirit that kept her alive, for truly, once the twins were born, she fell asleep, and asleep she stayed for all those years."

"So Ishbel has been asleep these past sixteen years?"

"She stirred a few years ago when the comet passed over and our young Khan'derin arrived but did no' wake until last week, when the Dragon-Star came again. I was with her, brushing her hair and washing her face as I always do, when suddenly she stirred and her eyes opened. Och, the surprise and joy! Fifteen years I have tended her, and all that time she slept as sweetly as ye could imagine."

"How . . . how was she when she woke?"

"Och, it was terrible. I had forgotten, ye see, that those

sixteen years she has been asleep were but a dream for her. All she remembered were the blood and the fire and the death, the terrible betrayal o' the Rìgh whom we had served so faithfully. And o' course, the death o' Khan'gharad. That was the last thing she remembered, how her lover died."

Meghan felt a great tide of ancient grief pour over her, and though she tried to fight it, tears began to slide down her wrinkled cheeks. She rested her forehead in her hand and struggled to control herself, but her grief had been stifled too long and the dam had finally burst.

After a while, she felt Feld's frail hand patting her shoulder and heard him say awkwardly, "Come, come, ye are wetting my book, and indeed it is far too auld and rare to be wetted with salt tears. I ken what it is ye did, and how that must grieve your heart, but really, what could ye do? Ye saved Ishbel's life and your own, and ye could have destroyed the Banrìgh, which indeed would have been a good thing, much as it pains my heart to say that the death o' any living thing could be a good thing."

"The mother-dragon told me Khan'gharad is no' dead," Meghan said, wiping her lined face impatiently.

"Did she so? Well, dragons do no' lie, though they can twist words in such a way that they might as well be telling an untruth. I canna see how he could have lived after ye opened a chasm at his very feet, but then the Banrìgh survived, did she no', and her black-hearted servant with her. Stranger things have happened. Take the waking of Ishbel herself. One moment she was asleep, the next awake and looking about her with those great blue eyes of hers. She knew you needed her, Meghan, though I do no' ken how. I tried to keep her here, even caught her in my arms and tried to hold her down, but she was too strong for me. A wee thing like Ishbel, too strong for me! Och, I am getting auld. She struggled and fought like an elven cat, and after she had won free, threw herself out the window o' her room! I thought she must be mad in her grief, and the confusion of waking after so long, and trying to kill herself.

"I was always a fool. Ishbel the Winged, to die by falling out a window! For light as a feather, she twirled and floated through the sky, and I watched her till she was beyond the Cursed Peaks, and out of sight. I could no' rest till she returned, I fretted and fumed, and young Khan'derin celebrated her coming o' age alone and not very happy, I am afraid. I felt I could not be easy until Ishbel was safe home again, though when she did return it was to sleep's arms that she turned, no' mine, and asleep she has been ever since." The old warlock sighed, and took off his glasses to rub them with the skirt of his robe.

Meghan and her old friend Feld talked long into the night, and he told her of some of the marvels of the Towers' library. It had been gathered together by the great twin sorcerers, Faodhagan and Sorcha, and Feld claimed it had some texts from Alba, the Other World, which they had brought with them in the Great Crossing. Written mainly in Latin, one of the sacred languages of the Other World, they were very difficult to read but Feld had persevered gamely.

"The twins lived in harmony with the dragons, ye ken, riding their backs and building the Great Stairway for them. Faodhagan was a great artist and craftsman, far greater than anything we ken, and a great wielder o' magic. It is he who built the dragons' palace, and the Towers o' Roses and Thorns, as well as many o' the other Towers too. Books in this library tell o' acts o' magic that are almost beyond belief. I have barely started my work, even after fifteen years here."

Suddenly Meghan felt so tired she could barely keep her eyes open, and she rested her head in her hands and her elbows on the table while Feld went on describing the treasures of his library. After a while she must have dropped off to sleep for she woke when he laid a hand on her shoulder, begging her forgiveness and leading her off to bed.

Her first night in a soft, warm bed for over a week did wonders for Meghan and she woke reinvigorated and almost happy. Although she and Feld had never been very close at the Tower of Two Moons, each preoccupied with their own concerns, it cheered her greatly to see a familiar face. It was also a comfort to know there was a great store of knowledge here that one day could help the witches re-establish the Towers, and perhaps even take them to greater heights of wisdom and understanding. The discovery of

Khan'derin was also a wonder and a joy, for here perhaps was a power equal to Isabeau's, and another young witch to fill the halls of learning both she and Feld dreamt of. Meghan washed her face and plaited her gray hair amidst dreams of a new Tower and a defeated Banrìgh.

There was a knock on the door, and Khan'derin came in bearing a tray with hot porridge and tea. She was wearing a loose white shirt, and her head was covered with a long-tailed white cap so Meghan could still not see her hair. The old witch smiled at her. "I am glad that I came," she said. "Indeed, twas grand to find the lost Towers o' Roses and Thorns intact still, and so rich in knowledge. So much has been lost. Feld tells me there are books here that came over in the Crossing!"

"Are all the other Towers really destroyed then?"

"I believe so," Meghan replied. "I sent carrier pigeons to those we knew still stood, and tried to contact their scrying pools in case any witches had returned after the Burning, but received no response at all. And I asked in all the villages and towns of Upper Rionnagan, and everyone says the Towers lie in ruins, with no living creature but rats and crows to disturb their emptiness. I hope one day we will rebuild them, but for now they are nothing but a pile of stones."

Khan'derin shrugged. "I never really believed in their existence anyway," she said. "The first I really heard o' witches was when I came here to the Cursed Valley and met Feld. He tries to teach me, but what do witches have to do with me?"

"A lot, I hope," Meghan said. "Bide a wee while I eat and we can talk."

Khan'derin remained standing. "I do no' want to hear what ye have to say."

Meghan was surprised and affronted. "What do ye mean?"

"The Firemaker had a dream that I was to leave the Spine o' the World and travel far away. I do no' wish to go."

Again Meghan was conscious of the fact that Khan'derin was an unknown quantity and that she must tread carefully. "Do no' your grandmother's dreams speak truth?"

"All dreams are visions o' what may be. We ourselves choose whether or no' to make dreams reality."

"What did the Firemaker dream?"

"She dreamt that I was to come face to face with my shadow."

"What does that mean, do ye think?"

"I did no' ken afore I met ye, but now I fear ye mean to take me to meet this girl ye keep speaking o', the one who is meant to look like me."

"Indeed, she looks enough like ye to be your mirror image. I am sure now that she is your twin sister, born to Ishbel the Winged, whom ye call the sleeping sorceress. Ishbel and the Dragon-Laird Khan'gharad were lovers, ye see, back in the Tower o' the Two Moons. When the Red Guards attacked the Tower, Ishbel was only a few weeks away from giving birth. I helped her escape, and she must have flown in search o' Khan'gharad's people then. The dragons say they found her on the slopes o' Dragonclaw—what ye call the Cursed Peaks—in dreadful pain. They helped her give birth then gave Isabeau into my care and ye into the care o' your father's people. I do no' ken why they separated ye."

"Because twins are forbidden, I imagine," Khan'derin said coldly.

"Perhaps . . . though I would have gladly taken ye both. Twins are no' forbidden in Rionnagan. I do no' understand why they are here."

"It is no' natural for two to be born o' the one womb. They are too close, the threads o' their destiny too tangled. They bring tragedy, for we are all meant to be born and die alone."

"Is this why ye do no' want to come with me? Ye do no' want to meet Isabeau?" Despite herself, Meghan's voice was incredulous.

"No' only that. I have just been scarred. I was to have joined the council next winter. Auld Mother says I am the youngest warrior ever to receive my scars."

"Is that what the scars are for? A mark o' fighting prowess?"

Khan'derin traced the scar on her right cheek. "This is for hunting. Last winter I made the greatest kill and so was given my first scar. This one," and she traced the left scar, "is for fighting."

"Fighting? Who do ye fight?"

"Our greatest enemy is o' course the Pride o' the Fighting Cats, who dared to trespass on our traditional hunting grounds and then made an assault on our Haven. The Fighting Cats are fools, trying to muscle in on our land."

"So the prides fight among themselves?"

Khan'derin stared. "O' course. We have always fought. What else is there to do?" When Meghan did not reply, she continued. "The Fighting Cats are jealous o' our Haven, which is large enough for all the pride, and high enough to be free o' any attack from the demons in the valleys. The Fighting Cats' Haven is much deeper north, on the ice plains, where spring is very late in coming and where the frost giants live. Their pastures are no' as lush as ours and, indeed, it has been a very hard winter."

"So ye are scarred as a sign o' hunting and fighting prowess?"

"Aye. All o' us are scarred, according to our calling. I chose to become a Scarred Warrior, which is why I do no' want to leave. Ye will want me to learn your tricks and treacheries, when all I want is to stay with my pride and fight for them and feed them, as is the way o' the Scarred Warrior."

"Was your father a Scarred Warrior?"

"Indeed, he was, the greatest o' them all. He received all seven scars, which I will too one day."

"What does this mean, the seven scars?"

"Only those who have the seven scars can order the Council o' Scarred Warriors. In my lifetime, I have heard o' only two Scarred Warriors with all seven scars."

"Explain to me again about how ye won your scars, and what it means. Ye said ye would have led the pride now?"

"No! No Scarred Warrior leads the pride, that is the job o' the Auld Mother. One day I will be Firemaker, and that is why I must win my scars. No, the Council o' Scarred Warriors discuss war plans and when to leave the Haven and head for the summer pastures, that sort o' thing. The Auld Mother decides, o' course, but she listens carefully to the Scarred Warriors."

"And ye are to be Auld Mother one day?"

"I am the only daughter o' the blood—at least I thought I was. Now ye tell me I have a sister. That is no' good. Who is to be Auld Mother and Firemaker?"

"I do no' ken. Surely that is still a long way off?"

"Indeed, I hope so. I need to win my scars first, and then be taught the way o' the wind, and how to travel in dreams."

"I canna teach ye that, but I can teach ye other things. How to talk to animals and understand the ways o' the earth. How to read omens and signs, how to ken what others are thinking."

"Feld has tried to teach me such things but I canna see how they will help me."

"If ye are to become Firemaker, they will help ye greatly. In the meantime, though, what o' your Auld Mother's dream?"

"I do no' want to leave the pride."

"Sometimes we must do what we do no' wish to do. Tell me what she dreamt and I will tell ye what I think."

"I do no' ken what she dreamt. All I ken is what she said to me as I was preparing to leave for the Cursed Valley. She said she had dreamed I was to leave the Spine o' the World and follow in the footsteps o' my father. She said I must test my wings."

"That is all I want ye to do," Meghan said. "I felt such an omen when first I met ye. I feel the Spinners are twisting the threads o' our lives together."

"So ye think I should go with ye?"

"Aye, I want ye to, Khan'derin."

She turned on her heel. "I will think on it."

Meghan spent the day in the library with Feld, finding out more about Tìrlethan and its strange history. The original inhabitants of this mountain country, who called themselves Khan'cohbans, or Children of the White Gods, lived in groups called prides. They were not human, though very similar in bodily structure, being closely related to the Celestine, the race of forest-dwellers who had ruled Eileanan before the time of the First Crossing. Faodhagan the Red had been fascinated by their ancient culture, and had spent much time with them after the establishment of the Towers. He had fallen in love with one of their women and had fathered twins with her.

So, Meghan thought, *Isabeau and Khan'derin are probably descendants o' his line, half human, half fairy. No wonder Isabeau's magic is so powerful!*

Later that day the white-clad youngster came up behind Meghan, startling her with her noiseless approach. "I have thought long on this, auld mother," she said reluctantly, "and if ye and my grandmother both think it is my fate to travel away from the Spine o' the World, then that is what I must do."

"I am pleased to hear that," Meghan responded gravely.

"I am very unhappy," Khan'derin said. "I have never crossed the mountains—I ken nothing o' your people or your land."

"They are your people too, Khan'derin, do no' doubt that for a moment. You may have been born into a fairy tribe, but human bluid runs strong in ye. From what I have learned, ye are the descendant o' one o' the First Coven, Faodhagan the Red, and that makes ye and Isabeau o' the very finest bluid. A ban prionnsa, no less. If that were no' enough, I sense much Power latent in ye. I canna allow that to go to waste. But there is no need for ye to be afraid."

"I am no' afraid!" Khan'derin snapped. "I just do no' think o' your people as being my people. The prides have kept to themselves for many hundreds o' years now. Only the Firemaker crosses the mountains, and then only when it is time to mate." She sighed. "Perhaps this means it is time for me to mate."

"Does that mean the Firemakers do no' marry and interbreed with the people o' the prides?" Meghan was fascinated.

"Sometimes. Khan'fella did. But mostly the Firemaker crosses the mountains in search o' a suitable mate. When she is with babe she returns to the Spine o' the World."

"What is a suitable mate?"

Khan'derin sighed. "A man, strong and wise, with blue eyes like those o' all the Firemaker's get and hair with red in it . . . that is what the Firemaker seeks." Meghan nodded thoughtfully. Khan'derin continued, "Children o' the White and Children o' the Red should no' mate, there is always tragedy if they do. That is how the Towers o' Roses and Thorns came to be deserted in the first place, and the valley cursed . . . So the Firemaker crosses the mountains when it is time, and the People stay behind, waiting in fear for her to return safely. Auld Mother says the only man o' our people to cross the mountains in generations was my father."

"And now ye follow in your father's footsteps, and indeed, that may no' be a bad thing."

"So where do we go?"

"I think I would fain return to my home first," Meghan said. She told Khan'derin how the Red Guards had attacked her home in the tree, and how anxious she was to return to see who and what had survived.

"Are ye no' concerned the soldiers will still be there?" Khan'derin asked.

"The animals will tell me," she answered.

Meghan spent the rest of the day with Feld, telling him some of her plans and asking his advice. The old sorcerer knew very little, however. He had lived all these years in the Towers of Roses and Thorns quite happily absorbed in his books and the care of the sleeping sorceress whom he loved like a daughter. He had thought it impossible that any of his former friends and colleagues could have escaped the Day of Betrayal, and had not tried to track any of them down.

Meghan also spent some hours sitting with Ishbel, holding her hand and wondering at the nest of hair that cocooned her. Ishbel's magic had always been strange. She had never mastered many of the simple acts of magic that is all most witches manage. She had never been able to light a candle or move an object or read its past. It was as if all of her magic was concentrated in that one Talent, the Talent of Flying, such a rare ability that the Towers had always been rather in awe of her. Perhaps that is why she and Khan'gharad had fallen in love, for he had flown the dragon's back and that too was a strange marvel and frightening to most witches.

Meghan decided it was time to go and brought Ishbel's hand to her mouth to kiss. "I am sorry," she whispered. "Sleep safely, my dear." Then, on impulse, she bent and kissed Ishbel on the forehead, between her eyes. The silver-haired witch stirred, and her eyelashes fluttered and opened. Ishbel looked about her with a wondering gaze and raised herself a little in the shining nest of hair.

"Meghan . . ." Her vivid blue eyes filled with tears.

"Ishbel, ye have woken!"

"I felt your presence here," she whispered. "I do no' want ye. Please go."

"I'm sorry, Ishbel . . ."

"I ken ye did no' mean to kill my love, my darling, but ye did, ye did!" Ishbel began to wail, tears pouring down her cheeks. "Och, he is dead, my Khan'gharad is dead!"

"Ishbel, the dragons say he still lives! Strange as it seems, they say he is no' dead. We could try to find him for ye, Ishbel, we could try."

"He's dead, he's dead," the silver-haired witch wept, and sank back into the nest of hair, burying her face in her hands.

"But the queen-dragon said—"

"Ye think I would no' ken if my love was alive? I ken he is gone from me, for I search and search, I call for him, and there is no answer. Go away, Meghan, I do no' want to remember, I want to sleep . . ." As she spoke, Ishbel's eyes began to close but Meghan shook her awake, rough in her urgency.

"Ishbel, we need ye! We are rising against the Usurper, we need your help! Now is no' the time to sleep. Things are afoot."

Ishbel gazed at her with wide blue eyes and said softly, "Ye have my daughters, is that no' enough?"

Meghan said frantically, "I ken Isabeau was your babe, Ishbel, she had your eyes. I did everything I could for her, I brought her up as if she was my own . . ."

"I ken, Meghan," Ishbel said, "and I thank ye for it. I heard your voice in my dreams, calling for help and so I came to ye, to judge her Tests as is fitting. But it was too much, too much. To see her all grown, when last I saw her she was still slimy with my birth fluids. To ken sixteen years have passed . . . that my love has been dead for sixteen years and still I live on . . . I canna bear it!"

"Ishbel, please!"

"Do no' think I hate ye for what ye did, but I canna bear to see your face. Too well I remember that day. It is seared into my memory. I canna bear to remember, I canna bear . . ." Slowly her words slurred and her eyes closed, tears still trickling from beneath their lids, her breath whimpering.

Meghan shook her fiercely again. "Ishbel, Ishbel, what about the Key? What happened to the Key?"

"I do no' ken," she whispered, not opening her eyes.

"What did ye do with the Key? Do ye have it still?"

"No . . ."

"What happened to it? Ishbel, ye must try to remember!"

"I do no' ken . . ." Her voice slurred into silence, and none of Meghan's pleas and admonishments and shakings could wake her, though her sleep grew more and more disturbed until at last Meghan desisted, sobs bitter in her throat. She was entangled now in the constantly floating hair as if in a giant spider's web and she was hard put not to fight it off with frantic fists. She stood still, fingers clenched by her side. Gitâ crept from her pocket, soothing and petting her, pushing his silken head beneath her chin. After a moment, she encircled him with her hand, and he buried his cold nose against her palm. "So be it," she said. "We keep on searching, and hope Isabeau is safe." Then she carefully disentangled herself and went back to her room.

After gathering her things together, Meghan left to say a subdued farewell to Feld, who looked as grave as she felt. "Feld, I may need ye in the end, when we raise our hands against Maya the Ensorcellor. Will ye help?"

"I am but an auld man, very tired—" Feld began.

Meghan interrupted him. "I am far aulder than ye, Feld. I remember when ye came to the Tower as an eager novice, still wet behind the ears. And I too am tired, so tired I sometimes wonder how I manage to keep this auld body creaking along. But this is no' the time to be worrying about such things! Our country is being ground to dust beneath the heel o' an evil sorceress, and for sixteen years we have nursed our wounds and wished for the grand auld days to return. Well, they canna return but we can start again. Eileanan needs ye, Feld. We need your wisdom and learning, we need your magical strength. Can I call upon ye when I need ye?"

After a moment the old warlock nodded, and his wrinkled face was ashamed. "Aye, Keybearer, ye can," he replied.

With Gitâ riding on her shoulder, Meghan made her way through the ruined corridors of the Towers. Cobwebs hung in splendid, dusty festoons from pillar to pillar, broken masonry littered the floor, and the old witch had to clutch her skirts tight around her boots to prevent them from snagging on the rubbish of centuries. Her spirits were very low, and Gitâ crooned to her softly, holding on to her ear with one black-tipped paw.

Suddenly there was a loud screech and a huge white shape took flight over her head. Meghan jumped and put her hand to her heart.

"No need to be afraid." Khan'derin's voice came out of the gloom. "It is merely a blizzard owl. They say the Red Sorceress had one as her familiar, and after she threw herself to her death from the heights, only her owl dared stay in the Towers."

"Is that what happened? Is that why this is called the Cursed Valley?"

Khan'derin came out into the dim light, dressed all in white fur, with a crossbow and quiver of arrows slung over one shoulder and a small satchel over the other. "The Red Sorceress slayed her twin brother and all who tried to stay her hand. Only when the corridors o' the Towers o' Roses and Thorns were red with blood did she kill herself. Everyone else fled, and for centuries no one would come near, for the halls were filled with the ghosts o' the slain. That is why I dreaded the dragons' command, and tried to stay with the prides when I had been told to come here. That is why no one else ever comes near."

Looking around at the ravaged carvings, the dismal curtains of cobwebs, the broken archways and dark, gaping doorways, Meghan could understand why. She shivered and pulled her woolly plaid closer about her, and was glad when they finally came out of the ruined hall into the gray gloom of the thorn trees. At least the air outside was fresh, and the spurs of the trees were budding with the promise of spring.

Khan'derin looked at her, and her cold, expressionless face seemed to stir with sympathy. "In summer, when I am bid to stay here, I spend as much time as I can outside. It is an uncanny place. I still find it so, even after eight years."

Meghan smiled at her in commiseration for the frightened eight year old she had been, but Khan'derin's face did not kindle in response, and Meghan's smile withered away. She hardly knew what to say to Khan'derin. Although her features were identical to Isabeau's, she could not have been more different. Meghan had not once seen her smile or laugh, she never spoke unless addressed, and she had all sorts of strange mannerisms. In silence they pushed their way through the entwining branches, Khan'derin clearing a path with her ax and knife.

On the opposite side of the loch, the dragon princess was practising aerial maneuvers, her green-gold body shining against the blue sky. As Meghan watched, she executed a perfect triple loop and, obviously pleased with herself, gave a triumphant bugle then swooped down above their heads, landing gracefully on the far shore.

Meghan smiled at the dragon princess, who gambolled playfully about, making it difficult for Khan'derin to strap on the harness. At last, though, they were mounted and ready, Gitâ huddled down in Meghan's pocket, trembling at the smell of dragon but comforted by Meghan's promise that they would soon be home.

Asrohc flew toward the secret valley. The journey which had taken Meghan seven days was accomplished in less than an hour, the dragon princess landing lightly on the wide rock by the waterfall. Meghan slid off the dragon with her hand clapped over her nose and mouth in a futile attempt to shut out the foul stench of corrupting flesh. All around her were the bodies of Red Guards, flyblown after a week in the sun, plus the corpses of animals who had died in the fighting or in the fires with which the Red Guards had tried to destroy the valley.

Asrohc looked round her with a certain dragonish pleasure, and began to paw at the body of the great stag who had once lorded over this valley.

Meghan held up her hand. *Please leave them be,* she said. *I will bury them, as is our custom.*

Khan'derin looked surprised at her words but was otherwise unaffected by the carnage around her. Meghan could not help comparing her to Isabeau, who would have been sobbing at the sight. A crested falcon flew down to her wrist immediately and told her much of what the Red Guards had done in their frustration and anger. Many of the valley's animal inhabitants were dead, most shot down for sport. The entire litter of elven cats was dead, their mother's tiny body studded with arrows, the bodies of her kittens scattered around her. The thick undergrowth had been scorched away, the great trees now merely blackened trunks. Once the dragon had flown away with a farewell bugle, what animals had survived came running out, their fur or feathers burned away in patches, most holding up a damaged paw or injured leg for Meghan to examine. She spent a few minutes petting them and crooning in their languages before making her way around the loch, her face grim, her mouth folded tightly. The way was now much easier without the flowering bushes that once had trailed their branches in the water, but by the time she reached the tree house, the hem of her skirt was black with ashes. At the foot of the great tree lay Seychella, her face covered by a red cloak to keep the birds of prey away.

"At least they had some decency," Meghan said, and lifted the cloak. Seychella's neck was twisted at an unnatural angle, but there was a smile on her decaying face. "They say to die in the Mesmerd's arms is to die in bliss," Meghan said, and dropped the cloak back.

She looked around at the ruin of her valley one more time, then lay her gnarled hand on the massive bole of the tree that was her home. "She is damaged," Meghan said softly, "but she still lives."

Gitâ was sitting on Meghan's shoulder, his bright eyes filled with distress at the death of his animal friends and the burning of the forest. Meghan stroked his fur and said idly, *Are ye glad now ye braved the dragons with me?* He laid his cold black-tipped paw against her neck and chittered loudly. *Will ye go into the house for me, Gitâ, and make sure these cursed Guards have no' left any nasty surprises for me? Be careful, though.*

Reluctantly Gitâ bounded down Meghan's body and crept into the entrance to the secret passage, which had once been concealed by a great thorny bush but now could easily be seen as a narrow crack in the rock. He did not come out for almost ten minutes but neither Meghan nor Khan'derin showed any signs of impatience. At last he came bounding out, chittering anxiously, and Meghan bent and picked him up, stroking his silky brown fur. *Thank ye.* "Come, Khan'derin, Gitâ says it is safe."

Inside bodies littered the kitchen, which stank of putrefying flesh. Khan'derin tied her white scarf over her mouth but again showed little distaste or discomfort. Most of the Guards seemed to have died in an attempt to breach the trapdoor through into the upper floors. They had easily broken the wooden bolt but had not thought to check whether an enchantment also guarded the door. The blast had killed nine of the Red Guards, and must have injured more for Meghan found several fingers, hands and unidentified globs of flesh that did not seem to belong to the bodies. There was also a small pile of dust and ashes that smelled strangely of the marshes, a not altogether unpleasant smell but completely out of place in the dry, cold air of the mountains.

Meghan bent and examined the pile of dust and bone remnants carefully, not touching it and not allowing Khan'derin to go near. After a while she carefully swept it up, keeping her mouth and nose covered and careful not to let any of the dust drift onto her skin. Only when the pile was completely gone did she stop to examine the rest of her house, and then she scowled at the sight of her smashed plates and ruined furniture, the marks of axe and fire everywhere in the small room.

"Well, let's get this all cleaned up," she said.

They toiled all the long afternoon to gather together the dead, both human and animal. Khan'derin was surprised that Meghan would show the same concern and courtesy toward the animals as she did to the slaughtered guards but said nothing, working hard and willingly in the hot sun.

They buried Seychella and the stag in the sun-dappled glen overlooking the loch. The other corpses were tipped into the crevice which Meghan had created during the fight with the Red Guards a week ago. By the time they had finished, the deep crevice was almost filled. Meghan bent her head and drew upon the One Power, then brought her hands together smartly with a loud crack. Slowly the lips of the giant fissure closed, burying Guard and animal together. Meghan then spoke the rituals of death over the graves, and scattered there earth, seeds and ashes, watered in thoroughly. Khan'derin watched with interest, sitting cross-legged in the shade, hands upturned in her lap, far less affected by the events than Meghan herself. When at last they were finished—filthy, sweaty and Meghan sick to her stomach—they walked back to the tree house in the gathering dusk, each pondering the mystery of the other.

In the fresh blue morning they began the task of cleaning and bandaging the many burns and wounds of the surviving animals. Khan'derin had done everything so competently till now that Meghan was surprised to discover she had no knowledge or aptitude for healing. Neither did she show any affection or pity for any of the wounded animals, who had been Isabeau's only friends. After a while, Meghan sent her away, expecting her to have a swim or explore, as Isabeau would have done. Instead, though, Khan'derin stripped off her tight leather suit and began a series of stylized movements similar to those the witches called *ahdayeh*. These were far more aggressive however, and executed with much greater skill and grace than Isabeau had ever demonstrated. Khan'derin worked for over an hour in the sun, kicking, punching, tumbling, working with a wooden stave she made from a branch, as well as with the strange variety of weapons she wore strapped to a leather belt around her bare waist. There was a sharp skewer, a mace on a short stick with a detachable head that could be swung around her head on a leather strap, an eight-pointed star that glittered as she flung it at a tree, then came straight back to her hand, a rope that she swung with amazing dexterity, and a long knife with one edge wickedly serrated. Meghan stopped her poulticing and bandaging to watch her. She was interested that Khan'derin worked naked, except for her weapons belt and a long-tailed linen cap that covered her hair.

Khan'derin paused, her white skin shining faintly with sweat, and looked around for a more interesting target. On a branch of a greenberry tree sat a bird, trilling happily in the sun. So fast her hand was merely a blur, Khan'derin threw the sharp-edged star at the bird.

With a cry Meghan flung out her hand and deflected the weapon before it could strike. "Any beast within this valley is under my protection," Meghan said gently. "Ye may no' kill here."

Khan'derin balanced on the balls of her feet, and brought

the star back to her hand. She looked at Meghan with interest, but said nothing.

By the time Meghan had tended every animal left alive in the valley, there were only a few hours of sunlight left. The wood witch straightened her aching back, and looked around for her new ward. "Khan'derin? Come and help me gather what provisions we can, for I want to set out at first light tomorrow." The white-capped girl rose from the log where she had been silently waiting, and came to Meghan's side. "It is early yet for there to be much to find, but this valley is fertile and the weather here generally much milder than elsewhere on the mountain, so one can usually find something," the old woman said.

"Ye wish me to gather foodstuffs?"

"Aye, o' course. What else would I be meaning?"

"I do no' gather. That is a chore for children and feeble old women."

"Suitable for me then, but no' for one such as yourself?" Meghan responded sarcastically.

"Exactly," Khan'derin agreed.

For a moment the old witch was taken aback. She glared at her incredulously, then said, "That may be the case on the Spine o' the World, lassie, but here, if ye do no' gather ye do no' eat. Come with me and I will show ye where the best plants grow."

Khan'derin did not budge. "I am a Scarred Warrior. I hunt and I fight. I do no' gather nuts like a squirrel."

"It's a little early for nuts, though the squirrels and donbeags will no doubt let me have some of their winter store. There's plenty else we can find, though."

"I am a Scarred Warrior." Khan'derin's voice rose a little, and her cheeks reddened, showing the white line of her scars along her cheekbones. "We do no' gather! It is an insult to ask me."

"I'll be insulting you harder if ye do no' come and help me!" Meghan said irritably. "What do ye think ye are going to eat on our journey if we do no' pluck what the valley has to offer and take it with us? It'll do us no good rotting on the ground, will it now? And we need to move swiftly, I want to try to catch up with Isabeau, we canna be foraging as we walk. Bring that basket, and I will tell ye what to pick."

The girl stood her ground.

"Khan'derin, pick up that basket and come and help me forage! I am too auld to be bending and digging for long, and if ye think I am going to let ye sit and watch me labor, ye're entirely mistaken."

With tightly compressed lips and scarlet cheeks, Khan'-derin picked up the basket and followed the wood witch through the forest. It had rained overnight, and a few early mushrooms had sprouted here and there. Sullenly she picked them, then pulled great copper-colored fungi off tree trunks, as directed by the wood witch. Here and there she was instructed to dig for roots and tubers, or to cut flower heads heavy with seeds, or to strip a branch of its leaves. By the time Gladrielle was rising, the sun just disappearing behind the far horizon, her basket was laden and she was hot and very dirty. Apart from the giving of brisk orders, Meghan had said little, and Khan'derin had been as silent as an elven cat.

Back in the tree house she was set to washing and cutting while Meghan swung down her great iron pot and laid out her skillets and pans. Khan'derin did all she was told, but showed no initiative or pleasure in the task, even though the kitchen was soon redolent with cooking fumes. She was clearly unhappy and, after sliding the bread pans into the coals of the fire, Meghan put out her hand to comfort her, saying, "I am sorry if ye find gathering and cooking an onerous task, Khan'derin, but indeed ye shall have to get used to doing many things ye have never done before."

As soon as her hand touched Khan'derin's shoulder, though, the girl flinched back, straining her body away. Meghan returned to the table with her mouth folded tightly, and kneaded the remaining dough with such vigor she was sure the bread would be flat. *At least, it will no' take up so much room in our packs,* she thought wryly.

Once all the provisions had been made ready, Meghan ladled out bowls of vegetable soup for dinner. She passed Khan'derin hers, and ate hungrily, her mind busy with plans for the morning. Suddenly she realized Khan'derin had not touched her meal, but was looking down at it with an expression of distaste. "For Eà's sake, eat your food else ye'll be starving yourself to death!" she snapped.

Slowly Khan'derin began to spoon the soup into her mouth, but her left hand remained tightly clenched in her lap, and Meghan had to bite back more irritable words, reminding herself she had no real authority over the girl.

There was another struggle of wills after the meal had been tidied away, for Khan'derin refused to change out of her conspicuous furs and leather. Again Meghan had to lose her temper before she would submit, and when at last she climbed down the ladder, dressed in a pair of Isabeau's old breeches, she wore still her white leather jerkin and her fur cap.

"Ye canna wear a cap like that traveling through Rionnagan!"

"I must," Khan'derin responded.

"But ye will draw attention to us, and make yourself out as a stranger, which ye must no' do! Besides, I canna bear to have ye near me wearing the skins o' dead animals. Please, will ye humor a poor auld witch and take the hat off!"

Khan'derin stared before her, then slowly and reluctantly reached up and took off the cap. Her red-gold hair was cropped close to the skin, as close as a knife could cut. Meghan was distressed at the sight of her shorn head, for witches believed their hair and fingernails, as part of their living bodies, contained residues of power. For this reason, witches were always careful to burn their fingernail cuttings or any hairs that stayed in their comb. "Your hair! Why have ye cut it so short? Have ye been ill?"

"The People o' the Pride do no' have hair like mine," Khan'derin responded unwillingly. "In the snow, my hair shines like a flame. A Scarred Warrior must slide invisibly through the white. Ugly red hair like mine would reveal me should my cap fall off. If I could, I would bleach it white like the manes of my people, but I am the heir o' the Firemaker, child o' the Red. I must accept my heritage."

"Ye must no' cut your hair again," Meghan said. "This is for two reasons. Firstly, we must stay as inconspicuous as possible during our journey. Ye must be like any other lass born in Rionnagan—and believe me, no lassie would shave her head unless she had been critically ill! Secondly, your hair contains power, just like any other part o' your body. Ye must learn to guard and protect anything that contains your living cells. Ye can be hunted down, or hurt from afar with a lock o' hair, or flake o' skin, or a discarded crescent o' fingernail. Remember that!"

For a moment Khan'derin looked as if she was going to resist, then she bowed her head. "Yes, auld mother, I'll try." She replaced the fur cap with the long-tailed linen cap that she had used for fighting, however, and when Meghan remonstrated with her again, set her mouth tightly. Later, she came down the ladder wearing one of Isabeau's old tam-o'-shanters, so faded it was almost white. Even when Meghan pointed out gently that there was no need to wear it indoors, she would not take it off. Later, when Meghan wearily clambered up the ladder for her last night in a bed for some time, she found Khan'derin, fast asleep, still wearing it.

When Meghan woke Khan'derin the next morning, it was pitch-black inside the hollow tree, and Gitâ was yawning widely, showing a long pink tongue. "We must make ready. I wish to Test ye this dawn, and ye must be prepared. I would fain have had ye suffer the Ordeal, but it was a hard day yesterday and as hard a one ahead o' us. Besides, this is no' a formal Test, for there is no other witch but me. Eà kens when we shall have another opportunity, though, and I must have some idea o' your abilities. The valley is guarded—if any more soldiers decide to come and have a look I shall ken at once, so I think it is safe to be using the One Power. Now, go and wash yourself, and meet me at the clearing where we first landed. I shall give ye the First Test o' Power, which is what children o' the Coven undertake when they are eight."

For a moment she thought Khan'derin was going to refuse, then the girl nodded, lowering her eyes so her expression could not be seen. "As you wish, auld mother."

In the clearing by the loch, where the water poured over the lip of stone to cascade in thin ribbons down to the cliff-face, Meghan Tested her new apprentice and found the results puzzling. Khan'derin easily, almost contemptuously, passed the Trial of Air, and when prompted by the wood witch, showed that she could also move that which was unmoving, proving she was strong in this element. She was, however, unable to even quiver water in a bowl, failing the Trial of Water. She knew none of the seeds or herbs or minerals, failing the challenge of knowing in the Trial of Earth, nor could she speak the first seven languages of beasts. Yet Meghan knew she could speak with dragons, which one must be able to do in order to pass the Sorceress Test of Earth. To speak with dragons was a rare and difficult challenge, for their language was quite unlike that of any other living creature, taking place entirely in the mind and without words or common perceptions. To be able to converse with dragons yet not with the birds and beasts of the field and forest was strange indeed.

Meghan already knew Khan'derin could light a candle, for she had seen her do it at the Towers of Roses and Thorns. To her bafflement, though, she found Khan'derin could not put the flame out with her mind alone. "It is the challenge o' the flame and the void," she said in puzzlement. "Ye must do it to pass. Think of darkness, coldness. Think of the dying o' the flame. Think of emptiness."

Suddenly she found herself shivering, and realized that not only had the candle-flame winked out, but the fire also, a thin veneer of ice forming across the bowl of water. She rubbed her thin arms vigorously, and said gently, "Think of warmth, lassie, ye're freezing me to death!"

With a wondering expression on her face, Khan'derin brought the fire flickering up again, saying, "I have never done that before. The fires in the Haven are never allowed to go out."

The last Trial, the challenge of clear seeing, Khan'derin had some trouble with, as all acolytes did, but at last she said tentatively, "Is it a star in a circle that I am meant to be seeing?"

Meghan smiled with relief and nodded. "Indeed, it is, lassie, and ye have done well. Feld must have managed to teach ye something. As we travel I will teach ye what I can, though any use o' the One Power will be dangerous with so many witch-sniffers about."

Having broken their fast in the goodwishing of the elements, they dressed and shouldered their packs, Meghan sighing at the weight. Indeed, her strength was not what it had once been. Gitâ rode high on the baggage, chittering farewell to the other donbeags, who glided from tree to tree ahead of them. The other animals clustered around Meghan, climbing onto each other's backs to better reach her.

She fondled the hare's long ears and stroked the otter's gleaming wet back. "Guard the valley for me," she said to the sad-faced she-bear, lumbering along by her side. The bear raised her woolly snout and moaned piteously, for she had lost her mate in the battle with the Red Guards. Meghan patted the massive paw, for the woolly bear's shoulder was far above her, and said gently, "Soon ye shall have a new litter of cubs to comfort ye," and was pleased to see the small eyes brighten. With another roar, the she-bear shambled off into the forest, and Meghan said smilingly to Khan'derin, "She says she must springclean her cave then, for she has been too dispirited to do it yet and it must be tidy for her cubs."

"Her coat would make a thick, warm rug," Khan'derin replied, and was surprised at the look of anger from the wood witch. Meghan gripped her flower-carved staff tightly and marched on, leaving Khan'derin to trail along behind her, conscious of having angered her but thinking it was her cheekiness in having spoken unbidden that was the problem.

It was some miles before Meghan's temper began to die, and Gitâ chittered softly in her ear. *She is only a babe, my beloved, she knows not what she says.*

She takes pleasure only in killing and hurting . . .

She is like the saber-leopard, Gitâ said. *It is her nature and her training. You cannot turn a saber-leopard into a donbeag.*

But Isabeau . . .

You have had the training of Isabeau. Remember this child has lived half her life with dragons, and the other half with hunters and warriors. It has not been an easy life, nor one to teach kindness.

No, that is true . . .

I have heard you say yourself that dark times are upon us. Remember the dragons see both ways along the thread of time. Perhaps it is a saber-leopard that we will be needing.

Meghan put up a hand to stroke her little familiar, who

rubbed his velvety head against her chin. *You are right,* she said in shame. *I should not always be comparing her to Isabeau and finding her wanting. Who kens what threads the Spinners are weaving into the cloth o' our lives?*

Isabeau the Apprentice Witch

After leaving Meghan on the slope of Dragonclaw, Isabeau and Jorge traveled south together, slipping down through the snowy valleys, the raven flying on ahead. Once or twice they had to find a holt while a contingent of Red Guards marched past, but the raven gave them plenty of warning and so no sense of danger ever worried them.

The journey was by necessity slow, the old man tapping his staff before him and pausing often to regain his breath. Isabeau grew so impatient she ran ahead, finding a rock with a pretty view to sit and wait for him. Great eagles soared far overhead, and on a rocky plateau below her, a pride of snow lions basked in the sun. Six tiny kittens, bundles of white fluff, bounded around, attacking their father's tufted tail and swinging from his magnificent black-edged white mane. The lionesses yawned, showing rows of sharp teeth, and stretched, one swiping at her kittens with a lazy paw. Isabeau watched entranced until Jorge at last caught her up, and then reluctantly went to find them a way down into the valley below.

She offered to help the old seer, but her help proved worse than her hindrance for she forgot to mention things like low branches or sudden drops, so that Jorge was rather bruised by the end of the first day.

"I will rely on Jesyah, who is used to my ways," he said with dignity, and Isabeau was happy to explore the path ahead and find them the perfect camp site as the light began to fade.

That first night, sitting around the campfire, Isabeau, curious as always about other people's magic, pestered the old man to tell her more about his Talents. Jorge was tired, but told her gently he was a seer, someone who could see both ways along the thread of time.

"So ye can see the future?"

"I can see future possibilities," the old man said quietly. "The future is like a tangled skein o' wool waiting for the first strands to be drawn and spun into a thread."

"Aye, that is what Meghan used to say." Isabeau remembered the long winter days confined within the tree house while the snowy blizzards raged outside. She and her guardian spent most of the winter spinning and weaving the white, silky fur of the long-horned *geal'teas* and the gray wool of the wild goats, making cloth for their own garments and to barter with when spring came at last. Meghan knew many plants which dyed the cloth in a range of beautiful colors—blue and yellow and crimson. It was these dyed cloths that they would sell, dressing themselves in the natural gray of the wild goats' wool.

Meghan always used the time spent spinning to teach Isabeau what she could about the history and politics of the land, or to tell her stories of the Three Spinners. There were many stories, of course, about babies bad-wished at birth by Gearradh, the cutter of the thread, but saved in the end by Sniomhar, the kindest of the three and the spinner of thread. One story Meghan told many times was about a beautiful girl who was summoned to the castle after her mother foolishly boasted of her spinning prowess. The laird was so struck with her beauty that he swore he would marry her if she could spin three rooms of flax into thread. If she could not, then she would die. Unfortunately, the girl had no skill at spinning and so she sat in the three rooms and wept. Moved by her tears, the Spinners appeared to aid her, asking only that she invite them to the wedding. Of course the girl agreed, and so the thread was spun. At the wedding, the laird remarked on the ugliness of the Spinners, one of whom had an enormous foot, one an enormous lower lip, and the other an enormous thumb. When he learned their deformities came from working the spinning wheel's treadle, moistening the flax and twisting the thread, he vowed his lovely bride would never spin again. Meghan had loved to tell her vain ward this story, for every time she would catch Isabeau anxiously examining her face in the barrel of water, in case her lower lip was swelling.

"Meghan always said the future is the unspun fleece, the present the moment it is spun through the spindle, and the past the spun thread. Then she said history is what the Weaver weaves from the many threads o' people's lives."

"Your guardian is a wise woman."

"So tell me what ye see," Isabeau begged.

"Ye may no' want to learn what I will say," Jorge answered tiredly. "Once the trance is upon me, I ken no' what I will see. It is no' always a good thing to ken what is to happen in the future, my lassie." But Isabeau continued to plead until at last the blind seer consented.

"It is good we have no' eaten yet. I need to be pure and empty so the sight can fill me like water fills a glass. We must be careful, though. I canna sense anyone nearby, but some of the Awl's seekers are very powerful and we do no' wish to bring them down upon us. Keep a sharp eye out, lassie." Jorge then washed himself carefully, stripping off his clothes till he was naked, only the flowing beard and hair covering his sunken chest and belly, the spindly legs sticking out comically below. He drew the magic circle around him with the sharp point of his dagger, and threw fragrant powder and leaves on the fire, so strange smelling smoke billowed up into the night sky.

Isabeau felt dizzy, the smoke stinging her eyes and throat, but she crouched silently as the flames leaped up, green at their heart.

Holding his staff before him, the clear stone at its head reflecting the flames, Jorge rocked back and forth on his haunches, staring into the bowl of water he had set between his feet, muttering to himself. Several times he leaped to his feet and stamped beside the fire, before dropping to his haunches again, swaying and chanting, "In the name o' Eà, our mother and our father, thee who is Spinner and Weaver and Cutter o' the Thread, thee who sows the seed, nurtures the life and reaps the harvest, feel in me the tides o' seas and blood; feel in me the endless darkness and the blaze of light; feel in me the swing o' the moons and the planets, the path o' the stars and the sun; draw aside the veil, open my eyes, by the virtue o' the four elements, wind, stone, flame and rain; draw aside the veil, open my eyes, by virtue o' clear skies and storm, rainbows and hailstones, flowers and falling leaves, flames and ashes . . ."

Isabeau began to feel afraid, the night bending over them, smoke swirling. Jorge's blind white eyes rolled in his head, and his skinny body curled over itself, twitching. He threw back his head and began to chant. "I see red clouds—the sun is setting and red clouds race across the sky. There is danger . . . a whirlwind is rising . . . I see a multicolored viper, striped like a rainbow. It attacks, jaws dripping with venom. Slash at it with your sword! Cut it! Ah, Eà! It throws itself into many pieces, and each piece attacks. There are ashes on the wind . . ."

Isabeau was very frightened now, having never seen anyone in an ecstatic trance before. "What do ye mean?" she whispered. But Jorge was deep in his vision and did not hear.

"Storm clouds are coming. The moon is being eaten, the moon is being eaten!" With a shriek the old man fell back, and Isabeau knelt beside him, chafing his cold hands and begging him to wake up. Although he stirred, his eyes did not open and he murmured a few words: ". . . The Laird o' the sea comes."

"Tell me what ye see about me?" Isabeau asked anxiously, afraid the old man would drift out of his trance before she learned anything at all. His eyes were open and he was staring up at the sky with blank eyes that leaked tears.

"Give me your witch knife," he said feebly, and sat up.

She passed over the narrow blade. The old man rocked back and forth, muttering. The smoke billowed into the sky, and he clutched Isabeau's knife, running his fingers over it. His voice changed, grew deeper. "I see ye staring into a mirror and your reflection reaches out and grips your wrist. I see ye with many faces and many disguises; ye will be one who can hide in a crowd. Though ye shall have no home and no rest, all valleys and pinnacles will be your home; though ye shall never give birth, ye shall rear a child who shall one day rule the land." His voice tailed away, and he blinked and looked up, his wrinkled face gray with exhaustion now the vision had passed. "Your destiny is indeed strange and mysterious, lassie. It fills me with fear—this vision is linked with others I have had—a child who straddles oceans and land; mirrors that break; moons that are eaten."

"What does it all mean?" Isabeau wondered, feeling excitement creep through her. A strange and mysterious destiny, he had said. A child that will rule the land.

He shook his head and wrapped his shivering body in his ragged plaid. "I do no' ken, lass. I only see what I see, and all the future is mysterious. Come, let us eat and sleep for we have another long day ahead o' us."

Isabeau spent most of the day close to the old man's side, hoping he could tell her more about her future. He told her no more, however, and grew angry when she became persistent. He did speak to her about the One Power, though.

"The One Power is in all things," the warlock said. "In trees and plants, in the air that we breathe and the water we drink, in our blood and our spirit, in the stars and the moons, in the red comet that has been brightening our night skies. But the One Power is no' inexhaustible. This is why we teach care in its use. When we draw upon the Power, we take it from all around us and within us. The greater the magic, the more Power is used."

"Why is it some witches can draw on a lot o' Power and others only some?" Isabeau asked. This was a question she had asked Meghan many times, but her guardian had only ever said, "Powerful is as powerful does." The blind seer was not much more forthcoming. "Why is it some men can throw a curling stone right to the end o' the pool and others can only throw it over the hog line?"

"Do ye mean that different people have different strengths?"

"Is that no' what I said?"

"So ye mean ye can only draw on as much Power as ye have strength to hold?"

"Is that what ye think?"

"I do no' ken very much about it," Isabeau said angrily. She wondered why it was that she knew so little, when she had been brought up by the Keybearer herself.

"Good, good," the old man said. "That's the first step."

Isabeau was so exasperated she ran on ahead, smashing leaves and branches with her stick.

Once they reached the foot of the mountains, they said their farewells as Jorge was turning to follow the line of the mountains west, while Isabeau was continuing south into Rionnagan.

"Will ye be all right?" she asked anxiously.

The old man took her hand in his and touched it to his forehead and then to his mouth. "Aye, indeed, lassie. I have been blind many years longer than ye've been alive, remember. And I have Jesyah to show me the way and warn me of trouble. The raven is wise and clear-seeing, ye must ken. It is not my welfare that should be o' concern to ye, but your own. Be careful and canny, lassie. It is a dangerous road that ye travel, and a vital task ye have undertaken. Guard the talisman well. I canna bear to think what would happen if it was to fall into the hands of the Banrìgh."

"Is it that important?" Isabeau was a little sobered.

"Aye, indeed. Perhaps the most important thing in the land at this moment. Meghan places great trust in ye, Isabeau Apprentice Witch. Do no' betray her trust."

"But what is it?" Isabeau touched the black pouch through the cloth of her shirt. "Why is it so important?"

"It is the key to unlock the chains that bind us," Jorge said cryptically. "Keep your courage high, Isabeau, and good wishes to ye."

"May my heart be kind, my mind fierce, my spirit brave."

The seer kissed her on the forehead, between the eyes. "Do no' fear, the time will come when the veil shall drop and ye shall see clearly," he said, then began to tap his way forward with his staff, the raven cawing a hoarse farewell as he flew ahead on midnight wings.

Isabeau put her hand to her head, which was ringing oddly, then set off down the path, unable to shake a sense of trepidation. *At least I'll now be able to make better time,* she thought.

In reality, she found the journey slow and difficult. She had come down from the heights and now was in the thick forest that skirted the edge of the range. Here the undergrowth was thick with brambles that caught in her hair or tore her shirt. Often what seemed a well-defined path petered out and she had to spend hours fighting her way through the thick woods before she again found a path that followed the fast-flowing burn. Other times she came upon a deep ravine which meant a long journey until she could find a place to cross. Once she thought she saw a nixie diving under the surface of a pool, tiny feet and a swathe of transparent hair disappearing in a swirl and a splash. Another time she came across a great woolly bear fishing in the icy waters of the burn. Warily she made a wide detour, having no wish to face down a woolly bear, renowned for both its savagery and its stupidity.

At night she heard the howling of timber wolves as they sang to the moons, and she huddled under her blankets, wishing Meghan was there to protect her. During the day, she often found herself growing uneasy, the back of her neck prickling as if she was being watched. Several times she began to lengthen her pace in an attempt to shake the feeling, only to have it return later, when she had at last begun to relax again.

As a result of her haste, she twice lost her way. The first time she found herself in a great valley like the one in which she had lived, surrounded on three sides by towering cliffs and no way out but the way she came in. A storm had blown up, as it did so often in the months of spring, and she sought shelter in a cave, only to come face to face with a pride of elven cats who did not take kindly to her clumsy intrusion. Luckily, Isabeau was conversant with their language and was able to back out quickly, apologizing and bowing, as she knew the small but savage black cats expected. The night was spent nervously and damply in a tree, for the bared fangs had been all too clear even in the dark of a stormy night.

The second time she followed a path for days, only to come out on a plateau looking down onto the forests of Aslinn far below. She cursed and swore, but had no choice but to turn and retrace her steps—she had come too far east if she could see Aslinn. She needed to head back and down to the south to find the way out of the Sithiche Mountains, the single break in the range called, appropriately enough, the Pass.

Isabeau should have known her way. She had made the journey down to the highlands of Rionnagan every year since she was a babe in arms. She had been confident that she knew the way, and indeed, all she had to do was bear southeast and wait for the lie of the land to take her into the fertile valleys and forests below. But in a year the landscape can change—storms and landslides make their mark, trees grow and fall, and even the animals of the forests change their paths as hunting grows scarcer. More importantly, Isabeau acknowledged reluctantly, her guardian had been with her on all her other trips and so Isabeau had not been responsible for choosing the path or the night's camp site. And despite Isabeau's knowledge of the languages and customs of the creatures of the forests, she was having more trouble with the wild animals than she had ever experienced when with Meghan. She reminded herself that Seychella had said all the creatures of the land were stirring. But that did not really explain why her previous journeys from mountain peaks to valley villages had always been so pleasant and easy, but was now the most arduous and difficult of her life.

Soon after she regained the track, the talisman she carried inside her shirt began to burn and tingle. For most of one day she ignored it, but the heat became too much to bear the further south she traveled, and so she took it out and stowed it in her pack where it could not burn her.

The track ran along the side of the fast-running burn which she hoped was the start of the great Rhyllster. If so, it would lead her straight down to the Pass and into Rionnagan.

Isabeau was hurrying down this track, trying to ignore the discomfort of the burning talisman which now scorched right through the leather of her pack, when suddenly a young woman dropped out of the trees right in front of her. "Sssh!" she hissed, and put her finger against her lips.

Isabeau immediately stifled her exclamation of surprise, but looked about her quickly for a possible route of escape. There was none: on her right, the bank dropped steeply to the rocky bed of the burn; to her left was a great stony bank, without foothold or handhold.

"Go back!" the girl said. She was dressed in a dirty green smock and long hood, and she had the greenest eyes Isabeau had ever seen, and the most freckled face. Her feet were bare and black with mud.

"Why?"

"Soldiers ahead. They will see ye. Quick, follow me!"

She darted past Isabeau and down the ridge, until she found a place where they could clamber up the bank.

After only a moment's hesitation, Isabeau followed her. The stranger leaped up the bank like a deer, and held out her hand to Isabeau to help her. After a breathless scramble, they were safe in the forest, though the green-eyed girl set off immediately on a wild race through the trees. They followed the line of the ridge, came at last to where it loomed over the burn, and there they flopped to catch their breath and watch the long line of soldiers marching up the track. There must have been more than a hundred, most on foot but some riding massive horses, with burnished helmets on their heads. If not for the stranger, Isabeau would have walked straight into them.

"They go to hunt the dragons," the girl said.

"How do ye ken?"

"I heard them talking."

"What's your name? I'm Isabeau. I have no family name, I fear."

The girl chuckled, and said, "Me neither. I'm Lilanthe. They call me Lilanthe o' the Forest. What do they call ye?"

Isabeau hesitated. She was now Isabeau the Apprentice Witch, but she could not tell this stranger that, so with a sigh she said reluctantly, "Isabeau the Foundling."

"Ye and me both, I fear," Lilanthe said gaily. "Nameless an' homeless, both o' us. Ye can be Isabeau o' the Forest too, if ye want."

"Isabeau o' the Mountains."

"Isabeau o' the Stones and River!"

"Isabeau o' the Sky!"

They smiled at each other and ran forward through the forest. That day they made the best time and had the most pleasant traveling that Isabeau had had all week. Isabeau had often craved a companion her own age to explore the woods with, and share secrets with. She had been alone all her life, the creatures of the forest and a bad-tempered old witch her only companions. It seemed Lilanthe felt the same.

"I have always wanted a friend," she admitted. "Someone who likes me all the time, an' never misunderstands me."

The next few days were more like a game than a real journey. They ran and sang and giggled and told stories.

Lilanthe was traveling to the south as well, though she only laughed and said she was exploring the river when Isabeau asked her why.

"Do ye no' have anyone to miss ye?" Isabeau asked.

Lilanthe laughed again and shook her head. "I'm free as a bird!" she cried, and ran down the hill with her arms spread, leaping over boulders and brambles and swerving as if tilting her wings to the wind. Isabeau followed, hallooing and laughing, her arms spread wide.

Knowing Lilanthe, like Meghan, was able to sense what lay ahead and so be able to avoid it, Isabeau was not afraid of being caught. As they traveled, she wondered why it was that she could not do this. Everyone had said she had power, but she had failed the Trials of Spirit, and would now be a prisoner of the Red Guards had it not been for Lilanthe. Again and again she tried to send out her mind, or sense what the other girl was thinking, but always her mind was a blank. Her excitement over Jorge the Seer's splendid prophecies faded into depression, deepened by her anxiety for Meghan. As if it was not dangerous enough for her frail old guardian to have set off to find the dragons, without having a hundred soldiers on her trail too! Isabeau wished she knew how to scry through fire or water or her witch rings as Meghan so often did. She could have warned Meghan about the soldiers. But Isabeau had never been taught to scry, and for the first time she wondered if this was because Meghan knew she had no ability in this direction. But a witch without the witch sense was no witch at all, and the further south the two traveled, the more subdued Isabeau became. Lilanthe's confession that she had been watching and following Isabeau for several days did nothing to make her feel better, though she realized Lilanthe could track virtually anyone through the forest and remain undetected. She seemed able to blend into the trees at any time, startling Isabeau by dropping out of branches or materializing behind a clump of flowering may when moments before Isabeau would have sworn there was no one there.

For four days they traveled together, and talked long and deep about their lives. Both were orphaned—Lilanthe's mother had died when she was a baby and she had been brought up by her father. Despite her openness on any other subject, Lilanthe would not talk about him at all, and shuddered a little when Isabeau tried to press the point, only saying, "Well, he's dead now, so it does no' matter."

Although neither mentioned it, both knew the other must have magic. Isabeau guessed Lilanthe was a wood witch like Meghan, for she seemed to understand the language of the birds and forest creatures as well as Isabeau did, and her woodcraft was superb. She was able to tell what had passed through a place merely by a sound or a smell or a warmth where there should be none.

On the fifth morning, Isabeau woke before dawn, though the stars in the sky were so bright, and the light from the setting moons so red that she could see round the clearing quite easily. She glanced across the gray coals of the fire, but Lilanthe was no longer lying in her bedroll. The blankets lay in a heap, and Isabeau could see the twisted material of her smock. But there was no sign of Lilanthe.

Isabeau was not perturbed, realizing her traveling partner must have slipped into the woods to relieve herself. Feeling the urge herself, Isabeau found a convenient shrub, then afterward wandered down to the pool in the center of the clearing and washed her hands and face. The sky was beginning to lighten and she sat and watched the pale colors ripple across the water.

Deep in thought, Isabeau rested her eyes on a beautiful weeping greenberry tree on the other side of the water. Trailing its long leaves in the water, the tree had a slim white trunk that bent and flowed in the breeze. It was easy for Isabeau to fancy the tree was really a shapely young woman just waking and stretching from sleep. Those long supple branches could be arms; the green tendrils her flowing hair, tangled with leaves and flowers. The knots in the bole could be eyes, just about to open. In a moment she would raise her trailing arms and rub at them.

Somehow, when the tree did raise its arms and stretch and the long eyes opened, and she realized it was Lilanthe, Isabeau was not surprised. There had been a moment when her mind's fancy and the truth of what she was seeing had merged, and everything fell into place. Why Isabeau never saw Lilanthe sleep; why she seemed so much part of the forest. She must be a tree-changer! Though Isabeau had always thought tree-changers looked far more treelike than human, and Lilanthe had certainly looked very human.

Her blue eyes met Lilanthe's green ones, and a look of despair and sorrow dashed across the other's face. With a cry she pushed back her hair, indisputably green in color and as thick and long as Isabeau's. Then she rose and ran, in a mad dash that saw no boulder or bramble in her way, nothing but the blur of tears in her eyes. Having run into the woods upset that way herself several times, Isabeau knew she had to follow her. She ran back up to the camp site, thrust her belongings and Lilanthe's into her pack, kicked dust over the fire and ran after her friend.

She chased Lilanthe into the forest for more than ten minutes, easily tracking her by the sound of muffled sobbing. Suddenly, though, all sound creased. There was no bird song, no chitter of donbeags or squirrels, no scamper of coneys. Isabeau came to an uneasy stop. There was no sign of Lilanthe. Isabeau took a few more cautious steps and then a few more, but saw or heard nothing.

After searching fruitlessly for several minutes, she sat down and realized she was hopelessly lost, not having noticed which way they had run. The forest all seemed the same; even the snow-capped mountains towering so close behind were all the same, the distinctive shape of Dragonclaw having long ago been left behind. Most of all, though, Isabeau was worried about Lilanthe. She had obviously done her best to appear human, hiding the betraying green hair beneath a long tailed hood, and pretending each night to roll herself for sleep in her blankets. The unmasking of her true nature had obviously upset her deeply. Perhaps it was because she knew of the Rìgh's decree against the fairies? Perhaps she was afraid Isabeau would turn away from her because she was an *uile-bheist,* maybe even denounce her. Isabeau got to her feet and again searched over the ground she had covered, but this time she did not search for a naked girl with green eyes, but for a slender white greenberry tree.

She found her almost immediately. Lilanthe must have realized Isabeau was not going to give up, and so had transformed herself back into a tree. Isabeau sat at her roots, in the shade of the beautiful long branches, and ate lunch. While she chewed her potato bread and cheese, and drank water from her flask, she mused aloud. "What could I have done to upset Lilanthe so badly? I must have said something. Maybe my face showed how surprised I was to see that she is a tree-changer, when all this time I thought she was human like me. I hope that's no' it, because Lilanthe was my first real friend and I'd so hate to lose her." Having not elicited any response, Isabeau sighed deeply and went on. "Maybe she's afraid I will no' like her anymore, which makes me so angry I want to shake her till all her teeth fall out."

The pale branches seemed to quiver, but that could have been the breeze. Isabeau began to wonder whether she was sitting under the right greenberry tree. "Maybe she's afraid I will denounce her to the Banrìgh's Guards. If only she knew. Why, she could denounce *me* at any time and I do no' go running off into the forest or make her go chasing after me through this bloody tangle o' thorns!"

Isabeau finished her cheese and plucked a dried apple from one of her canvas bags. The leaves swayed and a bumblebee came blundering through to sip from the tiny green flowers gathered along the stems. Isabeau sighed again, and then said with a quaver in her voice, "I'm so frightened . . . How could Lilanthe lure me off into the deep dark forest like this and leave me here all alone? I'm lo-oo-oost!" Although she was afraid she had overdone the break in her voice, cool white arms were suddenly sliding round her neck and Lilanthe was there again.

"Fool!" she said, laughing through her tears. "As if ye could no' find your way back again, after that trail ye left behind ye!"

"Och, thank Eà, Lilanthe, I was getting so sick o' chasing after ye! Why did ye run off like that?"

"I'm a tree-shifter!" Lilanthe suddenly exclaimed. "Not a changer. I'm half human. My da was one o' ye."

"Was your mother a tree-changer then?"

Lilanthe nodded, though fear was ugly on her face.

"At least ye ken who your mother and father were," Isabeau said bitterly. "I could be half frost giant for all I ken."

"No' with that hair," Lilanthe laughed, and then put up her hand self-consciously to her own, green as a new leaf. Then she sighed. "I be sorry, Isabeau, ye just do no' understand what it be like. My father used to beat me if I tried to change, would lock me inside so I could no' get to the forest. He used to sell me to the village men, for no one thought o' me as anything but an *uile-bheist*. When he died, they told the Red Guards, who came to get me. I had lived among them all my life and none would look me in the eye when they took me away. The soldiers used me as the village men had done, and taunted me with what the Questioners would do to me afore I died. Eventually I managed to escape: some fool let me put my feet to ground. Although they ken I was an *uile-bheist*, they never thought to ask what my fairy nature was. I hid in my treeshape for six days, and eventually they left. I have lived in the forests ever since. Five years! Five years I've been free, and I could never bear to leave the forest again."

"How auld were ye?" Isabeau whispered.

"Thirteen," Lilanthe answered. "Tree-changers develop much as humans do, I think. I was very much like a human bairn, in all but a few respects." She covered her face with her hands and gave a sharp gasp. Then her face was up again, and she was glaring at Isabeau with a wild look in her eye. "So there ye have it all. What are ye going to do?"

"Tell ye my story," Isabeau said comfortably. "Fair's fair. I was raised by a witch in a tree house deep in the mountains. I was taught much o' the ancient wisdom, and was only last week initiated into the forbidden Coven o' Witches. I think my guardian is in contact with the rebels, for sometimes we receive strange messages by carrier bird. I am now on a perilous quest for her, carrying a magic talisman to a spy in the Rìgh's castle itself. If we succeed, the evil Banrìgh will be toppled, and fairy and human can again live in harmony," she finished with a flourish, her blue eyes sparkling. "Now what are *ye* going to do?"

Lilanthe's eyes were brilliant. "How wonderful!" she breathed. "On a quest! Really?"

"Aye! Look, I'll show ye." Isabeau fished inside her shirt and brought out the black pouch. Opening its drawstrings, she pulled out the triangular talisman.

Immediately Lilanthe gasped. "I can feel its power!" she cried. "It's like a torch in your hand! Why is it I could no' feel it afore?"

"I think the pouch hides magic objects," Isabeau said frowning. "M . . . M . . . M . . ." She tried to say her guardian's name but her tongue seemed to twist about in her mouth and she could not. "I was told to keep it in there," she finished.

"Maybe that is why I could no' sense ye," Lilanthe said. "Normally I can sense anything living for quite a way, but with ye I could no'. I stumbled across your tracks and could no' believe someone was passing through my territory without me knowing it. That was why I followed ye—no' only because ye looked interesting, but because there seems to be some veil about ye so I canna read your mind. I wonder if it is the wee pouch, but if so, it must be very powerful."

Isabeau fingered her rings, which she had also hidden in the bag, then reluctantly stowed them away again. "I wish I could wear my rings," she said. "I canna wait for the day when witchery is no longer outlawed."

"Or when tree-shifters are no' hunted down like animals," Lilanthe said sadly. "It is lonely in the forest sometimes. I wish ye did no' have to keep going, or that I could travel with ye. I will miss ye once we reach the edge o' the forest."

"Me too," Isabeau said, feeling pity for her friend squeeze her throat. "But it is too dangerous."

"Are ye no' frightened?"

"Och, no," Isabeau said airily. "I only have to get to Caeryla, really, and then I'll have help."

"So ye really are no' going to tell anyone that I'm hiding out in the forest?" Lilanthe asked nervously.

"Of course no'!" Isabeau exclaimed, then mimicked her, "Are ye sure ye willna tell anyone I'm on a secret mission to overthrow the evil Banrìgh?"

Lilanthe laughed. "Oh aye, sure, I'll go up to the next Red Guard I see and say, 'I ken I be only a tree-shifter and ye are beholden to kill me, but if I tell ye where to find a witch, will ye leave me alone?' No, I'm going to stay right away from any soldiers, believe me!"

The two girls parted company three days later on the very edge of the forest. They hugged and kissed and wept a few tears, then Lilanthe melted back into the trees and Isabeau set her face toward the Pass. At last she reached the top of the last hill, and stood there in silence, smelling the wind. The Pass, a narrow ravine that ran through the last barrier of mountains, looked as though some crazed frost giant had chopped at the mountain with an axe, cutting a path through the very rock. It was not a giant's axe, however, but the Rhyllster, carving its way through the rock over many thousands of years.

The sun was setting rapidly, and the shadow of the mountains was falling upon the meadow before her. With a sigh, Isabeau decided she must spend another night in the forest, for the path through the Pass was narrow and dangerous and should not be negotiated at night. There was no other way down into the highlands of Rionnagan, for the mountains in this area were virtually impenetrable. Quickly she turned and scrambled back down the steep slope, looking about her for a safe place to camp. She knew there were few things in the forest that she could not contend with, but she was tired and hungry, and the forest held many strange creatures.

She found at last an old tree whose massive roots rose into large cavities like shallow caves. She propped her satchel inside the largest, then hid her pouches of herbs at the back. Carefully she built a fire and, with her finger, lit the twists of dry leaves and bark so a tiny blue flame sprung into life. Blowing gently upon the embers, she fed in more twigs and dry leaves until a small fire blazed between the roots of the trees. She thrust some sweet roots into the embers and put on her little pot to boil. Shadows danced like goblins over the twisted roots and the trunks of the trees about her, but Isabeau was not afraid.

During the night she was woken suddenly by a presentiment of danger. The fire had died, but the talisman she carried in its black pouch was burning hot, scalding her through the cloth of her shirt. Carefully she stretched out her hand and touched her knife, trying to scent what was in the air. She thought she could smell horses, and the next moment she could hear them, crashing through the undergrowth.

Quietly Isabeau tied her boots to her waist and gathered together her belongings. She could hear the riders now—they were swearing, and the bridles jingled. She kicked dust over the remains of the fire and, barefooted, swarmed up the tree. It was easy climbing, since the roots provided many handholds, and Isabeau was safely concealed in its branches by the time the party reached the clearing.

She heard the riders enter the clearing and, peering through the branches, could make out the shapes of men as they dismounted. There was a thud as some bundle across one of the horse's saddles was thrown to the ground, and the clink of metal as the horses were unbridled.

"In Truth, I hate this wood," one of the men said. "It fair gives me the creeps. If I did no' ken better, I'd swear there were spirits abroad this night."

"What sort o' spirits?" a woman's voice said, and the silky, menacing tone made Isabeau shiver. "If ye are no' careful, Carldo, people might start thinking ye believe in . . . spirits. People might start talking, and talk travels. Talk can travel places ye'd rather it wasna heard."

There was a tiny pause, and then Carldo said in a startled tone, "Och, but my Lady Glynelda, no one would think . . . everyone knows I was brought up right, I've been taught the Truth. No one would think otherwise."

"Still, one should be careful," Glynelda said. "The Awl does no' like those that speak against the Truth."

Carldo made a grunt of fervent assent, but the woman cut across him with a gesture. Then she spoke, very low, so that Isabeau could hardly hear her. "I can smell . . . enchantment."

Isabeau froze. A witch-sniffer! Terror ran like ice through her veins. What bad luck to come across a seeker. It might even be the one that had discovered the secret valley where she and Meghan had lived, forcing them to flee. She wished now she had lit her fire with flint, not magic, and she pressed back deeper into the shadows of the branches. The talisman seemed to be branding her skin, it burned so hot.

Another man spoke up. "This forest is probably stiff with enchantments, m'lady. Think on the monster we have already found. The Truth alone kens what evil things have bred up here in these cursed mountains. We mun keep our wits about us."

The group began to settle for the night. Isabeau heard the sound of other parcels being thrown down, and a whickering snort from a horse, which sounded like a rumble of discontent. She heard one of the men take his boots off, and another said something about starting a fire. Isabeau shrank back into the concealing branches, afraid the light would reveal her to the men below. She could escape them, of course, but would rather no one saw her passing.

By the light of the flickering flames, she saw eight men, six in the red cloaks of the Banrìgh's Guard; two dressed roughly in brown wool and leather, who sat together at one side of the fire. By herself on the other side was a woman wearing a severe red dress, buttoned high to the throat. She had a stern face, and sat with her back as straight as a ruler. Backed into the trees stood the horses, most of them rough hacks, one a finely-bred chestnut. One of the men hung a black pot over the fire, and Isabeau could smell meat. She wrinkled her nose in distaste.

"Should we feed the *uile-bheist*?" Carldo asked hesitantly.

"Feel sorry for it, do we?" another man said snidely.

Carldo shook his head violently. "No, no, I just thought it'd be better if it did no' die afore we got it to the palace. Surely she'd rather it be alive?"

After a moment, the seeker said, "True. Feed it then, if ye want."

Carldo got to his feet clumsily, and approached the shrouded bundle they had thrown down earlier. Isabeau leaned forward, watching him struggle to undo the rope that was passed several times around the object. At last Carldo managed to undo the knots, and pull aside the cloth. A young man lay inside, his mouth gagged tightly.

"Are ye hungry?" Carldo asked gruffly, pulling aside the gag. He was answered with an unearthly cry of despair and defiance that rose into the night like a clarion call. Quickly Carldo kicked him into silence.

"What in dragons' balls was that?" Carldo muttered. "I never heard such a thing!"

"Keep it quiet!" Lady Glynelda snapped, her voice frightened. "Do ye want all the creatures o' the forest down upon us? Feed it if ye must, only keep it quiet!"

Carldo looked as if he did not want to go near the prisoner again, but reluctantly he spooned some of the stew into a bowl and gave it to him, undoing his bound hands first and menacing him into silence. The prisoner ate hungrily, shoveling the food into his mouth with both hands. Carldo stood over him with his claymore in hand, looking uneasily out into the forest, which rustled and murmured with all its night sounds of wind and bird and branches tapping. Isabeau wondered if Carldo could still hear the echo of that strange song, as she could.

At last the bowl was empty, and although the prisoner gave a short squawk and motioned for more, Carldo took the bowl away and tied him up again. Isabeau busied her mind with plans of rescue. She wondered uneasily whether Meghan would approve if she knew—her guardian's instructions had not included the saving of a stranger with the voice of a bird. Then she smiled and shrugged. She had always been one to go her own way.

After a while, the party slept, the prisoner again bound and gagged. One man stayed on watch, but he sat with his back to her, staring uneasily out into the night. Slowly Isabeau slid out of the tree, and waited, crouching in the shadows, until his head was nodding. Then she slowly shook some valerian powder out of one of her pouches into her hand and lightly scattered it over him. He gave a snort and a start, but almost immediately began to snore. Isabeau smiled, and scattered a pinch over the others. She waited until the rhythm of their breathing had deepened, then slipped silently over to where the prisoner lay awkwardly on his side with the rough cloth draped over him.

"Do no' sing," she breathed into his ear, first in her own language, then in the language of birds. At the sound of the bubble of music, one of the men shifted uneasily, and Isabeau froze. She waited almost ten minutes, before saying again, "Do no' sing." She hoped he had understood.

Quickly the girl sliced the rope around his feet and hands, and rubbed them urgently, knowing how painfully circulation would return to his limbs. In the faint firelight, she saw that he was naked beneath the rough cloth, which made her blush with confusion. Isabeau had never had much to do with men, and the obvious differences between her body and his filled her with embarrassment. He clutched the cloth to his body and, looking the other way, she tried to help him to his feet, which were roughly bound in sacking instead of shoes. But it was no use, the prisoner was crippled by the long hours spent bound, and could not walk. Isabeau looked around quickly, and saw the horses resting in the shadows. They were awake, and watching what she did with some interest. The chestnut, a tall stallion with a fiery mane and tail, pawed the ground, then stepped forward daintily and nuzzled against her arm. She stroked his silky nose and said, "Thank ye," knowing the horse had understood what she wanted.

Isabeau had never ridden with a bridle and saddle before, being used to riding the wild horses of the mountains, not these tame, domesticated beasts. After some time struggling with the straps, she managed to unharness the stallion, and he tossed his beautiful head, and pawed the ground. She then unharnessed all the ponies, and as quietly as she could, dropped the bridles into a pile by the fire.

"Come," she said, and helped the prisoner to his feet. He stumbled, and she saw he was a hunchback, barely able to stand without assistance. One shoulder was humped higher than the other, and he could not straighten his back under the huge black cloak he wore wrapped close about him. Isabeau groaned to herself, knowing how much harder their escape would be, then led the sturdiest of the ponies to his side. She managed to hoist the prisoner onto its back, listening intently to the quiet snores of the men. He slumped forward, and for a moment the black cloak flared outward, as if caught by a fresh breeze. But the air was still in that quietness that comes just before dawn. Isabeau knew they must hurry.

Isabeau twined her hand in the bright mane of the chestnut stallion, which she guessed must belong to the woman in red, and indicated that the other ponies should follow. Once they were out of the clearing, Isabeau halted the stallion and, with soft whickers and nose-blowings, asked it to wait. Then she slipped back into the clearing, fumbling in her herb bag for the little parcel of valerian powder. She gently tapped some more into the palm of her hand, trying to judge the amount by instinct. Then she carefully scattered the powder into the slumbering fire, whispering, "Sleep, sleep." The fire flared up, blue and green, before dropping lower than before. Isabeau ran from the clearing before sleep should overcome her too.

Even though she had delayed the waking of the men for some hours, Isabeau was determined to put as many miles as possible between them. Riding the finely bred stallion, and leading the pony that carried the semiconscious prisoner, she whacked the other horses across the rump with a branch so they scattered. She then headed east, back into the mountains, then south again to avoid a narrow, treacherous ravine, at the bottom of which thundered a fast moving river. She had been forced to postpone the long, difficult journey through the Pass into the valleys below for they had a much better chance of concealing themselves in the forests than out in the open.

The man she had rescued was barely able to keep his seat, falling forward across the gray pony's neck. "Do no' let him fall," she warned the pony, who tossed its mane and trotted forward sturdily.

At last Isabeau felt it was safe to stop, and she busied herself making a fire and boiling some water, into which she cast a selection of herbs. The talisman was still burning and tingling, even through the material of its pouch, so she wrapped it up in her plaid and put it to one side so it would not bother her so much. The hunchback had fallen from the gray mare's back and now lay, half conscious, in the shade of an old tree. Isabeau was tired since she had slept little that night, but she ignored her own aching body and began to clean the scrapes and bruises around the young man's wrists and on his battered face. His arms were heavily muscled and she wondered if he was a blacksmith or miner to have developed his upper body so powerfully.

"What is your name?" she asked in her own language. He stared at her suspiciously.

"My name is Isabeau," she said, trying to sound kind and friendly. He did not respond, so she finished tying up his chafed wrists in silence, then gave him the herbal tea to drink in her wooden cup and refilled the saucepan with water. For a moment she almost dipped her finger in the water to boil it, before remembering with a blush, and hanging the saucepan on its hook over the fire.

The young man slumped forward again, his chafed wrists in his lap, his hairy black cloth covering him from throat to ankle. His hair was dark with an attractive white blaze at his brow, and his eyes were a curious yellow. Under the dirt and scratches, Isabeau thought he would be a very personable young man, if it were not for his deformity. She was glad she had rescued him from his captors.

"Who were those men?" she asked. "Why were ye their prisoner?"

He did not answer, looking down at the cup sullenly.

"They said they were taking ye to the Rìgh's palace. Why? Are they taking ye to the Banrìgh?"

Still there was no answer. Isabeau felt her temper rising. "I'm your friend," she said. "I rescued ye. Surely I have a right to ken what I rescued ye from?"

"I do no' ken who those men are," he said at last. "I do no' ken what they wanted with me."

"So ye can speak," Isabeau said, and tossed a handful of oats into the boiling water. "What is your name?"

There was a long hesitation, before he muttered, "They call me Bacaiche."

"Bacaiche," Isabeau said. "Does that no' mean . . . cripple?"

He gave her an angry look and snapped, "What o' it?"

Isabeau was quickly losing patience with her ungrateful charge. She stirred the porridge, and watched him as he raised the cup to his face and tentatively sniffed the liquid. "It's quite safe," she said sarcastically. "I havena poisoned it or anything." He shot her a quick glance, then just as tentatively sipped the fragrant brew. After a moment, apparently gaining confidence, he sipped again.

"Please tell me why ye were those men's prisoner," Isabeau cajoled. "I canna help ye if I do no' ken what's going on."

"I do no' need your help," he said rudely.

"Och, sure," Isabeau rejoined. "Ye were trussed up as neat as a chicken going to market when I first saw ye. Ye'd still be there, no doubt, if I hadna stupidly taken it into my head to rescue ye. And I suppose you're no' hungry. Ye wouldna like any o' this porridge now, would ye? Or some more tea?"

For once he had started, Bacaiche had gulped down the tea greedily, and was now looking rather longingly at the porridge bubbling away in the little saucepan. Isabeau had seen how little food his captors had given him the night before, and how hungrily he had devoured it. She swung the saucepan away from the fire, and spooned its contents into a bowl, stirring in some honey so the porridge turned brown and sticky. "Delicious," she said, swallowing a spoonful, her back now lodged comfortably against the fallen tree trunk.

He watched her, and said nothing. Slowly she ate another mouthful, staring off at the jagged peaks towering against the fresh morning sky. How many days would she be delayed, she wondered, by her decision to rescue this stubborn young man? She ate another mouthful, glad of the warm food after her sleepless night, and wondering how long he would sit there, mouth shut tight, eyes following every move of the spoon. Just as she was about to give in and pass him the bowl, he broke.

"I do no' ken who those men are," he said. "They rode me down and tied me up and said they were takin' me south."

"Why?" she asked.

He shrugged, and looked away.

"Who are ye that they would want to do such a thing?"

"Nothing. Nobody. I am just a poor herdsman."

Isabeau remembered the strange song he had sung last night, and how he had spoken in the language of the birds. She sat with the bowl in her lap, unsure whether to pass it to him or keep eating in the hope he would give her some more information. She knew he was no mere herdsmen. His face was so bruised, though, and his body so obviously painful, that her kind heart eventually won and she passed him the bowl.

He swallowed the porridge so greedily, scraping the bowl clean and looking at the empty bowl so wistfully that Isabeau put the saucepan on to boil again. Casting a glance at her companion, she saw his eyes were closed, and so she risked giving the water a swirl with her finger to make it boil faster. Making another round of porridge emptied her calico bag of oats, and her anxiety deepened. Her stores were running low, and she could not travel without food. She would have to forage as she went, and that would slow her considerably. Again she doubted the wisdom of her impulse. However, what was done was done, and she would just have to face the consequences.

The consequences came much sooner than she had expected. As she was packing away the meager remains of her rations, and rinsing out the saucepan, the stallion raised his head and whickered. Isabeau swung round and listened intently. Through the bird song and the soft wind, she heard the sound of horses' hooves and the clink of metal.

Quickly Isabeau gathered up her belongings. "We must hide," she said, and looked at the slumped figure of Bacaiche with grave worry. The bruises on his face were livid in the bright light, and he was obviously stiff and sore. "Hopefully it's nothing to worry about, but we canna be too careful. I canna see how it could be your captors—they couldna have found us so quickly, since we left them without horses."

Bacaiche struggled to his feet and stood leaning against the gray pony's flank, breathing roughly. The dark cloak he wore dragged in the dust behind him. With great difficulty, Isabeau helped him to mount. "This way," she said, leading the way out of the clearing and up the wall of the valley toward an outcrop of rock that would both afford them protection and allow them to see the whole valley.

Though small, the pony was sturdy and the stallion fleet of foot, so Isabeau urged them on without respite, her anxiety deepening as she realized that it was quite a large party riding up the path toward them. She could hear the jingle of at least six bridles, and the sound of men's voices. Once at the top of the hill, she called a halt and, hiding behind the rocky outcrop, looked down at the narrow valley. At the entrance a group of horsemen had stopped. Twelve wore the bright cloaks and helmets of the Red Guards' cavalry, and for the first time Isabeau felt a real prick of fear. According to Meghan, these men were her natural enemies, sworn to hunt down witches and magic creatures. The others were dressed in the brown wool and leather of local men. At the front rode the woman Isabeau had seen last night, her crimson dress buttoned high to her throat. She looked up at the mountains, and raised her head in a curious manner, as if smelling the wind. After a moment, the woman pointed south, and they all rode toward the clearing where Isabeau had made breakfast. It would not take them long to find the smoldering ashes of their fire beneath the dust she had kicked over it. The soldiers would know they had left only minutes before.

"They be the men who caught me," Bacaiche said hoarsely, pointing down at the two men in brown wool who were leaning out of the saddles, looking for hoofprints on the ground.

"How did they catch up with us so fast?" Isabeau wondered. Her sleeping spell must have worn off more rapidly than she expected, and they must have had friends nearby, though that still did not explain how they were able to follow her so quickly. For a moment, Isabeau could not decide whether they should try to outrun their pursuers or just hide and wait for them to leave. Then the memory of the woman smelling the wind came to her, and made the decision for her—if she was a seeker, escape was their only chance. Isabeau wished now she had not displayed her magic so obviously. Sleeping spells! Heating water with her finger! Would she never learn caution?

Isabeau wheeled the stallion round and led the way deeper into the forest. The shadows of great trees fell over them, and the ground began to steepen. Shaking their pursuers was not as easy as Isabeau had expected. The Red Guards were fast and determined, and seemed to see through every trick Isabeau used to hide their passage. She had stopped long enough to tie branches to the two horses' tails, yet the group of riders on their trail seemed hardly baffled by the scuffled marks left in their trail. Beginning to feel panicky, Isabeau let the stallion leave clear hoofprints on the bank of a stream, indicating they had crossed the water and were still heading south, when in reality the two horses splashed upstream for some considerable distance before doubling back. Sure that trick would mislead them, Isabeau was deeply troubled when the party followed them upstream with only a moment's hesitation.

She hastened their pace, glancing at Bacaiche, and wondering why he should occasion such a determined pursuit. The dark-haired man was swaying in the saddle, his face gray with exhaustion. Isabeau would not let them rest, however. All day they rode hard through the hills, till the horses were in a lather and she was herself almost faint with tiredness. She stopped only to check the position of the sun and to hide their trail, which had now looped back onto itself. After using every trick Meghan had ever taught her, Isabeau was now bearing back toward the Pass, not wanting to lose too much ground from her original direction. They did not stop for a meal till the sun was setting and they were only a few hours' ride from the spot where they had started out. Their pursuers, she hoped, would have continued riding to the north, and they could slip quietly down the Pass and into the great valley below.

During the brief stops to watch their trail, Isabeau had dismounted and foraged for food in the clearings. It was early in the season, though, and the winter had been harsh. She found only a few tubers which, even with the contents of her knapsack, could make them only a scanty meal. As she prepared the food, the stallion came and leaned against her, blowing gently in her hair. She fondled his soft nose, and looked up to find Bacaiche's yellow eyes fixed upon her. Again Isabeau told herself she must be careful. She knew nothing about her strange companion other than that he had been captured by the Red Guards, and that he spoke the language of birds. Although this seemed to indicate he was an enemy of the Banrìgh as well, she had no way of knowing whether she could trust him. Meghan had said to trust nobody.

Isabeau looked at Bacaiche as he huddled over the fire. He had wrapped the coarse material he had been found in around his waist like a loincloth, and the black cloak still draped his shoulders. However, it was bitterly cold at night in the mountains, with snow still glistening on the upper slopes. With the rest of his body naked, Bacaiche must be freezing. Not only that, how could Isabeau get through the Pass unnoticed with Bacaiche dressed like that?

She leaned over and began to rummage in her knapsack, pulling out her spare pair of breeches and a shirt. "Ye must be cold," she said, "Ye are no' that much taller than me, these should fit ye grandly." To her surprise, an expression of intense discomfort crossed Bacaiche's face. He shook his head. Surprised, she urged him, explaining her reasoning. "From now on there'll be villages, we canna afford to draw too much attention to ourselves. We must look like normal travelers."

As soon as she said it, she regretted it. As far as Bacaiche knew, she *was* a normal traveler, though only a moment's further reflection disabused her of this idea, leaving her rather cold and scared. She had not once acted like a normal traveler. A normal traveler would not rescue complete strangers from the Red Guards, or talk to horses, or know the tricks of evading capture. For the first time Isabeau doubted her ability to do as Meghan had asked.

However, before she could try to backtrack, Bacaiche had responded. "I am no' going to Rionnagan," he said. "I must head deeper into the mountains."

Isabeau was taken aback. It had not occurred to her that Bacaiche might have his own plans. "But . . . there's nothing in the mountains . . ."

"I have a journey o' my own to make," he said. He looked directly at her for the first time. "I came up through the Pass two days ago. They caught me coming through. The Pass is guarded."

Isabeau's heart sank, but she said, "We'll try to go through early tomorrow, at first light."

Bacaiche shook his head. The rosy firelight slid off his chest, highlighting his powerful muscles. "I must head back into the mountains."

"But why?" she asked in frustration. "I ken these mountains, there are few paths through them and those are still closed with snow."

He scowled. "All ye do is ask questions. Ye do no' need to ken what I do."

"I'm sorry," Isabeau said indignantly. "I was only trying to help."

"I dinna cross-examine ye," he retorted curtly.

"I just wanted—" she began, and then stopped, unwilling to explain further. "Very well, then, I'll ask no more questions. However, it's freezing in the mountains, ye must have some clothes. Will ye no' take them?" Isabeau held out the bundle again.

After a moment, Bacaiche took them and limped painfully out of the clearing, his black cloak trailing behind him. When he returned he had donned only the breeches, and the shirt hung from his hand. "It did no' fit," he said awkwardly, and looking again at the breadth of his shoulders, Isabeau could well believe it. He had wrapped the coarse cloth over his shoulders and around his chest, however, giving him some added protection so Isabeau was a little easier in her mind. She had not rescued Bacaiche for him to come down with pneumonia, she told herself sternly.

As they ate, Isabeau tried to find out more about Bacaiche without actually asking. However, all her conversational gambits were repulsed by her surly companion, so that she was quite exasperated with him by the time they had finished eating. Bacaiche, who had nodded over his stew, fell asleep almost immediately, but Isabeau was too anxious to sleep, although she had chosen their camping place carefully.

It was a clear, cold night. Lying on her back, Isabeau stared up at the starry sky and the two moons hanging close to the white peaks of the mountains. She thought about all that had happened to her in the last few days. Three weeks ago, the greatest excitement in her life was watching otters teach their babies how to swim. Now she was outrunning the Red Guards and rescuing ungrateful hunchbacks. A smile curved her lips, and she clenched her fingers about the talisman that Meghan had entrusted to her care. Isabeau was pleased with the changes in her life.

When Isabeau blinked her eyes open the next morning, she saw it would be a fresh, blue day. A thick dew had fallen, so her plaid was silvered and damp. A few stars still glimmered above the mountains, though the valley beyond the Pass was beginning to show dimly as the night faded. She stretched and yawned, then looked instinctively over at her companion to see if he was stirring yet. He was not there. There was not even a hollow in the grass to show where he had been lying. Chagrin filled her. Her unwilling companion must have slipped away during the night.

Sitting upright, she saw that he had taken the pony, and was very annoyed. Since she had been the one that had stolen the pony, the least he could do was ask her if he could take it, Isabeau thought crossly. She scrambled to her feet, then saw with dismay her pack open and its contents rifled. It took only a few minutes to realize he had taken her witch knife and the last of her supplies. Tears rushed to her eyes. She had been proud of her knife, forged in the fire of her Tests. Its loss, and her stupidity in trusting the stranger at all, saw the exultation and confidence she had felt during the lonely night dissipate in the morning light like the dew.

Since Isabeau had not undressed or taken off her boots, and she had no food to make breakfast, getting ready to move on was a simple matter of splashing her face with the icy-cold water of the stream and tightening her belt in the hope that would ease the dull ache in her stomach. The stallion was grazing the sweet meadow grass, but trotted toward her readily enough when she called. She wondered why Bacaiche had not stolen the stallion, but then thought the horse might not have let himself be caught. Crippled as he was, Bacaiche could not easily chase an untethered stallion.

Isabeau leaned her head against the horse's flank for a moment, enjoying his warmth and smell. "Well, we're better off without him. All he did was get us into trouble and eat all our food."

The stallion began to crop the grass again, unconcerned.

"What are ye going to do?" Isabeau asked. "I have to head south if ye would fain come with me."

The chestnut raised his head, and blew gently through his nose. He then rubbed against her again, almost knocking her off her feet. Tears of gratitude stung Isabeau's eyes. She told herself it was because she had a much better chance of escaping any Red Guards if she was on horseback, but in her heart she knew she had been dreading the long and lonely journey through the highlands. Already the stallion was as much a friend and companion as Lilanthe had been.

The quick and easy communication that had developed between Isabeau and the stallion was most unusual, for to speak the language of any beast was to understand and duplicate its subtle gradations of sound and movement and smell, and this was impossible for any human. No matter how Isabeau tried, she had no tail, no hooves, no ability to delicately shift the muscles under her skin like a horse could. Therefore, the accent of Isabeau's speech was necessarily odd and stilted, and occasionally incomprehensible. It usually took time and patience on both sides to establish understanding, which was one of the reasons why few witches ever learned the dialects of creatures such as saber-leopards, who were not known for their patience.

So although Isabeau spoke the language of horses fluently, she had never found it so easy to convey her meaning before. She and Lasair had quickly developed a sort of pidgin language, composed of words, whickers, and body language. This shorthand usually took great familiarity to develop, but was nothing like the communication between a witch and her familiar, which operated on a much more profound level. However, the ease with which they had established a connection made Isabeau wonder whether Lasair would one day become her familiar, a thought which filled her with pleasure.

Riding bareback was not the most comfortable way to travel, and Isabeau was already sore from their hard riding the day before, so she slung her plaid and pack across the stallion's back, and walked beside him down the long, green meadow. "I shall call ye Lasair," she said, stroking his red shoulder. "You're as bright as a flame. Your hair is almost the same color as mine. Maybe a wee darker." The stallion whickered in reply, and bumped her arm with his head.

Behind them were tier upon tier of mountains, the highest edged with snow; before them, the two high cliffs that marked the narrow Pass, the only path between the mountains and the highlands. She was nervous, remembering that Bacaiche had been captured here only a few days earlier. There was no sign of anyone else, though, and it was still very early. If there were Red Guards about, perhaps they would all still be asleep.

The meadow narrowed, the slopes about grew steeper and higher, and the sky shrunk to a narrow slice of pale blue between the cliffs. Isabeau's heart was hammering. There was no point in stopping, however, for she had to leave the protection of the mountains eventually. At last there was no meadow left, only a narrow chasm between the cliffs, the path winding along beside the rocky burn. When it became difficult to walk along beside the stallion, Isabeau mounted with the help of a large boulder, wincing a little as her sore bottom came into contact with his spine.

The path wound its stony way through the chasm, with nothing but the occasional raven to see her. At last she came to the far end of the Pass and stopped to observe the northern heights of Rionnagan, home country of the MacCuinns, Rìghrean of Eileanan. For miles they stretched, bare and gray, before dipping down into the more fertile valley below. There was no sign of life, not even a coney. All Isabeau could see was graygorse bushes and wild grasses, lonely outcroppings of rocks and the wide blue sky.

"Let's go," she said to Lasair, and the stallion obediently began to trot out from the shadow of the cliff, his ears pricking forward. They had only covered a few yards when a challenge was shouted out. Her nerves jumping, Isabeau looked round to see a sentry standing up in the grass, his red cloak whipping in the breeze.

The stallion danced a little and gathered his powerful muscles as if about to run. "Better no'," Isabeau said. "That would be suspicious."

Obediently the stallion halted, and the sentry strode toward them, his hand not far from his claymore, though it was obvious he did not expect any trouble. "Who are ye?" he asked. "Wha' are ye doing here?"

"Wha' I dae every spring," Isabeau replied tartly. "I been hunting for herbs and flowers. My gran says now's the best time t'gather for the sap runs strong in spring." She knew that here in the highlands women who understood herbs and plants were well regarded, being often the only ones who knew the secrets of healing. Every village had its skeelie, some more knowledgeable than others, though they were careful now to avoid any taint of witchcraft.

"Wha' sort o' herbs?" the sentry asked suspiciously.

Isabeau smiled coyly. "Harshweed for the healing o' bruises; and juniper, awful guid for indigestion; and black hellebore for auld Jento, who gets a mite queer in the spring." As she spoke, she showed him some of the plants in her pouch, one of which still had damp earth clinging to its roots, for Isabeau was too well trained to pass the rare hellebore plant without plucking it.

"Wha' does that dae?" the sentry asked.

"Stops the fits and madness," Isabeau said succinctly. "Only a wee bit, though. Too much be worse than the fits."

The sentry now seemed mollified, and though he asked her a lot more questions about where she lived and what she was doing in the wild Sithiche Mountains by herself, Isabeau was able to satisfy him. At last she was allowed to pass through unmolested, except for an overfamiliar squeeze of her knee and an offer to come and visit him if living with her gran got too boring. "For this be a queer uncanny place, and it gets that lonesome ye wouldna believe," the sentry confided. "There were a whole troop o' us here till a few days syne, but there be *uile-bheistean* in the mountains and I be left here all alone."

Isabeau smiled sweetly again, and rode off across the moor, her confidence much restored by the successful hoodwinking of the sentry. *Bacaiche could no' manage that much,* she thought smugly.

By the time the sun was high in the sky, however, her confidence was swamped by her hunger. Several searches through her pack found nothing but a few empty calico pouches and flour dust. Isabeau always had her herbs, though, and so she cooked herself up a thin but nourishing tea while the horse cropped at the short brush. Although it renewed her strength, the tea did not fill her empty belly and Isabeau knew she had to face one of the villages, despite what Meghan had said. "I must eat," she rationalized, and set about finding a village. She had finally worked out riding the horse was much more comfortable if she sat on her plaid, even though it meant her plaid was soon thick with chestnut hairs. A hairy plaid was far better than a bruised bottom, she told herself as she scrambled onto his back.

The moors were a high and lonely place, and so Isabeau set her back to the mountains and her face to the fall of the land. As soon as they stumbled across a little burn, Isabeau began to follow it and just as the sun was beginning to set, it lead her into a gray, dour village. A few women stood about the village pond, buckets at their feet, while thin children ran barefoot about the muddy village square. The houses were huddled together around the pond, threadbare chickens scratching at the dirt. As far as Isabeau knew, she had never been to this village before, since she and Meghan frequented the bigger towns on their excursions into the highlands, for there the villagers were less fierce and the news more plentiful. However, these highland villages were all very similar, with their gray stone walls and high-pitched thatched roofs. This one seemed very poor, for many of the walls were broken and patched with mud, and the women wore sacks over their shoulders instead of plaids. Their bare feet and legs were gray with mud to above the knees, and all had an expression of exhaustion and fatalistic acceptance. One was heavily pregnant, and she hauled the bucket up with a hand in the hollow of her back, dark smudges under her eyes and cheekbones.

As she rode in, Isabeau wondered what story could she tell and what she could trade for food. There were only her herbs, and many of these women would know as much about plant lore as she did herself. Nonetheless, she gave it her best, spreading out some of the buds and leaves on the ground, and slipping easily into the patter. "I also have some mother-wort, which as ye ken is excellent for calming the heart an' settling the babe in the womb—"

"If I wanted mother-wort I'd just gae an' ask the skeelie," the worn-faced mother-to-be said dismissively.

Isabeau's eyes brightened, for she might have something rare in her pouch that the skeelie would need and, in any case, one skeelie would always welcome another.

"Where be your skeelie?" she asked, and was told that she lived in a small cottage a few minutes' walk away from the village. "The skeelie will help ye, lassie," they all repeated. Isabeau thanked the women and set off down the muddy street, thinking how skinny the children were and how broken-down the houses looked. The winter here, on the edge of the highlands, must have been harsh.

The skeelie's cottage was set in a small copse of trees with a stream running through its back garden. It was small but its doorstep was scrubbed white as none in the village had been. Isabeau gingerly lowered herself to the ground, and let Lasair free to graze as he pleased. Before pushing open the gate and proceeding up the path, she cast an experienced eye over the contents of the garden and was impressed by the multitude of herbs and plants growing there. The skeelie could cure most of the village's ailments with what grew in this garden. Isabeau even recognized the pretty blue flowers of flax in one corner, a powerful plant that would have been difficult to grow in this cold climate. She laughed a little—here she had come, thinking she could give the skeelie a plant she did not have and it looked as though she would be begging her for something instead.

The door was opened before she had a chance to knock, so Isabeau was left with one hand foolishly raised in the air. "C'min, c'min," the old woman said breathlessly. "Wha' can I be doing for ye? Are ye having trouble with your menses, lassie? I have some tea made with ploughman's spikenard which'll clear that up right away."

"Why no' pennyroyal?" Isabeau asked. "I notice ye

have a good crop right by your door, while surely ye would have to travel to find ploughman's spikenard?"

"True, true," the old woman said, shooting Isabeau a shrewd glance from sparkling black eyes. "But I have no' made the pennyroyal tea, while I have plenty o' ploughman's spikenard left from a batch o' tea I made a few years ago. But I dinna think ye've come to see me to discuss pennyroyal and ploughman's spikenard. Ye hungry? It looks like it's been a few days syne ye've had a guid meal. I've some stew on the stove." Relief made Isabeau's knees weak, and she staggered forward with no hesitation.

"Will your horse no' stray, left loose like that?" the skeelie asked.

Isabeau shook her head. "Och, no, he's very well trained," she responded, and sat down in one of the cushion-laden chairs before the fire, holding her chilly hands out to the comforting blaze.

The skeelie moved briskly about the tiny kitchen, swinging the kettle over the fire, getting out cups and bowls, polishing spoons with a tiny cloth. As she worked she chattered away in her breathless voice, about the unseasonable cold, the hard winter, the difficulty in finding rare roots and flowers.

Isabeau let her body relax, suddenly realizing how very tired and hungry she was. When the skeelie passed her a cup of tea, she took it and sipped, frowning a little at the unfamiliar taste. The warmth of the fire and the comfort of the chair together made her bones as soft as butter. Then the skeelie passed her a bowl filled with fragrant stew, carrots and potatoes bobbing about in a rich, dark sauce. Isabeau ate ravenously.

"So what's a bonny young lassie like yersel' doing wandering the moors?" the skeelie asked, the firelight playing over her wrinkled face.

"Going south," Isabeau mumbled through the stew.

"Going south? So many young people seem to want to go south, though really there's nothing there, just a dirty city and the blaygird sea and pirates. Looking for work, I s'pose, in the city?" Isabeau nodded. "Just ye and your horse, heading south." Isabeau nodded again, cleaning out her bowl with a piece of unleavened bread and trying not to look hopefully at the pot still steaming at the side of the fire. "And have ye no family to worry about their bonny daughter all alone on the moors?" the skeelie asked, taking Isabeau's empty bowl and filling it again.

Now was the time for Isabeau to bring out the story about her elderly grandmother who lived on the moors, and sent her out in search of healing herbs. She opened her mouth to say it, and was surprised to hear herself say, "No, I never knew my real family."

"They died when ye were young?"

"No, at least, I do no' ken. I was found." Isabeau was surprised that she had spoken so freely. She glanced up at the skeelie, and saw her old face was calm, the black eyes vague and more interested in locating the rare pieces of carrot in her bowl than in watching Isabeau. Her uneasiness died.

"Ye were found! That be an interesting story. Most rare. I do no' think I ever met anyone who was found before. Who found ye?"

"My guardian. I call her my grandmother, but she's no' really."

"An' where does your guardian live? Wha' is her name?"

"M . . . M . . . M . . ." Isabeau tried to answer but found her tongue tangled in knots. She tried again. "She bides . . ." Again she found she could not speak, and her hand, which had risen from her lap to gesture toward the mountains, froze in the air. Isabeau tried again, but somehow her mouth could not enunciate the word "Dragonclaw." After a moment, her hand dropped, and she kept on eating, shaking her head a little as if to dispel the buzz of an insect in her ear.

"Ye live on the moors?"

Isabeau opened her mouth to say "Aye," but heard herself say, "No, in the mountains," and now felt real panic that she was answering so freely.

"In the mountains!" the skeelie exclaimed. "Ye mun have had a hard winter—we were snowed in and many died. Mainly the auld, o' course, and the very young. There was no' much I could do, with my garden frozen solid and the snow piling up around the windows. It mun be much worse in the mountains."

"We never really feel the cold," Isabeau said, remembering how snow only ever lay in patches on the slopes of her valley home. Even at the height of winter, the valley remained only thinly veiled with snow. For the first time, she realized how strange this was, and remembered how she had had to fight her way through snow on the other side of Dragonclaw when she had left.

"Ye mun live in a sheltered spot," the skeelie said, and took Isabeau's empty bowl away.

"Aye," Isabeau agreed.

"Yet I hear the mountains be harsh. It mun be a hard life for a young lassie."

"I do no' ken really . . ." Isabeau said slowly, wondering. Her life had never seemed hard; all she ever did was spin and sew, search for herbs, and listen to Meghan's teachings. Remembering the thin children and the tired women in the village, she thought her life was probably much easier than theirs. She had never gone hungry or lacked warm clothes or boots.

"Your guardian mun be a very wise woman, to live in the mountains with the cold and the storms, and no' suffer."

"Aye, she be the wisest woman. She ken everything about plants and beasts and the weather," Isabeau babbled. "She can tell if snow is coming by the smell o' the wind, and she—" Suddenly she found she could not speak again. Her thoughts seemed to unravel so she could not remember what she was about to say. "She's a very wise woman," she finished lamely.

"Wha' was her name again?" the skeelie asked, but again Isabeau was unable to answer, Meghan's name choking in her throat. She sat back in her chair, and found she could not even lift her finger to rub at her aching forehead. The shadows in the cottage were heavy now, rising over the two chairs by the fire so they looked alive. She was beginning to feel frightened, although even that emotion was very remote. Her tongue felt very thick and furry, and there was an unpleasant taste in her mouth.

The skeelie leaned forward. "I want ye to tell me about your childhood," she commanded, her voice strong and clear.

To her dismay, Isabeau did. All sorts of details poured out—what Meghan made her for her ninth birthday, how she had to spin wool for hours in the winter, how bored she got with Meghan's endless lessons. Again and again, however, the strange confusion came over her so she could not remember what she was trying to say. The shadows got thicker and more solid, the room beyond the circle of firelight vaguer and more insubstantial, and the skeelie more impatient, urging her for more information so at last Isabeau began to try to resist, and found to her horror she could not.

She told the strange old woman many things she would never tell anyone, but not one word about magic or witchcraft did she utter, nor could she say Meghan's name. Somehow she managed to resist revealing the more dangerous secrets of her and Meghan's life, and as she resisted, the skeelie became more direct in her questioning. Soon it became clear to Isabeau that the old woman herself must know something of witchcraft. This compulsion to talk must be the result of some spell that Isabeau had not even noticed being cast. Once Isabeau knew this, she let herself babble, talking about the everyday mundanities of their life, until at last the skeelie leaned forward in her chair, and fixed her piercing black eye on Isabeau's face. She said something in a strange tongue and Isabeau felt herself being drawn forward, her mouth working as she tried to speak but her tongue refusing to respond, as thick as a plank of wood. For almost a minute, words raced back and forth in her mind, damning words that could have had her and her guardian dragged before the Awl and condemned to a horrible death. But not one word did she utter. At last the skeelie sat back.

"I see," she said. "A very powerful ward."

For quite a long time she stared into the fire, her gnarled fingers twisting in her lap, then she sat back and said in her breathless voice, "Dearie me, wha' kind o' hostess have I been, bothering ye with questions when anyone can see ye're dropping off to sleep where ye sit. Ye mun forgive me, such a lonely life sometimes, biding here on the moors, it's no' often I have such a bonny, bright lassie to while away the time with. Come, come, let's tuck ye up in a bed for the night, and tomorrow it'll all look different."

Isabeau could only obey. She was so tired her bones refused to move in unison and she stumbled as she followed the skeelie to a bed made up in one corner of the room, in what looked like a cupboard set into the wall. The bed was hard but warm, and she could see the shadows of the flames dancing over the rough ceiling. She crawled in, and almost immediately was asleep.

When she woke the next morning to the sound of rain hammering on the roof, she had only the vaguest recollection of the previous evening. She remembered the delicious stew, she remembered talking about her childhood like she never had before, and she remembered the feeling of being asleep while she was awake. It was hard to distinguish her dreams from what had really happened. A vague sense of uneasiness remained, though, and so her immediate thought was to barter for some food and maybe a knife, and then be on her way. The skeelie had other plans however.

"Bide a wee, lassie, and I shall get ye some porridge an' cream for your brekker. I be baking some bread this morning; shall I pop in an extra loaf for ye?" Then she needed Isabeau's help in distilling some pure essences, and Isabeau found it hard to refuse. The skeelie was right, she should wait for the weather to warm, for the storm to pass, for the skeelie to have time to bake her some nut cookies. It was so comfortable in the little cottage, and she had never eaten such delicious food. The skeelie was a delightful woman, she showed such interest in Isabeau and all her thoughts and feelings. True, Isabeau sometimes felt uneasy or uncomfortable at her questions, but these feelings soon passed, and the skeelie could teach her things about plants even Meghan could not know.

The old woman made a delicious lunch that Isabeau could not bear to refuse, and before she knew it, night was falling and she could not leave. Again, each postponement of her leaving had seemed so natural and so difficult to refuse, that Isabeau felt only a vague uneasiness or impatience. That night, as she slept in the little box-bed, she dreamt only of summer on the moors.

Isabeau hummed as she sat on her heels in the garden. The air was very sweet and warm, bees buzzed around her, and the garden was thick with butterflies. After six days of storm and rain, the sight of clear blue skies and the feel of the sun warm on her face was a tonic for her spirits, which had been strangely depressed of late.

Manissia had sent her out into the garden with a basket and some scissors to cut flowers and herbs. Today they were going to start making the many teas and infusions that the skeelie used to heal the villagers nearby, and which she sold at the market. Isabeau had always been fascinated by the distilling of aromatic leaves, woods, and roots, and she was looking forward to seeing how Manissia's methods differed from Meghan's.

For a moment a strange unease stole over her, and then she shrugged the thought aside and concentrated on the rich smell of the earth, the spicy scent of rosemary and thyme, the sensuous pleasure of the sun on the back of her neck. Manissia was going to let her look at some of her strange books this afternoon, books with pages yellowing with age and filled with diagrams of the stars and planets, the two moons, and the sun. Meghan had never been interested in the sky, only in the earth, its animals, its plants . . . Again a frisson of anxiety crossed her, and for a moment she frowned and shivered, despite the sun, crossing her arms over her chest and rubbing at the goosebumps which had sprung up on her skin. Almost immediately the unease was gone, and she continued thinking happily about the skeelie's books.

Isabeau's basket was full, and her back beginning to ache when a sudden neigh made her stand and look around. The cottage was built in the shelter of a small copse of trees, with a stream that ran through the garden. Behind the house, a steep hill ran up to the great waves of purplish moors that undulated as far as the eye could see. A red horse was galloping along the crest of the hill, mane flashing bright in the sun. As she watched, the horse neighed again and tossed its head, rearing and striking the ground with its hooves. The horse was calling to her. Even at that distance she could recognize the sound.

"Isabeau!" the horse called. "Isabeau!"

Isabeau stood still in confusion. The horse neighed again and suddenly she recognized the sound. Lasair! How could she have forgotten Lasair? As she watched, the horse turned and ran back again, pawing the ground and neighing. There was a shrill sound to the neigh, almost panic. Isabeau dropped the basket and ran round the side of the house. At the bottom of the long garden was a hedge set with a gate.

She called Lasair to her, but though the horse neighed and tossed his head and ran back and forth frantically, he did not come any closer. Isabeau immediately went to open the gate to go out to him, but as soon as her hand touched the wooden clasp, all desire to go out suddenly left her, and she stood dreamily, brushing a tuft of grass gently with the sole of her boot.

Lasair had to neigh again, and then again, before Isabeau remembered, and then dismay and chagrin swept over her. How had she forgotten Lasair? And Meghan, her beloved guardian, and her journey to the south? All she could remember was the fire flickering on the creamy walls, the sound of rain washing against the windows, the skeelie's breathless voice as she served up another delicious platter of food . . . and her own voice. She could remember talking a lot. What had she told the old woman? Cold fear swept over. She must have been enchanted. But how? She had not felt any of the chill that came when power was drawn from the air and the earth, a usual sign of witchcraft. She had felt nothing, only an increasing comfort. If Lasair had not jerked her out of her dreamy state, she would have gone back in, eager for another afternoon with the wise old woman, not even thinking about the days slipping away.

Lasair was neighing again now, the sound shrill. Isabeau whickered reassuringly, and tried to think. After a moment she picked up a stick and knocked the clasp aside with it. Without letting the woven twigs touch her, she slipped through the roughly made gate and ran up the slope toward the horse. However, it was an effort—white butterflies danced in the sunshine before her and it was hard not to get distracted by their pretty flutterings, or by the beauty of the view. She forced herself to keep climbing, while the chestnut stallion ran back and forth along the crest of the hill.

Once Isabeau reached the top, she felt a dullness and sleepiness slip from her that she had not known was there. She took great gulps of clean, graygorse-scented air, while Lasair pushed his head against her roughly.

"She must be a witch," Isabeau said. "I never thought."

Lasair neighed and tossed his bright mane. Isabeau ran her hand through it, chastising herself. What was she to do? All her belongings—her pack, her precious rings, even the talisman that Meghan had given her, were still in the cottage. "I must go back," she said.

Lasair pawed the ground, shaking his head and neighing, but Isabeau knew she had no choice. How could she have left the talisman alone with a witch? Meghan had trusted her, and a month into her journey, she had lost her supplies, and her knife, and fallen under the spell of a simple skeelie!

She turned and hurried back down the hill, thinking, *I have to be strong. I have to keep a clear head. I have to be strong and brave and clear-headed the way Meghan would want me to be.*

When she pushed open the door into the cottage, the old woman turned from the fire, smiling. "Just in time for potato an' tarragon soup, my dear. Put the basket on the table."

Isabeau had forgotten the basket. She almost turned to go and get it, then she remembered. "Ye are a witch," she said.

"As are ye," the skeelie responded, ladling thick soup into an earthenware bowl.

Isabeau was disconcerted for a moment. "Ye put a spell on me. Ye made me forget what I was doing, where I was going."

"Did I, dearie? Well, twas very wet, miserable weather. Ye wouldna have wanted to be out there in that storm." The skeelie put the bowls on the table. "Eat up, lassie, ye're skin and bones still."

"No, I have to go."

"Well, if ye want, lass, though does it no' make sense to eat afore ye gae?"

It did of course, and Isabeau found herself looking rather longingly at the bowls, which were wreathed with tendrils of steam and smelling delicious. In anger she swept her arm across the table, crashing the two bowls to the floor so soup poured onto the thick rug.

"Now, dear, that's no' very nice. Wha' a way to repay my hospitality for the week! I'm ashamed o' ye."

"I'm sorry," Isabeau mumbled, feeling thoroughly ashamed. "I'll clean it up." She began to pick up the shards of pottery, burning her hand on the hot soup as she did so. The skeelie picked up a bowl and filled it with water from the barrel in the corner, passing it to her with a cloth. Isabeau was on her hands and knees scrubbing the rug before she realized. At once she threw down the cloth. "Ye've done it again! I said I was leaving."

"Well, o' course, dearie, ye can gae whenever ye want, though I do think ye should finish cleaning up that mess afore ye do." The reprimand in the skeelie's voice made Isabeau's cheeks burn, and she quickly bent over her task again. *I'll just do this, and then I'll go,* she told herself.

The skeelie had poured them some more soup, however, chatting away in her faded old voice. After Isabeau had cleared away the broken bowls, she felt she could not again refuse the old woman. *I will no' forget again,* she vowed, spooning down the soup as fast as she could.

"Gently, Isabeau, gently," the skeelie said. "Ye'll give yersel' wind bolting your food like tha'. Whatever did yer guardian teach ye?"

Immediately Isabeau was filled with panic. She had obviously told the skeelie about Meghan. How else could she know she had a guardian, not an old grandmother as the story was meant to go? She tried desperately to remember the last week but most of it was a blur.

Before she could say another word, Manissia suddenly raised her head. "The gate ward has been breached," she said. "Isabeau, it be no one I ken. Quickly, into the wall-bed!"

Isabeau immediately balked, gathering herself to say something that would express her contempt for the old hag; but the skeelie turned and said softly, "Isabeau, in the wall-bed."

Before Isabeau realized she was moving, she was in the bed, and the skeelie had slammed the doors so she was locked inside. Isabeau opened her mouth to cry out but found she could say nothing—her throat muscles were suddenly rigid. Then she lost all desire to protest, for through the crack in the door she could see two Red Guards standing in the doorway. They were cavalrymen, their helmets tucked under their arms, their red cloaks swaying.

"Dearie me, how I can help ye?" the skeelie was saying, in her breathless voice. "Are ye lost? The village is no' hard to find . . ."

"We have heard reports o' sorcery from hereabouts," one guard said gruffly.

"Sorcery? In this puir wee village? Och, no, I think ye two fine young men mun have been misled, there's naught here but sheep and bairns. C'min, c'min, can I get ye some tea? Where can ye have heard such a tale? Wha' would a sorcerer be doing here? Why, there be no money to be had in these here parts, and I'll have ye ken the people o' Quotil are guid, honest folks, no' the sort that'd rub shoulders with any wickedness like sorcery—"

"We heard a lass was seen round abouts here with a horse," the other soldier managed to interpolate.

"A lassie? Why, aye, a lass did drop by for some pennyroyal tea. Did she have a horse?" The Red Guards shouldered their way into the cottage, looking about pugnaciously. The skeelie bustled about, pouring tea and finding nut cookies, talking incessantly. "Aye, it be hard for a puir auld woman, up here in these lonely parts. Please ye, have a cookie. I'm too auld to be worth much anymore; the villagers are kind to puir auld Manissia, and buy my pennyroyal tea . . ."

"She be just a puir auld woman," one of the guards said.

"And what would a witch be doing up in these here lonely parts?" the other said.

They turned to go, grabbing a handful of cookies each on the way, but before the skeelie could do more than take a few steps toward the wall-bed, they were back, looking sheepish, a woman scornful at their backs. Peering through the crack, Isabeau saw a crimson skirt, and felt fear again.

"Ye feeble-minded fools," the witch-sniffer said contemptuously. "As easy to trick as a babe just beginning to waddle . . ."

The skeelie Manissia began her soft flow of words again, but the witch-sniffer ignored her, glaring around the small room.

"I smell enchantments," Lady Glynelda said. "The air is thick with enchantments, like smoke."

"That would be my whortleberry pie ye be smelling," the skeelie said. "Smell is thick, is it no'? Some find the whortleberry a trifle sweet but personally I think—"

"Shut up, auld woman," the seeker said nastily, and breathed deeply through her nose, frowning a little. "There's witchery here, no doubt, and we'll find it too." She began to instruct the guards to search the little cottage, and Isabeau could hear the sound of crashing and banging as they opened cupboards and emptied tins and canisters on the floor. Manissia kept up a flow of small talk, exclamations and pleas for gentleness, and offers of food and tea which seemed to irritate the witch-sniffer greatly. Pressing her eye to the crack, Isabeau could see little but her crimson skirt, as the witch-hunter stood waiting by the door, sipping the tea Manissia had pressed into her hand.

Suddenly there was a loud commotion and a thin wail from Manissia. "My valerian roots! Quick, they be burning! They be burning! That be all my stock. Wha' will I do when the villagers come asking?"

Plumes of sweet-scented smoke were pouring out of the fireplace, and Isabeau buried her face in her hands as it penetrated even through the closed door of the cupboard. She heard the witch-sniffer giving quick orders and the sound of boots clumping and metal rattling, then the commotion gradually faded away into silence. Suddenly the door was pulled open and Isabeau looked up with a start. She felt strangely dazed, and blinked for a moment in the bright light without making any move to escape. Only Manissia stood there, however, and, scrambling out of the cupboard, Isabeau saw to her amazement that the two Red Guards were both slumped in the chairs by the fire, snoring heavily and looking very comfortable. The seeker Glynelda was lying on the small settee by the front door, her arms crossed neatly over her breast, her red skirt decorously arranged.

"What happened?" Isabeau said stupidly, and ground the heels of her hands into her eyes, which felt gritty and tired.

"I gave them relaxing tea," Manissia said, quickly gathering together a loaf of barley bread and some cheese in a white cloth, and stuffing them in Isabeau's knapsack. "Then, silly clumsy auld me, I knocked my bundle o' valerian roots onto the fire, and dear me, it be the rare person who can stay awake after choking on a mouthful o' valerian root smoke."

"How come ye're still awake?" Isabeau asked, trying not to yawn.

"Och, I threw my apron o'er my head, o' course," Manissia said. "Now ye mun go, and fast, Isabeau. I do no' ken why the Red Guards are on your track, but I do ken I wouldna want any lassie o' mine to fall into that bitch's hands." She prodded the witch-sniffer's leg with one slippered foot. "As hard a face as I seen on anyone."

"What about ye?"

"Och, they canna hurt a skeelie," Manissia said cheerfully. "Now they've got a tummy full o' my tea, they be like spring lambs to the slaughter. They'll be down in the Quotil inn tonight, chatting to the locals about the simple auld lady that bides up in the copse. Poor auld thing, they'll say, a penny short o' a pound, but harmless."

"How do ye do it?" Isabeau asked, pulling her pack over her shoulder.

"Why, it's the Will and the Word," the skeelie answered, looking up at Isabeau with sparkling eyes. "Have ye been taught nothing?"

"Do ye mean . . . compulsion? I thought compulsion was no' allowed?"

"Och, so it be one o' the Tower witches yer're apprenticed to," Manissia said. "Very interesting. I thought they were all dead." Isabeau shut her mouth tight, wondering if she'd been indiscreet yet again. Manissia chortled. "Even the Tower witches are no' above imposing their will on others when it suits them, my dear. Besides, the Towers are gone now, and times are troubled. A puir auld skeelie has to use every trick she can to stay happy and healthy in these times. Now go!"

Already the witch-sniffer was stirring, although the Red Guards lay like the dead. "The trick now," Manissia mused as Isabeau slipped out the back door, "is to keep them from realizing they been asleep at all. Good wishes to ye, lassie, and come visit me again sometime . . ."

Lasair was cantering anxiously back and forth on the high green hill behind the cottage. Isabeau raced toward him, afraid they might be seen from one of the windows. She vaulted easily onto the stallion's back and they galloped away from the village of Quotil as if evil spirits were pursuing them. Lasair was very disturbed by the sight of his old mistress, afraid he would be caught again and subjected to the humiliation of bridle and saddle, spur and whip. So he ran like the wind, needing no urging from Isabeau, who was very glad to have the breeze of the moors again blowing in her face.

All day they rode, heading due south and staying away from the occasional village nestled into the side of a steep hill.

By sunset, they came over a high hill to see the wide loop of the Rhyllster shining between dark trees. Starting as a small spring deep in the Sithiche Mountains, the Rhyllster wound its way through the green valleys of Rionnagan to the sea, strung with lochan like diamonds. It was the lifeblood of the country, allowing produce from the farms to be ferried down to the towns and cities of the lower country, and metals, tools and city-made goods to be distributed in the highlands.

Below the hill where Isabeau stood, the river swelled out into a loch where pale mist drifted, concealing the dark waters. On the shore a large town spread out, just beginning to prick with lights as the dusk fell. Isabeau sighed with relief at the sight. It had taken her a month to make the journey out of the Sithiche Mountains to Caeryla, much longer than she had expected, thanks to the ensorcelment of Skeelie Manissia. Though Isabeau would not admit it even to herself, the talisman she carried in her pack was weighing her down with responsibility, and she would be glad of the chance of shifting some of that weight to older and wiser shoulders. For the last day it had been burning and tingling against her, and the closer she came to the loch, the more it hurt her. Now it was so hot to the touch that she had had to wrap it in layers of cloth before she could carry it. Even then it seemed to throb against her hip, and she looked forward to handing it over to Meghan's friend. She wondered whether she would still be waiting for her at Tulachna Celeste, more than a moon after Meghan had sent the message. She would have to worry about that when she got there, though, for first she had to make her way past Caeryla.

The sight of the town, piled inside its stone walls like children's wooden blocks tumbled in play, made Isabeau think of the last time she had been here, eight years earlier. She remembered it as a bright, cheerful town, hung with lanterns and streamers, its streets thronged with people, its loch perpetually drifting with mist. Clapping her heels to Lasair's side, she trotted down the slope of the hill toward the water, thinking of soft beds, hot stew and company.

It was a sharp disappointment, then, to ride up to the gates and find the streets beyond dirty and deserted. She hesitated a little before entering, having expected to lose herself in crowds. However, the lure of food and a bed was too much and she let Lasair trot under the overhang of the gate. At once a guard stepped out of the shadows, holding up a hand for her to stop. Isabeau's pulse quickened as she pulled the stallion up.

"Name?"

"Mari Collene, sirrah," Isabeau answered.

"Business?"

"Herb lore, sirrah. My granddam is a skeelie, and she sent me down to buy rare powders for the healing."

"Is that so, lassie? And wha' village be ye from?"

"Byllars," Isabeau answered, as Meghan always had.

"Byllars, hey? Ye've traveled a long way." The sentry stepped forward and peered at Isabeau's face. She smiled at him, and he smiled back, showing a mouth missing most of its teeth. "Well, ah, I s'pose it be fine . . ."

Just as she was about to spur the stallion forward, he reached up a hand and caught her bridle. "Just a moment, lassie, where'd ye get the horse? Wha' is the granddaughter o' a simple skeelie doing with a horse like this?"

"The stallion belongs to my da," she improvised quickly. "He did the local laird a great service and when asked wha' boon he would like, he asked for a colt bred from the laird's own stable."

For a moment she thought the story would hold, then the sentry suddenly stepped forward. "Let me see your hair." Before she could think of something to say, he had dragged her plaid away from her head, and her red plait fell down from under her tam-o'-shanter.

"Och, so I thought," the sentry said. "A redhead, just as she said."

Isabeau tried to yank the reins out of his fingers, kicking Lasair in the ribs, but the sentry raised one hamsized fist and hit her on the side of the head. Isabeau fell downward into a roaring darkness.

When she woke, it was dark and she was lying on a pile

of straw that stank of urine and mold. Panic rising in her throat, she tried to twist upright, but her hands were bound tightly behind her back so she could hardly move. She took several deep breaths and tried to locate where she was. It was cold and dank, and there was a stone wall behind her, slick with moisture. After a moment her eyes adjusted to the darkness and she could see, far overhead, a square where a few stars glimmered between straight lines that could only be bars. So, she was in some sort of prison. Isabeau ground her teeth. To be caught so quickly! She should have realized an alert would be out for the witch-sniffer's horse! The penalty for horse stealing was death by hanging, she remembered, and felt terror foul-tasting in her mouth.

After a few moments of writhing in anger and fear against her ropes, she fell back against the straw with a muffled groan. Dressed only in her breeches and a thin shirt, the cold of the stone floor struck up through the stinking straw. She strained against the ropes again and tried to unravel the knots by thought alone. However, without being able to see the knots it was impossible to undo them, and at last Isabeau wept in pure frustration. Once her tears were spent, however, she was able to think more clearly and she considered her situation carefully. Concerned as she was about the perilousness of her situation, it was the loss of the magic talisman and the betrayal of Meghan's trust that worried her the most. If she could only manage to escape and retrieve the talisman! All night Isabeau tested her strength against the ropes and turned over several plans, each more improbable than the last, and at last slipped off into an uneasy doze.

A few hours before dawn, she woke abruptly and lay rigid in the straw, straining to hear again the small noise that had disturbed her. At first there was only silence and then Isabeau heard again the scuffle and patter of paws that meant her cell had been invaded by rats. Most other girls would have screamed, but Isabeau felt relief fill her. Tentatively she opened her mind and sent out a simple thought-image of greeting.

There was an answering scuffle and she felt something warm against her legs. Isabeau shuddered despite herself but kept the slow trickle of mind-pictures that she hoped would be understood. The rodents did not have the sort of language that was easy for humans to speak, primarily because they relied on instinct, body language and smell, and try as much as she liked, Isabeau was simply unable to communicate the niceties of her meaning by the angle of her whiskers or a twitch of her tail.

Chew rope! she imagined over and over again, but it took a long time before they even listened, for the rats were consumed by a ravenous hunger that left little room for any thought. At last, though, a rat began to nibble at the ropes, drawn by the smell of blood from her chafed wrists. Soon Isabeau was able to wrench her wrists apart with a small cry of pain, and then undoing her ankles was easy.

The small seed of hope which had flared up soon died though, for Isabeau could find no way out of her cell. After the circulation had returned to her numb limbs, she struggled to her feet and began to explore the room. She seemed to scrabble around in the darkness for hours, without any benefit but the warming of her limbs, and the discovery that her cell was exactly eight steps long and four steps wide. There was a barred door in one corner, and the window set about fifteen feet off the floor, and that was it.

Isabeau had never before encountered a door bound by iron, and she found the metal was unresponsive to her magic. If it had simply been barred, like all the doors Isabeau had seen before, she would probably have escaped straightaway. However, the door was locked and the key removed, and Isabeau had no idea how a lock even worked. She probed it with her mind for a long time, but was unable to shift it. At last, exhausted, she slumped back into the straw and fell asleep once more.

When she woke the third time, the tiny square high in the wall was beginning to lighten, and footsteps were coming down the corridor outside. Isabeau quickly wound the rope back round her wrists to give the illusion that she was still tied up. However, the deception was unnecessary for no one came in. A tiny grate in the bottom of the door was opened and a wooden platter containing moldy bread and a jug of water was shoved through. Examining the unappetizing meal and remembering her daydreams of hot stew made Isabeau wince, but she had not had a good meal since she had left the skeelie's cottage and she was starving. Consequently she fell onto the moldy loaf like a ravenous wolf, throwing a few crumbs toward the rats who were glaring at her from the straw. After her hunger and thirst were appeased, she re-examined the door in the light of day. It was a massive door of oak, bound with iron, and fitted snugly into the doorframe. Isabeau was able to move the bolts back by stint of much concentration, but she still could not open the lock. She had just switched her attention to the rusty hinges when she heard footsteps marching down the corridor again. By the time her door was being opened she was back in the straw pretending to be asleep.

"Who forgot to shoot the bolts!" she heard someone say. "Lady Glynelda would have our heads if she knew!"

Mention of the witch-sniffer did little to reassure Isabeau, who made much of yawning and pretending to wake. Once her eyes were open she saw standing just inside the door two guards in the red jackets and green kilts of the common soldier. Beside them was one of the biggest men Isabeau had ever seen, almost seven foot tall and as thick as a tree. He wore a scarred leather jerkin and had a black hood over his head that caused a small whimper to escape her.

"I see ye be having your usual effect on lassies, Blyn," one of the Red Guards laughed. "Sometime I mun ask ye to teach me how ye do it."

The hooded giant gave a growl and the Red Guard stepped back involuntarily. Blyn then shouldered his way into the cell, which suddenly appeared half the size. Isabeau tried not to cower back on the bed of straw, but it was more than she could manage. She had never been so frightened before in her life. He stood over her and said gruffly, "Get up."

Although her knees were quivering, Isabeau managed to rise, keeping her hands behind her back so they would not notice the loose ropes.

The Red Guards stepped forward too. "Ye are under arrest on suspicion o' stealing a stallion which belongs to the Lady Glynelda, Grand-Seeker o' the Awl and Regent o' Caeryla. Ye are also charged with the most foul and heinous crime o' sorcery, and for using your sorceries to steal this horse. The penalty for such crimes is death by drowning."

Isabeau opened her mouth to protest, but the other Red

Guard stepped forward and slapped her so hard across the face that she fell back against the wall. "Ye will be put to trial this afternoon before my Lord Serinyza and his judges," he said, "and if the charges o' witchcraft be proven ye will be put to the Question thereafter. When the Grand-Questioner is finished with ye, ye will be executed by water."

Isabeau sobbed quietly, pressing her burning cheek into her shoulder. She had never been hit before, Meghan preferring to discipline her in other ways. The shock of the blow and the guard's confidence that she would be executed combined to fill her with something approaching despair. Then she realized the guards were still standing over her, leering quite openly at the glimpse of flesh below her torn shirt.

"I never stuck a witch afore, should be quite an experience," the soldier said, lifting his kilt.

Almost before Isabeau understood his words, the hooded guard had stepped between them with a grunt and a jerk of his thumb toward the door. Both soldiers protested his interference vociferously but he snarled, causing both to back away nervously.

"Havers, Blyn, ye should have said ye'd marked her out for yersel'," one said.

Their words caused terror to rear again in Isabeau's throat, and she measured the giant's size, wondering if she could take him by surprise and escape. To her relief, he went out after the guards and relocked the door. Hearing how the key turned in the lock gave Isabeau some idea of how it worked, and desperation lent her courage. As soon as the sound of the guards' footsteps had died away, she again began to probe the lock with her mind.

After delicate tinkering, she began to understand the mechanics of the lock, hearing little clacks as the levers within moved up and down. Sweat sprung up on her brow, for she was manipulating air in a way that she never had before. One by one she shifted the levers into place, and heard a loud click as the lock sprung open. She sat back on her heels, her head swimming, then turned her attention to the wooden bar across the outside of the door. It took much longer to throw back this time, and when at last it was unbarred, Isabeau was sick and dizzy with the exertion. She waited until her breath was calm again before daring to ease the cell door open.

Her cell was one in a row of ten, facing onto a dark corridor that ended in an iron-bound door at either end. Isabeau tiptoed to the left first, since that was the way the guards had gone. Putting her ear against the crack she listened intently but heard nothing. Silently she slipped back to the other end of the corridor and listened again. This time she heard a thin scream that was cut short at the end, and her blood ran cold. Without hesitation she retraced her steps and began to work on the other door. The lock finally clicked open and Isabeau, barely able to breathe for fear, slowly turned the handle and eased it open a crack. She could see or hear nothing and so at last opened the door wide enough for her slim body to slip through.

On the other side was a guard-room, with shields and axes hung on the wall, a fire burning merrily on the hearth, and a table with the chairs akimbo. On the table was a clutter of tankards, a sign that the guards could not be too far away. Isabeau began to creep forward, closing the door behind her. She was almost halfway across the room when she heard approaching voices and gruff laughter, and in blind terror she dashed across the room and dived behind the woodpile. There was just enough room for her to conceal herself behind the pile of logs before the giant Blyn returned with two other guards. All three were dressed in black leather trousers, a leather hood and studded leather straps that criss-crossed their bare torsos. Isabeau did not think she had ever seen a more sinister sight.

The three guards poured themselves some more ale and sat down at the table, one pulling out a pair of dice and throwing them on the table, calling out, "Flowers!"

And there they sat for another three hours, while Isabeau almost went mad with impatience. Only once did all three men leave the room together, and Isabeau was just beginning to scramble out when the giant returned with a tray of cold meat and bread. She was able to conceal herself again in time, though the close call had her heart thudding so loudly that it was a wonder the guard did not hear it.

The conversation between the guards was mainly devoted to beer and horses, though the occasional coarse joke was uttered and smirked over. They talked a lot about Lasair who, it seemed, was of the Angharar bloodline and so extremely valuable. Isabeau knocked her forehead against the ground in anger at herself for being so stupid as to steal a blood stallion and then ride it gaily into the biggest town in the northern highlands. She had been lazy, she decided, and arrogant too. She should have let Lasair go as soon as she could, and made the journey on her own inconspicuous feet as Meghan had intended.

"The Lady-Seeker is mad as hell that her stallion was stolen, and she sleepin' right next to it," one guard said, a beefy man with thick black brows over tiny black eyes. "Ye ken the Banrìgh gave her that horse? She wouldna want to lose it, that be for sure."

"That be some cheek," the other said in obvious awe. "I do think that lass mun be a witch, to be stealing the seeker's own horse."

"Obh, obh," Blyn said. "That's no' witchcraft. I heard o' horse thieves that could steal the Rìgh's own beast while he be sitting on it."

The other guards scoffed noisily, and for a while the conversation centered round the great horse thefts of all time. Isabeau almost dozed off, the stones of the fireplace hot at her back and the room filling with smoke and the smell of ale. Talk soon veered to town politics, however, and she roused herself in order to listen, for one never knew when local knowledge would come in handy. Certainly if she had known that the seeker Glynelda was so well placed in Caeryla she would never have come near the place!

How a seeker of the Awl could become regent over Caeryla was another problem vexing Isabeau's mind. The Awl had been set up after the Day of Betrayal to hunt down and prosecute witches and *uile-bheistean,* but it should have nothing to do with the lairds of Eileanan, who ruled their lands with almost as much right and power as the Rìgh himself.

Although the MacHamell family, lairds of Caeryla, were not one of the ten great clans descended from the First Coven, they were still very powerful with close connections to the Rìghrean. The sadly missed Lavinya, the mother of the current Rìgh, had been a Caerylian. Her sister's son had inherited the castle from his mother, and the last time Meghan and Isabeau had traveled to Caeryla, he had jumped the fire with the daughter of another great laird, causing much celebration in the town. What had happened to that young laird that there be need for a regent in his land?

By listening carefully, she was able to discover that the laird was dead and his young son had inherited the castle. The guards seemed rather sorry for Lord Serinyza, who apparently was kept very close, and allowed little freedom. How Glynelda had managed to be appointed regent remained a mystery, but she was obviously feared and even hated, given the way the guards' voices lowered when they spoke of her. Isabeau noticed that Blyn said nothing, although he encouraged the others to be indiscreet, pouring them more ale when their throats grew dry and occasionally muttering an encouraging rumble. The presence of the Red Guards at the castle was an obvious sore point, the two loquacious guards calling them Redcloaks in a contemptuous manner, and mocking their fighting ability. "Pretty nancy boys in their pretty cloaks," one of the guards muttered.

It was well after noon before Isabeau was finally able to crawl out from behind the logpile and continue with her escape. The dice game had finally come to an end, and one of the guards was stretched out on a bench in front of the fire for a snooze. The other two stretched and yawned and finished their tankards, before shrugging their weapons on again and going out the door. Luckily none thought to check the prisoners and so Isabeau's escape was still undetected. By now her confidence was beginning to return, and so she stretched cautiously and tiptoed across the room, being very careful not to make any noise that might wake the sleeping guard. Before leaving the room she gave it a quick search but could find no sign of her pack with its all-important talisman. She had no choice but to keep on searching.

Beyond the guard-room was another long room which seemed to perform the function of a kitchen, being hung with cured hams, ropes of garlic, large copper pans and a wide array of iron utensils. At first Isabeau felt quite faint, thinking the utensils some kind of instruments of torture, but once she saw the hams and garlic she relaxed. Once again she had to find a quick hiding spot as voices came near and she dived behind some sacks of flour and barley, trying to keep her head down. Luckily the owners of the voices passed right outside but did not come in, and she was able to crawl out a few minutes later, covered in flour dust but safe.

The kitchen opened out onto a square courtyard at one end, with another door in the center of the left wall. Isabeau risked a quick look out of the windows and saw the courtyard was filled with guards fighting with padded shields and clumsy claymores made of wood. Blyn was calling out instructions with his bass rumble and the other soldiers stepped back or attacked as he directed. On the opposite wall a man was strung up between two poles, his shirt torn and bloodied from what must have been a harsh whipping. He was either dead or unconscious because he did not move, despite the flies gathering thick on the torn, reddened flesh. Nausea swept over Isabeau, and terror, too, for if they punished one of their own so severely, what would they do to her?

Trying to control her trembling, she slipped back to the other door and cautiously opened it. Beyond was a much smaller room, hung with bright tapestries, and with a cushioned chair behind a table. On the table lay Isabeau's pack, the contents spilling out over the well-polished surface. With a glad cry she ran forward and seized the leather satchel, rummaging quickly through. Just as her fingers closed on the slender triangle, she heard the soft click of a latch behind her, and spun round.

A tall, very thin man was leaning against the doorframe with a most unpleasant smile curving his lips. "So," he said, "the witch managed to slip past three locked doors and a full contingent o' guards. It will be an interesting trial, will it no'?"

Isabeau slowly removed her hand from its hold on the black pouch, hoping the man had not seen how anxious she had been about the talisman. "I do no' ken wha' ye mean," she said, trying to look and sound stupid.

The man was not deceived and he pulled back his bloodless lips from his teeth in a terrifying smile. "My lady will be most pleased at this further evidence o' your witchcraft," he said. "She said she hunted ye as far as the Great Divide and back, and she's never known a slipperier fox. It was a mistake, ye ken, to anger her. Now, me. I have no temper. I find such displays of anger quite amusing. I see you have red hair—I hope you will lose your temper with me."

Isabeau said nothing, looking about her casually in an attempt to find some means of escape. Again the man smiled, and Isabeau's blood ran cold. "Do ye ken who I am?" he asked, and she shook her head. "I am Baron Yutta, the Grand-Questioner o' the Awl. That is a nice way o' saying I am their most creative torturer. I have been looking forward very much to meeting ye. I was most disappointed when I went to have a chat with ye and found ye had slithered away again. How did ye escape this time?

Isabeau found she could not speak. He smiled, and said, "Och, soon we'll ken the answer, bairn. We'll ken all the answers. I am looking forward to it so much. I hope ye will fight me—it is always a disappointment when my subjects break too easily. Are you afraid o' pain?"

Suddenly Isabeau's legs were moving of their own accord. She grabbed the pack from the table and bolted for the door. The Grand-Questioner moved smoothly to intercept her, smiling thinly, but she kicked him hard between the legs and was out of the door and into the corridor, straight into the arms of the Red Guards. They marched her back into the room, where Baron Yutta was leaning against the table, his face a little green but otherwise showing little effect from Isabeau's savage kick. Even his smile was still in place, although twisted.

"Take the witch to the questioning room," he said mildly. "We have a lot o' work ahead o' us."

Surrounded by guards, Isabeau was marched back through the long corridors and rooms to the cell block. Her legs were trembling so much she could hardly walk, and they prodded and pushed her forward with their spears, sometimes piercing her skin with the sharp points. This time she was marched straight past her cell and through the door at the other end.

The room was long and dark, the ceiling wreathed in smoke from the burning braziers. Here and there were tables with manacles attached, some with wheels at either end, the purpose of which Isabeau hardly dared guess. On one wall hung a young man, naked, his body marked all over with burns and bruises, his torso shiny with sweat and blood. At the sound of the door opening, he opened his mouth to scream but no sound came out, just a silent agony that swept over Isabeau in sickening waves. She began to retch and cough, but they pushed her forward so she sprawled into the stinking straw. As she lay there, trying to catch her breath in terrified sobs, the Grand-Questioner swept in, dressed now in long, red robes with the twisted emblem of the Questioners emblazoned on his breast.

"Strip her, chain her to that table," he said, pointing, "then leave us."

Despite all Isabeau's kicks and squirms, her breeches were stripped off, to the accompaniment of much fondling and squeezing, her shirt torn from her back, and her naked body strapped to one of the upright tables. One of the guards squeezed her nipple so hard that Isabeau screamed, and the Grand-Questioner smiled. "I like that sound," he murmured, so that the guards were encouraged, hurting her badly with their pinches and slaps. At last they reluctantly left, leaving Isabeau shamed and bruised, and more conscious than ever of Meghan's warning. "Do no' fall into the Awl's hands," she had said. "They will break ye like a doll."

Baron Yutta came and stroked her bruised cheek. "Puir wee one," he said, and lifted away her matted hair so he could look down at her body. Isabeau flinched away from his fingers, but he only smiled, running the great length of her hair through his hands like a rope. "It's never been cut, has it?"

Isabeau said nothing, just looked away over his head to the ceiling. There were all sorts of strange instruments hung from chains up there, and she shuddered.

He took her chin in his hand, and forced her to look at him. His eyes were a strange pale color, most unusual in this land of dark-haired, dark-eyed people. "So, tell me, who sent ye to rescue the *uile-bheist*? Are ye in contact with any o' the rebels? What are their names and where are they?"

Isabeau could not look away so she stared back at him with as much defiance as she could.

"Good," he crooned. "Fight me, witch. Resist me. I can tell ye are a stubborn lassie." He stroked her cheek with one finger. "I like that. Let us see how long ye can resist me." Isabeau tried to gather moisture in her mouth so she could spit in his face, but her mouth was dry as a desert.

He moved away, and began arranging tools on the long table. Several he put in the fire to heat, and one he took to a wheel and began to sharpen. At the sound the young man hanging on the wall jerked his head back in terror. The Grand-Questioner went over to him and stroked one finger along his cheek. "Ah, ye remember, my sweet pigeon. Ye ken what I have in store for the red haired witch, do ye no'?" Like a hypnotized coney, the man nodded, staring at Baron Yutta in terror. "Tell me, what would ye like me to do to the girl? The first touch is your choice. It is your reward, for screaming so sweetly for me."

The man began to throw his head from side to side. "Choose," the torturer said. When the young man said nothing, Baron Yutta put his hand up and gripped the young man's balls in his fist. "Choose," he said in his mild voice, twisting viciously. The man screamed and fainted, but the Grand-Questioner went back to his instrument table and got a small flask to wave under the victim's nose. When he coughed into reconsciousness, Baron Yutta smiled and stroked his cheek. "Choose," he said.

"Burn her, burn her," the young man screamed.

"Mmm, lovely," he said. "The flat o' the blade?" When the young man nodded, he kissed him on the mouth. "My sweet boy. Where?" Again the young man moaned and flung his head from side to side, and the Grand-Questioner took his balls in his hand and bounced them gently. "The back," the young man choked out.

"Ye disappoint me," Baron Yutta said. "Have ye no imagination? Lady Glynelda is unhappy with this witch. She wants her to be hurt."

"No," the young man panted, misery in his voice. "I canna tell ye where to hurt her. Do no' make me."

"Och, I think ye will. Ye do no' wish to displease me, do ye? Show me how much ye have learned about pain."

"No!"

Baron Yutta said nothing, just smiled as the prisoner

sobbed and writhed against his shackles. "I canna . . ." he pleaded, and still the torturer said nothing, smiling and running his fingernail gently down the boy's cheek.

"Burn her!" he cried. "I said burn her!"

"Aye, but where, my laddie? Where do ye want me to burn her? Show me what ye have learned."

"On the nipples!" he choked out, and rolled a despairing look at Isabeau. "Just don't hurt me anymore, please."

"Ye do have exquisite refinement," Baron Yutta purred. "Did ye enjoy that wee game we played? As a reward I shall do it to ye again. But the witch first."

Sick with horror, Isabeau shrank back against the hard table, watching mesmerized as the torturer turned the instruments in the glowing coals. An idea came to her and she concentrated on the brazier, thinking of the void. The Grand-Questioner turned quickly, and she realized he must recognize the faint chill of the air, the faint smell of enchantment, that meant magic was being worked. "Och," he said, "the witch works her sorcery." He saw that the fire had gone out, and she saw the first sign of anger in his face. "Clever," he said. "The question is, will I be able to light it again?"

He worked on the coals with a pair of bellows, while Isabeau thought furiously of the void. He tried to light a fresh fire with flint, but each spark just sank away into nothing. At last he turned back to Isabeau and he was smiling. "This is going to be interesting," he said. "We might leave the fire until ye are a little weaker."

Slowly he walked toward her until his pale, gaunt face and crimson robes filled her eyes. Again he tilted her chin in his hand and gazed deep into her eyes. She shuddered away from his touch but that seemed to please him. He stroked her cheek then slowly ran his hand down the center of her body, between her breasts, over her stomach and between her legs. As he probed inside her, he pulled down on the wheel with his other hand. An excruciating pain shot through her as the chains on her wrists and ankles began to stretch, and Isabeau screamed.

"Lovely," he said, and put his fingers inside her mouth so that she tasted the fluids of her own body. She bit them, hardly knowing what it was she did, and with a cry he snatched his fingers away, then laughed. Again he turned the wheel and her whole body jerked and spasmed. She fell into a red haze of semiconsciousness, and felt him fondle her again. Then an acrid smell under her nostrils jerked her back into consciousness.

"Who sent ye to rescue the *uile-bheist*? How did ye ken where the Grand-Seeker was?"

Isabeau was too sick to answer, and he leaned over her so his pale, mad eyes filled her vision. When she said nothing, he pulled the lever again, though not so hard, and pain screeched through her.

"Who betrayed us? Where is the rebel stronghold? Are there witches there? Who taught ye the One Power?"

Isabeau tried to think of something to say, anything. Her mouth formed Meghan's name but her tongue would not work. Again and again she tried to tell him, but her mouth would not speak. She remembered then how the skeelie had questioned her, with as little result, but she was in too much pain to try to reason why.

"Shall we try something different?" the torturer asked, and smiled his chilling smile. "How about the pilliwinkes? What would ye prefer, the rack or the pilliwinkes? It's your choice." Isabeau shook her head, sobbing, and he leaned against her. "Ye really do no' want me to choose, do ye? Trust me, what I would choose to do to ye is much worse than either o' those things. Tell me, my wee sweet one, what would ye rather, the rack or the pilliwinkes?"

"No' the rack, no' the rack," she cried, every joint in her body aching and throbbing.

He smiled. "So ye want the pilliwinkes? Interesting choice, my lass."

"No, no," she moaned, but it was too late, the Grand-Questioner was tenderly slipping the fingers of her left hand into a metal vice. He clamped it shut, despite all Isabeau's attempts to wrench her hand free, then twisted the handle so the metal jaws ground together, crushing her fragile bones at the lowest knuckle. Isabeau was racked with the most excruciating pain, her whole body convulsing with agony. With blood and bone marrow oozing out from under the vise, she threw back her head and howled, and through the red haze of pain and terror, saw a large iron wheel suspended on a chain just above the torturer's head. With all her mind-strength, she unhooked one end of the chain and watched with a strange detachment as the wheel came crashing down and struck the torturer on the back of his head. As he crumpled slowly toward the floor, she fainted again.

THE THREADS ENTWINE

Khan'derin the Scarred Warrior

Khan'derin sat as far away from the fireplace as she could, finding the heat of its flames on her face almost unbearable. It was a warm night, the stars overhead so close it almost seemed as if she could touch them. The old witch was telling her stories about her so-called twin sister. Khan'derin peered into her bowl, looking for something more interesting to eat than the withered carrots and turnips she found there. Finding nothing, she put the wooden bowl down with a sigh and tried to concentrate on what the sorceress was telling her.

Meghan obviously thought some of the things Is'a'beau had said or done were funny, chuckling a little to herself as she told the tale. Khan'derin wondered why the wood witch had not beaten her ward severely for such disrespect. Why, she had lost the skin off her back more times than she could tell for much lesser crimes. She thought Is'a'beau sounded like a cheeky good-for-nothing, and wondered at the obvious affection in the witch's voice.

She looked about her at the dark forest, rustling and murmuring with alien sounds, and wished she was back in the Haven, listening to war stories or tales of her hero father. Unconsciously she twisted the dragoneye ring on her finger, but stilled her hands immediately, hoping the wood witch had not noticed. Fidgeting was for untutored children, she reminded herself. A hunter should be able to sit for hours without twitching a muscle.

After a while, the old witch's reminiscences stopped and Khan'derin looked up to see the intense black eyes watching her. Khan'derin waited for her to go on, but there was silence. The little creature the witch carried around in her pocket sat up on its hind legs and made a chittering noise. Meghan's face relaxed and she smiled a little, chittering back in return. Khan'derin wondered if she dared ask a question; then, remembering the amusement in Meghan's voice over her obstreperous ward's antics, took her courage in both hands.

"Auld mother, forgive me, but is that your totem?"

"Gitâ is my familiar," Meghan explained. "He is my eyes and my feet, my protector and my friend."

"That is similar," Khan'derin said. She looked at Gitâ with increased respect, for if he was like her Auld Mother's totem, he was a powerful spirit indeed.

The old witch said, "In the dragon's hall, ye told me ye were found with a dragoneye ring on ye—May I see it?"

Reluctantly Khan'derin tugged off the ring and passed it to the old witch. Meghan turned it over in her hands and saw, inscribed on the inside, the word Iseult. She looked up in surprise and studied Khan'derin's face. "Iseult," she said.

The girl flushed scarlet, the scars on her cheekbones showing white. "My name is Khan'derin," she said in a muffled voice. "My grandmother named me!"

Meghan looked as if she was going to say something but evidently changed her mind, for there was a pause, and then she continued, "Ye also said the Firemaker found something else on ye, what was that?"

"My *sheyata,*" Khan'derin answered readily.

"What's that?"

"I am no' sure of the word in your language—charm, I think, or amulet. It was with me when the Firemaker found me. As soon as she saw it, she ken it was an amulet o' great power, and so she made sure it was kept safe all the time I was growing up. She gave it to me afore I went to the dragons for the first time, certain that it was o' significance. And surely it seems sometimes to compel me in directions I might no' have taken otherwise."

"Indeed?" Meghan said. "In what way?"

"Well, I did no' want to go to the dragons' valley. I was

frightened. So I decided I would pretend to go, then hide and follow the pride when it traveled to the Gathering. I did so want to see all the prides together, and watch the contests o' strength and skill, and see the dancing and feasting. I ken the Firemaker would be angry at first, but I am the bairn o' her heart and so would forgive me. So I set off as instructed and went halfway up the hill where I hid and rested. When I tried to go back down, though, my *sheyata* burned me right through my clothes, and sent tingles up and down my arm when I touched it. The further down the hill I walked the more intense the burning became, and the more painful. Whenever I stopped or walked in the direction I had been instructed, it did lessen. For almost an hour I tried to go back, but then I gave in and began to climb again. At once the burning went away and so I once again turned back. This time it was like a brand against my breast, and my whole body thrummed with pain. That time I accepted the *sheyata* and so came to the dragons' hall as the Firemaker had dreamed I should."

"That is interesting indeed. Is this the only occasion o' it compelling ye?"

"Och no, it has happened a few times. Only a few days ago, it began to buzz and burn, and the tingling only stopped after I was summoned to the dragons' hall to meet ye. But I can see no reason for that . . . Once it saved my life."

"Indeed?"

"Mmmm, aye. A few years ago. I was out hunting, and we were quick on the heels o' a herd o' *geal'teas* who ran out o' a narrow trail onto a wide slope o' snow. I was in the lead and was about to follow them when my *sheyata* began to burn and tingle again. Remembering the previous time, I stopped and examined it, and it scalded my fingers when I touched it. I tried to stop the others, but most ignored me and followed the herd onto the slope. Some heeded my warning, though it went hard to let such a fine herd o' *geal'teas* escape. Those that listened to me all lived, while those who ignored the omen died."

"What happened?"

"Avalanche," Khan'derin shrugged.

"May I look at it?" Meghan asked, and rather reluctantly

Khan'derin fished inside her shirt, and took out a small, black pouch, which she opened, tipping a triangular talisman, delicately wrought and inscribed with magical symbols, out onto her palm. Meghan took it in her hands, tracing the symbols with her fingers. Her whole face seemed to light up, her black eyes shining. Khan'derin watched in consternation and held out her hand for Meghan to pass it back. The witch did not seem to notice.

"What do ye ken about the Coven?" she asked instead, turning the talisman over in her hands.

"Only what Feld has told me," Khan'derin answered suspiciously, her eyes on her *sheyata*.

"The Book o' Shadows tells us that the leader o' each Tower must join together to create a Coven, working together to help witches across the land, exchanging apprentices and accepting students from other Towers so no knowledge shall be lost. The most powerful witch in the land shall be the Keybearer, and shall rule the Coven. Do ye follow me?"

"No," Khan'derin said.

Meghan sighed. "I canna believe that your people ken so little about witches. Are none o' ye taught the ways o' the Coven?"

"Why should we be? The prides are no' your kind, and went their own way for centuries before your kind ever came. The Towers o' Roses and Thorns have been deserted since the death o' the Red Sorceress many, many years ago. Who would have taught us the ways?"

"Well, then, ye say the Auld Mother leads your pride. Does every pride have an Auld Mother?"

"Aye, indeed."

"Well, imagine that all the Auld Mothers got together to talk about how they could best help each other—"

"Like they do at the Gathering . . ."

Meghan looked as if she'd like to know more, but nodded and went on: "Well then, the most powerful Auld Mother, the one with the most influence, would be like the Keybearer o' the Coven."

"The Firemaker."

"Perhaps . . . I ken so little about your people! I would fain ken more—"

"I do no' see what all that has to do with my *sheyata*?"

"Your *sheyata,* as ye call it, is part o' one o' the Coven's great artifacts o' power. It was wrought many years ago by one of my ancestors, Owein MacCuinn, he o' the Longbow. He was the first Keybearer. He wrought the Key in the sacred symbol of the Coven—a star contained within a circle."

"Like the one I suddenly thought o' the other morning, when you were . . . testing me?" Despite herself, Khan'derin was becoming interested, so much so that she dared ask a question.

"Exactly that. This medallion was worn by the Keybearer, meant to be the strongest and bravest and most compassionate o' all the Coven. Its history is no' all kind or true, however. No' all the Keybearers were the witch they should have been. Like many in a position o' power, some abused their trust, and battles were occasionally fought over the right to wear it. Nonetheless, the Key is an artifact o' great power, having been wrought by Owein MacCuinn and always worn by those with exceptional Talent."

The witch paused and sighed, before continuing in a subdued voice, "Some years ago, just before ye were born, at the time o' the Day o' Betrayal, I was given back the Key by Tabithas NicRuraich, who was then the Keybearer. The Tower of Two Moons, headquarters of the Keybearer, was being attacked by the Red Guards and she was afraid the Key would fall into the hands o' the Banrìgh, who would use its power for evil. Tabithas planned to confront the Banrìgh and engage her in a battle of power. I never saw her again."

Khan'derin leaned forward, her blue eyes very serious.

"The Rìgh later said she had been exiled, but I have never believed that. I think she died, and the Rìgh was trying to stop the people o' Rurach, who loved Tabithas dearly, from rebelling. Anyway, I had the Key and it was my task to keep it safe after the Day o' Betrayal. I used it to lock away something I did no' wish Maya to lay her hands on, and then, I broke the Key into three parts and gave two o' the pieces into the hands o' the witches I most trusted. One o' those was your mother Ishbel, whom ye have been tending for the past eight years. The dragons must have recognized the power o' the talisman and given it into your care. Perhaps they ken our paths would one day cross. Indeed the dragons can see all ways along the thread o' time."

"Ye canna have it!"

"I must have it, Iseult. Indeed I am sorry if it is important to ye, but there is far too much at stake here. Without your *sheyata,* the other pieces are worthless. And indeed, your *sheyata* wants to be made whole again—it knows the time is at hand. It will no' let ye take any step that is no' the direction it wants to go in."

"I said ye canna have it! It is my birth-right!"

"Indeed it is no'. If the truth be ken it is mine, for I am the Keybearer o' the Coven, and this is part of my Key."

Khan'derin thrust out her hand, calling to her *sheyata* silently, and the carved triangle in Meghan's hand gave a little jump and quiver. It did not move though, and Khan'derin stared at it in surprise.

The old witch smiled. "Even if it did no' want to stay in my hand, ye could no' take it from me. Ye are no' even an apprentice witch. Your powers are latent and untrained. I, on the other hand, have been practising magic for more years than ye can imagine. No one could take from my hand what I did no' want them to."

Khan'derin could hardly believe the *sheyata* had not responded to her call. Never before had her will failed to work on it, or any of her other weapons. For Khan'derin thought of her *sheyata* as another weapon, like a magic shield that warned her of danger and kept her out of trouble. Her grandmother had found the *sheyata* on her when she was a new-born babe. She could not believe that Meghan would take it from her like that, as if she did not know it was one of the few things Khan'derin had to call her own. How could the wood witch say so calmly that it was really hers, when it was obvious it was Khan'derin's?

The loss of her *sheyata* made Khan'derin even more sullen than before. For three days the pair traveled in silence, neither making any attempt to melt the ice between them. They saw no sign of any Red Guards and Meghan guessed the dragons had made a sweep of the area, killing any they saw. The wood witch did not try to talk about the twin again, much to Khan'derin's relief. She did not like the thought there was someone else in the world with her face and her ancestry.

Khan'derin spent most of her time dreaming of the snows. She was very homesick. It was so hot, and all the colors of the scenery were so bewildering. She had never realized there were so many shades of green, while the brilliant scarlets, oranges, purples and blues of bird plumage and flower dazzled her eyes, making her dizzy. On the Spine of the World there was only the blue of the sky and the white of the snow, the gray of rock and the dark green of the firs below the treeline. Color differences were so subtle as to be almost invisible. Here, her senses swam with the rich embroidery of forest life—the brilliant colors, the strong perfumes, the cacophony of bird song and wind rustle, the prickle of sweat on her body.

Khan'derin missed the daily routine of the pride, especially the thrill of the hunt and the triumph of the kill. She missed the comfort of being surrounded by many bodies, and of knowing exactly what to do and when to do it. Most of all, she missed her grandmother, a tiny woman—even smaller than Meghan of the Beasts—with the strongest will of anyone Khan'derin had ever encountered. The Firemaker had advised and directed her all her life. Even though Meghan was like an Auld Mother in her age and wisdom, the wood witch did not seem to understand any of the complexities of pride customs and manners. She never gave Khan'derin the directive to eat, so that for the first few nights Khan'derin had sat staring at her stew going cold, too afraid to eat a bite in case she displeased the sorceress. It was only after Meghan gave her a sharp look and snapped at her that Khan'derin had realized she was permitted to start. Meghan ate with both hands, and often drank between mouthfuls, as if not knowing that food and drink should never be taken together. Meghan interrupted her while she spoke, and did not seem to mind when Khan'derin spoke to her unbidden. She asked questions all the time, considered the rudest behavior possible in the pride, where personal privacy was extremely important because of the lack of privacy in everything else. When you had as many as forty people living together in the one system of caves, or traveling over the ice plains in pursuit of the migrating *geal'teas,* you did not ask them questions about their private thoughts all the time, as Meghan did.

She also interrupted constantly, so that it was very difficult to tell the answers in the accepted way. More than once, Khan'derin had almost forgotten the respect accorded an Auld Mother, and come close to raising her voice against her. Each time, though, she had remembered, and bitten her tongue and swallowed her words, so they sat in a hard lump in her stomach.

Worst of all, Meghan did not seem to think highly of Khan'derin's prowess with weapons, while Khan'derin was used to praise and admiration for these skills. The odd food they ate only added to her sense of homesickness. Not once since leaving the Cursed Valley had Khan'derin tasted meat. Usually her life revolved around the need to track and hunt, but she thought perhaps they were in too much of a hurry to spare time for hunting. Therefore, when she saw a coney bound away into the undergrowth some days into their journey, Khan'derin raced after it with joy in her heart. She killed it easily with one throw of her *reil,* and returned to Meghan proudly, its blood-stained body dangling from her fist. "We shall eat meat tonight," she said.

To her surprise, Meghan turned a look of hatred upon her, taking the furry animal and cradling it in her arms. Without saying a word, she knelt in the shade of a great tree and rocked the dead coney back and forth, keening gently. Gitâ scrabbled out of her pocket, chittering in his throat, and laid a paw on her arm in comfort. After a while, tears wet on her cheeks, Meghan took her small spade from her pack and began to dig. Khan'derin watched in absolute bewilderment, but said nothing. It took Meghan almost half an hour to dig a big enough hole to bury the coney in, then they continued on their way in gloomy silence.

That night, by the campfire, as they ate their potato bread and a thin soup, Khan'derin could barely contain her anger or contempt. She could not believe the old witch had wept over a dead coney and said the sacred rites over its grave. She could not believe she was again eating turnip soup when she had had a fat coney in her fist.

As if sensing her disgust, Meghan said softly, "Iseult,

happen I did no' make myself clear. Ye may no' kill while ye are with me. The animals o' the field and forest are under my protection."

"Do ye no' hunt or fish?" Khan'derin asked, puzzled. "What then do ye eat?"

"Roots, nuts, fruit, berries, herbs and leafage," Meghan answered. "Unfertilized eggs, milk, cheese, curds and whey. We eat very well." She began to pack away the remains of the food.

"Why is this? The Gods o' White created animals for people to hunt and to eat. Flesh keeps people alive, makes blood warm and fast."

"Ye will no' kill when ye are with me."

"But what about these enemies of yours? Do ye no' wish me to kill them for ye?"

"Only in defense o' your own life," Meghan responded, clearly troubled.

Khan'derin stared down at the thin soup in her bowl, which she had hardly touched. "Ye ask that I give up meat?"

"Ye will no' notice its absence."

"To eat flesh is part o' the sacred process o' life."

Meghan looked across at her, her hands stilling in their task. "Do ye mean that eating animal flesh is a ritual of your people?"

Khan'derin rocked back and forth on her heels. "Not exactly. We hunt, we eat—this is life."

"With me, ye shall both hunt and eat, but no' animals," Meghan said firmly. Khan'derin looked at her pensively but said nothing more.

That night, Meghan slipped her emerald ring off her finger and cupped it in her hands. The warm light of the fire flickered over it, finding odd glints and shadows in its depths. Meghan stared at it for a very long time, Khan'derin watching her from the shelter of her blankets. When at last she put it back on her finger, the witch's wrinkled old face was grim. Seeing Khan'derin watching her, she explained shortly that she was worried about Isabeau. She had taken the risk of trying to make contact with a friend of hers, who was waiting for the girl at Tulachna Celeste. Three weeks or more had passed since they parted company—

more than enough time for Isabeau to make the journey out of the Sithiche Mountains and down to Caeryla. Yet her friend had seen no sign of her. Meghan was anxious, both for the safety of her ward and because she carried part of the Key, whose loss would be disastrous.

"She has a *sheyata* like mine?" Khan'derin asked.

Meghan nodded, but said sharply, "Though it is no' hers, any more than it was yours, Iseult. She carries it for me, for I was afraid I might never return from the dragons' valley. I wish now that I had kept her with me, and the Key too."

"I am Khan'derin! Stop calling me by that name!"

"Your mother named ye Iseult, which in one o' the ancient tongues means 'the fair one.' Ye should be proud o' your name."

"I am proud o' Khan'derin."

"And that is good, for it is the name your grandmother gave ye. I do no' ken what it means, but I do no' wish ye to feel I am asking ye to reject your people. Ye must realize we are traveling into danger. I canna call ye Khan'derin . . ." the old witch stumbled over the difficult intonations, "for it is no' an islander name. I would draw attention to us and to ye, and that we must no' do. If I call ye Iseult now, we shall both be used to it by the time we reach civilization, and will no' betray ourselves. Besides, Iseult is much easier to pronounce!"

Khan'derin frowned and bent her head, but the sorceress laughed at her and patted her arm gently. "Ye are no' on the Spine o' the World now, my dear. Ye must try and pretend ye are a simple village girl and I am your granddam, that way no one will look at us twice."

Khan'derin jerked her arm away and rolled herself in her blankets to sleep, repeating the name to herself several times: Is'e'ult, Is'e'ult. She could not understand why Meghan thought it was easier to pronounce than Khan'derin!

The next morning the sorceress woke Iseult well before dawn, before the stars had even begun to fade. "We are approaching the Pass down into Rionnagan," she whispered. "I sense soldiers ahead, so we must travel very carefully. From now on we will travel mainly by night. I have called a friend to guide us."

Rubbing the sleep out her eyes, Iseult looked about her

but could see no sign of anyone but themselves. "Where?" she asked.

"In the tree," Meghan responded. Iseult looked up and saw a ghostly shape perched on a branch. "What is that?" Iseult asked, bemused.

"It is a horned owl, and it can see in the dark better than any creature I ken. I called it down so it can show us the safest path. Quickly now, for I sense something ahead, and I would rather be on our feet and ready than rolled in blankets and half asleep."

Iseult was up and ready immediately. They both shouldered their packs and set off through the dark forest, the owl gliding silently before them, calling out every now and then in an eerie wail. They passed an encampment of soldiers, flitting silently through the trees at the edge of the clearing, and reached the valley by the time the sun peeked over the edge of the mountains. Meghan had an odd look on her face, as if smelling the wind. "There is something . . ." she began, leaning heavily on her staff. "I think—"

She did not finish her thought, but seemed to make a decision. She called the owl down to her and thanked it, stroking its brindled head. Then she led the way briskly into the forest again, working her way along the shoulder of the hill instead of down the valley as she had planned. Iseult followed without question, though she loosened her weapons in their sheaths.

The forest began to fill with light, and birds called happily. Gitâ clambered out of Meghan's pocket and perched on her shoulder, clinging to her iron-gray plait with one black-tipped paw. Meghan stopped every now and again as if deciding which way to go and, by the time the sun was clear of the ridge, had taken them to the foot of a great cliff, choked with undergrowth.

Gitâ, I think there must be a cave or crevice o' some kind, can ye look for me?

The donbeag scampered down the length of her body and into the thick bushes. After some time, he returned, looking a little ruffled but chittering excitedly.

"Stay here, Iseult!" Meghan ordered, and followed the bounding animal into the undergrowth.

Iseult sat cross-legged on the ground, and began to polish

her weapons with a soft cloth, trying not to yawn. She was not used to walking for any length of time, particularly over such rough ground, and she was tired. Although the prides were seminomadic, spending all spring and summer following the herds along the alpine meadows, Iseult was a Scarred Warrior. They worked all winter to feed the People and guard them against the many dangerous creatures of the Spine of the World. On their wooden skimmers they flew over the surface of the snow, faster than a horse could gallop. When they traveled to other hunting grounds, they rode in sleds pulled by alpine goats, intelligent horned creatures whose hooves were designed for running on hard-packed snow. In spring and summer the Scarred Warriors rested, most in the beautiful valley of the Haven, Iseult alone with an old warlock and a sleeping sorceress in the Cursed Valley. She was used to the exhilarating freedom of skimming the snow-covered hills, not this hard slog through brambly thickets, stones turning under her boots, branches whipping back into her face. As a result her legs and back ached, her feet felt hot and swollen, and the pack weighed heavily on her shoulders.

After waiting ten minutes or so, and almost nodding off to sleep twice, she got to her feet and began to track the sorceress through the forest. It was a surprisingly difficult task, both because the wood witch automatically concealed her trail wherever she went, and because Iseult was used to tracking through snow, not over bare rocks and earth. However, Iseult was an excellent hunter, and at last she tracked the witch to a narrow crack in the side of the cliff. Careful to make no noise, she crouched outside to listen.

". . . I have been trying to make my way to ye for months, but I have been followed all the way from Lucescere, and caught twice now. These mountains are swarming with bloody soldiers, Eà damn them! No matter what I did, I could no' seem to get past them. For the past week I have been trapped in this valley, unable to find a way past that thrice-damned encampment." It was a male's voice speaking, and his voice was filled with anger and a kind of blackness that Iseult could not identify.

"So Maya knows o' ye?" Meghan's voice was flat.

"She must. She may no' be sure it is me, if ye understand what I mean, but she must be worried. They laid a trap for me, damn them, and I walked straight into it."

"They must have ken ye would lead them straight to me. I wonder . . . why did they no' just follow ye, keeping a discreet distance?"

"I've lost them several times afore now. It was just cursed bad luck that they picked up my trail again!"

"Things are beginning to make a lot more sense now. I could no' understand why there were so many legions o' Red Guards in the Sithiche Mountains. Even launching an attack on the dragons was no' justification enough for all these soldiers. I knew they did no' ken where I was—if they did, I would have been flushed out years ago! No, no, it makes sense now."

"I would have been with ye weeks ago, as I promised, if only they had no' been so hot on my trail."

"Why did ye no' scry me out and tell me what was happening? I was very worried."

"The Awl has my staff and knife, Meghan. They were taken from me the first time I was captured, and I could no' get them back. I was lucky to get free at all! They must be using them to focus in on me, spying on me as I speak through water. There is no other explanation. So many o' our plans have failed and it could only be that they were listening in."

"Could ye have a spy in your midst?"

"I do no' believe so. I ken all my men, and we have been through hellfire and back together. Besides, we have known for a long time they must have a seer in their ranks, and a powerful seer too."

"Indeed, that is true," Meghan said. "But we are being spied on now. Come in, Iseult, and do no' try and spy on me again. I dislike it very much."

Iseult straightened so abruptly she banged her head on the overhang of the cave. How had the witch known she was listening? She had not made a sound that could have betrayed her. Feeling rather shamefaced, an emotion she did not at all like, Iseult ducked her head and entered the tiny cave. At first her eyes were dazzled and she could see nothing, but then her vision cleared and she saw Meghan crouched by the side of a young man who was leaning up on one elbow and regarding her with an extremely unwelcoming look.

"By Eà!" he exclaimed. "No' ye! Just what I need, that damn nosy girl hanging around. Canna ye leave me alone, lass?"

Iseult's brows rose and she glared back at him, but said nothing, rocking slightly on the balls of her feet.

"I see," Meghan said thoughtfully. "So ye have met my ward Isabeau afore?"

"So she's a ward o' yours, is she? I should have known. Never met anyone who asked so many questions. By Eà's green blood, why did ye no' tell me ye knew my cousin?" he scowled at Iseult, who regarded him thoughtfully, but said nothing.

"Isabeau knows better than to mention my name to anyone," Meghan said frostily.

The man rolled his eyes and lay back on the ground, wincing a little as his shoulder came in contact with the earth. "You'd think then that she ken better than to tangle with the Awl! By Eà, she thought I was some stray puppy she'd picked up!"

Meghan's grim face relaxed a little. "She would," the witch said. Immediately though, her attention sharpened. "Did ye say she had run across the Awl? What happened?"

"They caught me about two days through the Pass, no' far from here actually, Eà blast them! They had a seeker, a damn unpleasant woman and the strongest witch-sniffer I've ever encountered. They'd obviously brought out the pick o' the herd to hunt me down. They beat me up pretty badly, and had me tied to a horse like a lamb trussed for the slaughter. Anyway, next thing I ken this pert uppity ward o' yours had snuck right into the Awl camp and had me untied and out o' there before I ken what was happening! They were hot on our trail, o' course, and she led them a fine dance through the highlands, back and forth and in and out like a donbeag."

Meghan clenched her fists. "The stupid lass!"

The man grinned. "And that I agree with," he said rudely to Iseult, who contemplated him calmly. "Anyway, I guess ye ken what happened then."

"I'd fain hear your version o' the story."

"Well, I cleared out, o' course. Took her supplies—sorry about that, but what could I do?" he said to Iseult. "I sure was no' going to follow that harebrained plan o' yours and head back down into the south. The Spinners ken it took me long enough to get out o' there!"

"So ye just left Isabeau there?"

"Well, she was grand, was she no'? She looks just dandy to me."

Meghan's face was the angriest that Iseult had ever seen. "This is no' my ward Isabeau but her twin sister Iseult," she said in a voice of ice. "And this stupid, bear-brained, crow-natured lump o' worthlessness, Iseult, is my cousin . . . Bacaiche. I dinna ken who is more stupid, your sister or my cousin! What was she thinking?"

"Ye mean this is no' the same girl as the one who freed me?" Bacaiche looked quite bewildered. "She looks the same, except for having cut her hair."

"She and Isabeau are twins," Meghan said coldly. "And I am very angry with ye, Bacaiche. Ye just abandoned Isabeau to the mercy o' the Awl! Ye knew she'd be fire fodder!"

"Well, I did no' ken she was your ward," Bacaiche said sulkily.

"And what difference does that make? She is young and inexperienced, and does no' realize the reach and power of the Awl like ye do. Ye stole her clothes and her supplies and left her for the Awl to find, and that I'll find very hard to forgive."

Iseult was interested to see the sulky expression that settled over the young man's dark face. So, he was in awe of his sorceress cousin.

Meghan slapped her hand several times on the ground, and Gitâ huddled in her lap, tapping at her arm with his paw. After a moment she began to stroke his glossy coat, and he pushed his quivering black nose into her palm. "Well, let us hope Isabeau has managed to escape," she said. "All we can do is travel as quickly as possible and try and catch her up. My heart misgives me, though, for surely she should be past Caeryla by now!"

"Why do ye no' scry her out?" Bacaiche asked.

"I canna," Meghan said. "She is protected."

"Obh, obh! I see! Well, that does make it difficult for ye then. Be comforted, though, it will make it harder for the Awl to sense her out as well."

"Indeed, that was the reason behind it," Meghan agreed dryly. "Now, are ye injured? I can feel pain emanating from ye."

"Arrow wound," Bacaiche said shortly. "In the left shoulder. Barbed head."

"How long ago?"

"Three nights."

"Fever?"

"Aye, unfortunately. I've been tossing and turning in this blaygird cave ever since."

"Well, let me take a look." Meghan pulled her pack toward her, and unknotted the leather straps so she could reach her pouches of herbs.

"Does she have to watch?" Bacaiche said in a long-suffering tone.

"Perhaps, Iseult, ye would no' mind fetching me water? We will spend the heat o' the day here, and start moving again once it's dark."

Iseult complied willingly, glad to get out of the stuffy cave and away from Bacaiche's sneer. By the time she returned, the water bags filled to bursting, Meghan had lit a fire and coaxed the smoke to disappear up a tiny vent in the cave's roof. Bacaiche was sitting up against the wall, bare chested, though his black cloak was still draped over his shoulders, and was wincing and swearing as Meghan probed at the arrow wound with sensitive fingers.

"Something major is afoot, Meghan, I swear it," he was saying. "All my reports show the Fairgean are rising, and there is nobody to stop them. The sea witches are all wiped out, and apparently their caves are now housing the Fairgean. Is that no' a horrible irony? And at the height o' the comet something happened, some spell . . ."

"Aye, I felt it too."

"So did the Lodestar."

"Aye."

"Jaspar must feel it too, must he no'? It must be tormenting him, the loss o' it."

"Aye."

Iseult noted the melancholy note in Meghan's voice and shifted slightly so she could see the wood witch's face. Meghan was staring into the fire, her wrinkled lids lowered over her eyes, her hands clenched. Gitâ crept back into her lap, and the sorceress stroked his velvety fur.

"Ye do hear it too, Meghan?"

Meghan nodded her head, not looking up. Staring from one face to another, Iseult saw a strong resemblance between them, despite the great disparity in age. Both were very dark, with a jutting nose and sharp cheekbones. Both had a white blaze in their hair just above the left brow, and a stern, stubborn mouth. The only difference was in the color of their eyes. Meghan's were a brilliant black, Bacaiche's an odd yellow color.

"I must free it," Bacaiche said restlessly. "It calls to me all the time, and it's fading, it's getting weaker. It has a pitiful sound, do ye no' agree? It says the time is coming."

"Aye," Meghan said and sighed. "My path is showing clearer before me all the time. I almost see the way clear . . . almost." Her voice drifted away.

"I canna see that!" Bacaiche said bitterly. "I sent a ship to Carraig to find out what news there is and the ship just disappeared. I sent another ship round to Tìrsoilleir and it disappeared too, even though it had on board one o' the few remaining Yedda that I've been able to find. The seas must be full o' Fairgean, all round the island. Even the pirates are too afraid to send out their ships, and indeed, what point is there, when the merchant ships are no' running? There's nothing for the pirates to rob."

"But what about trade?" Meghan asked.

Bacaiche shrugged his hunched shoulders. "I also went to *Tùr na Fitheach,* as ye instructed, but it stands empty, almost ruined. I did see ravens, though, and one followed me for many miles. It did no' make me feel easy."

"So when did the witch-sniffer pick up your trail?"

"At *Tùr na Gealaich dhà,*" Bacaiche said shamefacedly.

"Fool," Meghan said coldly. "Why did ye return to the Tower o' Two Moons? Ye must ken it would be watched."

"The Lodestar was calling me," Bacaiche said pleadingly. "I came from Ravenshaw through the Whitelock Mountains and it was too close . . . I could no' resist it."

"I told ye to be patient." Meghan's voice was cold and hard. "If ye are to win the Lodestar, ye must play the waiting game. How dare ye go to the Tower! She must realize we feel the Lodestar as much as Jaspar does. Ye led the Red Guards straight to me!"

"I'm sorry," Bacaiche said, and Iseult could tell apology was difficult for him. "It troubled my senses . . ."

"Destroyed your sense, more like," Meghan said, bandaging his shoulder tightly. "Bacaiche, ye will stay with me now. Too long I have let ye gallivant around, playing your rebel games and tickling the nose o' the Banrìgh. But there's too much at stake here. I do no' want ye out o' my sight until the Lodestar is safely in our hands. Do ye understand?"

Bacaiche nodded sulkily.

Because Bacaiche could not walk very well, crippled as he was, it took them another four nights to reach the Pass. He limped forward with an odd hop to his gait, leaning on a rough club he had made from a branch, and frowning angrily at Iseult whenever he caught her contemptuous gaze on him. Iseult was happy to leave his nursing to Meghan, though there was little else to do. Normally Iseult would have gone hunting, but Meghan had forbidden it, much to Iseult's disgust. Instead Meghan asked her to spend sometime foraging in the forest for roots and herbs to add to their scanty supplies, but Iseult was not familiar with the plants that grew this low down and, despite Meghan's lectures, still considered gathering the work of the very old or very young.

After the first day, when half the plants Iseult brought back were either poisonous, inedible or unripe, Meghan sent Gitâ with her. Although Iseult could not speak the donbeag's language, the little creature could at least prevent her from pulling up more of the noxious plants, and direct her to hazel-nut bushes or wild carrots. When they returned, Iseult was scowling and Gitâ was chittering exasperatedly, Iseult having apparently spent more time paddling in the stream than looking for food. Meghan had a few stern words with her and, as always, Iseult bowed her head and said nothing, her face carefully expressionless.

Gitâ chittered again, and ran up Meghan's long plait so

he could pat her earlobe. Meghan smiled and said, more gently, "Gitâ says ye played in the water like a baby otter—all squeals and laughter."

Iseult kept her eyes lowered, as was proper when speaking to an Auld Mother. "I have never immersed my body in water before," she said. "In my land all is white and cold; any streams which are no' frozen run too fast and are too cold for immersion. The loch at the Tower unfreezes in summer, but the thorns grow too thickly around it and, besides, I am always busy with my studies or looking after the sleeping sorceress."

"I see," Meghan said gently. "So ye do no' ken how to swim?"

"I am no' sure what that word means," Iseult answered politely.

Meghan sighed. "I wish Isabeau was here. She swims like an otter herself, and I am sure she would teach ye."

"I have no need o' . . . swims," Iseult answered gruffly.

She saw the wood witch looking at her in a puzzled way, as she often did, and thought the witch must find her as strange as she found the witch. She suspected the wood witch did not like her, perhaps because she knew how to hunt and kill; Bacaiche also disliked her for his own peculiar reasons, and Iseult was not used to being disliked. She had been a loved and cherished member of the pride, surrounded always by affection, and given great respect because she was the granddaughter of the Firemaker and so would one day rule in her place. Bacaiche was the rudest person she had ever met, either ignoring her or treating her with contempt. So Iseult ignored him too, although she found herself stealing glances at him as he limped along, slashing at the heads of thistles with his stick.

At first she had been on guard around him, because she sensed he was dangerous and unpredictable, and Iseult had decided her role was to protect Meghan, who was very old and frail and had such a strange reluctance to hurt or kill. Soon, however, she decided Bacaiche was more afraid of Meghan than of anything else, and was unlikely to harm her. His antipathy to herself she ignored, knowing he could not hurt her, particularly in his injured state.

Bacaiche was indeed a puzzle. He spoke with great arrogance, yet in moments of repose there was a look of such brooding unhappiness on his face that Iseult felt an unaccustomed sense of pity. She had realized the day she met him that he was a hunchback, his head set on a short neck below a great hump on his shoulders. As he was deformed, Iseult would normally have dismissed him as unimportant or even a bothersome liability. In her country all deformed or crippled babies were left out for the White Gods, and those injured in accident or warfare spent the rest of their lives limping around the Haven and trying not to get in the way. Life on the Spine of the World was not an easy one, and death always only a whisper away. Pity was not an emotion Iseult had ever been taught to revere. It was a sign of weakness. So she was astonished at the strange tenderness Bacaiche sometimes awoke in her, especially since his attitude to her had not improved on discovering she was not the meddlesome Is'a'beau. Occasionally he threw a sardonic comment or exasperated look in her direction, but otherwise they both worked hard at ignoring each other.

Every morning, after they found a cave or thicket in which to camp, Meghan sat by the newly kindled fire and stared into her sorceress ring, which she took out from the hidden pocket in the seam of her dress. Each time she came out of her trance her face was grim, her eyes hooded. Iseult guessed she was trying to find traces of Isabeau, though sometimes it was clear from later conversations that she had contacted other witches in other parts of the island.

Every morning, Bacaiche would announce that he too must try to make contact with his friends. One gray, pink-streaked dawn he even got out a bright, metal bowl and poured water into it, saying defiantly, "Dide will be frantic. I must tell him I am safe . . ."

Meghan took the bowl from him and poured the water into the big kettle that held their soup. "Ye were always clumsy and loud when scrying, Bacaiche, why do ye keep thinking ye may have improved? It's far too dangerous to be calling such attention to ourselves just now. And what if a seeker happened to be focusing in on your staff and knife? They would easily overhear ye, and then where would we be? The Underground can manage without ye a few more days."

That night, when Meghan ladled out their evening meal,

the soup was even more watery and tasteless than ever. Since they had been traveling in such haste, the soup that was their staple diet consisted largely of water, salt and herbs, which Iseult found extremely dissatisfying. She had even begun to look about her as she walked for plants that might add some substance to their meal, so hungry had she become. Little grew on the moors, however, and so Iseult vented her frustration by flashing angry glances at Bacaiche as she ate, which the hunchback returned in full.

After dinner, Meghan again took out her ring and Iseult knew how very anxious she must feel, to be risking so many attempts at scrying. While Meghan sat brooding over her ring, the silence between the other two companions grew thick and heavy. They fidgeted and sulked, neither willing to be the first to speak but both finding the silence difficult. Both were used to being comfortable with silence and this tension was alien to them, and awkward.

After Iseult caught Bacaiche's yellow eyes three times in quick succession, she began to stare steadily at the wood witch instead, wondering what she was thinking. The great stone glimmered in the firelight, seeming more black than green. Every now and then the witch turned the stone, so that a different facet would catch the light. Watching the stone, Iseult felt her body grow lighter, as if she was lifting and spreading outward. She almost drew her perceptions back, but the gleam of the ring was somehow mesmerizing. Gradually her awareness of the sounds and darkness around them increased, until she could hear every rustle and croak of the night as a separate disturbance.

Then she saw thoughts, as much a thread of colored beads as a stream of words. . . . *The countryside is boiling with soldiers, there is a sense o' unease, strangers are stopped and questioned, sometimes detained for no reason, no one thought an auld, blind beggar worth more than a few kicks and jeers, I have had dreams o' broken mirrors, in the taverns all the talk is o' the Fairgean rising, they say the sea witches are all dead, the whole o' Carraig is like an abandoned house with only ghosts walking, they say no good will come o' the dragon killings, they are feared the dragons will fly and flame again, like in the auld days, the grand auld days, whose houses would it be burned and ruined, no' the Rìgh's, oh no, so far away in his blue castle, his pretty young wife who never grows aulder, no' these gaudy soldier boys, trampling the new crops and seducing our sons and daughters, canna even find a quiet spot for a wee dram . . .*

Any uile-bheistean?

As soon as she heard Meghan's mind-voice, Iseult recognized it and realized that the wood witch was talking to someone through the ring. At once she understood many of the things Meghan and Bacaiche had said earlier, about scrying through fire or water, precious stone or talisman. Inadvertently she had been eavesdropping, but Iseult was anxious to learn what she could of these strange people and what lay ahead of her, so she continued to listen in on the mind-conversation of the two witches. They did not speak, as such, but rather conveyed what they meant by a series of emotions and impressions, stray words and images that followed each other in such quick succession, that Iseult had trouble understanding.

The other witch had continued: *No magical creatures at all, strange when ye think these mountains should be thick with them, all kinds and shapes, why even on my way I saw several nisses, as cheeky and crafty as ever, a tree-changer, and a cluricaun turning tricks in an inn for stray pennies. He had heard o' the Rìgh's latest Fairy Decree, but could no' believe it would hurt him, who had lived among humans for so long, I went back there o' course but he was dead, killed by the soldiers, hung upside down from the village pole by his toes, and the villagers would no' speak to anyone, no' even a blind man begging for alms, the winter has been hard, ye ken, and the Rìgh has posted bounties, a large one for ye, my dear, though ye are no' the largest, the reward for the Cripple is truly spectacular, enough for a dowry for three daughters, or a small but comfortable house.*

Tell them ye have heard stories o' a winged man, say he will come bearing the Inheritance o' Aedan and that radiance shall again flood the land. Say times o' blood and war are here, but the winged Rìgh shall come with dragons at his shoulder and the Lodestar in his fist.

Ye seek to start a prophecy . . .

Did ye no' see this, my friend? It may be only half o' the vision but let us beg the Spinners it is the true half.

If the tale spreads too far too fast it is me the Red Guards will be hunting.

The tale must spread far and fast, my friend. If the path becomes too hot for ye, slip deeper into the mountains, search out uile-bheistean *for me, and witches too, anyone that can advance our force, for do no' forget how we almost lost the Second Fairgean War, we must have the* uile-bheistean *on our side, if they join forces and rise it is between the pincers o' a crab we will be, find for me if ye can someone who understands the omens o' the sky, why the Child with the Urn washes the sky while the Fire-Eater is still swallowing, what all these omens mean.*

I will try . . .

Clearly as if it was before her, Iseult saw a regretful image of a small but comfortable room in a cave. She heard Meghan laugh and say, *Soon ye will be home, auld friend,* and then there was silence. The ring turned in the witch's hand and flashed green fire into Iseult's eyes, dazzling her, hurting her, she felt herself tumbling back toward the ground at frightening speed, and the witch's mind-voice thundered in her head, *Did I give ye the right to spy on me?*

Color rushed to Iseult's cheeks and she cursed her pale skin for showing her emotions so clearly, as she had cursed it nearly every day of her life. She straightened her pose, however, and looked Meghan back in the eye. "It was an accident," she retorted.

"Have ye never sent out your mind before?"

"Never like that. In the past I have sometimes . . . been aware o' where the prey is hiding, and sometimes thought I've known what people were feeling . . ."

"Well, that is all right then. Ken this, though, your intrusion was clumsy and loud, so loud that if we were no' all shielded, ye could have drawn the attention o' those who seek us. Also ken I could have stopped ye at any time."

Iseult felt dizzy and frayed around the edges. The unnatural clarity of her senses had faded, and her heart was pounding. She had only ever felt a similar sensation when skimming; especially on the hunt, when blood-lust and the speed and danger of the chase took her soaring out of her body in just such a way.

Meghan had turned to Bacaiche and was now berating him. "And what about ye? Why were ye *no'* listening? This is your land that is being torn apart, why are ye sitting there scowling and fidgeting and thinking lustful thoughts, when ye should be learning what ye can? Ye are the heir!"

"What about ye, Meghan? Is it no' your inheritance as much as it is mine?"

"Indeed, it is, and like ye, it is as much my curse as my inheritance. But I am auld now, aulder than ye can imagine, and the blood runs slow in my veins. We need a rìgh, no' an auld woman. We need a rìgh or banrìgh who will unite the land as Aedan once did. Ye are the only one . . . and ye are young, and if we can keep ye alive long enough, able to breed up heirs."

"And what if I do no' want to?"

"It's no' a matter o' want, Bacaiche. The Fairgean are on the rise, the Lodestar is buried, all the witches killed or scattered, our land is facing its most difficult time ever. If Jaspar dies without issue—and all my spies tell me he is wasting away—then there is no clear heir to the throne. Ye must remember that!"

"And what if we canna find the Lodestar! Your ward has disappeared with the third part o' the Key, has she no'? Without her the Inheritance o' Aedan is lost."

"We will find Isabeau and we will find the Key," Meghan said firmly, and neither of them dared argue with her.

They traveled swiftly the next few days, pausing for no more than a few hours at a time to eat or sleep. They were in the meadows now, with little to conceal them, but Meghan preferred to take the risk of being sighted than to waste precious days' traveling time. Luckily a storm had blown in, and the rain fell so heavily that the soldiers would have had to have been very close to have seen them.

Trudging along the side of the hill, her boots squelching, wet through to the skin, Iseult wished she had never agreed to come. By the scowl on Bacaiche's face, the hunchback felt the same.

It was just on sunset on the first clear day in a week that the omen occurred. Meghan saw a hawk plunge from the sky, rising a few seconds later with a coney in its talons. She frowned. "I have such a sense o' danger," she murmured. "I feel a shadow across me—something is happening!"

Iseult lengthened her stride, gazing about her with keen

eyes, and wondering if the copse of trees ahead could be concealing a legion of soldiers. Suddenly she cried out and staggered, her hand to her head. She would have fallen if Meghan had not caught her arm and held her. As it was, her knees buckled and she slid to the ground, Meghan's arm about her back.

"My head!" Iseult put her hand to her forehead, as if feeling for blood.

"What is it? Are ye hurt?" Meghan demanded, kneeling beside her, and probing her brow with gentle fingers.

"I feel . . . like I've been hit," Iseult said faintly. "Ow! It hurts!"

"I can see no wound or bruise," Meghan answered. "Are you all right?"

"I do no' ken . . . I feel strange. My head aches."

"Can ye go on? Do ye need to rest? I wonder . . . I have a feeling . . . I think we should keep on moving, if ye can, Iseult. Let us move quickly! I'm afraid something may have happened to Isabeau."

Unable to prevent resentment from choking her, Iseult stumbled to her feet and kept on walking, her hand to her head, which throbbed with invisible pain.

They reached the long meadow above the Pass just before dawn, and paused in the edge of the forest to examine the lay of the land. Although she was pale under the faded tam-o'-shanter, Iseult sat down with her usual grace.

Meghan's lips tightened as they looked down on another encampment of Red Guards, the flags on the peaks of their tents fluttering in the dawn breeze.

"How many o' these blasted soldiers does she have?" Bacaiche scowled. "She must have conscripted every able-bodied man in the land!"

"The dragons wiped out a full legion o' three hundred at Dragonclaw, and we saw signs o' more on our way down. These must be fresh troops," Meghan mused.

"How are we to get round them?" Bacaiche asked. "They've camped right at the mouth o' the Pass, and there's no other way through."

All three lay on the ground and watched the camp begin to wake, Bacaiche and Meghan arguing about the best course of action. After a moment Iseult rolled her eyes and slipped away, knowing they would argue all morning if she let them. She slid down the hill on her stomach and approached the camp cautiously from the rear. It was easy to see the Redcloaks were not used to fighting wars. No guard was set, and the tents had been set up haphazardly, with little regard for security, so Iseult's task was easy. Within ten minutes she had found what she was looking for and was slithering back up the hillside, taking her time so as not to overexert her tired sore body. By the time she reached the lookout, the whole camp was astir, fires being lit, horses fed, and breakfast cooked.

"She probably got frightened at her first sight o' soldiers and ran away," Bacaiche was saying sourly.

"I do no' think so," Meghan said, and Iseult was pleased to see her face was creased with concern.

She slipped into place beside Meghan and was warmed even more to see the witch's face relax in relief. "I have uniforms," Iseult said, and dropped her armload of red jackets, cloaks and white breeches, the cavalry uniform of the Banrìgh's Guards.

"Where did ye get those?" Bacaiche asked, flabbergasted.

"From the back o' a tent." Iseult sounded as though the answer was obvious. "The only way we can get through their lines is if we camouflage ourselves. They're obviously a collection o' raw recruits from the way they're milling around down there. I would say no one kens anybody else, so ye and I should be able to conceal ourselves without too much trouble. Meghan, I dinna think there is any way ye could be disguised as a common soldier, particularly no' with all that hair. So we have two choices—ye can either try and talk your way through as ye are, which I think may be risky given all that ye've told me about recent events. Otherwise, we could wrap ye up in one o' these cloaks and ye could be a haughty leader. We can hang your plait down inside the cloak, see?"

"And what are we going to do when they notice all these clothes missing? They've got to belong to someone," Bacaiche said disagreeably.

"Och, no, I took these from the storemaster's tent," Iseult said gently, as if talking to a child. She passed them to Meghan who turned them over in her hands.

"They still have the seamstress's label on them," she said. "I would say they have been freshly made."

"It is no' a very well organized camp," Iseult said disapprovingly. "They are all very nervous. They seem to spend a lot o' time looking at the sky, and muttering about dragons."

"Well, that is to be expected, I suppose, if they have heard about the revenge the Circle o' Seven wreaked for the death o' their pregnant queen." Meghan considered the problem seriously, and wished that she had the power of illusion—sometimes her talents seemed so unspectacular compared to some of her former brethren. *Still, they perished and I survived,* she told herself, and thought about possible diversions.

"There is one problem that I think ye at least should have considered, Meghan," Bacaiche said in an injured voice. "Your ward here was worried about the problems o' trying to disguise *ye* as a soldier. Have ye considered the problems o' concealing these?"

And to Iseult's complete astonishment, Bacaiche sat up, tossed back the dirty cloak, and spread out a great pair of black wings. As long as his body, they gleamed in the dappled sunlight, rising high above his head.

"Bacaiche! What if someone saw! Hide yourself," the wood witch snapped.

Bacaiche folded back his wings. Even then, he looked magnificent; suddenly the burly shoulders and thick neck seemed perfectly in proportion, the haughty expression inevitable. He stared at Iseult with a dangerous gleam in his eyes. "How do ye propose to hide my wings, Iseult o' the Snows? Or my talons?" And leaning down he stripped away the rough sacking to show taloned feet, like an eagle's claws. "I canna imagine the Banrìgh designing a uniform that would hide *my* deformities, can ye?"

Iseult could only gape at him. She could not understand how she had not noticed before. True, he had nearly always had that revolting cloak wrapped tightly around him, but still!

"Ye see our problem now, Iseult," Meghan said dryly. "Bacaiche is rather hard to conceal, particularly under close scrutiny. The Banrìgh must ken by now that the rumors are true and there is indeed a winged man roaming the countryside and causing trouble everywhere he goes."

Iseult could not find words. She gaped at Bacaiche, who folded his arms and stared right back at her.

"I had planned to take Bacaiche to a friend o' mine who can help us. However, I did no' expect the countryside to be crawling with Red Guards, nor for the stupid lad to blow his cover by returning to *Tùr na Gealaich dhà*. If we can just get to Tulachna Celeste, then I think we shall be safe, at least for a while . . ."

Her words tailed off and Iseult guessed she was worrying about the missing Is'a'beau. Her guess was confirmed when Meghan said, half to herself, "I keep getting such dreadful feelings. Isabeau is in danger, I ken it!"

Iseult turned her attention back to the camp, and began to think. "If we canna hide Bacaiche, we should no' try," she said. "When they caught ye coming up through the Pass, what did they intend to do?"

"The Grand-Seeker had caught me herself," Bacaiche said sourly. "She was going to take me back to Caeryla, turn me over to the Grand-Questioner for a while to wring out details o' the Underground, then send me, broken and bleeding, down to the Banrìgh at Dùn Gorm. Ye can be sure I did no' want to do that!" And he shuddered, the black wings rustling. Iseult found she had to avert her eyes from him if she was to think at all, so turned her eyes resolutely back to the camp.

"So if any o' the troops up above had caught ye, they too would try and take ye to Caeryla?"

"Bound hand and foot and slung from the belly o' a mule," Bacaiche grinned.

"Then that is what we will do," Iseult said, and passed Meghan the great crimson cloak and the plumed helmet she had stolen from the camp.

"What do ye mean?" Bacaiche snapped, rearing backward.

"I mean we will tie ye hand and foot and sling ye from the belly o' a mule." Iseult answered. "Can ye get us a mule, auld mother? I think we will need horses too."

"Och, I can call us horses," Meghan responded, smiling rather grimly at her new ward. "There are many herds o' wild horses in these mountains. But they will have no saddle or bridle, nor will they be shod, and I canna believe the commandant o' that camp will believe our story if we ride up on unbroken, unbridled horses."

"So what do we need? I could steal them from the camp."

"Surely they would notice?"

"No' if we had a diversion o' some kind . . ."

"The only diversion I've been able to think o' that would work is an attack by a dragon, and indeed I do no' think they would penetrate this far. I convinced them to attack the Red Guards at their very gate, but I think they would see an attack on soldiers at the Pass into Rionnagan as a declaration o' war, and I just canna see the mother-dragon sanctifying that."

"But if we can make them think the dragons are on the way . . ."

"What are ye talking about?" Bacaiche demanded, and huddled back into his cloak.

"Getting through the Pass, o' course," Iseult responded, making no attempt to disguise her impatience. "Meghan, can ye call up the diversion? Including horses? I'll go down and steal us some . . . what did ye call them? Bridles? You'd better tell me what they look like and where I'm likely to find them."

When, some time later, Iseult returned to their hiding spot in the trees, she dragged with her a wide variety of riding tack, including a gorgeously decorated saddle with a high pommel.

"Do no' tell me no one's going to miss that!" Bacaiche said.

"We need to make Meghan look like one of their commanders. That is what they use, though it's as foolish as those gaudy clothes they wear—such easy targets they make. I itch to practice my archery on them." She was looking the most alive they had ever seen her, her blue eyes sparkling, the scars sharp against her flushed cheeks. "I hope I got everything we need. I really could no' tell what was what!"

Meghan had spent the time sitting cross-legged in the shelter of a great tree, her eyes closed, sending out her thoughts to any animal she could find. She was dressed in the uniform Iseult had brought her and looked surprisingly like a seanalair of the Red Guards with her strong nose and piercing eyes, her long braid hidden beneath the helmet and cloak. Iseult dressed herself quickly in the red coat and white knee-length breeches, stowing her clothes—or rather Isabeau's clothes—away in her pack, and hoping no one would notice the shapeliness and hairlessness of her calves.

The horses came first, galloping and whinnying, their manes tossing and their hooves drumming. While Iseult and Bacaiche anxiously kept an eye on the camp in case an overvigilant sentry noticed too soon, Meghan spoke to the great stallion of the herd, who reared high over her, his hooves dangerously close to her head. The conversation seemed to go on forever, and Iseult could tell the stallion did not want any human being to cross their leg over his back, or the back of any of his herd. Meghan spoke to him gently, and let her natural charm for animals sway him. At last he cut out three old mares from his herd, and let Meghan saddle and bridle them, before leading the rest of the herd in a mad dash down the valley toward the camp.

The stampede of horses had exactly the effect Iseult had hoped. The camp was thrown into confusion as soldiers ran to get out of the way; the seanalair stamped about, shouting orders that no one listened to; some of the soldiers tried to catch the horses with rope, but were run down for their pains. Everyone was shouting and pointing back into the mountains. Quite a few watched the sky in fear, thinking—as Iseult had hoped—that it was a flight of dragons that had put the herd of wild horses into such a swelter.

The stream of animals that followed seemed to confirm their fear. Stags galloped out of the forest; flocks of birds flew overhead, squawking loudly; coneys bolted and donbeags scampered. Even a pride of elven cats showed their faces before slinking back to their holt.

"Can ye speak the language o' dragons?" Meghan asked her cousin, who was watching the effect of the animals' flight on the soldiers with glee.

He shook his head. "No, my education was interrupted quite young, if ye remember," he responded sarcastically.

"Ye can, though, can ye no', Iseult?"

"O' course."

"Good. I want ye to make a bugling sound, as loud as ye can. Dragon on the warpath—ye ken what I mean. I will try and enhance the sound, though that is no' something I've ever had much need to do. I've seen it done, though, in plays and musicals put on at the Tower, so I ken it can be done."

Iseult nodded, took a deep breath, and waited for Meghan's signal. When it came she opened her mouth and gave the most blood-curdling cry imaginable. It sounded just like the clamor the dragons had made following the mysterious spell on the night of the comet. Meghan, concentrating hard, was able to magically enhance the sound so it echoed from the hills. Immediately there was chaos. The animals that had been pretending to run in terror immediately began to in earnest, and the screeches of the birds, the terrified whinnying of the horses and the hoarse bellowing of the stag could not have been bettered. Down in the camp the horses were rearing and bucking, trying to escape, while soldiers milled about in a state of panic.

They galloped down into the camp at full pelt, whipping up the horses and glancing nervously behind them. It was only the calming presence of Meghan that kept the three wild horses in thrall, though their rearing and bucking and the wild rolling of their eyes seemed added proof that dragons were in the area.

"The dragons!" Iseult shouted in as deep a voice as she could, hoping she sounded convincing. "They've wiped out our entire legion!"

In a moment she was surrounded by a mob of soldiers, grasping the bridle of her mount and bombarding her with questions. Bacaiche, much to his angry disgust, had been bound to one of the horses by Iseult, who had taken some pleasure in ensuring the ropes were authentically tight. Iseult continued to babble about dragons and was gratified to see the many fearful glances cast back in the direction of Dragonclaw. No one seemed to notice the mismatched tackle or that the horses were unshod.

"We need to get through to Caeryla!" Meghan commanded. "The Grand-Seeker must be informed o' the latest developments, and we have a very important prisoner for her. Prepare yourselves to move north—ye are the last legion left in the Sithiche Mountains. Ye must mobilize to attack the dragons!"

For a moment it seemed their trick was going to work, for the soldiers stood back to let them through, while others went running to get the camp on the move. However, the seanalair had not been idle and he came striding up immediately, saluting Meghan with a fist to his heart and then to his forehead. "Seanalair MacGrannd at your service!"

"Seanalair Collene at yours!" Meghan responded, and Iseult hoped she had said the right thing.

"What is all this talk o' dragons?" he frowned. "Come to my tent and make a report."

"No time, Seanalair MacGrannd," Meghan answered, impressing Iseult with the timbre and resonance of her voice. Obviously the wood witch could mimic the sounds of other humans as well as those of animals. "The dragons struck our camp just on dawn two days ago. The Grand-Seanalair sent us to get reinforcements, and to take the prisoner to Caeryla. I fear the dragons are on our trail."

Iseult felt the soldiers stir all around her, and wished Meghan had not insisted that she hide most of her weapons in the pack strapped to the horse's saddle. She felt uneasy and vulnerable without them.

"I doubt very much that the dragons would come this far south," Seanalair MacGrannd said, and Iseult's heart sank. "I want to hear your full report afore ye go through the Pass. We were given strict instructions to allow no one through."

"And we were given strict instructions to get this prisoner to Caeryla as soon as possible!" Meghan snapped.

"I am seanalair o' the legion, and I command ye to dismount and give me your report!"

Meghan sat very straight on the back of the restive mare, her red cloak stirring in the breeze. Iseult got a brief glimpse of the end of her plait trailing below the hem of the cloak, and hoped no one else had noticed. "Very well, if ye insist, Seanalair MacGrannd, but may I tell the Grand-Seeker Glynelda that our delay was at your instigation?"

Seanalair MacGrannd fell back a step, dismay clear on his face. "The Grand-Seeker demands your presence?"

"Indeed! We have here an *uile-bheist* that she is very anxious to have put to the Question. Any delay will displease her greatly."

The seanalair looked at Bacaiche, bound tightly to the saddle, his mouth gagged. "He does no' look like a *uile-bheist* to me?"

Meghan nodded wearily at Iseult. "Show him."

Iseult dragged back the cloak to show the great wings, now strapped tightly at Bacaiche's side, and the taloned feet. Bacaiche took a swipe at the seanalair with one claw, and shrieked through his gag. The leader of the legion leaped back, surprise all over his face. "What is he? I never seen the like!"

"Nor have any o' us!" Meghan responded. "Now, I must be on my way. The Grand-Seeker was very anxious indeed to examine him!"

"I can imagine," the seanalair said, and waved them through. As they galloped down the path that led between the great cliffs and so to Rionnagan, Iseult could hear him shouting as he ordered the camp to be struck and the soldiers to march north. None of them looked very happy about it.

"If we're lucky we may cause a rebellion as well," Meghan said, and she was laughing. "Well done, Iseult, that plan worked like a dream!"

Resting a few miles on, sheltered behind a great clump of graygorse, Meghan and Bacaiche argued long and hard about what to do with the uniforms. The horses had been let go on the other side of the Pass, as Meghan had promised the stallion of the herd. They would make their way back that night, under the cover of darkness. The saddles and bridles were thrown into the ravine, disappearing under the foaming waters of the Rhyllster. Bacaiche thought they should stay in disguise, arguing that the local peasants would be in much greater awe of them, and so more likely to replenish their supplies and not give them trouble. Meghan disagreed. She thought it would not take long before the Grand-Seeker heard of their trick, and so would know Meghan and Bacaiche were within reach of her. Both were considered such great enemies of the Banrìgh that she would be itching to bring them in. There was also the danger of running into another legion of Red Guards, and their seanalair may not be as easily tricked as MacGrannd. She thought they should try to keep quiet as possible, staying under cover and slowly heading toward Tulachna Celeste.

While they argued Iseult said nothing, just polished her weapons and strapped them lovingly to her belt again. Meghan turned to her. "What do ye think, Iseult?"

The girl shrugged. "Never use the same trick twice."

Meghan stared at her wonderingly, then nodded. "True," she said. "What do ye suggest?"

"Dispose o' the uniforms. If we are caught with them, it will be proof o' wrong-doing. I can always find more if we need them. Travel at night. If we need supplies and canna find our own, only one o' us should go into a village at a time, for they will be looking for a group o' three now. Stay on high ground, and keep an escape route in mind. Without knowing the lay o' the land, I canna suggest any more."

"What are ye, some kind o' Berhtilde?" Bacaiche sneered. Iseult did not understand what he meant, but stared back at him expressionlessly till he looked away.

"She certainly seems to ken warfare," Meghan said, and her voice was both admiring and concerned.

"I am a Scarred Warrior," Iseult said proudly.

In comparison to the mountains, the highlands of Rionnagan were easy to traverse, with their wide, empty moors that stretched away under gray skies. Their supplies were down to nothing after the hard journeying through the mountains, and so Meghan decided to find a village where she could trade for oats, flour, curds, fresh vegetables and other essentials. Wanting to avoid the larger villages she followed the high crest of the hill away from the river, so they were heading as much east as south, toward the rising sun.

The air was filled with the fresh scent of the green-gray grasses and the trill of bird song. Bacaiche lifted up his voice and sang with the birds, and Iseult listened entranced. On the Spine of the World, birds were rare and those that survived the snow blizzards and the bitter cold had only rough cawing voices, which sounded desolate and cruel. The melodious lilting of Bacaiche's voice brought a most unaccustomed lump into her throat.

Soon they saw the dark smear of smoke against the sky and their pace unconsciously quickened. Iseult looked at

Meghan and saw the donbeag now rode on her shoulder, clinging to the witch's long plait with one paw, and patting her cheek with the other. "Ye and Bacaiche had better find a holt, my dear, and I'll go down and see what I can find," the witch said, and tension was evident in her voice.

"I shall go with ye," Iseult said. "It may be dangerous."

"All the more reason for ye to stay."

"I am the Scarred Warrior. I shall guard ye."

"I would rather ye stayed and guarded Bacaiche."

"I do no' need some slip o' a lass to guard me!" Bacaiche retorted angrily.

Iseult looked at Meghan and said, "I shall come with ye."

Meghan hesitated for a moment, then nodded reluctantly. "Very well, but ye must keep quiet and do exactly what I tell ye."

"Aye, auld mother," Iseult replied meekly.

Together they walked down the long green slope and toward the village, Iseult keeping several paces behind the sorceress. It did not take them long to realize the plume of black smoke came from the burned-out remains of a cottage nestled in a copse of trees some distance away from the village. A crowd of villagers was gathered outside the cottage, looking mournfully at the smoking ruins. A pedlar in a rickety old cart had drawn up at the fringe of the crowd, and the locals were explaining the situation to him vociferously.

"She did be the best skeelie in these here parts," said one thin, old woman with gray braids wrapped around her head. "Eà damn those red-coated soldiers! Why could they no' hang some other village's skeelie!" When the other villagers shushed her rather nervously, she shook her round gray head and muttered bitterly, "Wha' is the island coming to?"

Taller than most of the crowd, Iseult was able to see over their heads to the dangling body of an old woman who had been hanged from the lintel of her own gate. As small as she was, it took some careful maneuvering on Meghan's part before she found a good vantage position. As soon as she saw the dead woman, an expression of sorrow crossed her face, puzzling Iseult yet again.

"So wha' brought the Red Guards to this Truth-forsaken

corner o' the world?" the pedlar asked, and a chorus of voices answered him.

"They were after a horse thief as stole the Grand-Seeker's own horse!"

"Some red-haired lassie . . ."

"They said she be a witch," a worn-faced woman said, her hand to her swollen belly.

"Och, aye, I heard aboot that!" the pedlar exclaimed.

"The Grand-Seeker were in a true *fiadhaich*! Swore she'd track the witch down hersel'!"

"She had no' need to murder our skeelie," the woman with the gray braids said.

"They said Skeelie Manissia helped the witch escape the soldiers," one man said with uneasy authority, fingering the chain of office around his neck. "That is why they hanged her."

"They had no call to hang our skeelie who has bided in these parts for all o' her life, and her ma and granddam too. Wha' shall we do without a skeelie? Manissia was one o' the best, and now we have no one to serve us."

The village mayor looked uneasy. "The Grand-Seeker said Manissia had employed witchcraft to help the red-haired witch escape. The penalty for witchcraft is death, as ye all ken."

"And wha' if Manissia had a few witch tricks up her sleeve!" the woman retorted, her cheeks red with fury. "She served us and our village faithfully all her life. Why, she even brought ye into the world, Jock MacCharles, for all the good tha' did her!"

The exchange had been so heated no one had notice Meghan and Iseult at the fringe of the crowd. However, at the woman's scathing words the mayor looked about uneasily, and his gaze fell upon Iseult's head of short, red-gold curls, just beginning to peek out from beneath her tam-o'-shanter.

"There she is!" he cried. "It's the red-haired witch, returned to the scene o' her crimes! Catch her!"

Everyone turned and stared, and Iseult dropped automatically into her fighting crouch, her hand flying to her weapons' belt. Meghan was quicker, however. In a cracked, querulous voice she cried out, "Och, no, guid sir, that do be my granddaughter. There mun be some mistake."

"It do be the same lass," one of the middle-aged women cried. "Though she has cut off all her hair."

"No, indeed, it canna be the same lassie," the pedlar interrupted. "For as I drove oot this morning I heard the red-haired witch had been caught riding into Caeryla. Can ye believe it? Rides the Grand-Seeker's own horse into Caeryla, bold as brass. I did hear she was to be put to trial by Lady Glynelda hersel'."

"They mun have caught the wrong lass!" the mayor exclaimed. "For this is the lassie that stayed with Manissia. I saw her ride through Quotil myself."

"It mun be an uncanny likeness," Meghan frowned. "For Mari has been by my side for the past six weeks and we have never been in Quotil afore."

The crowd dissolved into argument, the mayor shouting at some of the crofters to grab Iseult, but Meghan standing her ground and swaying the crowd by pure force of character.

"She be my granddaughter," she said in her cracked voice.

"She be her granddaughter," someone in the crowd repeated obediently.

"She is no' the witch ye seek."

"She is no' the witch we seek."

"The witch ye seek has been captured."

"The witch we seek has been captured." By now the whole crowd, including the mayor with his fat red face, was repeating Meghan's words with glazed expressions on their faces.

"Ye shall let us pass now."

The crowd parted without a murmur and, vastly impressed, Iseult trotted along behind the sorceress's small figure. Casting a quick glance back at the crowd, she saw the eyes of the pedlar in his rickety cart lingered on them, and she hastened her step, anxious to be out of sight. As soon as they had rounded the curve of the hill, Meghan lost her querulous voice and bent figure, and strode along upright once more.

"That crowd is used to coercion," she mused. "I would say Skeelie Manissia, Eà guard her soul, has had that village wrapped around her finger for years. If she had tried that trick on the Grand-Seeker, though, I am no' surprised she was hanged. Such bonny tricks will no' deceive a seeker."

They reached the camp where Bacaiche lay hidden soon before sunset, but Meghan did not give them a chance to eat or sleep. "Isabeau has been here," she told Bacaiche curtly. "A skeelie helped her escape, but was hanged by the Awl for her trouble. That is her cottage burning. The villagers say nothing o' ye, which makes me think your capture was no' public knowledge. All they said was a red-haired witch had stolen the Grand-Seeker's horse. I canna believe Isabeau was so stupid!"

Bacaiche opened his mouth to say something but Meghan rounded on him. "Ye should be grateful to Isabeau! If she had no' rescued ye, it would be on the way to the Banrìgh that you'd be. Now she is captured and in trouble, and she has no' your experience. She's rarely been out o' the valley. I am so angry with ye, Bacaiche; ye ken she had put herself in danger for ye, and ye abandoned her to the Awl!"

"I dinna want to be saddled with a pesky lass! I dinna ken who she was!"

"What will they do to her if they catch her? Beat and torture her, rape her, most like, for she's a bonny lass! Then it'll be a hanging like that poor auld skeelie back there, or worse, the fire. Fine way to treat the lass who rescued ye!"

Bacaiche said nothing, just looked as stubborn and sullen as Iseult had ever seen him. Meghan was not finished, though. She pinned him with her eyes and said contemptuously, "Ye say ye want to win the Lodestar, Bacaiche. When the time comes ye must be ready and able to wield it. The Lodestar requires greatness o' heart and spirit. Do ye really think ye could wield it now?"

Bacaiche swallowed his words, turned on his heel and marched on.

They were eating as they walked, Meghan too ridden with anxiety to let them stop, when Iseult suddenly screamed and fell to the ground. She cried out again, as Meghan hurriedly dropped to her side. "What is it? Are you in pain?"

"My arms, my legs, I feel like I'm being torn apart!" Iseult cried and rubbed at her shoulders and hips.

"By the Centaur, what's wrong with the lass? She'll bring

the soldiers down on us if she screams like that," Bacaiche said uneasily.

Meghan pulled a tub of ointment from her pack and began rubbing it vigorously into Iseult's joints. "I do no' ken. Rheumatism o' some kind? There does no' seem to be much inflammation . . ."

Suddenly Iseult sat bolt upright, moaning with pain, clutching her left hand in her right. "Oh, gods!" she cried. "My hand!" She rocked back and forth in pain, then suddenly fell sideways into a faint.

White-cheeked, Meghan chafed her hands between her fingers, calling her name. "It must be Isabeau!" she cried. "Iseult must be linked with her somehow. I canna think what else could be wrong, and indeed I've been feeling most unsettled in my mind about her. Quickly, Bacaiche, we must be going. Can ye carry Iseult? Oh, Eà, please, let Isabeau be safe."

When Iseult finally came to her senses, Bacaiche was staggering along under her weight, swearing viciously. "Put me down," she said. "Please."

"Och, ye've decided to wake up, have ye? About bloody time! I've just about broken my back heaving ye along!"

He dropped Iseult to the ground, but her legs gave way beneath her and she hit the earth with a thud. She felt sick and dazed, and her whole body ached, particularly her throbbing hand. She examined it carefully but it looked the same as ever and all her fingers opened and shut as usual.

Meghan came and helped her to her feet, shooting her cousin a furious glance. "How do ye feel?" she asked. "Can ye walk?"

"Aye," Iseult said, though she was not at all sure that she could. Tears welled to her eyes, and she lowered her head so none would see. After a few deep breaths they subsided, and with an effort of will, Iseult climbed to her feet.

"Here, drink some o' this. It'll make ye feel much better," the old witch said, and gave Iseult some of her healing *mithuan,* which Iseult gulped down gladly.

"Let me lean on something," she said faintly, and Meghan passed over her tall staff, carved intricately with the shapes of vines and flowers. Soon the dizziness subsided and Iseult was able to walk more easily, though occasionally she looked down at her hand and flexed her fingers as if surprised to find them still there.

As the sun dipped below the horizon, Iseult stumbled and fell again, a wave of blackness crashing over her. When she at last regained consciousness, she was unable to stop the tears that flowed down her cheeks. "What's wrong? What is happening to me?"

"I think you are experiencing whatever has happened to Isabeau," Meghan said, stroking the damp red-gold curls off her forehead. "Come, lie still for a moment. Tell me, have ye ever before experienced pain or dizziness that had no cause that ye could see?"

"A few years ago, I felt sharp pain in my ankle that kept me limping around for a day or two, although I had no' injured myself in any way." Iseult lay still, enjoying the comfort of the old witch's hand on her brow.

"Isabeau broke her ankle a few years ago, jumping off a branch trying to fly," Meghan said thoughtfully. She frowned, and searched the swiftly encroaching darkness as if willing it to reveal to her what was happening to Iseult's twin. "Isabeau is in dreadful trouble," she murmured. "I can feel it. Iseult, I'm sorry, but we must go on. Can ye manage?"

"I am a Scarred Warrior," Iseult replied coldly. "O' course I can go on."

Although they had rested little in the past few days, the old witch set a pace that both Iseult and Bacaiche had trouble matching. All night they marched on through the darkness, and as Iseult stumbled forward in a daze, she glanced at Meghan's tiny upright figure and marveled at the old woman. For days she had thought her just a frail old woman, so gnarled and bent she looked as if a touch must crumble her to dust. She had been affronted by her gruffness, puzzled by her weeping over dead animals, made uneasy by her talk of twins and power and prophecies. As each day passed, though, she had discovered hidden strengths in the old woman. She was surprised to find the ceremonial respect a wise old woman should be accorded give way to a more sincere affection. She was not an Auld Mother like the ones Iseult knew, but more like her own grandmother, mysterious and powerful, commanding by strength of will rather than strength of body. Iseult decided Meghan was another Firemaker, and therefore rare and precious. She needed to be protected and served, and Iseult was the only one capable of doing so. Such was the duty and privilege of a Scarred Warrior.

JORGE THE BLIND SEER

Jorge lay back in the rough hay and made plans. He had abandoned his discreet course and had instead headed toward the villages and towns. The thick forests that skirted the Sithiche Mountains had given way to long, falling vistas of green hills, gleaming here and there with thin threads of water. To the west the Whitelock Mountains reared snow-tipped needles of stone against the sky, the two ranges meeting at a tall, perfectly symmetrical mountain called the Fang, the highest mountain on Eileanan. Its point was wreathed in clouds most days, but there were many stories of how the Fang sometimes spat fire and smoke into the heavens.

The road Jorge was following wound between lush orchards and meadows where black-faced sheep and shaggy goats grazed. The fruit trees were all in blossom and, although Jorge could not see their ethereal colors, the air smelled delicious and he breathed deeply of the good air as he walked, giving thanks to Eà for the new season. He took his time, stopping to chat with the shepherd boys in the meadows and the crofters tending their patches of tilled soil, and begging for food at nearly every farmhouse he passed. To everyone he met, he muttered his rumors and prophecies, and was surprised at the reaction he received.

It seemed the story of the Winged Man was well known in these parts, the stories brought by pedlars, jongleurs and boatmen from the south. Tales of his exploits had spread: the Winged Man was the real leader of the infamous underground movement, the Cripple just his lieutenant. His band was composed of both fairy and human, including many witches who had escaped the persecutions; the Winged Man was himself a witch, and could perform great acts of magic.

The people of Rionnagan were not like the stodgy crofters of Blèssem or the Berhtildes, the grim maiden warriors of Tìrsoilleir with their mutilations and sacrifices. Magic was bred in their bones and steeped in their blood. Rionnagan was home to the great MacCuinn clan and the ancient headquarters for the Keybearer, and so Rionnagans had never adjusted easily to the destruction of the Towers. Tales of a winged warrior gladdened their hearts, and they had happily fed and housed the old man who came bearing more tales of the hero's exploits.

Jesyah flew down, the wind of his passing stirring Jorge's hair. He gave an exultant caw that spoke of refuse and rubbish. A village was ahead, with a busy marketplace—heaven for a hungry bird. Jorge sighed and hauled himself to his feet. The raven could not understand Jorge's aversion to begging or rooting through old scraps. He did not understand that Jorge had never grown accustomed to his abrupt change in status. The great seer and sorcerer was now merely a wandering beggar, his only home a drafty cave.

The warlock heard the market first, a babble of rough voices, gossiping and shouting out wares. Then he smelled it—manure and sweat and blood and the fresh earthy scent of vegetables and the bright smell of corn. Jesyah hopped along in the mud before him, then flew up to a rooftop as Jorge felt his way forward with his staff. He called out his beggar's wail, rattling his bowl before him, following the sound of kind voices and avoiding the kick or jeer of the unkind while he scanned the crowd with his witch sense. This village was the last before the steep ridge of the Whitelock Mountains, almost lost in the beginnings of the forest. There should have been many kinds here, but though he saw signs of halfbreeds, he could tell from their smell that they lived in anxiety in case it should be discovered. There were no fairies here, no *uile-bheistean*. Here and there, though, he caught quicksilver glimpses of something else, something which made his blood quicken in excitement. There was a great Talent here, he was sure of it, the thrum of power like mercury in his nostrils.

He thrust his shaggy white head forward, stumbling through the crowd, trying to catch the source of the power. By its quickness and mobility, it could have been a will o'wisp or even a nisse. But the magic did not seem like that of any of the lesser fairies. It was distinctly human, although with traces of fairy in the mix.

Just as he thought he had located the source of the magic, it rushed toward him with a scamper of feet and a boy's giggle, and two boys cannoned into him, knocking him over.

A young woman scolded the boys and helped him to his feet, brushing the mud off his tattered clothes and beard. "I be sorry, the boys do make such mischief."

The boys scrambled to their feet, laughing and punching at each other. Jorge moved his head helplessly, trying to understand the thwack he heard. The boy with the magic drew himself up and said wonderingly, "Mam, he be blind. The puir auld man is blind. Och, should I no' . . . ?"

"No, no, come away, lad," the woman said hastily, and grabbed him by the arm. She apologized to Jorge again, and dragged the boy away. Jorge heard him say, "But Mam—"

Jorge gave himself over to begging for food scraps and coins, of which he received surprisingly many of the first and none of the latter. Generous but poor, he noted, and sidled round the edges, spreading his rumors and muttering his prophecies.

One young woman bent and whispered in his ear, "Hush, auld man, there be soldiers in the village, looking for *uilebheistean*. They will think ye a witch."

Jorge heeded the warning, for he was keen to seek out the young boy again, and if the Red Guards caused trouble, he would have no chance. Once the market was packing up and the air growing chill, Jorge tottered forward, asking the raven if he had noted where the lad had gone, as asked. Unnoticed by the crowd, Jesyah had followed the child and his mother back to a house outside the village, and he took Jorge there now, slipping silently through the gray fields.

Jorge cast out his mind and caught the panicked thoughts of the mother as she scolded the boy. *Ye mun no' talk about such things where anyone can hear ye, ye mun no' think ye should heal everyone who is sick or lame or blind, they will take ye away, they will hurt ye and kill ye if they ken . . .*

The word *heal* sprang out of the muddle of thoughts, and Jorge stood still in amazed hope. If the omens and dreams were true, another war was ahead of them, a fiery and bloody war. Of all Talents that would be needed in the dark days ahead, a healer was the best. And it was such a rare Talent—to heal with the laying of hands rather than knowledge of herbs and minerals, medicines and poultices. For how else could a young boy heal? He must have the touch . . .

His knees were trembling as he went up to the front door, and he had to lean on his staff as he knocked softly. There was a startled scuffle inside, and then a long pause. Jesyah fluttered down to his shoulder as the front door opened.

"Mercy me, if it is no' the blind beggar!" the woman exclaimed, and Jorge felt warmth flow over him as she pushed the door further open. "Come inside, then, for it'll do none o' us any good if the Red Guards see ye here and come for a look."

She took him in, settled him by the fire and fed him soup with Jorge hardly saying a word. She did not seem to notice the raven perched on his shoulder or the filth of his rags. Jorge was touched by her simple generosity. When he had finished eating, he looked up and said softly, "I have come about the lad." He felt the woman stiffen. "I ken he has power, I can see it."

"Ye are but a blind auld beggar, what can ye see?" she cried furiously.

"I see what your eyes canna," Jorge said gently. "Do no' ask me what I see for then I am compelled to tell ye, and ye may no' want to hear what I shall say."

He heard her sit down heavily, and then felt his hand taken between hers. Her palms were rough and callused. "What should I do? What should I do?" she murmured.

"Ye must leave the lad in my care."

She said faintly, "But why? I've kept him safe enough till now."

"The Rìgh has sent out seekers to find anyone or anything with magical powers. Your bairn blazes like a torch.

If seekers pass through this valley, they will find him, have no doubt about that."

She moaned a little, and her fingers moved uneasily over his. "What can *ye* do, though?"

"I can shield him and, if need be, I can protect him."

"Ye be a witch."

"I am what I am, my dear. Rest assured no harm will come to the lad if I can do anything to prevent it. He will be safer with me than here."

"No, how can ye say so? He should be with his mam. Who can protect him better than me?"

"What will ye do when the Red Guards come? How will ye stop them?"

"This village looks after its own."

"The village would be burned to the ground, and any who raised their hands to the Guards hanged."

"We could hide him."

"Ye do no' understand. I am blind, yet I could follow your son's path as he ran through the market, I could follow ye here. If I can, so can others." As he said the words he felt the woman slump and knew he had won. He wondered if it compromised his oath of truth-telling not to mention his second sight was exceptionally clear, and could see many things others could not, even the Seekers of the Awl, few of whom had any profound Talent.

Just then a door banged open, letting in a blast of cold air. The child ran into the room, his radiance spreading before him. Jorge took a deep breath, and gripped his staff.

The boy saw him and skidded to a stop. "Look, Mam, the auld blind man is here. Has he come for me to touch him?"

Jorge scrabbled back in sudden alarm as the child advanced toward him, holding his palms out as if to lay them on the old man's head. To Jorge, the child's hands seemed to blaze with incandescent power, and he knew that if the child touched him, his eyes would be healed. Jesyah rose screeching into the rafters, and Jorge scrambled away over the bench, knocking over the fire stand so that pokers and brushes crashed into the hearth.

The woman took his shoulders. "It is all right, auld man, it is true. He can heal ye, though how such a thing could be I canna understand."

"No, no, he must no' touch me," and Jorge bolted away again as the child advanced on him, his hands held out.

"But ye are blind, I can make ye see, truly I can," the boy said, trotting after him. His hand caught the edge of Jorge's plaid, and the seer felt a moment of pure panic. Jesyah dropped down from the rafters like a black lightning bolt, and the boy screamed, dropping to the ground and covering his head with his arms.

"I be blind for a purpose," Jorge panted, scrambling over the table and knocking his hip painfully.

Jesyah fluttered back to the rafters, and both the woman and her son regained their feet, though still nervous of the raven. He could sense their doubtful glances, and the boy said, rather sadly, "Ye do no' want to be healed?"

"No, lad. I can see things with my blind eyes that I would miss if my everyday sight returned. I have been blind for far longer than ye have been alive, or even your mother for that matter. I am content to stay blind."

The boy sat down on the bench, and said happily, "All right then, I will no' touch ye."

"Does he try and touch anyone who is sick or maimed?" Jorge asked.

The young woman nodded, then realizing the seer could not see, answered in a subdued voice, "Aye, my laird."

"I am no laird, just a blind beggar who needs a strong lad to help me find my way."

"Och, I can! Can I, Mam?"

"Ye want to go away from me?"

"Only for a wee while, Ma. Besides, I told ye. I have had dreams o' war, and ye ken I shall be needed."

Jorge felt his mouth drop open, and sensed the rueful glance the woman sent him. "Ye do no' ken what it is ye want, old man," she said. "Tòmas is no ordinary lad. Ye shall have trouble keeping him safe."

"How auld are ye?"

"I am eight," Tòmas said with perfect composure. "Well, almost!"

"Would ye fain accompany me on my travels?"

"Will I have to beg?"

"No' if ye do no' want to, though I have found it an excellent way o' gaining vital information. People ignore a beggar, ye see."

"People never ignore me."

"Well, we shall have to teach ye how to be ignored, my lad, for attention is the one thing we do no' want."

"So ye are really going to take him?" his mother said, and her voice was an odd mixture of anger, sorrow, regret and relief. "Can I no' come too?"

Jorge shook his head. "I be sorry, but three is a crowd, and it is difficult for a crowd to slip through the lines o' Red Guards without being noticed."

"Wha' are ye going to do with him?"

"I am going to take him back to my home in the Whitelock Mountains, and I am going to teach him how to control and conceal his Talent. He shall be my apprentice and my helper. Then, when the time comes, we shall put him to work. For your laddie is right, a war is coming, and the omens are no' good. We live in dangerous times, my dear, and a healer is a rare and precious commodity. Ye need no' fear I will let any harm come to him."

"Are witches going to come back then?" the boy asked in his high, piping voice.

"If Eà permits," the blind seer answered.

Isabeau the Captive

Isabeau woke in a red haze of pain, moaning a little as the dark silence gradually peeled away. She could hear deep, rough voices exclaiming in consternation and fear, and in numb incomprehension, lay and listened to them.

"The Grand-Seeker shall have our heads!"

"Call the castle guards! Tell them the witch has killed the Grand-Questioner."

"Find someone to carry the body away. Do no' step in the bluid, ye fool!"

Isabeau whimpered, and turned her head away from the light that was stabbing her eyes with brightness.

"The witch is coming round." There was fear in the rough voice. "Should I knock her out again?"

"Nay, leave her be; they'll want her conscious for the trial. Leave her chains on, though."

"If she could kill the Grand-Questioner chained up like that, why did she no' escape?"

"Probably heard us coming," the other soldier replied, and then exclaimed, "O' course! That's what we can tell the Grand-Seeker. The foul witch would have escaped if we had no' heard something suspicious and come to investigate."

"I dinna hear anything."

"Fine, ye can tell her that if ye want. I heard a noise, though, and came running, in time to stop the witch from escaping again but too late to save the Grand-Questioner."

"She mun be powerful indeed, to kill Baron Yutta." Again there was apprehension in the soldier's voice.

His companion spat noisily on the floor. "Sooner we fed her to the *uile-bheist* o' the loch, the better as far as I'm concerned. Shame, though, she was a bonny lass."

"No' so bonny now."

"Och, I wouldna touch a witch, no matter how bonny. Happen my crown jewels would shrivel up and fall off and then where would I be?"

Isabeau was passing in and out of darkness, a strange roaring in her ears. The soldiers' coarse laughter came in undulating waves, sounding bizarre and demonic. She tried to curl up, and found herself unable to move, cold iron at her wrists and ankles.

"She's moving." The light came closer so she moaned and turned her head from side to side. "He made a bloody mess o' her hand. Take a look."

"Death to all witches," the other said piously.

"She's only a lass. Canna be much aulder than my sister, who's only fifteen. In Truth, that must hurt! Nasty." He released the vise, and as blood rushed through to her mangled fingers, Isabeau screamed and fainted again.

When she drifted back into consciousness, Isabeau was lying on the floor, a blanket thrown over her. She shifted a little, glad to find she could move, and huddled into the coarse material, bitter cold striking up against her naked flesh. For a moment she could not remember what had happened but then she saw a cloak-shrouded figure on the floor and the memories came flooding back. She wished they had not. When she tried to curl up against the memories, all her body screamed in protest and she gave a faint sob.

"Quiet, witch," Blyn's gruff voice said. "Do no' move or speak, else I shall knock ye unconscious again. Your trial has been brought forward, for ye are far too dangerous to be allowed to live another night."

Isabeau was so dazed and in so much pain that she could make little sense of what the hooded guard was saying. All she wanted was to sleep again, and she closed her eyes with a sigh. She heard feet tramping about her, and more voices, then there was silence. She must have slept a little, for next thing she knew she was jerked awake by the acrid stench of smelling-salts under her nose.

"Come, it is time for your trial. Get up."

Isabeau opened her eyes and shrank back in fear when she saw the sinister hood of the guard. "Do no' put on the bairn act with me," Blyn said. She shook her head, her blue eyes dilated with terror. He gave her something to drink, and it burned down her throat like fire. Her gaze cleared, and the weakness receded a little. Sick with trepidation, she looked down and felt her stomach convulse. Her left hand was a bloody mess, more like an otter's flipper than a hand. The fingers and thumb were all smashed near the joint, splinters protruding through the swollen and blackened flesh. Isabeau knew enough about healing to realize she would be crippled, at the very least. At worst, she would lose her hand, especially if it were not treated soon.

"We'll have to get that strapped up," Blyn said. "Canna have ye bleeding all over our laird's castle. Ben, get the leech!"

Isabeau managed to sit up, leaning against the leg of the rack. She stared with fascination at her hand. After a long wait the leech, a fussy little man with a tasseled cap on his head, came sidling in, looking with distaste at the blood-stained instruments of torture. "No need to bleed the witch, since she's going to be executed tonight anyway. I'll just get her cleaned up."

"I am no' a witch," Isabeau said clearly.

The hooded guard and the leech exchanged disbelieving looks, then she was made to drink some foul-tasting liquid that made her head spin. The leech cleaned her wounds carefully, roughly splinted her fingers, and bound the whole lot up in bandages. "That should stop the bleeding for a while," he said, packing up his bag again. "Long enough to get her through the trial, anyway. Why they bother I do no' ken, for its clear she be a witch, murdering the Grand-Questioner like that, chained and bound as she was!"

"I dinna kill the Grand-Questioner!" Isabeau said desperately. "It was an accident. The wheel just fell loose."

Again they exchanged glances over her head, then the guard said with a ponderous laugh, "Tell that one to the judges!"

Just then the door of the torture cell swung open and a contingent of Red Guards marched in. Blyn immediately stepped back and stood with his arms crossed over his massive chest.

"Can she walk?" a guard demanded, and the giant grunted in response.

They hauled her up, and after a few moments Isabeau was able to stand. "I need to wash and tidy myself," she said, staring the Red Guard in the eye. After a moment he nodded, and she was taken to the Grand-Questioner's room, where her pack still lay on the table. It was difficult to wait until he had closed the door behind her, but as soon as they were gone, she flew to it and rummaged through. Heart pounding, her fingers closed over the magic pouch and she grasped it to her breast, giving fervent thanks to Eà.

The recovery of the talisman gave her fresh life, for only the Grand-Questioner had examined her pack and he was now dead, his knowledge gone with him. If only Isabeau could manage to convince her judges of her innocence, or escape again!

With renewed hope, she went through her pack and found the little bottle of *mithuan* she carried there. By clenching the bottle between her knees, she managed to wrench the top off and drank down several mouthfuls, feeling it race through her system, bringing with it new strength and a lessening of the pain. Slowly she washed her face and as much of her body as she could reach, trying to remove the stink of Baron Yutta's touch and the filth of her night in the cell. She could not wash her hair, for that was an operation that took many hours, but she shook out the straw and lice as well as she could with only one hand, and twisted the long rope into a rough knot at the back of her head. As her wits returned, so did her memories, and she cried as she washed, the tears slow and hot and shamed.

Once she was as clean as she could make herself, she dug out a little jar of ointment that smelled strongly and burned like fire when she rubbed it on, relieving the pain in her joints greatly.

Pausing often to rest, she dressed in the gray gown that she carried in her pack and pulled the demure white cap over her hair, tucking as much of her hair as she could beneath it. She hung the pouch, laden with its precious cargo, inside her dress, next to her skin.

As she prepared herself she went over her story, searching for flaws and polishing up details until she felt certain she could lie convincingly. She had no compunction about lying, despite her vows, for she knew death was the reward for truthfulness, and Isabeau had no wish to die just yet.

She was marched out of the cell block and into the courtyard where she was hoisted into a cart drawn by a huge old carthorse. Because of the injury to her hand, the guards did not bind them, but secured her firmly to the cart with a rope around her neck. Isabeau braced her injured hand against her, as the cart rumbled out of the courtyard and into the streets of the town.

Immediately Isabeau was aware that her trial was not going to be a quiet little affair. The streets of Caeryla were lined with people, some who booed her and threw rotten fruit at her, some who looked on with anxious pity. Unable to deflect the missiles with her magic for fear of betraying herself, Isabeau endured in silence, holding her head high.

"Bluidy witch!" the crowd catcalled. "Evil sorceress."

Isabeau did her best to look like a simple country lass who did not understand what was happening to her, but inside she burned with rage, wanting to let fly with fireballs, as she had done during the battle with the Red Guards after her Test.

The carthorse strained to pull the weight of the vehicle up the steep cobbled streets to the castle, which was perched on a high crag of land overlooking the town and the misty waters of the loch. Several times Isabeau was almost thrown to the floor as the cart lurched over the stones, but she managed to retain her balance, biting her lip bloody against the pain in her hand. A young boy threw a tomato at her and caught her full on the cheek, causing the crowd to jeer, but she shook it off and stared defiantly at the people. One young man, dressed in a bright blue jerkin, looked at her with a start of recognition, and Isabeau turned to watch him as the cart rolled on, sure that she had seen him somewhere before too. The thought only increased her unease.

At last they were inside the castle walls, and the guards were pushing her into the great hall where public trials were performed. The walls were lined with curious onlookers, and on a beautifully carved seat on a dais sat a young boy, no more than seven years of age and very dark, with black hair and eyes and smooth olive skin. Isabeau curtsied to him and bowed to the judges, two men and a woman in crimson. With a chill of the blood she recognized the witch-sniffer Glynelda, and was glad that the Grand-Seeker had never really seen her. That was her only hope.

A herald stood up and made a long formal greeting to lords and ladies both, then read the charges, couched in convoluted terms. Tired and aching in every joint as she was, Isabeau could hardly understand them, and so when she was asked what she said in response, faltered. "I'm sorry, but I dinna understand wha' it is ye be saying."

The crowd murmured, laughing a little and Isabeau flushed. The Laird Serinyza leaned forward and said in a high, clear child's voice, "Ye are accused o' witchcraft."

Isabeau shrank back. "Me? Witchcraft?" She let tears well up. "But I'm naught but a country lass, my laird. I be Mari Collene, from Byllars, and my family be well known in our district for piety and lawfulness. Indeed, my da once saved our laird from drowning, and so we be allowed in the keep, to bring our goods and chattels in for bartering."

As she had hoped, the naturalness of her story had an impact on the crowd, who muttered among themselves. Once again she thanked Meghan's obsession with secrecy, which meant Isabeau's story was virtually water-tight. There was a Collene family in Byllars, a small village in the highlands, and a Collene had saved the local laird from drowning, resulting in the said privileges Isabeau had just quoted. The Collene family even had a skeelie who was always off somewhere hunting herbs and who usually had a grandchild or two about her. The family was written in the district records and there were several granddaughters named Mari, which was why Meghan had picked that name for her ward. Isabeau had been practising this story since she was a babe in arms.

One of the judges leaned down and fixed her with a stern eye. "Ye are accused o' stealing a horse by the foul practice o' witchcraft, young woman, and o' rescuing an enemy o' the state. Ye then resisted arrest and several times attempted to escape our rightful custody, again by the use o' your foul sorceries. As if these crimes are no' heinous enough, ye are also charged with the murder o' the Baron Yutta, Grand-Questioner o' the Anti-Witchcraft League. What do ye say to that?"

"I never stole no horse," Isabeau sobbed. "None o' it's true. Och, please believe me, m'laird. I've been beaten and tortured and locked up, and I've committed no wrong-doing!"

"Ye rode into Caeryla on a fine blood stallion. Do ye expect us to believe a simple country lass like yourself would own such a thing?"

"Och, no, yer lairdship. The horse is no' mine." The words caused a sensation, but Isabeau went on bravely. "But the horse did used to be my da's until he was stolen, many a long year syne."

"Are ye now accusing *me* o' stealing?" the Lady Glynelda said in tones of such ice that Isabeau began to stammer and falter in earnest.

"No, no, my lady, I would never say such a thing, no. But happen ye did buy the horse from someone who bought it from someone who did, that be all I am saying."

"Ye ken that the stallion Garlen once belonged to the Banrìgh herself, and is o' the very best stock?" the Grand-Seeker said in contemptuous tones, but Isabeau nodded eagerly.

"Och, aye, he be a fine stallion, my lady, o' the Angharar bloodline." Isabeau then rattled off the bloodlines of the horse, thankful both for the guards' conversation she had overheard, and her own excellent memory. Again she could tell she had impressed the crowd, although the judges remained skeptical. They asked her more questions about the bloodlines, hoping to trip her up, but Isabeau was very careful, and grateful for her thorough knowledge of horses. All the horses on the island were descended from those brought in the Great Crossing, since horses were not native to Eileanan, but only a few were descended from Cuinn Lionheart's six great stallions. It was from that stock that Lasair was descended, bred on the wide plains of Tìreich by the great Horse-Laird Ahearn himself.

"And how does a country girl ken this much about horses?" the witch-sniffer asked. "It is obvious she is a professional horse thief."

"I be no horse thief!" Isabeau cried angrily. "Och, I beg your pardon, my lady, but the Collene family be a respectful family and nobody has ever said such a thing o' us. No, my da is employed in the laird's stables, and we do be horse trainers and breeders for many generations." This last part was not true, the real Collenes being huntsmen, but Isabeau thought she could get away with that one. "Lasair was given to my da as a wee foal, as a boon gift for the saving o' the laird's life."

"What did ye call the stallion?" the seeker said, frowning.

"Lasair. That be his name." She told them she walked the many miles to Caeryla in order to run errands for her da, and her skeelie grandmother, until she came upon Lasair grazing untethered on the moors. Recognizing him immediately, Isabeau had called the stallion to her, and ridden it the last few miles to the town, where she had been planning to ask advice about what to do with him. Although the stallion had been stolen from her da many years ago, he had a new brand on his flank and she, Mari, had not known what the legalities were about a horse stolen years earlier.

Back and forth the questioning went, but they could cut no holes in Isabeau's story. Suddenly the seeker picked up a large paperweight and threw it at Isabeau's head. Isabeau's instinctive reaction was to deflect it with her magic but she remembered in time, and let it come. It hit her hard between the eyes and down she went, bleeding.

Immediately the court was in an uproar, and Laird Serinyza protested angrily. The seeker herself was a little disconcerted. "I'm sorry, my laird," she said. "That is a common trick to catch out a witch, who usually can deflect such things."

"I be no witch," Isabeau sobbed, trying to staunch the flow of blood with her hand. "I said I be no witch. Why ye hurt me so?"

Laird Serinyza instructed the leech to attend to her, and soon Isabeau's head was bound up and the tumult in the courtroom had died down. Isabeau made much of her injury, sobbing still and holding her head. Between her sobs, she told the court again of how she had been tortured and held up her bloodstained, bandaged hand for them to see.

The witch-sniffer reminded the court of how Isabeau had tried to escape, using her witchcraft to do so.

"I picked the lock with my hairpin!" Isabeau exclaimed, and the Grand-Seeker shot her a look of such loathing that Isabeau felt fear close her throat.

The judges began to argue in low voices. The Lady Glynelda had to admit she had not seen the thief that stole her mare, that it had been night and she had been asleep. In high-flown language she described how she had tracked them by following the traces of enchantment she had found in the air, and the physical evidence such as hoofprints and the marks of a fire where the thief had stopped. She said the thief had helped an enemy of the state escape—a foul *uile-bheist* their beloved Banrìgh was anxious to recapture, before he spread more evil. She had been bringing the *uile-bheist* back to Caeryla for judgment, and he had escaped in the night with the help of the thief who had turned all their other horses loose. It was only by commandeering the Red Guards watching the Pass that she had been able to follow them at all.

Laird Serinyza asked the Grand-Seeker whether she could smell any scent of witchcraft now, and the witch-sniffer nodded her head. Isabeau's heart sank. Hours had passed since she had last used the Power, and she had washed herself thoroughly, but evidently that was not enough.

"Och, aye, there's a smell here, for sure," the seeker said. "I can smell the stink o' it, and all the hair on my neck is bristling."

"That could be the serpent," the young laird said calmly. "I have been taught it is a magical creature, and this castle is always filled with the mists from the loch. That may be what brings the scent o' enchantment."

The witch-sniffer scowled, as if hating the idea that any magical creature be allowed to exist. Indeed, Isabeau wondered why they had not hunted it down, considering any magical creature was anathema to the Awl, but thought perhaps it was too convenient as both executioner and the town's defense.

"It is true there is always a stink on this place, my laird," said the seeker, "but this is something different. I examined the cell where the witch had been incarcerated, and there were clear traces of witchcraft, a quite different thing to the smell of a fairy-serpent. The lock stank o' it."

Isabeau's heart dropped. She wondered how it was witch-sniffers were able to smell magic so clearly. Was it a Talent? Or were they trained in some way? Surely, if it were an inherent ability, they too were witches?

The trial dragged on. The judges were now arguing about Isabeau's story, the Lady Glynelda insistent that she was lying, some of the other judges half convinced by Isabeau's story. One, in particular, stood up against the Grand-Seeker, an elderly man with ordered waves of white hair and a green velvet doublet. He said wearily, "Have we no' tired o' feeding our people to the serpent o' the loch, or sending them to Dùn Gorm to be burned? She seems a mere country lass, and surely too young to have been taught the Skills the Grand-Questioner is so sure she's been displaying. The laws o' the Truth promise that none shall be Questioned without first having been proved guilty. Yet she has been put to the rack, and given the pilliwinkes, a cruel torture for no proven crime. And we have no positive identification, no first-hand witnesses. Everything is said to be proven by the fact that she used sorcery, yet she is so young, how could she be capable of such Craft and Cunning?"

For the first time Isabeau felt hope, but she stood demurely, head lowered.

"Ye are very free with the terms o' the witches, Laird Bailey. They slide off your tongue with great familiarity and comfort." The Grand-Seeker's voice dripped with poisoned honey.

"Ye must forgive me, Lady Glynelda Grand-Seeker. I am an auld man, and sometimes the times o' my youth are clearer to me than my middle years, and so my language also. I just wish that we should be careful and canny in our judging—make sure we do not cry 'witch!' when the peculiar effects o' chance may be all that is at play."

"Chance! Indeed, I can see today is no' as clear to ye as your past, my laird, when ye think chance can have had a hand in this. Chance that my horse is stolen and this lass happens to be riding it? Chance that she escapes us again and again, although I have the best trackers in Rionnagan?

Chance that she is hidden by a village witch or that she kills Baron Yutta?"

The young laird held his hand up for silence. "Please, let us stop this bickering," he said, and immediately the judges fell silent, though they did not look too pleased to be told what to do by a seven-year-old boy, dwarfed by his huge chair. "I think I have a solution," he said. "The accused says she found the stallion loose on the moors and it recognized her, coming to her when she called. Surely if that were true, it would prove the stallion knows the accused and therefore that she is telling the truth. Why do we no' call in the stallion?"

A flood of relief broke over Isabeau, though one of the judges sneered and said, "Really, my laird, calling in a horse as a witness is ridiculous . . ." Laughter broke out here and there in the packed hall, while the murmurs of conversation rose high. Eventually, however, the young laird prevailed, and Lasair was brought in, whinnying and flailing out with sharp hooves at the man who led him. He whickered anxiously at Isabeau, who dared not reply. Laird Serinyza instructed the Grand-Seeker Glynelda to come down from the dais and stand in the square with Isabeau and she did so, her face stiff with outrage. A few of the crowd snickered and she glared round at them with anger clearly written on her face. The crowd fell silent.

Lasair was led to the center of the room, where he reared, so that the groom had to fight to retain hold on his rein. Then the groom let go, and Isabeau held out her hand and whickered, saying, "Lasair," while the Seeker called impatiently, "Garlen!"

The chestnut tossed his beautiful head, and dashed over to Isabeau, leaning against her and whickering anxiously.

Lady Glynelda was saying crossly, "In Truth, I've never called the damn horse in my life. That's what I have a groom for!", and the Lord Serinyza said, "See, the stallion does ken her," and Isabeau tried not to grin in relief. The whole room seemed to relax, and Isabeau held her breath, sure now she would be freed. The Laird was the highest authority in his holding, the highest point of law except for the Rìgh himself.

"Is there any more evidence to be brought to bear in the

charges o' horse theft, sorcery, resisting arrest and murder?" the herald said.

"Aye," the Grand-Seeker shouted, "and I think this will close the case." She held something up between two fingers and everyone in the courtroom strained forward in an attempt to see, but whatever she held appeared invisible, making the witch-sniffer seem rather ludicrous. Seeing the boy's puzzled look, Lady Glynelda got to her feet and walked over to the dark-haired laird perched on the edge of his huge chair. The young laird's face fell and Isabeau's heart with it. The Grand-Seeker smiled.

"I found this caught on a branch near where the *uile-bheist* we had captured was lying asleep," she said in tones ringing with triumph. "It proves the accused was skulking in the bushes while we made camp! We ken that witchcraft must have been used to free the *uile-bheist,* so it therefore proves that the accused is a witch!"

Isabeau strained desperately to see what it was the Grand-Seeker was holding up so triumphantly before the courts, while murmurs of, "What is it?" ran round the room like a plague. No one could see anything in the witch-sniffer's hands. "It also proves that the accursed witch enchanted and stole my stallion Garlen and the ponies o' the trackers, who hunted down the *uile-bheist* for us. To these heinous crimes are added the wicked and abominable murder o' the Grand-Questioner o' the great Awl, also by the foul practice o' sorcery!"

Only then did she walk over to Isabeau and show her what she held in her hand—a long thread of bright red hair. Then she yanked Isabeau's tam o'shanter off, pulling on her hair so hard that Isabeau fell to her knees with a scream of pain. With great ostentation, the seeker compared the strand to Isabeau's ruddy tresses. "Of these charges the accused is proven guilty!"

Isabeau tried to wrench her hair free, but the seeker tightened her grip so Isabeau thought she'd pull her hair out by the roots. "Look at the length o' this hair! I would wager my entire year's salary that these luscious locks have never been touched by scissors. This girl is a witch! No' a doubt! And she freed that *uile-bheist* we hunted down in the mountains, and she killed the Grand-Questioner when he tried to discover the nature o' her witchcraft. I say drown her! Feed her to the *loch-serpent*!"

As the crowd began to chant "Drown her! drown her!", Isabeau kicked the Grand-Seeker sharply in the stomach, wrenched her hair out of her weakened grasp, and leaped onto Lasair's back. Before anyone could do more than cry out, the stallion was galloping down the great hall while the screaming crowd tried to get out of the way. One man leaped in front of the wild-eyed horse and was knocked down for his trouble. While the Red Guards ran after, shouting and waving their spears, the Grand-Seeker Glynelda screamed, "Stop her! She's stolen my horse again!" and the young laird on his throne laughed till tears ran down his cheeks.

With freedom heady in Isabeau's mouth, they were out of the massive doors and bolting down the steps. Ahead of them, a castle guard struggled to shut the high gates that divided the castle from its town, but Isabeau spurred Lasair on and the stallion galloped over the guard so he shrieked and fell, arms over his head. Then they were into the town, hooves loud on the cobbles. Dogs and chickens scattered before them, and they knocked a cart of vegetables into the path of the Red Guards behind them. Over a low wall they jumped, Lasair showing his breeding in the smoothness of his motion. Down a narrow alley, through a maze of twisty streets and at last the sound of pursuit began to fade. Isabeau risked a look behind her and saw only an empty lane.

"We've done it!" she whickered, and Lasair neighed, only to be answered by another horse as they rounded the corner into a square filled with red-clad soldiers. Isabeau dragged at the stallion's mane and the horse wheeled and headed back into the narrow lanes, but again the pursuit was loud behind them, and now it was on horseback. Lasair was losing his freshness and once his hoof slipped in some unidentifiable slime so that he almost lost his footing.

They shot out into another big square filled with people and Isabeau had to rein Lasair in sharply or risk killing someone. Across the square a man driving a gaudy caravan raised his hand and she thought she heard her name being called, but hot on her heels were two Red Guards, both young and both relishing the chase. Isabeau kicked Lasair on, trying to weave through the crowd, looking everywhere for some means of escape. A hand came up and gripped her reins and she caused the leather to burst into flame, so the soldier dropped them with a yell. A spear came whizzing toward her and only her training saved her, her hand coming up and deflecting it away into a wall.

She was trapped now, her back to the wall, only Lasair's flailing hooves keeping away the guards with their long spears. And Isabeau was very tired, barely able to keep her seat, blood seeping from the wound between her eyes, and her injured hand throbbing sickeningly. She made one last valiant effort, kicking Lasair forward in a great surge of speed, but the young Red Guard spurred his horse forward and the stallion slammed into its bulk. Isabeau lost her balance and lurched out of the saddle, the paving stones rushing up to meet her.

When Isabeau was slapped into consciousness, it was sunset. She was lying on a wooden landing place in a puddle of cold water, while mist wreathed about them and the waters of the loch rocked against the jetty.

"I wanted ye to ken what was happening," the seeker hissed into Isabeau's face. "Ye thought to make a laughing stock o' me!" And she slapped Isabeau hard, so her head snapped back onto the wooden floor.

There was a crowd of people about, including the young laird looking scared, and the great bulk of Blyn, his face still covered with the sinister black hood. Isabeau was so dazed and in such pain from her injuries that she hardly registered what was happening. She was half pushed, half carried to the edge of the jetty, the waters below black, obscured by the drifting mist.

Long speeches were made, but Isabeau did not register a word, just stood dully, staring into the fast-dropping darkness. Suddenly there was a cry, and everyone scurried back from the edge.

"It comes!" the laird cried, half in excitement, half in dread.

Isabeau looked up blearily to see a great sinuous neck, topped by a tiny head, approaching fast through the pale tendrils of mist. The head moved this way and that, as if smelling the air, and everyone screamed and ran off the jetty, except Isabeau, bound hand and foot, the grim-faced seeker in her red robes, and the hooded executioner. The serpent of the loch had arrived.

In fascination Isabeau stared up at it, then she was pushed hard, between the shoulderblades, and she fell, the dark waters closing over her head with a swirl.

MAYA THE BANRÌGH

The Banrìgh sat at the long ornate table, crumbling her bread and nodding her head in agreement to what the laird beside her was saying. The Prionnsa of Blèssem and Aslinn, Alasdair MacThanach, was protesting the cessation of trade with the other islands in the archipelago, but his words seemed to have no effect on the Rìgh, who stared morosely into the dregs of his wineglass. Maya touched his elbow with her arm, but he took no notice, and so Maya was forced to answer the laird herself, something she was always loath to do.

She knew the laird of the MacThanach clan was concerned about how he was to sell the yields of his rich fields after he harvested in late autumn. Traditionally, the land of Blèssem shipped its grains and fruits round Eileanan's coastline to the other countries and across the eastern seas to their neighboring islands. Eileanan had a monopoly on grains such as wheat, corn and barley because, according to the old stories, the seeds for such crops had been brought to this planet by the First Coven, and were not native to the islands.

As she spoke the soothing words he desired, she saw the Prionnsa of Carraig, Linley MacSeinn lean over and mutter something into the ear of his neighbor. Maya regarded him thoughtfully. Although she could not hear what he said, she could guess he had said something scathing about the loss of the sea witches. The Yedda of Carraig had been for centuries the only weapon the islanders had against the

Fairgean, having the power to mesmerize the sea people with song. However, the destruction of the Tower of Sea-Singers in Carraig had meant there were no Yedda left to sing the trading ships to safety. It was for this reason that the merchants no longer dared set sail from the shores of Eileanan, for outside the rocks of the harbors the Fairgean waited.

"Ye have a solution to our problem, MacSeinn?" she asked, and had the satisfaction of seeing him blanch.

"No, no, Your Highness," he answered. "Though I still no' have word from His Highness about the Fairgean's invasion o' my lands. It has been four years syne I fled here, and nothing has been done!"

"Rest assured, the Rìgh is no' idle," Maya responded and wished her husband would wipe the foolish smile off his face and take note of the conversation. "His Highness has sent more scouts into Carraig, as ye ken. We have no' yet heard news, but it has been a long and snowy winter, and the mountains have been impassable. Now that the Time of Flowers is here, happen we may receive some news." She turned back to her barely touched meal, but the laird of the MacSeinn clan was not satisfied.

"It has been four years, Your Highness! Four years since my clan had to flee our land because o' the foul, murdering *uile-bheistean*! I want to ken when the Rìgh is going to raise the navy and drive them back to the sea where they belong!"

A red tide of anger filled Maya's ears and eyes. She glared at the loud-mouthed laird and hissed, "We canna send out the navy for the same reason the merchant ships loll at anchor in the harbor! The seas are thick with Fairgean, who would hole and sink the ships as soon as the sight o' land falls away!"

"If the Yeddas were still alive, this would never have happened," blurted out Lord MacSeinn's young son, and immediately went fiery red as sharply indrawn breaths were heard all round the great table. The Prionnsa of Carraig went quite pale, for what he might mutter to his friends and family was not safe to repeat at the Rìgh's own table. Jaspar seemed not to have heard, however, and although Maya's instinctive reaction was to have the whole MacSeinn clan thrown into the dungeons, she controlled her temper. If Jaspar had not reacted to the treasonous statement, she could not exert her power so publicly as to arrest one of the island's great prionnsachan and his family. She gave the young lad an admonishing glance, and Lord MacSeinn a warning one, before returning her attention to her plate.

On her other side the Rìgh sat slumped in his chair, staring at his untouched meal and sighing at something only he could hear. Maya kicked him with her foot, aware of the curious glances of the court that ate and drank and whispered poisonous gossip all around them. He did not seem to notice. She sighed. It was becoming harder and harder to reach him, when once he had hung on her every word. He seemed to be retreating into a twilight world, where only his childhood memories and the far distant song of the Lodestar had any meaning for him. The tangled affairs of the court and country, the vying for position among the lairds and minor prionnsachan, the return of the Fairgean, none of this seemed to concern him anymore. The Rìgh was happy to leave everything to his wife, but it did not suit Maya to rule so openly. She worked best in secrecy and subterfuge, in planting a suggestion here and a hint there. And now that the many threads she had spun over the past sixteen years were slowly twisting together, Maya would have liked to be free of such petty matters as the merchants' fears, the weavers' taxes and why young children were being snatched out of their beds at night, never to be seen again. Maya was particularly vexed at the moment by many of the lairds insisting on keeping their young with them, even at the high table. The outbreak earlier by the young MacSeinn would never have happened if people were not so foolishly troubled by the tales of ghosts that came at night and silently spirited away their young. He should have eaten at the lower tables, as did all the other pages!

Maya did not feel well. The heat was bothering her as it never had before, the roast pork made her queasy, and the drone of voices made her head ache. Anxiety was always with her, a knife blade twisting beneath her breastbone, and sometimes she longed for the dim peace of a country farm wife, with nothing to worry about but the crop and her husband's moods. As she sighed again, and dropped her uneaten bread back on the plate, her elbow suddenly slipped, falling onto the edge of her plate so her entire meal was tipped into her lap, splattering both the laird on her left and the Rìgh on her right with gravy. Maya almost betrayed herself with a most unbanrìghlike curse, but caught herself in time, smiling and making some light comment about her clumsiness, before getting up and leaving the room. *Some blasted witch bad-wishing me again,* she thought, and knew she must be distracted indeed to allow such a small thing to slip under her guard. Normally Maya could turn the bad-wishes of the witches away without any effort, but now her belly was swelling with the babe, she was feeling so unwell and so preoccupied, it seemed they were slipping under her guard all the time. For the past few months, ever since the comet had passed through the skies and she had enacted the Spell of Begetting, Maya had been dropping things, bumping her hip, stubbing her toes, spilling sauces, knocking over ornaments, and tripping over her skirts. It seemed as if every witch in the country must be bad-wishing her!

Suddenly Maya's eyes narrowed, and she wondered if she had inadvertently stumbled across the truth. Perhaps the thrice-cursed witches could read the omens in the sky as well as Sani could. Maybe they knew that all her plans were only now coming to a head, that soon—if all went as planned—the land would once again belong to her people, and all these humans would be slaves.

When she came into her quarters, her servant was waiting for her, her pale eyes snapping with impatience. "Thank Jor ye've come at last, Maya. What have ye done to your dress—more bad-wishing? Canna ye rid us o' these pesky witches?"

"I'm trying, I'm trying," Maya grumbled, stripping off the food-stained skirt and throwing it on the floor. Then her eyes brightened. "Sani, ye should really try no' to swear by the god o' all the seas! Imagine if someone should hear ye!"

Sani shot her a venomous glance and opened her mouth to retort, only to shut it again for, really, there was nothing she could say. She had castigated Maya many a time for exactly the same thing.

Feeling much better, Maya finished undressing and slipped into the pool in the center of the room. "Careful!" Sani warned sharply, but Maya was past caring. She had not been able to go down to the sea for several days, and felt as knotted up as a tangle of twine. She let the salt water lap against her parched skin and slowly let herself relax.

Sani clicked her tongue with anger, and locked the door. "I feel uneasy," she said. "Such chills have been running down my spine! I fear me something has gone wrong."

Maya rolled luxuriously, sending waves splashing over the edge of the sunken bath.

"So I have my Banrìgh's permission to use the mirror?" Sani said sarcastically, and Maya indicated that she did, too happy to be in the bath to take offense at the tone. The tiny old woman crossed the room, and unlocked a drawer in the tallboy that sat next to Maya's bed. Reverently she drew out an oval hand mirror, its handle sinuously shaped like the tail of some slender fish. She sat at the table, laying the mirror down carefully, and making a secret sign above it. For a long time she stared into its silver face, while Maya swam back and forth and wished for the sea. Then the old woman suddenly stiffened, and went pale. "Maya, Maya! The dragons! What will your father say?"

"What has happened?" Maya said, surfacing again.

"The dragons have retaliated. They have wiped out the entire legion o' guards we sent against them!"

Maya felt dread run through her, and sank back into the water, shivering. "Did the dragons . . . burn them?"

"I fear me, aye."

Suddenly Maya was angry. "But I thought they would no' attack the soldiers o' one o' their precious MacCuinns! We were assured they would no' attack! What o' their sacred pact? Did they try to take them by surprise? How can this have happened?" She thrashed from side to side, causing great spouts of water to splash into the room.

"I do no' ken," Sani said. "I focused in on the Seeker Thoth, but all I could see was smoke so I rose higher, and saw the pasture filled with the bodies o' the slain, all charred and torn. Higher I rose, until I could see the battlefield, and there was a dragon, his nostrils still steaming, his chomps all bluidy, chewing on the body o' one o' your soldiers."

Revulsion shot through Maya, and with a flip she was out of the pool, water streaming from her sleek body. At that moment there was a knock on the door. "Quickly, my daughter," Sani ordered, and she carefully covered the mirror with a cloth and went to the door. Maya struggled to her feet, then wrapped herself in her bedgown before Sani opened the door.

"Why do ye interrupt the Banrìgh when she is bathing?" the old woman scowled.

The cook Latifa stood outside, holding a tray. "I be sorry, Mistress Sani, I just noticed our Banrìgh did no' eat any o' her dinner and thought happen she needed something to tempt her appetite and knowing how important it is she keep her strength up and all, I just—"

Sani took the tray and shut the door in her face. "Aye, just thought she'd take the chance to spy through our keyhole more like! I wonder how long she was standing there, listening."

Maya wrapped the gown around her more securely and lifted the lids on the tray. To her relief, there was fish, lightly cooked, and rice wrapped in seaweed, just the way she liked it. "Och, Latifa is harmless," she said lightly. "She's so auld now she probably could no' hear a thing anyway. Keep an eye on her, though, just in case." She sat at the table, careful not to bump the mirror, and began to eat. "Try to contact the Grand-Seeker Glynelda. Find out what is happening up there in the Sithiche Mountains that everything should go so wrong."

Sani obeyed, rocking back and forth before the mirror and muttering to herself. At last her sight seemed to clear, for she sat straight and leaned into the mirror, her face grim. "Greetings, Grand-Seeker. What is your report?"

"Things are going according to plan, my lady, although we have no' been able to capture the Cripple as ye instructed. We had him in our hands, though, and indeed ye were right, he is an *uile-bheist,* winged like a bird."

"If ye had him in your hands long enough to establish he has wings, why is he no' on his way to us?"

"He was rescued, my lady, by rebels and witches. We have many soldiers out hunting through the hills, and the region's best trackers, and are confident we will soon have him in our hands again."

"That is no' good enough!" Sani snarled. "Ye should never have let him escape!"

"We caught one o' the witches who freed him, my lady!" the Grand-Seeker Glynelda said eagerly. By leaning over as she ate, Maya could just see the watery reflection of Glynelda's face in the mirror. "She was given to the monster o' the loch, as is the custom up here."

"How did she ken ye had him? Ye were meant to move in quiet and stealth!"

"I do no' ken, my lady." Glynelda's consternation came through clearly.

"Why no'? Was she no' put to the Question?"

"Well, aye, she was, my lady, but she killed the Grand-Questioner, and anything he discovered before he died, died with him."

Maya and her wrinkled old servant looked at each other in absolute consternation. The Grand-Questioner, Baron Yutta, had been one of the most powerful sorcerers in the service of the Banrìgh, and as careful and canny a servant as anyone could hope for. His predilection for causing pain had been spotted by Sani early on, and he had served her the best of any of the Awl, ferreting out witches and revolutionaries as easily as a hound scented the trail of a deer.

"Ye should have brought her here!" Sani said angrily. "She was obviously a powerful sorceress to have freed the leader o' the rebels, then killed the Grand-Questioner. Ye are a fool! Why did ye no' have her shipped down to us? We would have been very interested in questioning her ourselves."

In the dim reflection, they saw the Grand-Seeker wetting her lips. "She was a slippery, tricky witch, my lady. We chased her all over the highlands, and she almost escaped us three times. It was only my personal attention to the case that resulted in her capture. I was afraid she would escape again if we allowed her to live. There was another reason too. The hunting down o' the magic monsters has made the people here very uneasy. They have lived with their misbegotten dragons and serpents for so long they fain no' see them destroyed. It was a public show o' power and discipline, my lady."

"Are ye sure the witch is dead?" Maya whispered, and in a louder voice Sani repeated her question.

"Och, aye, my lady. I watched over her execution myself. She was bound hand and foot and thrown in the loch, and the *uile-bheist* was already waiting, scenting his food." As she spoke of the loch's serpent, her mouth screwed up as if she had tasted something nasty. "She would have been devoured before she could even have drowned."

"Was the witch auld, very auld, and wee? With black eyes?" Maya asked, and again Sani repeated her question.

"No, my lady, she was young, only a lass still, and red. That was how I spied her out—I found one o' her hairs at the campsite after we discovered the prisoner was missing. I was able to follow her, using the hair, and then prove she was the one we sought. Red hair is no' as rare in the mountains as it is on the coast, my lady, but it is still rare enough."

"So have ye found any signs o' the Arch-Sorceress Meghan, she who talks with animals and commands the earth?" Sani asked, at Maya's prompting. "My Banrìgh is still very anxious that the Rìgh's renegade cousin be found. If she is alive, the Rìgh still has hopes o' bringing her to the Truth; and if she is dead, well, then we shall bury her with all due pomp."

Glynelda hesitated, then said softly, "My lady, the Seeker Thoth did send me a message some weeks ago. He said that he had stumbled across a conclave o' witches, performing their foul rites at the height o' the comet's passing, and did storm their stronghold with the help o' the Gray One. One witch at least was killed, maybe two, although the second body was no' found. By use o' their perilous talents the other witches escaped, but he has promised me they will be found. He said then that one o' the witches caused the earth to open beneath their feet, and all the beasts o' the field and forest came to her call and fought at her direction."

"Meghan!" Maya breathed. "It must be her!"

"Why, Grand-Seeker, did ye no' contact us with this news? Ye ken how anxious the Rìgh is for news o' his cousin."

"My apologies, my lady, it is just I hoped to contact ye with better and more concrete news. Always we hear o' sightings o' the auld witch but always they are just stories. I wanted to be sure afore I reported."

"And why has several weeks gone past without any o' these witches being captured? How many did escape?"

"I suspect the witch we captured last night was one o' those witches, for we did track her down through the lower range o' the Sithiche Mountains and through the Pass to Rionnagan, and that was the way some o' the witches did seem to escape. Thoth followed the one we feared was the Arch-Sorceress, both because he knew she was important and because she was heading toward the Dragon Stair, and he feared her intentions."

"So, Meghan, your fine fingers were meddling in my affairs again!" Maya hissed.

"And what news o' the dragons, my dear?" Sani asked sweetly.

"My messengers have no' yet returned, but I will soon have news, and am confident that we will hear all the cursed dragons have been wiped out," the Grand-Seeker said complacently.

Sani leaned forward so her mouth was only inches away from the enchanted mirror. "Ye are wrong, Glynelda. And ye will suffer for your mistakes! Ye said the dragons would no' attack our forces, that they would respect the ancient pact made with Aedan Whitelock and we could destroy them all. Ye were mistaken, and the Banrìgh does no' like mistakes!"

Even in the dim, rippling surface of the mirror, they could see the Grand Seeker's face become ashen, her eyes black with fear. "What . . . why? What has happened?"

"The dragons struck at the legions and wiped them out. As we speak they lick their bluidied chops as our troops lie in pools o' their own blood. The dragons have the taste o' human flesh now. Can ye tell me they will no' like it?"

"How could this have happened? That fool Thoth! He must have grown overconfident—"

"And who gave us all reason for confidence?" Sani asked softly. "Who assured us that all the dragons would wait afore retaliating, that their *honor* would mean they would no' break the Pact o' Aedan Whitelock until it was too late?"

The Grand-Seeker had shown her fear for only a moment. Though still pale, she said confidently, "Ye asked me to tell ye all I ken o' dragons, my lady, and that is what I did. But I am no' a dragon-laird. I canna tell the minds o' so awful and alien a creature. All the books on dragons were burned with the ill-fated Towers and the cursed witches. When ye did ask me I told ye what I ken—that the dragons do be slow to move but terrible in their movement; that they do honor the Rìgh's mighty ancestor and, unlike humans, will honor its spirit and no' just its word; that females are rare and breeding difficult. How am I blame?"

"Ye should have overseen the slaying o' the dragons yourself!"

"But ye did instruct me to find the winged *uile-bheist* and bring him to ye," the Grand-Seeker said. "I did but follow your orders."

Sani was growing tired of the Grand-Seeker and she allowed it to show on her face. "Beware, Glynelda, that ye do no' displease me," she whispered. "Ye are Grand-Seeker. I elevated ye above all others because I believed ye capable. I fain no' be proved wrong."

"No, my lady." The Grand-Seeker licked her lips.

Sani waved her hand across the surface of the mirror and they both watched as the surface grew bright and clear again. Afterward they sat in silence, until at last Maya said, "Meghan is a sea-urchin spike in my side. We must hunt her down."

"Ye think she had something to do with the unexpected attack o' the dragons?"

"Och, aye, Meghan's fingerprints are all over this one!"

"We have been hunting her for sixteen years, Maya, and she keeps slipping through our fingers."

"She went underground. That is why we have no' heard o' her for so long. By Jor, I had hoped she had died!"

Sani said nothing about the curse, just stared into the mirror again. "Do ye wish me to see what I can scry out?"

Maya nodded. "Try for Meghan again. She may have let her shield slip in the excitement o' the moment."

"And then we must contact your father," Sani said maliciously.

Maya felt her cheeks whiten, but refused to give Sani

the satisfaction of seeing her beg for more time. "Contact the other seekers first, and set them on the trail o' both the Cripple and the Arch-Sorceress. No! Better still! Call in the MacRuraich, it is time he worked for us again," she commanded. "And then let me speak to my father myself."

LILANTHE OF THE FOREST

Lilanthe stood at the edge of a great escarpment, looking down at the plain undulating away three hundred feet below. She recognized the precipice from Isabeau's geography lessons as being the Great Divide, a narrow, steep wall of stone which formed an effective barrier between the forbidden land of Tìrsoilleir and the western lands of Eileanan. Sadly she wondered what the blue-eyed witch was doing now. She hoped her quest was going well, and treasured her promise that when Isabeau returned she would seek Lilanthe out again. As Isabeau said, who knew what pattern the Weaver was designing? Perhaps their threads would cross again sooner than that.

Lilanthe had lost faith in the Spinners long ago. She could not lose faith in Eà, for it was in her flesh that Lilanthe dug her roots each night and from Eà that she drew her nourishment. But the Spinners, it was easy to disavow them when all their spinning and weaving had brought her only pain and heartbreak. Nonetheless, she hoped Isabeau was right and that their paths would cross again. In the meantime, however, Lilanthe was finding it difficult to recapture her mood of happy, aimless traveling. She was restless and lonely, and filled with admiration at what she saw as Isabeau's strength of purpose. She had followed the ridge of the escarpment out, wondering idly what Tìrsoilleir looked like, but the pale hills and fields looked much like Rionnagan, only flatter. There was no sign of any warrior-maids, though she could see a few tall spires in the distance, marking the location of their kirks. Although the Alainn Falls were as spectacular as people said—wide sheets of white water crashing three hundred feet down into a loch of turbulent foam—she grew quickly tired of them, and began to wonder what she should do next.

The Sithiche Mountains curved in the shape of an upside-down smile around the gently falling hills of Rionnagan, with Dragonclaw a sharp tooth protruding from its upper lip. To the east, it crunched into the Great Divide, whose steep cliffs few could climb. If she followed the edge of the clifftop back round for some days, then turned back to the south, she should be able to find a way down into the forests of Aslinn, where Isabeau thought she might be safe. That way she could leave the Sithiche Mountains, now swarming with legions of soldiers, without having to negotiate the Pass. That way also, Lilanthe reasoned, she would be curving back round to the east, where Isabeau had gone.

She gave one more wondering glance at the dizzying drop before her, listening to the distant roar of the Alainn Falls across the curve of the horseshoe-shaped cliffs. Then she began her journey again, loping easily along the rocky edge of the plateau, the stones hard on her bare feet. For several days she followed the curve of the ridge, angling eastward and then south. Here the sharp pointed Sithiche Mountains eased down into softer hills, their feet shrouded by the thick forests of Aslinn. Lilanthe found herself looking forward to being surrounded by trees again, and began to dream of a clearing with a loch, a view of the mountains and thick, rich soil.

First, however, she had to find a way down the cliff-face, for there was no other way to reach the forest below. At last she found a spot that looked promising, where a narrow waterfall had once carved a path down the steep walls. A landslide had diverted its course, leaving behind mossy rocks and the occasional patch of herbs, for the water had brought with it soil that clung to cracks and crevices. Lilanthe knew she could send out tendrils of roots from her hands and feet to cling to the earth, and so slowly lowered herself over the side.

The cliff-face was almost three hundred feet high, and

where it was not perfectly perpendicular it leaned out over the valley, so that Lilanthe's descent was fraught with danger. Several times her questing rootlet could find no crack to insinuate itself into, and once she found herself clinging in terror to the wall, unable to find any way to continue. She had to slowly shape-shift until she was more tree than girl; then slowly, slowly stretch out all her branches and roots until at last she found a handhold and could swing her flesh-wood body over, an exercise in control rare for the tree-shifter. At last, though, she reached the ground, and stood thigh-deep in the pool beneath the waterfall, washing away the sweat and terror of her descent and cooling her overheated sap.

Aslinn was as beautiful as Isabeau had promised. Great mountain ash trees towered above the floor of the valleys, with crystal waterfalls splashing down from the mountains to form meandering streams and pools below. Songbirds darted through the clear air, trilling madly, and once Lilanthe saw a bhanais bird flying through the canopy, trailing its crimson and gold tail, which was more than three feet long. She traveled more slowly, but could not find her perfect clearing. Small lochan abounded, and on a clear day the backdrop of snow-tipped mountains and green hills was as beautiful as any daydream. The soil was rich with leaf mold and tasted wonderful. The problem lay with Lilanthe. Her fits of loneliness and self-pity came more often now, and she had fallen into the habit of brooding, ignoring the beauty around her as the old Lilanthe would never have done.

One morning when she woke and began to twitch her roots in preparation for rising, she cast out her mind as she always did and was surprised to find that she was no longer alone. Only a few hours away she caught traces of consciousness—a group of people and animals, their mind-thoughts quite loud and brash. As always fascinated by any other intelligent life, Lilanthe found herself slipping through the forest toward the thoughts.

It was a camp of traveling jongleurs and minstrels, making their way east from Rionnagan. The camp was just stirring, small children scampering about naked, heedless of the cool mountain air, women lighting fires or washing their faces, men scattering seed for chickens in hutches or lighting up their pipes as they gossiped over the fire. Lilanthe crouched in the bushes at the edge of the clearing and watched in fascination. Soon the smell of cooking food wafted toward her, and her mouth watered. Even though Lilanthe drew much of her nourishment from the soil in which she dug her roots, she still had a stomach, much like humans, and she definitely had taste buds. Lilanthe had not eaten a hot meal since she and Isabeau had parted company, having a natural fear of fire and no inclination to try lighting one.

The jongleurs ate their meal in leisure, talking and laughing and smoking all at the same time. One of the small children turned somersaults all round the adults, finally tumbling to a heap just at the very edge of the hot coals. Cries of alarm rang out, and the child was rescued and dusted off, before being slapped hard across the legs and tossed overhead to its mother. The sun was climbing high before they had packed up and harnessed the stocky horses to the caravans again. They headed east, and Lilanthe followed them.

By the third day she had identified the relationships between most of them. There were six caravans, most filled to the bursting with at least three generations of family—one with four—ranging from a toothless old crone to the child whose mishap Lilanthe had witnessed the first day. The caravans were rarely entered, containing instead the few possessions of the jongleurs: their props and instruments, their bright, ragged clothes, battered cooking implements, and sacks and barrels of stores, including one of whisky, which had been called firewater in Lilanthe's home village. One night they tapped the barrel freely, and there was dancing around the fire, and much story-telling and laughter. Lilanthe crept right up to the group that night, hiding beneath one of the caravans, huddled into the sleeping blankets of the family who would later bed down beneath the scant protection of the caravan's wooden floor.

Her favorite jongleur was young, with bright black eyes and a tangle of dark hair. His beard and mustache were just beginning to grow in straggles, giving him a rather raggedly look that went well with his patched sky-blue jerkin and dirty crimson trousers. He captured Lilanthe's interest primarily because of his juggling skills. The way the golden balls spun out of his hand in ever more complex patterns intrigued her, and she often followed him when he slipped away from the camp to practice in private. He juggled all the time—pots and pans when he was meant to be washing up, stones and pebbles that he carried around in his pocket, daggers and swords when he practiced routines with his sister. She was a slender child, with eyes as bright and black as his, though her hair was browner, with red glints. Both of them were trained acrobats as well, and watching their somersaults and tumbling runs sometimes astounded Lilanthe, who had never seen such agility in human creatures before. They were more like cluricauns than children, particularly when they played among the tree branches, swinging and somersaulting from limb to limb.

Their father, a heavy man with blood-shot eyes, frightened Lilanthe and she often slipped away when he was in sight. He was a fire-eater and watching someone swallowing a gust of flame was more than the tree-shifter could bear. It was he who told the loudest stories, and played the fiddle in the danciest tunes, and often squeezed the bottoms of the other women in the party, hitting their men on the shoulder in a comradely way. He had no wife of his own, and did not seem to notice his pinching ways irritated the other men. His mother traveled with them, though, and she was the only one that could control his bluster, especially when the firewater ran through his veins. Unlike everyone else in the party, his mother did not sleep on the ground under the caravans, but inside, only coming out when the fires were lit and the tea made.

Lilanthe did not know why the jongleurs exerted such fascination over her, except perhaps they eased her loneliness a little. She found their antics often made her laugh, so that she had to bury her face in her hands so no sound would escape and betray her. When she was in tree form, it was easier, for her laughter expressed itself in a little shiver of her dangling branches, which could easily have been the wind. Sometimes she thought she saw the young man looking in her direction, but each time his eyes seemed to drift past her and she would let out her breath, sure he had not noticed her.

One day he slipped out of the camp early, before anyone else was awake, and Lilanthe transformed herself into her human shape to follow him. He went some distance, leaving the green road the jongleurs were following, until he found a clearing with a still pool. He leaned above the water, and Lilanthe felt his mind cast out, searching. She brought her mind in very small and still, like a hunted coney frozen in the grasses. He was searching a very long way away, though, and she thought he may not have noticed her. She should have been shielding herself. It never occurred to her that one of these simple traveling entertainers could have such range or power. He must hide himself very well for her not to have recognized it straightaway. She remembered Isabeau and how completely she had been shielded, and thought she must remember humans could hide their minds as well.

She felt the young man bring his mind back into his body, and she let her bare feet press deeper into the earth. The delicious shiver that was shifting rippled over her skin and she opened her pores to the sun and the air. She was almost changed, her eyesight and hearing dimming, a mass of other perceptions taking over, more sensitive than any of her human senses, when she felt him sit back and look at her. Deep in her mind he said, *Shall we introduce ourselves?*

The shock alone slowed Lilanthe's shift, and only a few panicked thoughts tumbled over each other before she reversed the change. Her feet stirred and flexed, her arms thickened and swelled back into warm flesh, and then she was looking at him with her eyes wide open in fear.

"It's all right," he said out loud. "I shall no' hurt ye, or tell anyone. I ken they hunt creatures such as ye, and kill ye for being what ye are. Ye need no' be afraid. I am Dide."

She said nothing, wondering if she should run. Now he knew, shifting was no escape for he could damage her with fire or axe, and she would be helpless, her roots deep in the soil.

"I have seen and felt ye watching us," he said, and rose carefully to his feet. "I do no' think anyone else has, except probably my granddam and she o' all people would no' harm ye. Do no' be afraid. Wha' is your name?"

She would not answer, and so step by slow step he approached her, as she backed deeper into the underbrush and wondered again why she did not run. Soon he was close enough for her to smell his human, meat-eating stench, and to see how bright his eyes were, like the eyes of a donbeag, liquid and black. "Please trust me. I am very glad to find someone like ye, truly I am. I am Dide. I am your friend."

"I am Lilanthe."

He stood still. "Good morrow to ye, Lilanthe," he said. "Are ye hungry?"

She nodded her head, for indeed her human stomach did feel empty and she had had little time to forage the last few days. He put his hand in his pocket and pulled out a withered apple for her. When Lilanthe would not take it from his hand, he laid it on the ground and stepped back. Quickly Lilanthe snatched it up, and smelled it before tentatively nibbling on its sweet rubbery flesh.

"Let us talk," he said, and slowly crouched on the ground. "Quietly, though, for soon the camp will wake and then Nina shall come looking for me."

The morning talk was the first of many for, despite being discovered, Lilanthe continued to follow the caravans deeper into Aslinn. Twice a day, and sometimes more, Dide slipped away so they could meet. He talked more than her at first, for he was trying to win her trust. He told her about his childhood, traveling the lands of Eileanan in a caravan, performing tricks and acrobatics for thrown pennies or a free night in an inn. He tried to reassure her that her secret was safe with him.

"No' all humans agree with the Fairy Decree." Dide was perched on the end of a log, while Lilanthe sat a good seven steps away, her cheek resting on her knees, her arms wrapped close about her. "It's a travesty o' the Pact o' Aedan, killing fairy creatures, and the Rìgh should ken it. Syne the Lodestar was lost, nothing has gone good in this country. That's why we have to find the Lodestar again. The Rìgh is dying, everyone kens it. Some dreadful disease is sucking the life out o' him, and the mind and soul with it. Why, we saw him a few months ago when we played in Rhyssmadill, and he was gray as ashes, with a foolish grin on his face like a bairn. Enit said then he would die within the year, and she is never wrong." Enit was Dide's grandmother and she was never far from his conversation, being Dide's greatest friend, along with his sister Nina.

"If the Rìgh dies without an heir, there'll be civil war again, for sure. That is why the Fairgean are slowly building a position in the north and east, for once Rìgh Jaspar dies, there'll be no one to take the crown and, besides, without the Lodestar, we have no true defense against the Fairgean. All the Yedda are gone . . ." Seeing the incomprehension on Lilanthe's face, he regained the track of his conversation. "Wha' I'm trying to say is, there's no need for ye to be afraid o' me. I dinna agree with the Rìgh's decree, in fact, I hate it, I'm fighting to stop him . . ." He paused again, then said in a rush, "I'll tell ye all about it, for then you'll see I'm no enemy, but your friend. I love the fairy, I canna believe the Rìgh wants to exterminate them, or why. Ye were here long afore the Great Crossing, when we humans came to this land."

"Well, I do no' think I was," Lilanthe said cheekily. "I'm only eighteen years auld."

Dide was delighted at the flash of personality. "I mean the fairy . . ."

"I'm half human, ye ken. My father was like ye, it is only my mother who was a tree-changer."

"I think most o' us have a twist o' fairy in us somewhere." Dide sounded uncertain.

Lilanthe's face was sullen again. "Most wouldna admit it."

"Once they did. Why, they say the MacAislins were more than half nisse and tree-changer, for these forests were once thick with them, and the children o' Aislinna have lived here for more than a thousand years. The family is mostly gone now, o' course, but that was why they adopted the Summer Tree as their emblem. That's why I'm here actually—my master has sent me to make contact with someone at the MacAislins' Tower, for he has had word the tower is occupied again, and he hopes it'll be one o' the family, or maybe one o' the Dream-Walkers returned."

The warmth and life had returned to Lilanthe's face, and she leaned forward, her leafy hair streaming over her shoulders. "Who are the Dream-Walkers?"

"Aislinna's tower is the Tower o' Dreamers. It was ruined at the Time o' Betrayal, o' course, though rumor has had it for years that many o' the dreamers slipped away in the night and so escaped the massacre. Some can travel the dream road forward, ye see, and so may have had forewarning. Our hope is the story is true, and now that the Tower has been forgotten, one or even more have returned. My master saw someone, ye see. He went to the Tower o' Ravens and used the Scrying Pool there, trying to contact each Tower in turn. He surprised someone at the Tower o' Dreamers, but frightened them away. He was no' able to make contact again."

"How do ye ken all this?"

"I ken my master well. He lived with us for many years. I can contact him and he can contact me, as long as we each are near water. Each dawn I try and reach him, but lately he has been silent. It troubles my heart."

"Who is your master?"

"Have ye heard o' the Cripple?"

"No."

"Well, I am surprised. Though ye are a creature o' the forest, I s'pose, and so happen may no' have heard o' him. He is the leader . . . o' the rebels. He's the one who masterminds any move against the evil Banrìgh and her Red Guards; who rescues captured *uile-bheistean,* or witches, even silly auld skeelies or cunning men who have made too much trouble and are accused o' witchcraft because o' it. Slowly we gather strength, slowly our plans mature; soon a new weft shall be threaded."

"And then what will happen?"

"That is the question, indeed. If things go to plan, we shall depose the evil Banrìgh, and go in search o' the Lodestar. Once that is in our hands, we shall drive the Fairgean away from our shores, and humans and fairy can live in harmony again."

"But are the Fairgean no' *uile-bheistean* too? They were here long afore the Great Crossing, surely, just like the tree-changers an' the nisses."

Dide's olive skin slowly colored until even the tips of his ears were red. "I suppose that be true. The Fairgean never signed the Pact o' Aedan, though, did they? And they've tried to overthrow us for a thousand years."

"But Carraig was their land, was it no'? Originally, I mean. At least, that is what I remember being taught, by both my ma and pa. All that north coast, Siantan too. They need to come to land to give birth and raise their bairns, and those rocky shores were their home."

"They're brutal, though, Lilanthe. They have never agreed to any pact. They just keep fighting until one or the other o' us are all dead. We beat them off, and years later they come again, hordes o' them."

"I wonder where they give birth to their babes now?" Lilanthe mused.

"On the shores o' Carraig, no doubt, after killing all the Yedda, and virtually wiping out the entire MacSeinn clan! They say there is only the lord himself left, and his son and a handful of retainers. And did ye never think it was rather suspicious, the way the Rìgh's Decree Against Witchcraft wiped out the Yedda, which made it *so* easy for the Fairgean to invade Carraig?"

"No," Lilanthe said.

There was a pause, Dide's color high, his black eyes sparkling. Then his temper dropped a little, and he said, a little gruffly, "Anyway, the point is, there's a new thread being woven into the tapestry. I am no' your enemy, I'm your friend. I want to help ye."

"How?"

Again Dide was a little disconcerted. "I . . . do no' ken. I suppose I mean, help all *uile-bheistean,* free them from the Fairy Decree, renew the Pact o' Aedan."

"That's wha' Isabeau wanted to do too," Lilanthe murmured under her breath.

The effect of her words was electrifying. Dide sat bolt upright, and said, "Ye ken Isabeau? Red hair, blue eyes? Always laughing?"

"Aye! Ye ken her too?"

"I did many years ago, when we were bairns. I thought I saw her again, recently, in Caeryla. I hope it wasna her."

"Isabeau was heading toward Caeryla. She was meant to meet someone there—"

"Well, I hope it wasna Isabeau! Though when I called her, she looked round . . ." Dide's face was suddenly shadowed.

"Why? Wha' happened? Is she all right?"

"Well, if it was Isabeau, she's no' all right at all. She was on trial for witchcraft. They were going to feed her to the *uile-bheist* o' the loch. We rode out just afore sunset, and all anyone in Caeryla could talk about was the red-headed witch. Her execution was going to be the spectacle o' the month. Everyone was going!"

Lilanthe scrambled to her feet. "Och, no! No! She canna have been caught. Why did ye no' help her? Why did ye no' do something?"

"Wha' could I do?" Dide asked. "There was only me, and she was being escorted by a whole troop o' soldiers, no' to mention most o' the townsfolk o' Caeryla. I wasna even sure it was her, I just saw the red hair—"

The tree-shifter burst into an agony of crying, and turned and ran into the forest. Rather alarmed, and feeling a little teary himself, Dide ran after her, but Lilanthe had disappeared into the forest. That night, he helped pack up the caravan with a heavy heart, and though he cast out his mind anxiously, there was no trace of Lilanthe.

For three days the jongleurs traveled along the green road, following the meandering stream and camping every night by its still pools. Dide was in a quandary. He dared not show his fever of anxiety, for his long absences and abstracted silences were already a cause for teasing from the other jongleurs, and he must always be careful to appear like the others, unless they guess his traitorous secret. The penalty for being involved with the rebels was death, and Dide wanted no suspicion attached to him or his father's caravan. In addition, the chance the witch who had been executed in Caeryla might be Isabeau distressed him, for although it had been eight years since they had met, he had always remembered her and wondered if they would meet again.

Every morning he slipped away to go and stare into one of the pools in case his master should be trying to reach him, or in case Lilanthe returned. On the fourth day, he watched the dark waters shimmer into silver with the growing light without any sense of pleasure at its beauty, when he became aware of another, alien consciousness. With a spurt of joy he looked up and there was Lilanthe, her green hair knotted, her face streaked with mud, her eyes almost closed from crying.

"I want to join ye," she said. "I want to be a rebel too."

Thoughts tumbled madly in Dide's mind. His initial reaction was to tell her not to be silly, but part of Dide's job was to find his master new recruits, particularly those with magic of their own. He also recognized the depth of Lilanthe's grief, though he did not fully understand it. "Then I'd better take ye to meet my granddam," he said. "She'll ken wha' to do."

Maya the Ensorcellor

Maya sat in her room, staring out at the sunset, trying to control the little shivers that were running over her body. It was time to contact her father, and the prospect filled her with fear. It was useless to remind herself she was Banrìgh of Eileanan, the most powerful woman in the country. It was useless to tell herself she was far from her father here in Rhyssmadill. The very thought of having to speak to him filled her veins with terror.

Maya's father was a man to be feared. He came from a race of warriors, proud of strength and contemptuous of weakness, their lives circumscribed by long-held traditions and strict magics. Even though it was many years since Maya had lived with her father, having been handed to the Priestesses of Jor when little more than a toddler, the very thought of him was enough to make her bowels clench. Sani knew this, and brought out the antique mirror with a malicious glint in her tiny pale eyes.

The fish-tail mirror was very old, the metal now green with tarnish, although the oval surface was still bright. Not a single scratch marred its polished face, and when Maya held it between her hands and stared at her own reflection, her face took on a mysterious beauty that seemed somehow alien.

Using the mirror as a focus, as Sani had taught her, Maya stared into her deceptively serene face and called out to her father. His many names and titles fell off her tongue in stilted, musical phrases. On and on she sang, and her reflection sunk away beneath cloudy ripples. Still she called to her father and, through the distorting veil, his face approached, dark with fury. He was roaring, his mouth wide open, his tusks gleaming yellow.

"Why have you not contacted me before?" His song sounded more like the pound of breakers on an icy shore than the delicate lap-lap of Maya's voice.

She tried to strengthen the timbre of her melody. "It was not safe."

"Not safe! Are you not in control there? Are you not Banrìgh?"

"The palace is full of mutinous lords and spying servants. I could not risk exposure at this time. The tighter my grip, the more suspicious they become."

"Weak and foolish as all women are. When shall I have my way? What is the news?"

"The Fairy Decree is working its will, and fairy creatures of all kinds have been surrendered to us. Most are useless, but some . . . some have proved of use. We have had many rebels and witches revealed to us, for they have pity on the fairies and betray themselves unwittingly. The biggest coup was discovering another rebel stronghold in Rurach, and wiping the entire rats' nest out. The fools had returned to the Tower, and of course I had kept a watch on it. Blèssem and Aslinn are completely under our control as ye ken, and although Rurach and Tìreich remain a little recalcitrant, it really does not matter, since we prevail on other fronts."

"And what of our ancient enemies, the dragons?"

Maya would have liked to look away but she dared not. "The dragons have risen."

Her father threw back his head and roared again, and the mirror was filled with the unsavory sight of his tongue and tusks. "So be it," he said at last. "Each time we have struggled to regain what is rightfully ours, the dragons have set their will against us. I am displeased, though, *daughter*." He spat the note out with contempt and, indeed, for him to remind her of her lowly status was to insult her. To him and his kind, daughters were mere pawns in the games of power they all played so relentlessly. If times were hard, it was the girl babies who were drowned so there would be more food for the boys. If a female child survived to adulthood, she had no control over her future, being mated to whatever male her father or brother favored at the time. Manliness was proved by displays of brutality and strength, and the dividing up of food, space and women decided by manliness. Maya had only escaped by a strange twist of fate which had seen her given to the Priestesses of Jor, who recognized power in her and thought to use it for their own ends.

"You have failed," he continued. She did not allow her expression to change or her gaze to falter, but she could not prevent the sweat from springing up on her forehead. "You were supposed to flatter the dragons with those glib and slippery words you *women* use so well. You were meant to send them fine gifts and smooth promises until their guard was relaxed, and then fall upon them with the poisoned spears. What did you do wrong?"

Maya fixed her eyes upon his, and said smoothly, "A contingent of guards, searching out witches in the Whitelock Mountains, panicked when a dragon came down to investigate their presence. They had their poisoned spears with them. I am sure His Highness would be glad to know the dragonbane worked just as he predicted."

"Of course, it worked, fool. And do not expect me to believe the Circle of Seven have risen merely because a dragon was killed. Accidents do happen. Such a thing could easily be explained by the men succumbing to dragon-fear, as they so cowardly do. The dragons know they cannot come too close—"

"The dragon was female, and with child."

He snorted with disgust and scorn. "I suppose that would make their cold blood boil, they have such strange notions. Why did you not send a conciliatory troop to the dragons' valley? Once they had let your heralds in, you could have fallen on them then."

"We did," Maya stuttered, "but they would not accept our heralds."

"Not accept your heralds! Not accept the heralds of the Rìgh of Eileanan? You must have insulted them grievously indeed. No, there is something you are not telling me. What of those other sea-urchin spikes in our flesh? What of the Arch-Sorceress? What of her?"

Despite herself, Maya licked her lips and swallowed. "We have reason to believe the Arch-Sorceress Meghan NicCuinn reached the dragons before us and spoke against us. We had tracked her down to her secret hideaway beneath the shadow of Dragonclaw, and there surprised her and some of her Coven in their filthy secret rites. Some of the witches were killed, though they called on the powers of earth and fire. The Arch-Sorceress escaped, though we have caught and executed one we suspect to be her apprentice, a powerful witch. We are now hard on the Arch-Sorceress's trail, and confident we shall soon have her by the heels."

"Oh yes, confident. Confident as you've been before. Nigh on twenty years you've been confident of destroying her, and I've seen nothing but empty words. So she spoke to the dragons against you, and now the dragons are risen. By Jor! That I should be forced to rely on a puny female as my instrument! Pluck out this spur for me, or else, by Jor, I'll have your blood!"

"Aye, Your Highness." Maya bowed her head, and tried to keep her face serene.

"And what of the Cripple? I notice you say nothing about him. I hope you have not failed me there too?"

"We did locate the leader of the rebels in the mirror, using his witch knife and staff, and so were able to spy on him and know where he was traveling, sure he would eventually lead us to Meghan. Many times he did trick and deceive us, and each time we drew the net tighter about him."

"So? Last time we spoke these were your same words. I want to know if the net drew tight enough to hold him. I told you last time not to risk losing him in those Jor-cursed mountains, where one valley looks much like another. I told you to capture him as he came through the Pass, and twist the Arch-Sorceress's hidey-hole from him there. Did you not do this?"

Maya was sweating again. "Aye, Your Highness, only—"

"Oh, I see. Another excuse? How have you failed me now?"

Maya spoke rapidly. "Meghan's apprentice foiled our plans. She rescued him the night of his capture, and led our men on a sardine chase while he escaped into the mountains. We caught her, though, and executed her."

"While the Cripple has slipped through your fingers again. Why have you not been able to relocate him?"

"He has stopped scrying."

"So he knows you are watching him!"

"It would seem so."

"And would you have told me this if I had not asked?" he sang in a deceptively mild voice. She tried to think how to reply, but he curled back his lip, showing his gleaming tusk, and began to roar again. Maya almost flinched back. When at last he was finished, he panted, "Curse your feminine mysteries. Curse your sleek, sly ways. That I should have to leave such matters in the hands of fools and weaklings! That the proud children of Jor should have fallen so low to depend on a imbecilic half-breed woman!"

"We are closer to victory than we have ever been, Father!" Maya fixed her father with a burning gaze. "Do you not always say that the tidal waves of Jor's wrath roll slow, but to sand the rocks shall be ground?"

He eyed her with a fierce, pale eye and then laughed chillingly. "True enough. But know this, come winter, when the birthing is done and the pup is swimming, then we shall come! You had best be sure I am glad to see you, and that wrinkled-up, oyster-faced priestess-hag too!"

Then he was gone, and Maya's own reflection came swimming toward her through the rippling depths of the mirror. She was shocked to see how ashen was her face, how frightened her eyes.

Sani was frightened too. "Ye fool! Just because he is on the other side o' the land is no excuse for provoking him in such a way! His arm is very long. Do no' think ye are so high and mighty powerful, my fine lass, just because ye ensorcelled a rìgh into marrying ye. Ye are still nothing! Ye are still a worthless halfbreed daughter, less than a grain o' sand to the great rock o' His Highness, Lord o' all the Seas, Master o' Storm and Tidal wave, Rider o' the Sea Serpent! Let me tell ye, if ye endanger yourself ye endanger me, and do no' think I will allow ye to bring me down!"

"Enough!" Maya screeched. "My father's arm may be very long, but mine is still closer." And she struck out at the little old woman, knocking her against the table so that the mirror shot over its polished surface.

The old woman raised herself slowly. "Be careful, my dear. Be very careful." She picked up the mirror reverently, and wrapped it again in its faded silk. "I am your only friend here, remember, and the only one to take your part with your father. What if I tell him the many details ye so cannily left out o' your accounts?"

Maya felt like screaming, but she drew herself up to her fullest height so that she towered over the old woman, and said silkily, "I suggest *ye* be careful, Sani. Remember, I am still Banrìgh here."

"Och, aye, my dear, how could I forget? Just remember, come winter, your father shall come, and your precious Rìgh shall be dead. What shall ye be then?"

Maya had nothing to say. It had been a mistake to lose her temper. She had known the high-priestess Sani all her life, had indeed been brought up by her, and so had a very healthy respect for the shrivelled-up old woman. Sani forgot nothing and forgave very little. Biting her lip, Maya picked up her plaid and threw it over her shoulder, saying briskly, "I am going for a walk. I feel in urgent need o' some fresh air."

"Enjoy your walk, my lady," Sani said smoothly.

As Maya strode down the hall, she almost fell over the old cook's back as she rubbed industriously at a brass door handle. "Sorry, my lady, but as my dear mam always used to say, nothing gets done proper unless ye do it yersel'! The lassies on this floor do be getting terrible lazy! Is anything wrong, my lady?" Maya shook her head, and marched on, wondering again if Sani could be right about this old woman spying on them. Looking at Latifa's serene old face it seemed impossible, but in Maya's present mood, she could have lashed out at anyone. Turning on her heel, she said quietly, "Do no' let me find ye hanging about my private quarters again without leave, do ye hear me?"

Latifa looked up in distress. "But my lady—"

"Do ye hear me?"

"Well, aye, my lady."

"Good!"

* * *

The long ride to the sea from Rhyssmadill only exacerbated Maya's temper. She had to make her way through the thronged streets of the city with her plaid over her head so none would recognize her and wonder why she rode the streets at night, alone. Although the last light still glimmered on the waters of Berhtfane, it only showed her the thickly clustered masts of the ships that dared not venture outside the river mouth. The streets were filled with boisterous sailors who drank away their savings even though no one knew when the merchant ships could again set sail. With a sour twist to her mouth, Maya quit the city as quickly as she could, angling through the thick forests and greedily sniffing the salt of the air. She was trapped, she saw it now. What would happen if her father's will prevailed? She would be Banrìgh no longer, powerful no longer, free never again. With a sharp stab of anxiety, Maya dismounted, leaving her horse to graze freely, then ran the final hundred yards to the edge of the forest, scrambling up the defensive bank built there to gaze at the sea.

The tide was out, and miles of bare sand scattered with the rubbish of the ocean stretched before her. She dragged off her clothes, and ran out onto the silvery shore, racing for the water so far away. It was now fully dark, and the light of the two moons was very bright. She could see the water clearly, a dark blue under the starry sky. The wind against her nakedness was wonderful, the scent of salt, the lure of the water. Soon she was in the waves, swimming strongly.

Maya tried to remember how she had felt when she first came, how proud she was to be chosen for this task, how determined she would succeed. How simple all her choices had been! Now, despite all her training and upbringing, despite all that she thought she wanted, she wished things could stay as they had been. To have Jaspar love her again as he had first loved her; to be Banrìgh with all the love and trust of her people, as they had loved and trusted her in the beginning. *If only my father and Sani would just disappear, and leave me alone. Then I could be happy,* she thought.

Maya was used to the intrigues of a court where power was so concentrated in the hands of so few, that to gain what one wanted one needed to resort to subterfuge and scheming. As she swam with precarious joy through the waves, the vast night sky overhead, she began to plan and slowly the scowl disappeared, to be replaced by something very close to a smile. *There was still a chance . . .*

JORGE THE BLIND SEER

As Jorge, Jesyah and Tòmas traveled deeper into the Whitelock Mountains they found the journey grew ever more dangerous. In the Sithiche Mountains, the Red Guards had all been marching toward Dragonclaw, so once Jorge started traveling away from the dragons' peak he had left most of them behind. The Whitelock Mountains were notorious for its troublemakers, however, and so the Banrìgh's soldiers were thick on the ground, and suspicious. Jorge began to wonder how best to conceal Tòmas's Talent, for to his eyes, the little boy blazed with power like a torch.

"If we come across any seekers in this part o' the world, they are bound to sense the child," he said to Jesyah one evening. The raven gave a questioning caw, hovering a few feet above Jorge's head.

"If he is close by me, aye, I can, but the lad keeps running off, and I canna hold a shield over him then." The raven gave an indifferent caw, and flew on.

Jorge did try to impress upon the boy how important it was that he not be discovered, but Tòmas was not quite eight,. and quicksilver seemed to run in his veins. It was difficult for the old man to keep up with him, and Jorge did not want to draw attention to them by yelling after Tòmas as he darted here and there. He began to wish he could leash the boy like a lord's gillie leashed the hounds before the chase.

Each day they covered as much ground as they possibly

could, Jorge rising before the sun and pushing on well after sunset. After several weeks, Jorge wondered how he had managed so long without his new apprentice. Tòmas delighted him with his wonder and excitement, his curiosity and willingness to learn, while his innocent utterances made Jorge chuckle. Jesyah the raven grew quite jealous, but Tòmas won over even the enigmatic bird, feeding him special tidbits he found on the side of the road, and scratching his glossy black back, which Jesyah could not reach with his claw.

While they stayed in the protection of the mountains, they were fairly safe for villages were few and far between, and any stray contingent of soldiers easily avoided with the help of the keen-eyed raven. Soon, however, they had to strike south, heading down into the highlands of Rionnagan toward Lucescere, the Shining City. It was this part of their journey that filled Jorge with anxiety, but if he wanted to spread rumor and dissension, the marketplace of Lucescere was the place to start. had business there that could not be avoided.

Lucescere was the largest city on the island, and the most ancient. When the First Coven had first arrived in Eileanan from their home on the other side of the universe, they had built the Tower of First Landing on a rocky crag near the ruin of their ship. Often called Cuinn's Tower, the ancient stone citadel was built around the body of Cuinn Lionheart, who died in the Crossing. On the barren flats around Cuinn's Tower a rough settlement was built as the five hundred or so migrants struggled to survive.

Unfortunately, the settlers did not understand the wide seasonal swings of the tide, affected by the contrary pull of two moons. Their first winter saw the settlement drowned in the rush of the high tide, many lives lost with it. Only the Tower, built on what became an island, survived. Owein MacCuinn crammed the survivors into the Tower and sat out the bitter cold and isolation, sharing out the meager rations and guarding against disease so that surprisingly many of the people managed to live through that first great test. When spring at last came and the sea began to flow back, expedition parties were sent into the hinterland, following the shining curves of the Rhyllster high into what would become Rionnagan.

In Rionnagan they found what they were searching for—fertile lands, a plentiful supply of fresh water, and a building site that could easily be protected. For the new settlers discovered that seasonal tides, unfamiliar food and homesickness were the least of their problems. The native inhabitants of Eileanan were not all pleased at the invasion of humans from another planet, particularly the Fairgean, who arrived at their spring pastures to find them occupied. A brutal, warlike race of sea-dwelling nomads, the Fairgean did not give up their hold on the coast of Eileanan easily, and for the next two hundred years the First Fairgean Wars raged. Lucescere, built on a great pinnacle of rock thrusting between two waterfalls, was never broken, holding off the Fairgean and their allies for over a thousand years.

It was the sound of the waterfalls that first alerted Jorge to the nearness of their objective, then the smell of water and the spray against his face. He heard Tòmas give a cry of awe and delight, and felt with his stick for somewhere to sit down, emotion choking his throat.

"There is the most amazing waterfall," said the little boy, who had become used to describing everything he saw to his blind master. "It seems to fall forever; ye should see it! And at the top is a castle, with great soaring walls and pointed towers with bright pinnacles like flames. Their roofs must be made of gold or bronze to shine so in the sun. And rainbows hang all around its foot, and below is darkness and mist."

"What else can ye see, my lad?"

"There is a big loch, all shining and bright, at the bottom o' the waterfall, and an auld city, all twisty streets and houses all on top o' each other, built into the cliffs. Why did they no' build the city on the shores o' the loch, Jorge? So much room, yet the city is crammed up on top."

"Why do ye think?"

Tòmas did not know, despite having lived all his short life in a country pulled apart by inner turmoil and war.

"For defense, lad. Lucescere has a river on either side, and high mountains at its back. It can defend itself against any attacker, human or fairy. And that, o' course, is the reason why nobody in their right mind would build too close to a burn, no matter how bonny. Burns, lochan and rivers are dangerous. The Fairgean can penetrate deep into the land by swimming up the rivers, and many a foolish human has been drowned by venturing too close to a body o' water. They canna leap a waterfall like the Shining Waters though, and so, no matter how many o' the Fairgean infiltrate Lucescere Loch, the city o' Lucescere is safe."

"Can we go down to the loch?"

"Maybe. They say the Rhyllster is the only river in Eileanan the Fairgean have no' seized. Though how anyone could ken about the rivers o' Tìrsoilleir is beyond me. It's been many a year syne we heard anything from beyond the Great Divide."

"Why have the Fairgean no' invaded the Rhyllster?"

"The Rìgh's proclamations say it is because they fear his power, though syne the loss o' the Lodestar that canna be as true as it once was. The navyshipmen believe it is because o' the gate they have constructed at the mouth o' the Berhtfane. The merchants whisper it is because the Fairgean canna leap the series o' locks and canals the witches constructed to control the tides, and indeed it is true we have seen no Fairgean syne. The most pervasive rumor is that it's because our mysterious Banrìgh is really a Fairge and some foul subtle plan o' theirs is only now coming to fruition."

"How could the Banrìgh . . . ?" stuttered Tòmas in amazement, and Jorge realized his country loyalty to the High Crown was bred deep.

"Stranger things have happened. Indeed, if it is by horrible mischance true, it answers many questions that seemed unanswerable."

"But Fairgean have tusks! And scales!"

"Only when in their seagoing form," Jorge reproved. "And even then they look amazingly human. And they shape-change to come on land, ye ken that."

"But my mam says even then they do no' look . . . anything like us."

"They are no' like us, foolish lad, so why should ye think that they should? No, a Fairge in their landshape is just as strange and bonny as they are in their seashape."

"I've never heard them called bonny before. People mostly call them repulsive."

"Well, I doubt many villagers in the Sithiche Mountains have seen a Fairge."

"Still, my uncle's wife's brother's cousin has seen the Banrìgh and he said she was very bonny. He did no' say anything about scales. And I thought she was the daughter o' a Yedda, and can sing the heart out o' a man, just like a Yedda."

"The Fairgean sing too. That is why they are so susceptible to the song o' the Yedda."

"But surely if she were a Fairge, everyone would be able to tell? I think that's a stupid story."

"Unless some magic was at work. We never really have understood the magic o' the Fairgean. They are a mysterious people." Jorge heaved himself to his feet, and faced toward the spray, breathing deeply of the water-scented air. "Come, lad, I will need your help negotiating this steep slope. Set your face toward the city, and try and keep close."

They made their stumbling way down to the cobbled road, ridged with battlements, that wound along the hillside toward Lucescere. Already groups of laborers were making their way back to the city, picks and hoes over their shoulders, their tired faces grimy with the dust of the fields. It was almost sunset, and only the heights were still lit with sunshine, the valley below sinking into shadow.

As he tapped his way over the uneven stones, Jorge again pondered the dangers his new apprentice presented. He had to find a way to shield the boy. Witch-sniffers abounded in Lucescere, hired frequently both by the city officials and soldiery and by private citizens to hunt out bad-wishers, curse-mongerers, fairy halfbreeds, and anyone with rebel tendencies. Lucescere had long been considered a cesspool of rebels, witches and thieves by the Crown and, despite a large contingent of Red Guards, a ruthless baron, and regular surprise raids, the Guild of Seekers had long been considered the most effective method of control. Hiring a witch-sniffer was also an excellent way to rid oneself of an enemy, since anyone accused of witchcraft had little chance to defend themselves. It was therefore dangerous for the old man and the boy in Lucescere, and Jorge remembered clearly Meghan's story of how Isabeau had once brought them near disaster in an inn in Caeryla by changing the outcome of a dice game. Although the story made Jorge smile to himself, his wrinkled face was worried. Tòmas's magic was bright and loud, and he had no idea of discretion, wanting to help and heal all he came across. Jorge's strength and magic were insufficient to shield him, particularly if the child drifted too far away from him.

As they approached the Bridge of Seven Arches, which soared over the river to the city, Jorge's face relaxed a little—he had thought of someone who might be able to help. As if sensing the old man's subtle relaxation, Tòmas ran ahead singing, and Jorge stared after the sound of his bare feet affectionately.

"*You grow fond of the lad,*" the raven said in his mind.

"*I have been too long alone.*"

"*My companionship over the past years not, of course, counting.*"

Jorge did not reply, just sent the raven a mind-smile, and Jeѕyah flapped on ahead leisurely, uttering a hoarse caw of laughter.

The bridge was wide enough for twelve men to march side by side, and more than two hundred feet long. Broken and defaced statues leaned here and there, though most were gone, destroyed in the riots of the Day of Betrayal. Underneath its seven massive arches, the Muileach River thundered toward the falls, where it mingled with the waters of the Ban-Bharrach River. Where the two rivers poured over the crescent-shaped lip of the cliff, rainbows shimmered in the sunset air. It was these ethereal shimmers which gave the Shining Waters their name, and so also the city.

Guards lined the bridge, examining the faces of those that passed and poking spears into any carts or baskets of produce. Occasionally they would jerk someone out of the crowd and interrogate them, sometimes with mere prods with the hafts of their short spears, sometimes with fists and boots. By now the bridge was crowded, with the bells ringing out to announce the closure of the city gates. Jorge mingled with the throng, the child close to his side, his cold little hand tightly clasping Jorge's plaid.

"Do no' be afraid," the old man whispered. "They will no' notice us." And they did not. With everyone pushing forward, anxious to be safe inside, Jorge and Tòmas were able to slip through quite easily. The bent old man with his dirty beard and blind eyes was a familiar sight on the Bridge of Seven Arches, and no one noticed the wide-eyed little boy peering out from the tattered folds of his robe, or the raven flying overhead, dark against the bright cascades of water.

Beyond the iron-bound gates, twenty feet tall, they plunged into the dirty, noisy city. The great road wound on through the jumble of buildings toward the abandoned palace with its bronze-topped domes and the half ruined Tower of the witches, but Jorge did not follow it, turning left into the poorer parts of the city instead. Here the streets were narrow and dark, the cobbles thick with mud. Only occasionally could Tòmas see a strip of stars shining faintly overhead, for the houses leaned so close their crooked roofs sometimes touched.

The little boy stared around him with amazed eyes, for he had never seen a town bigger than his little village, nor so many oddly dressed people. Used to gruff crofters dressed in brown wool, he was fascinated by the bellfruit sellers with their wide crimson pants; the merchants in their long robes selling teapots, jeweled knives, perfumed oils, powdered spices and wooden bowls; the butchers shouting out their prices, scrawny carcasses hung from hooks over their shoulders. Lucescere was famous for its dyes, and so the people were dressed in clothes dyed crimson and blue and saffron yellow. Even the beggars were more brightly dressed than anyone Tòmas had seen before, though their clothes hung in tatters about their bodies. Ragged children ran screaming and laughing through the crowd, their legs muddied to above the knees from playing in the ooze that covered the cobblestones. Jesyah the raven fluttered down to scavenge through the piles of refuse, and was chased away by a stout matron in a grubby apron, wielding a broom.

The boy shrank even closer to his master's side, so that the old warlock could barely take a step without stumbling over him. Luckily Jorge needed little assistance in these streets. He could sense people much more easily than he could natural obstacles such as rocks or low-hanging tree branches, and he had been born in the slums of Lucescere. He knew every winding alley, every half hidden archway, every secret of its labyrinthine structure. Deeper and deeper into the ancient city they wandered, their senses assaulted by the noise, the smell of dampness and refuse, the occasional touch of spray on their faces. They were close now to the falls, and their roar sounded like some angry dragon.

They came to a tall, narrow gate set deep under a overhang of gabled roofs. Jorge felt his way along the wall with one gnarled hand until he found the bolt and handle, then opened the gate a crack and slipped though, Tòmas close behind him. Unexpectedly, the gate led not into a courtyard or front hall, as might be expected, but into a narrow alley that ran between the backs of houses, piled high with boxes, crates, broken furniture, mops and brooms. Through this obstacle race they made their way, Jesyah fluttering down to perch on Jorge's shoulder, his beady eyes bright.

Under a massive pile of moldy sacks and broken crates, Tòmas uncovered the round lid of a grate as Jorge had said he would. Reluctantly the boy followed the warlock down the hole, trying not to breathe as the raw smell of the sewers closed over them. He was astounded to discover another city beneath the one they had already explored. A maze of dark tunnels ran off in every direction with, here and there, what seemed to be a pile of old bones and rags but proved instead to be someone sleeping, or gnawing on a crust of bread. Through this dark maze they made their way, stumbling over recumbent forms and trying not to step in the foul stream that trickled down the center of every drain. Occasionally bursts of song and laughter came down one of the openings, but mostly it was quiet and dark.

By the time they arrived at their destination, Tòmas was stumbling, rubbing his eyes with his fists and yawning widely. Jorge had made his way through the tunnels with no hesitation, coming at last to a ladder that dropped sharply into a round duct. "Come on lad, almost there," he whispered. "Quietly now."

The ladder seemed to lower itself into darkness for an age. Tòmas followed Jorge's lead, though the blackness swallowed him up like a great throat. For ten minutes or longer they descended the steep steps, then Jorge felt earth beneath his feet. He lifted Tòmas down the last few feet, then summoned blue witch light to his staff.

They were in a large cave, filled with shadows that moved and flowed around them. The air was thick with spray, for the mouth of the cave was concealed behind a wall of water. They had gone so deep below the city they were no longer on the island between two rivers, but actually behind the Shining Waters.

"Ceit Anna?" Jorge called over the roar of the water. "Are ye there?"

There was silence, though a shadow seemed to detach itself briefly from the darkness, before disappearing again. Although there was no sound, Jorge looked in that direction. "Ceit Anna?" he whispered.

A hoarse voice answered him. Although it spoke in the common language, the voice was oddly accented, rising and falling in cadences quite unlike the accent of Tòmas's native village. "Jorge the Sightless. You bring a stranger to my cave. I gave you no such right."

"Greetings, Ceit Anna. I beg your pardon. He is only a lad, and harmless."

"I gave you no such right."

"He is my apprentice. It is on his account I have come."

"You want my help?"

"Aye."

"Why else would you be here? What do you want?" There was a slither of sound, and Tòmas clung to Jorge's side, burying his face against the rough cloth of his plaid. Jorge stood straight.

"Can ye no' tell, Ceit Anna?" There was a challenge in his voice.

There was a dry chuckle, and a tall, spindly shadow darted across the floor. "The lad has magic. Strong, pure magic. He smells delicious."

"What can ye tell me about his powers?"

"They are strong . . . his hands . . . the magic is in his hands." The shadow seemed to be circling round them. In a paroxysm of terror, Tòmas huddled closer to Jorge, but was unable to resist watching the flicker of movement, the occasional dry rustle of sound. "He is too young and foolish to know how to hide himself—that is why you have come to me."

"Ye are the mistress o' illusions," Jorge said softly.

She laughed, a dry, papery sound like a leaf blown by the wind. "Once, perhaps, Sightless One. No longer." Slowly the moving shadows resolved themselves into a tall figure, far taller than Jorge, with spindly arms and legs, black, leathery wings, and a great mane of wild hair. The slanted eyes took up most of her face, and shone in the blue witch light like an elven cat's. She stooped over them, and Tòmas felt a thin finger touch his cheek. He buried his head against Jorge's thigh, but she trailed her fingers over the back of his head and down his spine. "I have never encountered a Talent like his," she mused. "It is wild, a wild Talent in a human lad. Interesting. He must have fairy blood mingling with his. Let him look into my eyes."

Tòmas buried his face deeper, but inexorably the long, stick fingers turned his head and the frightened blue eyes looked into the narrow face of the nyx.

Her eyes were black and lustrous, without any whites, her pupil a narrow slit, set at the same sharp angle as her eyes. In the semidarkness they shone with an unearthly light. Tòmas stared at her wonderingly, and found he could not look away, though his heart beat suffocatingly fast.

"Well, well, well," she said with a chuckle. "Traces of Celestine, no less. What is your Talent, lad?"

Tòmas slowly put out one finger and laid it on the papery skin of the nyx. She shuddered and moved away. "This is no ordinary lad," she said. "His touch sings to my heart. All my weariness has melted away, my blood dances around my old body."

"He heals by the laying o' hands," Jorge said. "He tried to cure my blindness."

The nyx chuckled, and drifted back into the shadows. "I see him chasing you around a room, you with your robe all kilted up and your skinny legs kicking."

Jorge nodded. "Ye see rightly. Indeed, I barely escaped, he was so determined."

"He will be difficult to conceal."

"That is why I came to ye, Ceit Anna. I beg your help."

"Many times you and your brethren have come to ask my assistance. Each time you have made promises of rescue and redemption; each time you say the persecution of fairies will end. I am the last of my kind, Sightless One. I am old. I am tired. When I pass again into the night the nyx shall be no more. Why should I help you? Your kind has feared my kind for centuries. We have been hunted down, persecuted, subjected to the light so that we dissolve. I have no wish to help anymore."

"It would be a dreadful thing if the nyx should be no more," Jorge said anxiously. "Indeed, I hope this is no' true. I have searched, Ceit Anna, as I promised ye. The mountains are wild, though, and the nyx canny. If they did no' wish me to find them, what can I do? Ye must trust me a wee longer. Have I ever betrayed ye? The day is at hand. The nyx are patient. Many times ye have told me this yourself. The nyx can wait and plan, when others rush in. Will ye no' be patient a week longer?"

"I am patient," Ceit Anna replied in her hoarse voice. "I am merely bored with your constant importunities. Why will you not leave me alone?"

"It is seven years or more since I was here," Jorge said. "The spell ye wove for me then was a powerful spell. It was a very great favor. It is because o' your kindness then that we are so close to freedom now. I would no' come to ye if I could think o' anyone else who could help me."

The nyx drifted back and forth before them, her slanted eyes gleaming. She turned to the boy once more and bent over him, and Tòmas stared up at her and held out his hand to her again. This time she let him touch her, and he laid both palms upon her narrow skull, his fingers deep in the snakes of hair. When at last his hands dropped she made a low keening sound in her throat.

"I am tired no longer," she said wonderingly. "Indeed, it is a wonderful power that he has. Hope seems to flow from his touch. I could almost believe nyx still walk the night and fly the wind. I could almost believe the Celestine still command the forests." She sighed. "Very well. For his sake, not yours, Sightless One. For the sake of the Celestine."

She drifted soundlessly back into the darkness, and Jorge let out all his breath in a glad sigh. The nyx were always difficult to deal with, and Ceit Anna more difficult than those Jorge remembered.

"What is she doing?" Tòmas asked in a tremulous voice.

"Ye may go and watch, if she lets ye. She seems to like ye, so maybe she will let ye stand by."

"What is she?" Tòmas whispered. "She's no' a person, is she?"

"No, she's a nyx," Jorge replied. "Her people lived in this land long afore Cuinn Lionheart brought our ancestors here. She is a spirit o' the night, a very powerful one. Speak respectfully to her, for her magic may well save ye."

It took a long while for Tòmas to find the courage to explore the dark cave or to follow the nyx, but eventually he did. Jorge had sat down against the wall and was asleep, his long beard spread over his chest. Though Tòmas had been walking all day and half the night, he was too excited to rest and was not yet fully accustomed to sleeping on the ground. In addition, he was very curious about the nyx. He had seen cluricauns and nisses before, for both were common in the highlands of Rionnagan; they were both small charming fairies, prone to trickery and thievery, but generally harmless. The nyx was so tall, her limbs so long and thin, her eyes so dark and bright, her personality so powerful that, despite his fear, Tòmas was fascinated.

The witch light had gradually faded while Jorge slipped into sleep, but Tòmas's hands shone with a strange faint silver light. He held his hands out in front of him and they cast a feeble shadow on the wall before him. Tòmas had never noticed any nimbis of light around his fingers before, and the sight made him quiver again with fear. Curiosity was still stronger, however, and so he stumbled forward, trying to pierce the darkness with his shining hands.

Jesyah hopped forward with him, turning his sleek head every now again to regard the boy with one bright eye.

The nyx was sitting at the very back of the cave, where the darkness was thickest. As Tòmas approached her, his hand grew brighter and brighter so that he was able to see quite clearly. She was playing cat's cradle with her hair.

"Close your fist, my lad," she said. "We want no light in this weaving."

Obediently he closed his fingers and the light dimmed, though he could see his knuckles shining red as if he held a candleflame in his palm. After a moment he sat down. He could see little, only the hunched shape of the nyx within shadows, the quick movements of her hands as she twisted her hair about her fingers, the occasional frightening gleam of her eyes.

"I am making you a pair of gloves," Ceit Anna whispered. "Once I wove a cloak of illusions this way, and seven days and seven nights it took me. Afterward I was drained of life, an empty husk of shadows. I do not think I could undertake that weaving again, and not pass into shadows myself. Your hands are small, though. I shall make the stitches tight, tight, so none of your light spills through. And afterward ye will touch me again, and I shall feel as though I can ride the night winds, as I once did and shall no more."

"Why no'?" Tòmas's voice was shrill in the darkness.

"I do no' wish to ride alone," Ceit Anna said sadly. "Once the night was filled with the whisper of the nyx. Now the wind is desolate, desolate."

All night Tòmas sat by the side of the old nyx, and listened to her stories of the darkness, while she wove him a pair of enchanted gloves from her hair. She told him of caves where the nyx had hung in their thousands, their wings rustling, their voices murmuring. She told him of the magic of the night flights, when the light of the moons were hidden by thousands of nyx wings. She told him how soldiers had come, with hammers to knock out the walls of the caves so sunlight had poured in. She told him how her brethren had fled the cruel light, knocking their wings against the walls of the cave, fighting to shelter in any dark corners or cracks. Most had dissolved into a black dust that drifted away on the wind.

"We are not meant for the light of day," she said in her hoarse voice. "We are children of the night, and to night we all return."

Sometime during her stories, Tòmas fell asleep, and when he woke she had slipped away, leaving in his hands a tiny pair of black gauntlets, closely knit with spiral patterns weaving around the wrist. When he put them on, they fitted perfectly and for a moment his hands felt cold and numb. When he went to wake Jorge and show him, the old seer could not see him.

"She has wrought a fine thing," Jorge said at last when Tòmas had taken his gloves on and off several times. "The cloak she made for me was far larger but no' so complex or subtle a creation. That was meant only to conceal, to hide what lay beneath it and present an illusion to the world. These gloves hide ye even from my sight. They will protect ye from any seeker, no matter how clear their second sight. And no doubt they have other properties which we will discover in time for a nyx weaving is a wonderful thing—"

Tòmas was very hungry, as they had not eaten since midday the previous day. He interrupted the old man to rub his stomach and complain, and so Jorge laughed and bade him lead the way up the ladder again and into the sewers below Lucescere. "I have a friend who will feed us," the old man said in his quavering voice. "But keep those gloves on, and keep by my side. I do no' want to lose ye."

The two travelers made their way through the city to a chandler's premises where a soft tattoo of coded knocks on the side door saw them whisked inside into a great warm kitchen where Tòmas was fed to his heart's delight. Jorge began to tell all his news to the chandler's wife, a massive woman with arms as thick as Tòmas's entire body and a voice like a foghorn. So deep in conversation were they that Tòmas was forgotten and he spent a happy few hours exploring the extensive pantries and playing with a litter of kittens he found there. One of the kittens had a swollen, weeping eye, but even though Tòmas handled him thoroughly, his magic had no effect. After casting a quick glance around to make sure no one was watching, Tòmas eased off his glove and touched the kitten's head with one finger. Slowly the dried pus softened and melted away, and the kitten was able to open her eye again. Delighted, Tòmas jammed his glove back on again, but the brief flash had been enough for Jorge, who scolded him soundly for taking it off at all. With the kitten snuggled securely in his pocket, Tòmas was able to accept the scolding meekly.

That afternoon they went out into the city again, in search of money and food to refill their empty packs. The blind seer led them through the narrow streets to a great square, where stalls of all sorts were set up, and bands of ragged jongleurs roamed, juggling apples and bellfruit, and pulling coins from behind people's ears. Jorge found an empty spot to crouch, and began to wail out his beggar's song, calling for coins and good wishes. In between verses, he listened to the gossip of the marketplace and planted a few seeds of his own. The afternoon sped past so quickly it was only when Jorge began to pack up that he realized Tòmas was no longer crouched beside him.

With the enchanted gloves muffling the boy's magic, Jorge had no way of knowing when the boy had crept away or how long he had been missing. Cursing fluently, the seer called down Jesyah and instructed him to search the marketplace. He then began his own search, casting out his mind anxiously and tapping his way through the thinning crowds. Jorge was well known in these parts, and so many people called greetings to him, some kindly, some not. To all that were kind, Jorge asked if they had seen a small blond boy. Fair hair was rare enough in this land of dark-eyed, dark-haired people for him to be sure Tòmas might have been noticed. All his queries were in vain, though, and Jorge cursed the nyx for creating a concealing magic so strong it would hide his apprentice from his own eyes. By the time night was falling and the torch-bearers were filling the square with orange smoky light, Jorge was close to tears. Lucescere was not the city for a young boy to be lost in.

Scruffy pushed against a well-dressed man in the crowd and felt through his heavy coat the fat, hard shape of a well-filled purse. A smile flickered over his face but he drifted away as the man looked round sharply, feeling the presence of someone too close for comfort. By the time the man's hazel eyes were scanning the crowd, Scruffy was well away, a piebald puppy galumphing at his heels.

"We'll eat tonight, Jed," Scruffy whispered, pulling at the puppy's flea-bitten ears. They followed the man through the marketplace, never hovering close enough to attract any attention, but never losing sight of the plump man in his fur-lined cloak.

The puppy was just four weeks old, and the only thing in the world that Scruffy had to call his own. He had rescued the puppy from being eaten, for meat was scarce after the long, hard winter and many a lady's pet had found its way into a thief's cookpot. Painfully thin as the puppy was, it still meant the best meal the thieves had had for a long time and they had not been happy at Scruffy's interference. At first Scruffy himself was unsure of why he had rescued the little dog, or even why he did not eat it himself. After a night spent with the warm little body snuggled under his shirt, he did not wonder any longer. He just knew the puppy was his and had to be protected.

Scruffy was an orphan, and like many children in Lucescere, lived off what he could beg or steal. His mother had been a maid in the royal palace, his father a gardener. When the Rìgh left Lucescere and took his royal court down to the new palace by the sea, they had been left without jobs, despite their families having been employed by the MacCuinns for generations. By the time Scruffy was born, his father was one of the famous band of Lucescere thieves, his mother a prostitute. In Lucescere there was not much else for an ex-lady's maid to do. By the age of five, both his parents were dead, and the little boy was left to fend for himself as best he could. It had not taken long for Scruffy to adjust to living on the streets, and the thieves of Lucescere had a strict honor code that protected their own. Scruffy thought his life was a good one, even though cold and hunger were his daily bed-mates.

The chance for Scruffy to steal the man's purse came as the Lady of Lucescere's litter was carried swaying through the marketplace. The plump man stopped to stare, as indeed did everyone in the square, for the lady had chosen cloth of gold curtains for her litter and they glittered in the bright sun. Servants beating drums and blowing pipes led the procession and followed after, and the litter itself was born on the shoulders of four gaudily dressed men. Fascinated as he was by the sight, Scruffy took the opportunity to press up close to the man, slip his hand in his pocket and gently remove the purse. He was just slipping his hand free when Jed caught sight of a kitten perched on a young boy's shoulder, and with a hoarse bark of rage, launched himself forward. The cat shrieked and dived for cover, and the puppy promptly gave chase, his ears flapping wildly as he skidded and lost his footing in the mud. Scruffy gave a shout and followed after, afraid of losing the dog in the crowd, as the plump man clapped his palm to his empty pocket.

"Thief! Stop, thief!" he called, and Scruffy felt his heart sink as he put on speed.

Stealing in the marketplace was always dangerous, for the shopkeepers had an unwritten agreement to help stamp out thievery. At the shouts of "Stop, thief," many tried to grasp Scruffy's shoulder or bowl him over so they could pin him to the ground. Luckily, though, this was Scruffy's home ground and most of the beggar children swarming the great square were members of Scruffy's gang. As thin as matchsticks and dressed in a wide assortment of dirty rags, they dodged and weaved through the crowd, tangling the fat man's legs or knocking over a basket of apples so the city soldiers slipped and fell. Distracted by the sudden swarm of dirty children, the pursuit fell behind, and with a slap to the palm of Jay the Fiddler, one of his lieutenants, Scruffy dived into the labyrinth of alleys beyond the square.

Clasping the heavy purse hard to his chest, Scruffy ran after the determined white bob of Jed's tail, leaping over a basket of bellfruit and ducking his head to avoid being brained by two men carrying a loom. It was only sheer persistence that prevented Scruffy from losing sight of his dog, but at last he ducked into a dark alley to find the puppy wagging his stumpy tail and barking loudly at the outraged ball of fuzz perched on a narrow windowsill.

"Bad dog, bad dog," Scruffy said, and fumbled for the length of string tied around the puppy's neck. Jed avoided his grasp, however, jumping up and down in a vain attempt to reach the kitten, who sat down and calmly began to wash. Scruffy made another lunge and caught the end of the string just as a small blond boy came running into the alley.

"Kitty, kitty," he called.

"Your scat?" Scruffy demanded belligerently.

"Aye," the boy replied sunnily and held out his arms so the kitten jumped straight from the windowsill onto his shoulder. Jed whined and rubbed around the boy's feet, making Scruffy jerk on his string with jealousy. He eyed the little boy with distaste. He was blond and very neat, with wide blue eyes, and a good pair of boots. Scruffy had never owned a pair of shoes and he eyed them with contemptuous envy. The little boy also wore a pair of black gauntlets, like a falconer, and Scruffy huddled his own dirty, scratched paws under his threadbare jerkin.

"Your bloody scat almost got me caught."

"Your dog almost ate my cat."

"I could've got into real trouble!"

"Ye were stealing."

Scruffy was taken aback. "Wasna."

"Ye were. I saw ye."

Scruffy darted forward and punched the little boy in the face, so he reeled back and fell, blood trickling from one nostril. To Scruffy's horror, Jed barked at him and bounded forward to lick the little boy's face.

"What ye go and hit me for?" The blond boy sat up, one hand to his bleeding nose. "I wasna going to tell anyone."

The kitten, finding itself face to face with Jed, hissed and arched its back. The puppy bounded forward joyfully, barking, but the little boy said, "No, dog," and obediently Jed flopped to the ground, giving his hand a lick.

That was too much for Scruffy. "Jed! Come here!" he commanded. His puppy whined and wagged his tail but did not move. "Jed! Do as ye're told! Come here!" Reluctantly the dog wriggled through the dust to Scruffy's feet, but cast a longing look back at the little boy, who was scrambling to his feet.

"Wha' a runt!" Scruffy said contemptuously, and pushed the little boy. Again he fell over, and Scruffy leaned over and began to pull his boots from his feet.

"Do no' take my boots!" the boy said in dismay, tears beginning to trickle. "I need to walk such a long way. I need my boots."

Scruffy sat down and tried to squeeze his broad, flat feet into the boots, only managing the task with some difficulty. "Och, dinna I look grand!" he crowed. "I look like a laird!" Flushed with his success, he began to pull at the boy's jacket and then tried to wrench one of the gloves off, even though there was little chance he could fit his hand in it. For the first time the little boy began to fight back.

Scruffy had been so consumed by jealousy and instinctive dislike he had not been keeping an eye on the mouth of the alley, and had virtually forgotten he had been chased all through the marketplace. He was just grinding the little boy's face into the ground, and trying to undo the clasp of his woolly plaid when there was a shout, and he looked up in horror to see the fat man in the furred cloak pointing at him, a whole group of blue-clad town guards with him.

"That's the lad who stole my purse!" the fat man shouted.

Scruffy looked about him in panic, but the alley ended in a high wall with only a small window breaking its height. There was nowhere to run, and none of his gang was around to help him escape. He let go of the little boy and gathered the puppy up in his arms, conscious of the weight of the purse in his pocket. If he was caught, the best he could hope for was a branding or to lose his right hand. At the worst, he would be hung.

As the town guards fanned out, closing off any means of escape, he launched into action. Running full-tilt at the guards, he head-butted one in the stomach, dodged around him and through the gap. Ordinarily Scruffy would have been able to escape, for he was quick and canny, but he was hobbled by the too-small boots and laden down with the squirming body of his puppy tucked inside his shirt. The guards caught him halfway down the street.

The little boy was also held tightly by a guard, the fat man proclaiming he must be an accomplice. When his purse was found in Scruffy's pocket, the fat man was very pleased. "Take them to the city dungeons!" he cried. "I will speak to my cousin Baron Renton myself!"

The city dungeons were deep below the old palace, which had been abandoned when the Rìgh moved the court to Rhyssmadill fifteen years earlier. The current Baron of Lucescere occupied only one wing of the massive building, the Guild of Seekers another, with the rest being allowed to fall into ruin. Scruffy and Tòmas, frightened as they were, could not help but look about them in interest as they were taken through a pair of great gates and up a neglected drive, planted on either side with tall trees, just budding with white blossoms. With the snow-capped mountains behind, the glittering domes and turrets of the palace looked very beautiful, set as they were in acres of wild gardens, with the Tower of Two Moons, greatest of all the Witch Towers, rising straight as an arrow in the background.

"I've only ever looked through the gates and ye canna

see much," Scruffy whispered, limping in the tight boots which were chafing his feet unbearably. "My da was once a gardener here, ye ken."

"Where is he now?"

"He's dead," Scruffy answered, just as he was knocked sideways by a blow from a guard, who yelled at him to be quiet.

They had little chance to see much of the inside of the palace, for they were marched straight through to the guards' barracks and then down to the dungeons. Deeper and deeper they descended into the bowels, darkness and a horrible smell closing over them. Tòmas shrunk closer to Scruffy, who was surprised at the protectiveness that swelled up inside him. They were eventually thrown into a long room of cells, filled to the brimming with men, women and children, some chained to the wall, others free to roam about their small pen, clutching the wooden bars and peering out at the blaze of torches that accompanied the guards.

This was the thieves' gallery, they were told by a young man who recognized Scruffy as the son of Adair the Bold. "Well, young Dillon, following in your da's footsteps? Well done! Shame your da is no' here to see it, he'd be that proud!" Culley, the young man, was here for thieving, as they all were, and had been there for almost three years. "Baron Renton do be busy wi' other things. I was told we would be tried and judged when there were too many thieves in here and they needed the room. I would say that would be soon."

The long gallery was indeed crowded with prisoners, most sunken-eyed and pale, as if they too had been locked up for years. Many were sick, coughing hoarsely, and one old man lay in a pile of rags, his waxen features silhouetted against the slimy stone wall, his breath rattling in his throat.

Following Tòmas's gaze, Culley's mouth twisted. "He's been like that for days now. It will no' be long, and we'll have a corpse stinking up the place. Shame. He was a grand auld man, King o' the Thieves, afore he was caught. No' that they ken, the fools. None o' us'd betray him. He was taken wi' his daughter, who stole the Lady's jewels right off her finger without her noticing a thing! She was no' got for that, but for spitting at the seanalair. The jewels are safely stashed away somewhere, no doubt o' that."

Culley was a garrulous young man and obviously glad to have a new audience, tired as he was of talking with his cell-mates, who threw in sarcastic comments every now and again, but generally sat in silence in the foul straw, too broken by hunger and fear to move much at all. Scruffy listened in interest, but Tòmas was concentrating on the old man, lying like a corpse in his sepulchre cell. One of the old man's bare feet was almost within his reach, and so while Culley was telling Scruffy he'd be lucky if he ever saw daylight again, Tòmas took off his gauntlet and reached his hand through the bars to touch the old man. He could not reach, so had to lie almost prone, stretching his arm as far as he could. Scruffy noticed what he was doing just as Tòmas managed to touch the old man's toe. His rude comment was halted as a wave of color seemed to wash over the dying man. The pink bloom of health began at his toe, and washed right over his body, finishing at his face. The old man stirred and coughed, then sat up tremulously. His daughter, who had been cradling his head and weeping quietly, cried out in surprise. He shook his head and seemed to smile.

"Come closer," Tòmas said. "It is better if I can touch your head."

The old man and his daughter looked at him in blank surprise, then the old man shuffled over and knelt so Tòmas could put his hands through the bars and lay them on his head. This time the change was dramatic. Color sprung up in the old man's cheeks, his eyes brightened, his stooped shoulders straightened, and he rose and stretched. "I feel bloody grand!" he cried. "Where we be? Wha' has happened?"

The entire gallery was thrown into chaos. Sick prisoners stretched out their hands to Tòmas through the bars; whispers and exclamations ran round like wildfire; and the old man's daughter knelt at Tòmas's feet, thanking him and crying out that here was magic, magic had returned to Lucescere at last.

Locked in his cell as he was, Tòmas could not reach all the prisoners, but he laid his hands on all those he could and those he could not moaned and pressed up against the bars. Scruffy and Culley stared at him in awe. Soon those too far away from Tòmas to be touched were rattling their bars, calling to him, begging him to touch them. One prisoner, a huge bearlike man with a leg all swollen and weeping with pus, managed to pull one of the wooden stakes out of the ground. A cheer went up and, with a loud groan, he managed to knock another out of the way. At last he was kneeling in the straw on the outside of Tòmas's cell and when Tòmas laid his hands on the giant's curly black hair and all the infection melted away, the old bruises and cuts disappearing, and he could stand on his leg without pain, a cheer went up.

The black-haired giant was able to break open Tòmas's cell and the boy hurried around the room, touching everyone he could reach. One by one the cells were broken open. Strength and hope filled every prisoner in the room, and they began to test the door at the entrance to the gallery. No one had responded to the noise and excitement in the prisoners' gallery, and Culley shouted, "The guards never stay down here when they could be up drinking and feasting in their guard-room. If we can get free . . ."

The thought of drinking and feasting was an added spur to the prisoners, and the extraordinary strength Tòmas's touch had imparted to them, at last had the wooden door broken down and the prisoners streaming out into the dank corridors beyond. The old man, minutes before close to death, naturally took the lead, and the escaped thieves followed him, mindful of his years as King of the Thieves, leader of their guild.

The escape was not to be that easy, however. Three hours after breaking down the door they were still wandering in the labryinthine dungeons, though their numbers had been swelled by other prisoners freed from their cells. The high excitement and bravado was beginning to fade into fear of the consequences, and arguments between the escapees were turning ugly. Tòmas was exhausted by his healing efforts and could barely stumble along, and all were painfully aware it was almost time they were all fed. Once the guards came with the trays of slop, they would find the door broken down and all the prisoners escaped.

They had paused to rest in one of the endless identical

corridors, and the thieves were arguing amongst themselves about the best way to go.

"We've been in this corridor before!" Culley was asserting belligerently. "I recognize that stone."

"How can ye recognize a stone in the wall? They all look the same!"

"We should be markin' our passage," Scruffy said. "Does anyone have any chalk?" Of course no one did, nor a knife they could scrape marks with, nothing that could show them the path they'd already taken. Tòmas lay curled on the damp stone, his head on Scruffy's thigh, his eyes closed. He was breathing shallowly, his soft face white with exhaustion.

The corridors were nearly all lit with strong-smelling torches that were placed sporadically along the way and could burn for days without being replaced. As they all argued, the torch nearest to them suddenly went out and they were plunged into darkness. Immediately a scared hush fell over the band of thieves. Tòmas sat up, yawning and rubbing his eyes.

The thieves were whispering, "Wha' should we do? Where are we? We're lost!"

To Tòmas's surprise a finger touched his hand briefly, then withdrew. A voice said in his mind, *"come, lad."*

"Ceit Anna?" he whispered.

"None other. Come."

"Wha' about the others?" he said. At his words, the thieves had fallen silent and although he could not see them, he could feel them staring in his direction.

"What do I care about a gaggle of thieves? Come."

"Please, Ceit Anna, I canna leave them."

The nyx sighed, and Tòmas felt her leaning over him. *"Very well, but only because the guards are close, and they have lights and I do no' like the light. Bring them if you wish."*

Tòmas took the nyx's hand, and he felt a shudder go through her at his touch. His hand was still bare, the gauntlet tucked in his pocket with the kitten, who had been miaowing pitifully for sometime now.

"Take my hand, Scruffy," Tòmas commanded. "She canna bear the light so we mun go in darkness."

"Who? Wha' are ye talking about?"

"A . . . friend. She will help us get free. Trust her, she likes the guards less than any o' ye."

And so, linked by hand, the long line of prisoners made their escape through the endless tunnels of darkness. Again and again one of the thieves' courage would fail and the line would halt while arguments went on, but each time the nyx said indifferently in her dry-leaf whispery voice, "Leave them. They will die in these tunnels, but no one will care," and each time the thief would hastily grasp someone's hand again and on they would go.

It was many hours before the nyx at last halted, and said to Tòmas, "*We are under the great square. If they climb up into the sewers they should be able to find their way out.*"

Tòmas told Scruffy, who told Culley behind him, and so the word passed down the line. Most of the thieves obeyed the nyx, and scrambled up one of the great pipes, thanking Tòmas over and over again, bowing to him, and kissing the edge of his cloak. "It was no' me, it was Ceit Anna who got us out," he said tiredly, but the thieves were too afraid to even try to see the nyx through the gloom.

Scruffy, the old man and his daughter, Culley, the black-haired giant, and a handful of others stayed.

"Do no' send us away, my laird," the old man said. "Your magic is a wonderful thing. We would stay wi' ye and have ye tell us wha' ye wish us to do."

Tòmas was only seven years old, and very tired and hungry. He clung to Ceit Anna's hand and could think of nothing to say. Scruffy took it upon himself to answer. "Ye can hang round if ye want, but do no' be expecting him to touch ye again. He's worn out!"

The nyx bent and whispered in Tòmas's ear. "Jorge is waiting for ye in my cavern. Once he told me what had happened, I came to find ye. It is lucky ye took off your glove, for otherwise I might no' have been able to follow ye. No one knows these tunnels like I do."

The old seer did not scold Tòmas, just gathered him in his arms, hugged him tight, fed him milk and porridge, and put him to bed. While the little boy slept, the kitten curled up at his side, Jorge spoke to the remaining thieves, and his words resounded. He spoke of how a winged rìgh was coming, how the Lodestar would be saved, and a new era of peace and enlightenment would dawn on the land.

"But the Lodestar was destroyed in the Day o' Reckoning!" the old thief's daughter cried.

"It was no'. It was saved by Meghan NicCuinn and hidden until such a day could come when it might be used again. The Lodestar shall again protect the people o' Eileanan. Magic shall again be revered and used for the good o' the people."

By the time Tòmas woke at noon, hungry again and eager to see Jorge, the thieves had gone to spread the word through the city. Only Scruffy remained, Jed curled up on his lap chewing a strip of dried meat. "Your auld man let me stay," he said jubilantly. "I'm to travel wi' ye!"

They spent the afternoon resting and preparing for the next stage of their journey. Scruffy had reluctantly given back Tòmas's boots, and had bound his feet up in rags in an attempt to protect them from the stones of the road. Jorge took the kitten back to its mother and returned with a leather satchel full of supplies donated by the chandler's wife, which made Scruffy's eyes widen in excited anticipation. Jorge was looking worried, for the streets had been filled with blue-clad city soldiers, searching for the escaped thieves, and a "lad, fair, charged with the foul practice o' witchcraft." The Guild of Seekers had also mobilized, causing the old man's face to furrow up like crumpled paper.

Jorge had planned on slipping out of the city the way they had come, mingling with the crowds of people crossing the Bridge of Seven Arches before Lucescere's gates shut at sunset. The legions of soldiers marching the streets and guarding the gates and the great crowds of excited citizens made this plan impossible, however, and he racked his brains trying to think of an alternative plan. The Ban-Bharrach and the Muileach Rivers were too fierce to be crossed without the bridges, and the only other way out of the city was through the palace grounds, far too risky to be attempted.

Seeing the worried expression on the old man's face, Scruffy cheerfully asked what was eating his goat. Absentmindedly Jorge explained his problem, only to have the freckle-faced lad grin and say, "Och, no need to fraitch yourself. That be no problem. We'll slip out the Thieves' Way." In answer to Jorge's question, Scruffy explained that the thieves had to have a secret way to come and go without the soldiers knowing, and that as the son of Adair the Bold, he naturally knew the way. "Me and the gang'll help ye, master," he said.

So, rather reluctantly, Jorge agreed to put himself and Tòmas into Scruffy's very grubby hands. Leaning on his gnarled staff and holding Tòmas's gauntleted hand tightly, he followed the beggar boy out into the crowded slums and was perturbed to hear the ragged cheer that rose up from the throng. Crowds gathered behind them, calling blessings on their heads and reaching out to touch Tòmas. Small gifts of flowers, cakes, bundles of scented candles and skins of wine were thrust into their hands, and mothers held out babies for Tòmas to touch. The little boy clung close to Jorge's side, but Scruffy swaggered boldly, exchanging ribald comments with the crowd and waving to those he knew.

Soon a ragged band of children was swarming round them, saluting Scruffy and asking for news. Jay, the most able of Scruffy's lieutenants, began to play on his fiddle, and the discreet withdrawal which Jorge had planned turned into a procession of laughing, dancing, shouting townsfolk. Stout matrons and thin whores waltzed together on the muddy cobblestones; bellfruit sellers dropped their great flat baskets and danced jigs, their legs bare and hairy under their bright robes; a crippled beggar hopped wildly on his one good foot, waving his twisted stick and knocking off a plump merchant's tam-o'-shanter; children sang hastily composed rhymes of winged warriors and healing hands.

The procession wound its way through the muddy alleyways, torches hissing in the constant gray drizzle. Resigned, Jorge shrugged, clutched his rag of a blanket closer around his shoulders, and limped along, his dirty beard flapping in the wind. There was nothing he could do but trust in Scruffy's gang to alert them to any soldiers and to hide them in the crowds. Besides, it did his old heart good to hear Lucescere singing the praises of witches again. Lucescere had always been proud of its magical heritage, the one-time home of the MacCuinn clan, the most powerful family of witches in the land.

Jorge heard the sound of marching feet before his ragged guide did, but even as he reached forward to grip Scruffy's shoulder in fear, the beggar boy had begun deploying his troops. Jay the fiddler boy kept marching forward, playing his violin with such skill and passion that the townsfolk kept dancing and singing in his train without realizing their hero, the little boy with the sky-blue eyes, was no longer with them.

Scruffy pulled back a grubby curtain and ushered Jorge and Tòmas through, as two boys promptly began to play knucklebones in front of it, hiding their passage. As the soldiers ran into the square, a crowd of small, very dirty children ducked and weaved about their feet. A few of the soldiers staggered, and one almost fell, grabbing hold of a pile of crates to steady himself and bringing them crashing to the ground, spilling their contents across the mud. All was confusion, and by the time the saighdear had sorted out his troops and begun questioning the crowd, there was no sign of the blind beggar with the raven on his shoulder, nor of the little boy the soldiers were seeking so desperately.

The Baron of Lucescere had put a high price on the head of the Lad with the Healing Hands, once the stories racing round Lucescere had reached his ears. Worse, he had threatened his soldiers with a whipping and a severe cut in their pay unless the source of all the rumors was tracked down quickly. Baron Renton knew that his rule over Lucescere was tenuous, and only maintained with great brutality and the excellence of his spies. Lucescere had been a trouble spot since the Day of Reckoning, filled with witch-lovers and rebels who worked constantly to undermine his protector the Banrìgh Maya, and therefore him. Sixteen years of harsh rule and the public burning of any witches found had done little to cement his domination, and the Baron knew the boy's so-called miracles would be enough to cause an open uprising. Not only would he then lose the life of luxury and power he enjoyed so much, but any failure on his part would not please the Banrìgh, and he knew he must keep pleasing her at all costs.

So, despite all Scruffy's diversions and tricks, it was a hard chase through the narrow alleys of the slums, soldiers seemingly around every corner. Once or twice they were sighted and the chase grew fierce, Jorge having to pick up his ragged robes and run. Once he only escaped after diving through the half open door of a carriage-way, Scruffy slamming it shut and bolting it behind them so that the soldiers had to use their shoulders to break it down. By the time the door was smashed through, the alley beyond was empty, though if the soldiers had thought to look up they might have seen a small bare foot disappearing over the edge of the gutter as Scruffy chivied his charges over the rooftops. Another time Jesyah was almost spitted on a spear after dive-bombing the soldiers as they emerged into an open square. Distracted by the flurry of black feathers and the raucous screeching of the raven, the soldiers failed to see an old man tapping his way round a corner, a mangy puppy at his heels. Instead, the soldiers hurried in a different direction, tricked by the sound of running footsteps that turned out to be merely two beggar children playing.

By now Scruffy had led them down into the poorest part of the city, the huddle of shacks and shanties built into the side of the cliff below the waterfalls. Here the roar of the Shining Waters was so loud Scruffy had to yell to be heard, and their clothes were dampened by the constant spray. The uncobbled pathways were knee-deep in mud, and they made their way across the reeking slime by stepping on unsteady bridges made by broken planks and stones. Here there were no singing crowds, no gifts of bread and wine. Thin girls huddled in corners, coughing and hiding their bruised faces behind filthy rags. Men with scarred faces that caused Tòmas's heart to race with fear peered from doorways and fingered notched daggers before melting away. The puppy Jed kept up a low growl in his throat, causing Scruffy to bend and stroke his black-patched head. In several places the water roared down right past them and they had to cling to the slimy cliff wall to avoid being swept away. Far below them was the loch, while above the dark cliff loomed over them, broken by the white rushes of water. The air smelled foul, and Tòmas kept his gloved hand clapped tight over his mouth.

"Where are ye taking us?" Jorge asked, his voice trembling a little. Although he too had grown up on the streets of Lucescere, he had rarely been in this part of the city, known as a cesspool of disease and crime. Only those who wanted to hire a cut-throat or arrange for the burning down of a rival's warehouse would venture here, and even then they would hire one of the Guild of Thieves as a go-between in preference to braving these streets themselves.

"Ye'll see," Scruffy answered, then embarrassed, said, "I mean . . . ye'll find out soon enough."

Once or twice they were accosted, and each time Scruffy, his voice shrill with fear, cried, "In the name o' Adair the Bold and the King o' Thieves, let me through," and each time they were allowed to pass. By now the key members of Scruffy's gang had caught up with them—the thin-legged Jay who had played the fiddle so beautifully, a lass called Finn who called out cheerful insults to the men lurking in the shadows, the two freckled lads who had played knucklebones, and a younger boy, only about nine years old, who hung close to Scruffy's shoulder. They came and went like shadows, reporting to Scruffy who would then send them off on yet another errand, to return five or ten minutes later with another summary of the location of soldiers or witch-sniffers.

"I've thought up a diversion," Scruffy whispered into Jorge's straining ear. "It's dangerous but I think it'll work. I found a lad that looks much like our Tòmas . . . He and a few o' the other lads have led the soldiers back toward the palace. They'll think we're trying to get through the maze and out into the mountains that way. Finn says they've taken the bait, and the whole lot o' them are running like mad toward the auld Tower."

Soon the narrow track led past the last of the shanties and came to a halt at a bulge of rock, the water running down in a black clamor. Tòmas stopped in fear, unable to see how they could travel any further; while Jorge turned his blind head from side to side, unable to hear or sense anything but the tangled energies of the waterfall.

Scruffy edged his way forward, feeling round the bulge of rock. His foot slipped in the ooze and he almost fell, causing Tòmas to cry out in terror. He had found a handhold, though, and hung there grimly, water crashing onto his head and shoulders with the force of a hammer. With a massive heave, he pulled himself round the bulge of rock and was gone. Tòmas gave a little mewl of distress, but Finn was crouched by his side, reassuring him, and the oldest of the beggar boys—a thickset lad called Anntoin—was guiding Jorge's faltering steps forward.

The old man was not at all troubled by the slippery maneuverings required to get round the bulge for, blind as he was, he could not see the stomach-dropping fall to the loch so far below. With Scruffy pulling from one side and Anntoin pushing from the other, he got round quite nimbly, and then it was Tòmas's turn. The little boy could not help crying a little from fear and tiredness, but with Finn's encouragement and a length of old rope from Anntoin's belt tied round his waist, he slowly crept forward until the rock was pressing against his belly. Water pulverized his head and back, threatening to unbalance him, but Scruffy's muddy hand was waving from behind the outcrop and Anntoin was holding him steady. He reached out and grasped Scruffy's fingers and with a squeak, felt himself tugged round, feet flailing. He landed on his hands and knees at the mouth of a cave, great sheets of water pouring past like they had outside Ceit Anna's cave.

One by one the other children clambered round the rocky outcrop; Jed was heaved round, with the rope tied round his thin belly, then they all cautiously filed into the cave.

"Got the torches, Finn?" Scruffy asked, and with a nod and a smile, the girl pulled three long twigs, wrapped with cloth and pitch, from under her ragged skirt. Scruffy's flint was wet and so it took them a long time to light the torches, which stank foully when at last they spluttered into flame. They lit up the dark cave, however, showing a narrow crack at the back.

"Welcome to the Thieves' Way," Scruffy grinned, and took the lead.

In single file they followed him through the narrow passage that wound through the rock on which Lucescere was built. Occasionally they could hear the thud of boots overhead or the distant sound of shouting, reassuring sounds in the thick musty silence of the caves. Once they heard a dry rustle and Tòmas looked round excitedly. "Ceit Anna?" he whispered, but there was no answer and the sound did not come again.

Here and there the passage widened into a low cave, or split into different directions, but Scruffy seemed to know his way, padding forward soundlessly on his bare feet. After about twenty minutes they came to a junction and Scruffy was just moving forward when a long arm suddenly shot out and seized him by the neck. Before he could even squeal, a long, wickedly serrated knife was pressing into his throat and a hoarse voice said humorously, "Now where do ye think ye're going, Dillon me bold?"

Scruffy was unable to speak, but Finn dashed forward and kicked the unseen assailant squarely between the legs so that he gasped and bent over, the knife lifting from Scruffy's throat. The puppy Jed also tried to save his master, biting at the man's bare calf, but although Scruffy tried to wriggle free the man had recovered in an instant. Although his voice was even hoarser than ever, it did not lose its humorous tone. "Do no' go making any mistakes now, laddie," he said. "I'm a gentle man mesel' and no' wanting to hurt a passel o' brats, but I am no' the only one round here, and we do no' like just anyone saunt'ring our highways. So answer me quick, laddie, or I'll be getting angry and ye do no' want that."

Scruffy shrugged his shoulders sulkily, and tried to ease the pressure of the knife against his throat. "Ye be hurtin' me, Culley," Scruffy whined, but the man just tightened his hold. "I be helping the auld man and the bairn get outa Lucescere afore the witch-sniffers get hold o' them. The streets be swarming wi' soldiers and if the bloody Baron gets hold o' them they'll burn for sure . . ."

The knife lifted, and the man slid out of the shadows so that he could get a good look at the little party. "Aye, that be the lad," he said, and Tòmas recognized him as the thief they had befriended in the dungeons. Culley seemed to ruminate, his bearded cheeks rolling as he chewed his tongue, then he said abruptly, "Better be taking ye to see His Highness, for it's up to him to decide. Ye shouldna have brought strangers along our way, but since it's the lad that did save us, I be sure His Highness will no' be too hard on ye . . . C'mon, Dillon me bold, I'm sure ye ken the way . . ."

They were pushed and pulled through the tunnels at a great rate, at last coming to a high-roofed cave where men of all shapes and sizes lolled around a massive barrel of whiskey. By the looks of it, the barrel had been breached many hours before, for the men were full of jollity and temper. On a rough wooden seat by the fire was the old man whom Tòmas had healed in the dungeons, the one they called King of the Thieves. Standing behind him was his daughter, a wild-eyed, wild-haired woman with a cutlass thrust through her girdle, and a *sgian dubh* protruding from her boot. She recognized Tòmas immediately and came forward in a rush of gratitude which did much to disarm the hostility of the robbers milling around.

The King of the Thieves knew all the beggar children by name, a feat which both impressed and unnerved them. Finn, in particular, was disconcerted, her disquiet deepened even further when the old man continued smilingly, "And do no' worry, lassie, I be sure ye had nothing to do wi' the death o' auld Kersey and if ye did, well, who am I to be blaming ye?"

Finn went white, and shrank back into the shadows, but the old man only nodded and smiled and turned to Jorge. "Och, it be the blind prophet himself, inciting revolution in my city. No' that I be minding, o' course, chaos and confusion helping the honest thief to make a living. Still, all these soldiers do me no good and the cursed witch-sniffers are even worse. If I find ye've led them to me, well, a quick death is all ye'll get from me."

Scruffy shook his head violently, and told the thieves how he had organized a diversion in the shape of another small fair-haired boy. "Och, that'll be young Connor, I imagine," the old man said and, with an expression of awe, Scruffy nodded, telling how Connor and his sister Johanna had been deputized to lead the soldiers astray.

"Och, well, let us just be hoping they are no' caught too soon," the daughter said. "They'll rip the lad to pieces for deceiving them."

The unhappiness on Scruffy's face deepened.

The old man lit a strange pipe, which bubbled and hissed as he pulled on it. Foul-smelling smoke billowed round them, and they coughed and wiped their watering eyes. "Dillon me lad, ye ken I do no' take kindly to strangers being shown the Thieves' Way, or even being told about it. This is my kingdom down here and I decide who gets to walk my roads. Normally I'd be telling the boys to toss ye o'er the cliff and the Shining Waters would be doin' their justice, but my heart is divided on this one. I do be real grateful to this here lad for the touch o' his magic hands that got us all out o' that blaygird dungeon, and got the King back to his rightful throne." He patted the timber of his seat. "However, I canna be letting just anyone wander my roads, without hindrance or payment, and if word got out that I'd let ye, weeeelll . . ."

Jorge stepped forward and bowed his gray head. "Your Highness, please forgive us our intrusion on your private ways. If it were possible, we would have chosen to walk elsewhere, but since the lad here touched and healed those in the thieves' gallery and led them to freedom, the soldiers have been hard on our tails."

If he had hoped to remind the old man of his debt to Tòmas, the thief's next words seemed designed to remove any hope of being allowed to pass. "Och, that be true, the lad's accused o' witchcraft, is he no'? Wi' a price on your heads. I mun be thinking o' the profit that'd be bringing me."

Scruffy bounced forward, indignation running high, not noticing the twinkle in the old man's eyes. "Och, ye canna be betraying him to the redcloaks for blood money! He's only a wee lad and he saved ye!"

The King of the Thieves smiled and drank deeply of the cup he held in his hand. "I can be doing whatever I please, young Dillon," he said, when at last he raised his head again. "Though so bold ye are I'm reminded o' your da, the brazenest piece o' swagger the Thieves o' Lucescere have ever ken! Well I remember how he came to me when ye were just a runt, and your ma lying wi' the whore sickness eating her vitals away. It's Dillon the Bold ye be, just like your da!"

As Scruffy's chest swelled and he drew himself up an inch or two, the thief's expression darkened. "That's no' to say I like the boldness though, lad. Ye be so sharp ye'll cut yersel' one o' these days. Keep a humble tongue in your head, else ye'll be carrion meat afore ye're grown. If I be letting ye pass it's for the lad's sake, and the auld warlock, who I remember well from aulden days before this blaygird upstart Banrìgh got the country into such a mess and mucken. So for his sake and the wee laddie's, I'll let ye pass and no' because ye got a bold tongue, young Dillon!"

In confusion Scruffy nodded and bowed, and after they'd all toasted the King of the Thieves and the Lad with the Healing Hands with gulps of raw spirits, they were kindly but firmly escorted through the warren of caves to a small aperture which lead out onto the dark hillside. Scruffy was unusually silent, but when one of the beggar boys made a cheeky remark, a flash of his old spirit returned. "That be enough from ye, Artair, else ye'll be thrown out o' the gang, no mercy! And do no' be callin' me Scruffy no more, Dillon the Bold I be now!"

Margrit of the Thistle

Far to the south, in the misty fens of Arran, a boat pushed its way between rushes and slid quietly into the still waters of the Murkmyre. Sitting in the prow of the long, narrow dinghy was a still-faced woman, her back stiff, her hands folded calmly in her lap. She wore a black dress with a dark plaid pinned at her breast by a silver brooch in the shape of a thistle.

Thick mist coiled around the boat, obscuring the surface of the loch and caressing her face with damp fingers. Margrit NicFóghnan, Banprionnsa of Arran, lifted her face to its touch, frowning in pleasure. The boat slipped noiselessly around a marshy headland and the delicate spires of Tùr de Ceò drifted into view. Margrit's frown deepened. She loved the first view of the Tower of Mists after the long, wearisome journey through the marshes; its sharp-pointed, scrolled towers rose out of the bank of mist like a palace out of a fairy tale, a reminder to her of her royal heritage and proud ancestry, never to be forgotten.

With a slight sound the boat slid into position at the jetty and, without hurry, Margrit of Arran rose and disembarked, pulling the plaid closer around her shoulders. Servants and retainers lined the steps in silence, bowing and curtsying as she slowly walked up the steps toward the great arched door of the Tower. Standing on either side of the door were two Mesmerdean, their beautiful inhuman faces impassive, their four arms folded over their chests. More than seven feet high, they seemed strangely insubstantial, as if there was nothing below the loose gray robes that drifted and swirled about them in an unfelt breeze. Their multifaceted eyes stared at Margrit and she stared back without fear. They did not bow.

Engraved on each half of the door was the thistle device and the motto of the Clan of MacFóghnan: *Touch not the thistle.* Margrit frowned as she passed through the doors, and her fingers lifted to briefly touch the thistle brooch at her throat.

The great hall within was luxuriously appointed with rich carpets from Lucescere in crimson and blue and gray, and statues carved from the white marble of Rurach. The walls were hung with vast tapestries depicting great scenes in the history of the MacFóghnans. There was many of Fóghnan herself, one scene depicting the great ship of Cuinn sailing the magical storm that bent the fabric of the universe and brought the First Coven to the Far Islands. Fóghnan was depicted with a falling star above her head, symbolizing her great prophecy which had led them to this world. Another showed her leaving the wrecked ship upon arrival, her face stern and proud, while Owein MacCuinn wept like a child over the dead body of his father and shook his fist after her as she refused to bend to his authority. In the background a tidal wave was beginning to gather, looming over the crowd of frightened migrants—the great tide that would kill so many of those that had braved the Crossing. All of those who went with Fóghnan survived, and thereafter no one dared doubt the truth of her prophecies.

Other tapestries showed the magical summoning of Tùr de Ceò on an island in Murkmyre, deep within the shifting maze of the fenlands, and Fóghnan's death at the hands of Owein MacCuinn's youngest son, Balfour. Margrit smiled as she glanced up at the tapestry on her way through to her throne-room. The blood ran bitter between MacFóghnan and MacCuinn, who had learned one did not touch the thistle without pain. Balfour too had died soon after, of a mysterious ailment that saw him frothing at the mouth, his body arching backward in agony, his drumming heels tearing the earth up in great clods. MacFóghnan's twelve-year-old daughter, named Margrit as many NicFóghnans would be, had taken up her mother's staff and knife and assumed the duties of the Tower. Many years later, when Aedan MacCuinn had united the warring lands and peoples of Eileanan under the rule of the Lodestar, only Arran, Tìrsoilleir and the Fairgean had refused to accept his authority. Years of war had followed, but not even the Lodestar could pierce the mysteries of Murkmyre and the ever-hungry marshes had swallowed up the armies sent against her. The Clan of MacFóghnan had survived, as it always would.

The anger provoked by the memory of Fóghnan the Thistle's death brought Margrit into the great throne-room smiling. At the sight of her dimples, her son paled, standing up hurriedly. Aged in his early twenties, he seemed younger because of his awkwardness and lanky height. At the sight of him Margrit's smile deepened, and Iain began to look for a route of escape.

"Och, ye're back, M-M-Mother!"

"I see your powers o' observation are improving, at least." Margrit crossed the room with a slow, stately glide and arranged herself on the great throne of ornately carved wood piled with purple velvet cushions.

"H-H-How was your journey?"

She considered his question, straightening one of the massive rings on her fingers. "As I expected. The seeds o' dissension I sowed these last few years shall yield us a profitable crop."

He nodded, and began to back toward the door. She watched him through lowered eyelids, and then as he laid his hand on the panel, said, "And how have things progressed here, my son?"

"Och, well, well . . . K-K-Khan't-t-tirell will no doubt have m-m-much to tell ye . . . Shall I send for . . . h-h-him?"

"Och, no. I would prefer my son, heir to the Tower, to tell me. Have a seat, Iain."

Iain sank into one of the upright wooden chairs lining the hall and looked at her in trepidation. He told her all he could remember but, as always happened when he had to speak to his mother, his wits fled and so it was a garbled tale that emerged, all dragons rising and Mesmerdean dying and rebellion here and rebellion there. When he had stammered and stumbled into silence, she smiled at him, then laughed. Her laugh was particularly sweet and musical. "Go and call K-K-Khan'-t-t-t-tirell," she mocked. "At the very least I ken he will make sense."

Iain shot out of his chair and was almost at the door again when she said softly, "Why, o' all my lovers, was it your father that finally managed to impregnate me? True, he had the face o' an angel, but the wits o' a fool, and now his addled seed has grown into a halfwit! If I could bear another babe, I would drown ye in the marshes, as I should have done when ye were born. Since ye are my only offspring and the future o' the Tower would drown with ye, ye will be glad to ken I have arranged a marriage for ye. She is strong and canny and has magic, and is willing to suffer your caresses in order to be the first lady o' Arran. Do no' fear she will be disappointed when she meets ye, for I have told her all about ye."

Iain went scarlet and tried to speak, but his stammer defeated him. Margrit watched his strangled attempts with a smile on her face, and said smoothly, "I am glad ye are so transported with delight, my dear. She is a NicHilde and so o' the best blood, even though the Tìrsoilleirean no longer acknowledge the existence o' magic or the lineage o' the descendants o' the First Coven. She is arranging her affairs now, and will be with us soon. Ye have one duty only, and that is to get her with babe. Now get out o' my sight!"

Once her son had scuttled out of the room, Margrit sank back into the cushions and, still smiling, toyed with the silver tassels that hung from her black velvet gown. Soon her chamberlain slid into the room, a tall, lean man with a long mane of white hair tied back with leather. The architecture of his dark, fierce face was sharp and angular with prominent cheekbones, his eyes so heavily hooded that their color could not be seen. On either cheek, three thin white scars stood out clearly against his olive skin. His looks would have been enough to have aroused suspicion of fairy-blood, without the heavy, tightly curled horns on either side of his forehead.

"My lady requested my presence?" He spoke with a thick, halting accent, though his sweeping bow was the very model of courtly grace.

"Khan'tirell, indeed I am glad to see ye, for my halfwit

son has been babbling away and I need someone to make sense o' it for me. He said the dragons have risen."

"Indeed, Your Grace, matters did no' unfold as we wished in the Sithiche Mountains."

"Why no'?" Her voice was mild.

Khan'tirell told the story efficiently and well. The Mesmerd she had chosen had accompanied Seeker Thoth deep into the Sithiche Mountains to assist him in his move against the dragons. That the Mesmerd had had a mission of his own had not of course been revealed to the seeker, as the Lady Margrit had suggested. The Mesmerd had become aware of a significant amount of magic being expended and so had subtly directed the Red Guards in that general direction. They had come across a party of witches practicing their Candlemas rites in a well-hidden valley that had, of course, been easily penetrated by the Mesmerd. The witches had escaped, all but one.

"Why only one?"

"The Arch-Sorceress Meghan NicCuinn was there, my lady."

"Ah, I see. Go on."

The chamberlain shifted his shoulders slightly as a small frown marred the smoothness of Margrit's face. "The Mesmerd was killed by a magical ward the Arch-Sorceress had set to guard her residence."

"How? Why did the Mesmerd no' sense the ward?"

"I do no' ken, my lady, having only heard the report from Seeker Thoth. I imagine, though, that she hid the more powerful ward below a simple device and so tricked the Mesmerd."

"Then it deserved to die," Margrit said indifferently.

When she learned that Meghan had reached the dragons before the Red Guards and had somehow convinced them to attack the legion, Margrit laughed. "She's wee, but she's feisty," she said appreciatively. "So Thoth is dead? Damn it! I spent time cultivating him. Still, he was never the only arrow in my quiver. The rising o' the dragons is a different matter. That I am concerned about. Even angry about. Meghan should no' be meddling in my affairs. I had hoped she was dead, the doddering auld thing. I am pleased to hear she is still alive, for that will give me the pleasure o' arranging her death." Margrit paused and stroked her cheek with one finger. "The dragons are slow to rouse, but once roused, they are terrible," she mused softly. "Have they flown over any o' Rionnagan or Siantan? That would at least be some consolation."

"No, Your Grace. After killing the Red Guards, the dragons returned to their palace and flew no more."

"Strange. Very strange."

Khan'tirell told her then that the Mesmerdean were very distressed at the death of their comrade. Mesmerdean did not die easily, and they had spent the month since in the strange rituals of their mourning. All the Mesmerdean traveling in other lands had returned and they refused to leave the marshes again. As if that were not trouble enough, the children in the Theurgia chose this moment to stage a rebellion, locking themselves in their wing and throwing stones and hard bread at all who came near. Khan'tirell had eventually overpowered them, of course, and severely whipped the ringleaders, and killed the most recalcitrant, who unfortunately had also been the most Talented. He had been confident that she would like him to teach them a lesson, however.

"Ye did exactly right. How dare a gaggle o' snotty-nosed farm kids stage a rebellion on my land?"

"Ye forget, my lady, that a number o' them were stolen from the families o' lairds and rich merchants, and quite a few are direct descendants o' the First Coven."

"Poor and dispossessed now, however," Margrit smiled. Khan'tirell bowed his head. "What did they want?" she asked curiously.

"To return home, my lady."

"Fools! Do they no' ken my Theurgia is the only one left on the entire island? They'll get no training elsewhere. Make sure their rations are all cut."

"It has already been done, my lady."

"Now, let me tell ye what transpired from my journey to Tirsoilleir. It is as I hoped. The Fealde o' Bride was pleased, no, anxious to receive me—she is even prepared to overlook my suspected use o' enchantments, uneasy as such suspicions make her. They are tired o' marching up and down the streets o' Bride, shouting "Deus Vult!" and dreaming o' great victories. Four hundred and score years is more than enough time for them to forget the last time they challenged the might o' the MacCuinns. Now that the Rìgh wanders in a dream land, and the Inheritance o' Aedan is destroyed and the land divided, the Tìrsoilleirean grow ambitious. The Fealde wants to strike at something, and what better than the earth-worshipping infidels? I made her bargain hard, though, for my permission to march her armies through Arran."

"What has she offered?"

"Gold, o' course, and jewels. The continued independence o' Arran, plus a fair proportion o' Aslinn and Blèssem as well as the Strand, since o' course they do no' wish to defend the coast. A NicHilde to mate with my idiot son, plus all the forbidden works locked away in Tùr na Sabaidean. They say they have a fine collection o' works from the Other World, as well as many texts on the mysteries. Also permission to recruit in Tìrsoilleir for my Theurgia."

"Do they no' ken ye have been "recruiting" in Tìrsoilleir for years?"

She frowned, playing with the tassels on her gown. "Of course no'. If anyone had seen or heard the Mesmerdean stealing children they would have dismissed them as a trick o' the eye or the result o' too much whiskey."

"I thought the Tìrsoilleirean frowned upon intoxicating liquor."

"Och, they do, Khan'tirell! They are a pious people. I've had a terribly boring few months, pretending to be as mealy-mouthed as they are. Ye ken they must pray in the Kirk as many as three times a day? Still, religious fanaticism has its purposes, and they will prove an able army. In the meantime, I will speak with the Mesmerdean. We canna have them skulking in the marshes. I want fear and distrust in the countryside and I want every bairn with a scrap o' magical ability here under my eye!"

The Mesmerdean came slowly and with arrogance, but Lady Margrit was too wise to show anger or impatience. She knew she did not command the Mesmerdean, that their obedience to her will was due only to some purpose of their own that, for this time at least, lay parallel with hers. When they pleased they would melt back into the marshes, and she would lose her most potent weapon.

Only the elders came, twenty-one of them, dry, shrivelled husks without the unearthly beauty that the Mesmerdean nymphs possessed. Many did not wear the delicate gray robes that Margrit had designed for them, and she smiled as she lay back in her chair, for she saw this as a subtle insult. They rustled their silvery wings together and stared at her from great, shiny eyes that were indeed thousands of eyes, clustered closely together.

Communicating with the Mesmerdean was difficult. They had no language that another species could learn for they did not speak and the multitonal humming they made by rubbing their wings and claws together was impossible to copy. However, Margrit had lived in the fens of Arran all her life and knew what every twitch of wing, gesture of claw and timbre of hum meant, and she knew they read her energy forces as easily as she read words on a page. One did not talk to the Mesmerdean for they heard no words, and by talking, hidden emotions could be revealed by the fluctuations of one's emotional energies. So Margrit sat on her throne and the Mesmerdean watched her and she watched them and gradually the rustle of their wings began to roll and vibrate and their eyes gleamed with metallic hues.

Margrit listened to each quaver and trill, and she frowned and thought of the rich plains of Clachan again seeping with water, a great labyrinth rustling with the sedge grasses of the marsh; and she smiled and thought of the people of Clachan and Blèssem sinking back into the arms of the Mesmerdean, eyes closing in bliss; and she frowned and thought of long trails of glistening eggs laid in the mud of the marshes. As she thought and imagined, the quality of the trill deepened and harmonized, until soon there was but one shrill note left. She gazed over the elders and found the one, and his wings were back and erect, his head thrust forward. She bowed her head, and imagined Meghan the Arch-Sorceress crumpling back after a Mesmerd's kiss and immediately the quality of the song changed, quickening and intensifying. They knew who Meghan was, for Mesmerdean shared their experience as one, linked together by a sense as precise as their eyesight and their emotional radar. When the Mesmerd had died in Meghan's tree house in the Sithiche Mountains, each and every Mesmerd had known.

The Mesmerd she had bowed to bowed in return, and though his wings stayed erect, the quality of his hum became a counterpoint to the others, and they were in harmony. As silently as they had glided in, the Mesmerdean left, and Margrit frowned and bit her thumbnail. She had again won them over, and though one of the families—the family of the nymph who had died in Meghan's tree house—would stay in the marshes until the mourning was done, the others would return to their forays into the surrounding countries. And when the mourning was done, the egg-brothers of the dead Mesmerd would go in search of Meghan and kiss her life away.

Iseult the Scarred Warrior

Meghan would not take Iseult with her into Caeryla. No matter what she said or how much she stood her ground, Meghan was adamant. "No, Iseult, it is too risky. Your face is too much like Isabeau's, and it seems that, despite my warnings, Isabeau has got her face very well known in these parts. Ye must stay here and look after Bacaiche."

"I will no'," Iseult said.

"Do no' be a fool," the sorceress said. "And do no' think ye can follow me, for I shall ken, Iseult. Ye swore to do as I said."

"I will go with ye."

"Ye shall no'.'

"I will."

"Ye shall no'."

"I will."

"No, Iseult. Ye shall stay here."

And somehow, Iseult the Scarred Hunter, for the first time in her life, found herself staying behind in the camp like a child or a cripple. At that thought, her gaze went to Bacaiche, and saw by his face that he had known exactly what she was thinking.

To relieve her overflowing feelings, Iseult went hunting as soon as Meghan had disappeared over the fold of hill. Bacaiche, barely able to walk because of his deformed feet, crouched in a moody silence by the pool, throwing pebbles into its murky depths. Iseult wondered idly how he could stand being tied to one place so much, then lost herself in the joy of the hunt. When she returned, flushed, sweaty and triumphant, two coneys dangling from her fist, he glowered at her from under his brows, and said, "The penalty for poaching in these parts is a whipping."

"I will no' be caught," Iseult answered serenely as she gathered kindling together.

"I do no think we should have a fire so close to the town . . ."

"No one will see my fire," Iseult retorted, and indeed, so dry was the kindling she gathered and so cleverly positioned was the fire that only a vague heat shimmer could be seen above the coals.

Bacaiche snorted in disgust, got to his feet and limped away in the ugly half hop, half step that was his gait. Iseult smiled, skinned and gutted the coneys expertly, and hung them on a spit above the fire. Twilight was drifting through the trees in a violet hush, the sky banded with the last colors of sunset. Iseult stretched, glad to feel her muscles aching, and eyed the pool. In moments she had stripped and was wading into the water, enjoying its cool freshness against her skin. Of all the many new things she had experienced in the last few weeks, this was her favorite. None of the pride would ever dream of immersing their bodies in water, for on the Spine of the World it took only three minutes to die once you were submerged. Here the water had the caress of silk, not the bite of frost, and Iseult had discovered the pleasure of being really clean.

After washing away the sweat and dirt and coney blood, Iseult floated on her back and looked up at the sky as, one by one, faint stars pricked into being. Her keen hunter's ears heard Bacaiche's awkward gait as he stumped through the undergrowth, but she ignored him, revelling in the feel of the water against her nakedness. It was only when his shuffle died away that she stood up, and looked for him, aware that he had been left in her care.

He stood under one of the trees, staring at her in a way Iseult did not fully understand. His gaze was both angry and yearning, miserable and exultant. For the first time in her life Iseult felt fully conscious of her body. Her arms felt heavy and awkward. Unsure what to do with her hands, she plucked a reed and turned it in her fingers, looking at him still. For a moment she thought he started forward; then, with a curse, he turned and lurched away into the undergrowth. Iseult waded out, dressed herself, and turned the coneys on their spit, all the time wondering about the expression on his face. She had seen desire on the faces of others in her pride, but never directed toward herself. She was considered very ugly, being so pale and freckled. Only her red hair was acceptable, and only then because it was a sign of the Firemaker, and not because it was considered pretty.

There had been desire on Bacaiche's face, she decided at length, but it had been mingled with other emotions she found more difficult to understand. When Bacaiche at last came back to the fire, she said nothing, just handed him a coney leg and a roast potato. They ate in silence and went to sleep in silence, and woke the following morning in unbroken silence.

By now Iseult was beginning to feel concern at Meghan's long absence. She found a graygorse bush on the edge of the copse of trees, and lay beneath it, staring out at the valley with its misty loch and gray-walled town. Bacaiche prowled restlessly around the camp. He had flung off his cloak in an excess of impatience, and Iseult again noticed that much of his crippled appearance disappeared with the cloak. He stood taller and his beautiful wings sprung out as if released from tight bonds. Again the thick neck and broad shoulders seemed balanced by the spread of black feathers, and it was only his taloned feet that made movement difficult. Iseult felt her curiosity about him grow, but was still unable to overcome her inbred reluctance to ask questions.

Bacaiche prepared them some food when the sun was high overhead, and they ate together in the shade of the trees. It was now a day and a half since Meghan had gone down to Caeryla, and Iseult had decided to wait until dark before going down in search of her. She had become so used to the silence between them that when Bacaiche spoke, she was quite startled.

"Ye are no' much like your sister, are ye?" he said. "She had a mouth like a donbeag, chitter chitter chitter all the time."

"I do no' ken," Iseult replied. "She does no' sound much like me."

Bacaiche hesitated and she realized that he too was consumed by curiosity, but reluctant to trespass on subjects that might be painful to her. She said in a rush, "I do no' much like the sound o' her, but things are so different here. I do no' think she would last long on the Spine o' the World." It was the first time she had spoken voluntarily, and she felt Bacaiche turn and look at her. She kept her eyes downturned.

"Life is hard on the Spine o' the World?" he asked tentatively.

"The Gods o' White are sometimes cruel and sometimes kind, and rarely can we see the reason behind their choices," Iseult replied. "But we are free, and the sky is sometimes blue and bright, and the hunting good, and sometimes there is storm or avalanche, and the hunting is bad. Such is life. At least we ken who are our friends and who are our enemies, no' like here."

"We too ken who are our friends and who are our enemies."

"If that is so, why did ye steal from she who had helped ye, and leave her to be hunted in your place?" Iseult felt that she could ask him a question since he has asked one of her.

Bacaiche's face darkened and he looked away sullenly, but eventually he answered, "That was wrong o' me. Sometimes I feel so angry and bitter none are my friends I forget that other people have pain as well."

Iseult knew he did not mean the pain of his deformities, but the pain around his heart, and she nodded. "It is easy to be kind when life is good."

"May I ask ye a question?"

"Ye just did," Iseult answered with a smile. It felt strange, as if her face was stiff, and she wondered how long it had been since she last smiled. Certainly not since she came to this hot, bright land. He smiled too, and it transformed his face, which had always seemed rather hard and cold.

"Another then. I wanted to ask about your relationship with my cousin. I ken ye and your sister are her wards, but ye say ye have never met your sister. I do no' understand."

Iseult considered the question, then sat up in a single fluid movement. She assumed the storyteller's position, legs crossed, spine straight, hands upturned in her lap.

"I was found on the slope o' the Cursed Peaks by the Firemaker, Auld Mother o' the Pride o' the Fire-Dragon, at the time o' the flaming Dragon-Star, which crosses our sky every eight years. Realizing I must be the child o' her son, who had long ago disappeared in the land o' the sorcerers, she raised me as her heir and granddaughter, until I was eight years auld. At that time I was given in *geas* to the dragons, and brought to the Towers o' Roses and Thorns. I was to care for the sleeping sorceress and study in the libraries during the green months, which is traditionally the time o' rest for the Scarred Warriors. During the white months, I stayed with the pride and hunted and fought, as is the way o' the Scarred Warriors, whose craft I had chosen. For eight years, my life was thus. Then the time o' the Dragon-Star came again, and the prides left for the Gathering, leaving me at the Tower o' Roses and Thorns with the sorcerer Feld and the sleeping sorceress. I was no' pleased to be left behind again, and wondered whether I would ever find a mate, for my sixteenth birthday having passed, I should have been jumping the fire with other women o' my age. The dragons called for me, however, and said an Auld Mother had come in search o' the sleeping sorceress and I should take her there, and look after her. That was the first time I did meet the Firemaker Meghan, who is your cousin. It was only then that I did hear I had a sister still living, which is a very bad thing indeed, for who shall inherit the godhead when my grandmother dies?"

Bacaiche looked a little confused, but he nodded. "I see. Too many heirs now, are there? No wonder ye resent the idea o' a sister."

"Twins are cursed," Iseult answered shortly. "The Gods o' White will be angry that one was no' given to them." There was silence for a moment, then she relaxed her pose and said, "Ye have asked o' me a question, which I did answer fully. Now I request a question of ye."

Bacaiche frowned, but nodded his head in an abrupt jerk. "I suppose that's fair."

"I have never seen a man with the wings and claws o' a bird before. Ye say the Firemaker Meghan is your cousin, yet she has no wings or claws. Were ye born this way?"

"No," he answered.

When she realized that was all he intended to say, anger sparked her blue eyes. "On the Spine o' the World, a question is a request for a story," she said coldly. "If one decides to answer, one must answer fully, for how else is the question answered?"

"I do no' come from the Spine o' the World," he answered, and looked away from her.

She nodded, and got to her feet. "That is true." Without a backward glance she walked away, and gingerly crawled back under the graygorse bush, scanning the empty valley for any sign of Meghan.

After pacing the clearing for close on half an hour, Bacaiche came and crouched beside her, ignoring the vicious thorns of the bush. "I'm sorry. It is hard for me to speak about it." Iseult did not reply. "I have killed a man for asking just that question," he went on in a troubled voice. "Most o' my life I have been hunted down, pursued, reviled, for something that is no' my fault." Iseult still said nothing.

He went on, his voice thick with passion. "It is the cursed Banrìgh. This is all her fault, all o' it! Sometimes I long to close my fingers around her throat and squeeze till there is no life left in her! She could beg and plead, and I would no' care. I would smile at her and kill her with as little mercy as she killed my brothers. The foul witch! She has the whole land ensorcelled!"

They were silent a very long time. Bacaiche said at last, almost in a whisper, "I was no' born like this. For the first twelve years o' my life I was a lad much as any other lad is. I had a home, a family who loved me, every toy and luxury I could want. Then I was ensorcelled. What ye see today is the remnants o' an enchantment so strong and so mysterious than no one can find the cure. No' even Meghan."

"Ye were put under a spell?"

"It was Maya. She could no' bear for Jaspar to love anyone but her. She smiled at us and spoke sweet words, and he was angry that we did no' like her, and said we were silly and jealous, and should ken better. One night she came to us, smiling still. I woke from a deep sleep to see her standing over our beds. I was half asleep still, and watched as she turned Feargus and Donncan into blackbirds.

Before I even had time to cry out or try and escape, she had transformed me also. It is strange to try and scream, and have only a bird's squark come out, or try and run, and find your body does no' work the way it should. She threw us out the window of our bed chamber, and set her hawk upon us. I saw Feargus caught almost immediately, and I flew as fast as I could, though I had not yet learned to manage my wings. Behind me I heard Donncan's cry and knew he had been caught too, and then the hawk was above me. I could hear it and feel its shadow upon me, and I folded my wings and dived into the forest. In the trees, the hawk could not catch me and so I escaped.

"The next few years are all a blur. Slowly, my memories, my language, my knowledge of who I was, all were lost. I became a bird, fighting for the worm and living my days between heaven and earth. At last I had lived so long in the body o' a bird that nearly all sense o' being a man was lost to me. Eventually I was captured and caged, sold to a family as a songbird, to be fed seeds and bits o' bread and sing for their pleasure. It was there the auld jongleur woman Enit found me and rescued me. Somehow she recognized me, and tried to save me. She has a way with birds, can sing them to her hand; perhaps she saw I was a man trapped in a bird's body, or perhaps she saw the white lock remained still. Who knows? All I ken is that she brought me to Meghan, and together they tried to break the spell, but could no'. Meghan says she has never encountered a spell like it before. They tried all they knew and more still, and at last brought back my body, though marred as ye see it now. That was eight years ago. I have been this way ever since. I barely remember that—for weeks I was a wild bird, trapped in the body of a man. Enit had to teach me to speak again, and to use my hands and legs, and all that time I was kept in a tiny caravan, too afraid to go outside. While Enit tamed me again, Meghan sent the blind prophet Jorge to find me this cloak o' illusions. Only then was I was at last able to walk in daylight."

"I see. Do ye wish to be like other men again?"

"I will never be like other men. Even if my body was like that o' others, my soul will never be. I was half-bird too long."

"So the . . . Rìgh o' your land is your brother?"

"Aye, Jaspar is my brother. I am one of the Lost Prionnsachan of Eileanan, that the minstrels sing o' in cold, winter evenings . . ." His mouth twisted wryly.

"So Bacaiche is no' your name?"

"No, I am the Prionnsa Lachlan Owein MacCuinn, fourth son of Parteta the Brave."

"I am Khan'derin, gessepKhan'lysa o' the Fire-Dragon Pride, Scarred Warrior and heir to the Firemaker."

He glanced at her coldly, and looked away.

"Did ye never try and reach your brother, tell him what happened?" Iseult asked.

"Isn't that a whole new question?" he sneered. "I have told ye my story, what more do ye want?"

Iseult nodded and moved away. Like many stories, Bacaiche's tale had raised as many new questions as it had answered. She knew that the telling had been difficult for him, however, and so she asked no more questions, returning her gaze to the valley. As if reminded of his past, Bacaiche began to sing again, and his blackbird's voice pealed out clear and melodious, charming Iseult anew.

It was a long, hot afternoon, tense beneath the spiky branches, as gradually the sun crossed the sky and still the slope was empty of Meghan's small fierce body. Iseult stood it much better than Bacaiche, used as she was to stalking prey in much harsher conditions than these. The heat bothered her but the restless swish of Bacaiche's wings as he fidgeted and fretted created a cool breeze that helped considerably. It was almost sunset when Meghan at last appeared beside them, remarking sardonically that she'd been able to hear Bacaiche's mutters a mile away. Both jumped at her words and were badly scratched by the graygorse's spikes.

"Where did ye come from?" Bacaiche asked. "We've been watching and watching and we never saw a sign."

"As if ye could see me approach if I did no' want ye to!" Meghan said harshly. Iseult looked at her anxiously. Gitâ was nestled up against her neck, always a sign Meghan's mind was troubled, while her face was as grim and shadowed as Iseult had ever seen it. Meghan answered her unasked question. "Isabeau was executed last night, at sunset."

To her surprise Iseult felt a stir of pain, but she told herself it was the darkness on the Firemaker's face.

"Apparently she killed the Grand-Questioner when he tried to torture her, even though she was fastened to a torture-table at the time. She did no' go lightly, at least."

Iseult was impressed—Is'a'beau could not have been such a softling, after all.

"They fed her to the serpent o' the loch, apparently," Meghan said. She was gathering her pack together. Bent over, her hands busy at her task, she shot a look at them. "So, ye took advantage o' my absence and killed, Iseult?"

Involuntarily Iseult met her gaze, heat sweeping over her cheeks. "Aye, Firemaker."

"And what small animal did ye murder? Coney, by the smell o' ye."

Iseult clenched her fingers. "Aye, Firemaker."

Meghan shouldered her pack, and started walking quickly through the trees. "Stay well behind me, then, both o' ye. The smell o' ye makes me sick to my stomach."

Iseult slung her already loaded satchel onto her shoulder, picked up the long staff of ash she had taken to carrying, and followed in silence. She felt Bacaiche lurching along at her shoulder, and stared straight ahead.

"She's taking it hard," he whispered, but Iseult would not reply.

Down below the valley was filling with mist, only the opposite peaks still touched with light. Within an hour the mist had risen enough to cover their forms, and Meghan led them out of the copse of trees and down the slope toward the loch. Iseult looked around carefully. She was surprised that Meghan had not waited until they were further away from the township, bright with torchlight and still clearly within sight. There would be patrolling soldiers this close to the town. The loch's shore was bare of trees that would conceal them, and if the mist should waver, they could be seen.

Meghan had a purpose though. She lead them inexorably to the shore, planted her staff in the mud, and stared out at the misty surface.

"What are we doing?" Bacaiche whispered, looking about him with some anxiety. The shadowy loch, wreathed with mist, was a sinister place, thick with mystery and magic. "Is there no' an *uile-bheist* in this loch?"

"O' course. That is why I am here." And from Meghan's

thin form came an eerie ululating cry that echoed around the shore. Again she raised her voice, and again the long, sobbing cry rang out. Iseult felt her skin crawl.

Out of the mist loomed the serpent of the loch, its tiny head high above them, its long sinuous neck swaying back and forth. It opened its mouth and wailed, and it was all Iseult could do not to fall back in terror. In the Spine of the World few fairy creatures could survive the bitter cold. Apart from frost giants, she had no experience with *uile-bheistean,* and had no desire to make a closer acquaintance. She held her ground, however, and felt gratification when Bacaiche stepped back involuntarily.

Meghan and the loch serpent wailed and bobbed at each other for fully ten minutes. Iseult concentrated on keeping a watch for any passers-by, but they were undisturbed. Listening to the eerie ululation, Iseult thought to herself that anyone who might be nearby would surely be too afraid to come any closer.

When at last the strange conversation was finished, Meghan's small dark face was alight. "Come, let us go," she said, and grasped her staff with more vigor than Iseult had seen in days.

"Where are we bluidy well going now?" Bacaiche asked bad-temperedly.

"In search o' Isabeau," she answered.

"Isabeau is dead," Iseult said as gently as she knew how.

"Och, no, she's no'. Isabeau has my mark upon her. The loch serpent did no' harm her."

"Then . . . where is she? What happened?"

"That is what I am going to try and find out," Meghan said, and the usual grimness of her voice was drowned beneath her evident joy. "Isabeau must have escaped, for else we would have heard. All we have to do now is find her."

THE THREADS ARE SPUN

Isabeau the Hunted

The shock of the cold water and the scald of the talisman against her hip roused Isabeau as she plunged into the loch. Immediately panic filled her, and she struggled against her bonds. Finding they would not yield, she gathered her will together and tore the ropes apart. For an instant she felt the world contract about her, and her inner self was a hard, clear stone, unnaturally conscious of water, weeds, darkness, and the rush of currents. Then it seemed she would swoon again, her lungs and head bursting, multicolored lights swirling in her head. The pain of her hand and her own will was all that kept her conscious as she kicked feebly to the surface.

There was a loud kooning sound and she saw far above her the long neck and tiny head of the *uile-bheist* of the loch. Torchlight flickered on the water as the soldiers leaned forward, searching the waters. Terrified, Isabeau shrank back under the barnacle-encrusted poles of the jetty and began to swim as silently and quickly as she could in the opposite direction. Injured as she was, she could barely keep afloat, and gave a half hysterical sob at the thought of the *uile-bheist* bearing down on her. Then it was on top of her, a huge sinuous creature that opened its mouth to wail again, showing a mouth full of tiny, pointed teeth. The long neck bent and, although she swam as hard as she could, Isabeau felt its length brush against her. Then the mouth closed on the cloth of her shoulder and she was being towed along, water swelling on either side. For a moment Isabeau was stiff with astonishment, then she realized, with shocked gladness, that the *uile-bheist* was towing her to safety.

"Do ye think it got her?" she heard one guard say, and the other chuckled, and said, "Look at that thing, ye think a wee girl like that could outswim it, bound hand and foot? No, she's monster bait, for sure." Isabeau smiled tiredly, and cradled her injured hand against her body, letting the loch serpent tow her.

For long, anxious minutes they swam through the heavy mist, Isabeau craning her ears for any sound. There was none. She could hardly believe the *uile-bheist* had rescued her, and she wondered what it wanted. She did not know the language of loch monsters and although she tried sending out a mind-message, she had no way of knowing if it understood. Did the shock waves from her breaking her bonds attract it? Was it not hungry? She prayed to Eà, mother and father of them all, to protect her.

The loch serpent swam for what seemed like hours, the fog thick about them. Isabeau slipped off into a feverish daze where voices seemed to speak to her through the mist—Meghan scolding her; the witch-sniffer sneering at her and hurting her; the Grand-Questioner Yutta, his cavernous face leaning over her, the stench of blood in her nostrils. She was half woken by the loch serpent's eerie call as, with a flourish of foam, he beached himself, and bent his neck so she slid forward and onto soft sand. Just before nightmares filled her eyes, she heard his haunting call again.

The next few days were a feverish blur. The bitter cold of the water, the lack of dry clothing and food, and the throbbing pain of her injuries combined into a whirl of dancing lights and darkness that kept threatening to overwhelm her. She knew she had to keep going, though. The Grand-Seeker might send out a party to search for her body, or she may even be discovered by sentries. Although all she wanted to do was rest her aching head on Eà's breast, Isabeau kept staggering forward.

Sometime during the next day, she tended her hand with some herbs she found in the forest, and ate some berries off a tree. Her hand throbbed with an eager pulse that made her sick to her stomach, but she kept on following the burn, barely conscious of her surroundings.

The water will lead me true, she kept telling herself. *Soon I will be at Tulachna Celeste. Soon I will be safe.*

Isabeau was too deep in fever to recognize the signs that would have told her she was no longer following the Rhyllster. Where the river ran through a wide, gradually falling valley in long, sinuous loops, with the Tuathan Loch filling most of the center, Isabeau was following a fast-moving burn that ran through thick trees. Where the Rhyllster ran almost due south, she had the sun on her face in the morning and at her back in the evening. Isabeau's woodcraft and general knowledge of geography should have alerted her.

Each hour that passed, however, made Isabeau less and less coherent. Soon she was walking with no clear thought other than that her muscles must keep working. She lost the burn and wandered through thick woods with nothing on her mind but the beat, beat, beat of her blood, the beat, beat, beat of her boots. Night came again, and then it was day, and Isabeau lay where she had fallen many hours earlier, with the talisman burning no hotter than her forehead. In the throng of nightmares that beat around her, she thought she saw Lasair, dreamed they galloped like the wind, dreamed they were together again. In rushes of sound like storm trees strode over her, sky broke, darkness was filled with whispering faces, she was as small as a pea, she was large as a world, shapes flinched, sounds roared, colors blurred and rolled, nightmares chased her.

She woke with a start, and was conscious at once of coolness. She was lying on her back in a dark room, and someone was wiping her face with a blessedly damp cloth. She tried to speak but was so parched her tongue felt like a lizard in her mouth. The person tending her held a cup of water to her lips and she gulped greedily, trying to follow the cup when he moved it away. Her body felt as frail and light as a dandelion seed, so that the effort of raising her head exhausted her and she let it fall back onto rough pillows.

"Obh, obh!" he said in a gruff, reproving tone. "Sick you'll be if ye swallow too much o' the water."

She became aware of the pain in her hand, which throbbed with an urgent pulse. Through blood-stained bandages she could see her fingers, grossly swollen and blackened, and her heart sank with fear. The streaks of infection were already racing up her wrist, and she could feel her whole arm aching. He followed her gaze. "Paw hurt bad," he said.

At his words, she peered more closely at him. Her vision gradually steadied, and she realized with a shock that this was no human tending her. Although she had never seen one, she made a guess at a cluricaun. He was about three feet high, sturdy, with a triangular face that had a slightly guilty expression on it, like a cat caught with its paw in a jar of cream. He was dressed in rough clothes like a farmer's boy, and she could see they had been clumsily altered to fit. Round his neck hung a jangle of different objects—keys, flashy rings, buttons, the top of an inkwell, and a christening spoon. They all sparkled and flashed, although it was dim in the room, and she saw they had been carefully polished. As he turned his head she saw his ears; large and covered with soft, brown hair, they swiveled from side to side like an elven cat's. If not for the ears, he would have looked rather like a very short, very hirsute man.

As he moved away from her, she saw a long, slender tail sneaking out of his clothes, waving about as he moved around the room. She lay back, cradling her hand against her, and let her gaze rove around. Behind her was a high wall, made of ancient blocks of stones that were now much broken and discolored. She could dimly see the shape of a narrow doorway, with leaves clustering close outside. She wondered vaguely where she was, and felt her eyes begin to close, sleep swooping in.

Suddenly Isabeau remembered the talisman, and tried to sit up with a jerk. Pain flashed through her and her vision swam, so that she sank back with a groan. Whether it was the expression on her face or whether the cluricaun could read her mind she did not know, but immediately he fished out the black pouch from his pocket and sheepishly handed it over. "It be marvelous bonny," he said wistfully. "I do be wanting to wear it on my chain, but as soon as I take it out it shrieks so loud I am afraid, and put it back."

"It shrieks?" Isabeau was surprised, having never heard the talisman emit a sound before. She clutched the black pouch to her and felt, with waves of relief, the familiar triangular shape through the silky material.

"Indeed, and though we do be far from anyone here, a witch-sniffer could hear it if they be close enough. So I did no' keep it." The cluricaun sounded regretful.

"What about my rings?"

A sly expression crossed the cluricaun's face. "Do no' be trying to sit up now, or it's your head that be whirling off, and then where will ye be?"

Isabeau covered her eyes with her hand, exhausted by even such a slight effort. "I have to get going," she murmured. But she was asleep again before she even finished the words.

When she woke it was daylight and she could see her surroundings more clearly. She was lying on wide flagstones, with broken walls on either side. The room must once have belonged to a great building, for she saw faces and patterns carved here and there into the walls, and part of a great arch, now filled with rubble. The cluricaun had turned the corner of the long room into a snug little home, with a real bed, lanterns hanging on the wall, and a small fire built in a fireplace big enough to roast an oxen. Smoke puffed out, filling the room with a fragrant blueness that stung Isabeau's eyes. A barrel of water was set near the pointed doorway, and herbs, onions and a cured ham hung from the walls on hooks. Although her eyes had been open only a few seconds, the cluricaun bounded to his feet, which she saw were bare and rather hairy, and brought her some hot broth, which she ate greedily, steadying the bowl against her throbbing arm.

"How long have I been here?"

"The moons have swelled and shrunk again and are almost ready to swell again. Long time ye tossing and turning on my floor—too long ye are by far for my bed, and too heavy for me to lift ye."

"A month! I've been here a whole month! No, I canna have! It's impossible!" Isabeau tried to sit up, but her weakness overcame her and she sunk back, plucking at her blankets in distress, the broth forgotten.

"Eating, eating," the cluricaun reproved, and tried to force the spoon into her mouth. "No eat, no go anywhere."

Feeling tears stinging her eyelids, Isabeau tried to obey, but panic was setting in. She had already taken far longer than she should have to make the journey out of the Sithiche Mountains, and she hardly dared hope that Meghan's friend would have waited for her. With as much patience she could muster, she swallowed the broth the cluricaun forced between her teeth, trying to ignore the spoonfuls which splashed over her. A savage bout of coughing shook her, and she lay back afterward, feeling weak.

The cluricaun waved a rag around, trying to disperse the smoke, chanting, "House full, room full, canna catch a spoonful!" He gazed at her anxiously as if wanting her to respond in some way. Not having any idea what he was talking about, Isabeau was silent, while he chanted again, mournfully, "House full, room full, canna catch a spoonful!"

"I must go," Isabeau said when she was finished. "I am so horribly late."

"Where is it ye are trying to be?" asked the cluricaun cheekily.

"Tulachna Celeste."

His slanted eyes widened. "Well, ye are several weeks ride from there," he said. "If no' more."

"But how? I was only a day's journey away from it afore."

"Tulachna Celeste is in Rionnagan."

"Where am I?" Anxiety made Isabeau feel sick to her stomach.

"Aslinn, o' course."

"Aslinn! How can I be in Aslinn!"

"That's where ye be. The bonny forests o' Aslinn. The wild and bonny forests, where dreamers wander. I will show ye if ye do no' believe me."

Isabeau could not walk, though; her legs were too shaky. The cluricaun gave her water, and chuckled. "I think ye will no' be traveling anywhere just now."

During the next three days the pain in Isabeau's hand increased steadily and, despite attempts to clean and dress the injuries, the sickly smell of infection hung around her, turning her stomach. The cluricaun, whose name was Brun, brought her herbs and once she tried to lance the infection with his blunt little knife, to ruinous affect. Isabeau's anxiety and impatience increased with her pain, but her body was so weakened with the fever, she had trouble crawling from her bed to the little bucket Brun had set aside for her lavatory. There was no hope of setting out to Tulachna Celeste until she regained her strength, no matter how she fretted.

In the interim, she lay on her bundle of furs on the floor, staring at the cluricaun's home, and wondering at the beauty of the architecture. He had taken over one corner of a great room with a vaulted ceiling so high Isabeau could barely see its rafters. Skins and furs scattered the stone floor and provided partitions that made the corner around the huge fireplace quite cozy, despite the drafts that whistled through the broken walls. At the other end of the room, the ceiling had fallen and only blackened rafters remained, showing a cloud-streaked sky. Odd faces grinned at her from the stonework, while over the massive fireplace was a complicated stone shield, surrounded by stars and with faint traces of words emblazoned underneath.

The little cluricaun stayed close to her during that time, anticipating her every need. If she felt a pang of thirst, he was there with a beaker of water before she had even acknowledged her need. If she was cold, he would stoke up the fire, and when the pain in her hand grew so fierce that she wept, he brought her pain-numbing herbs. A strange, merry creature, prone to capering around the flagstones and laughing at his own jokes, he sidled up to her one day, his hands behind her back. "Guess what I have found for ye, Is'beau."

"What?" Isabeau sighed.

"It has marble walls as white as milk, lined with skin as soft as silk, within a fountain crystal clear, a golden apple does appear."

Isabeau shrugged her shoulders impatiently. "I do no' ken, Brun. What?"

"Walls as white as milk," he prompted. "A golden apple within."

"Havers, Brun, I do no' ken. A pebble?"

"Nay, Is'beau." A ludicrous expression of disappointment crossed his hairy face. "I found ye an egg. A beautiful white egg, full o' goodness, to make ye better."

He showed her the gleaming white egg, cradled in his palm. "See, walls as white as milk."

"That's lovely, thank ye, Brun." Isabeau said, and rested her head on the pillow again.

A crestfallen expression crossed Brun's triangular face, and his tail twisted anxiously behind him, but Isabeau was too weak and nervy to make the effort to soothe him.

Once Isabeau was strong enough to walk a few steps, Brun helped her through the pointed doorway and across the ruined garden, all broken stones and overgrown berry bushes. With several stops to regain her strength, Isabeau was finally able to sink down to the ground, wrapped in rough-woven blankets, in the warm, sheltered spot Brun had chosen for her, with stone at her back and feet, and a clear view into the valley. Then she saw clearly enough that she was in Aslinn, for as far as the eye could see the massive boles of mountain ashes rose, towering hundreds of feet above her. The ruined castle where Brun had made his home was built on a high, green hill and from her vantage point, Isabeau looked down over a small burn shining between tree trunks. To the north she could see the distant blue peaks of the Sithiche Mountains, and to the west the high cliffs of the Great Divide, streaked with ribbons of waterfalls. Isabeau could not believe it. Somehow she had traveled far to the east, leaving the open hills of Rionnagan behind her.

"I must have been wandering in fever for days," she murmured aloud.

Just then there was a shrill neigh and, to her joy and amazement, she saw Lasair galloping through the trees toward her, his mane and tail blazing in the sunlight. He cantered up the slope of the hill, and danced to a halt before her, neighing and shaking his bright mane and butting against her breast with his nose. "How . . . ? Where . . . ? What . . . ?" she stammered, and the cluricaun looked at her in astonishment.

"When first I see ye, ye had two heads, six feet, one each side and four beneath, and one tail blazing."

"But . . . I left Lasair in Caeryla . . ."

"So ye did come from Caeryla? Well, when I saw ye, ye were galloping like the wind, and ye were clinging to his mane, and he came to drink at the burn and ye fell from his back and lay on the grass as if ye were dead. I did come to ye, and found ye burning with fever and bleeding from your head and hand, and so at last I did take ye back to my home and tend ye there. Your horse has been fretting and fuming ever since, running back and forth in front o' the Tower and wailing like a banshee."

"I remember dreaming o' Lasair . . ."

"What a fever it mun have been," Brun chuckled. "Fall asleep in Rionnagan, awake in Aslinn." He performed a faultless forward roll, then looked at her from between his legs, his face even odder when upside down.

"What am I to do?" Isabeau was in despair. She had failed Meghan, failed her miserably. It was surely too late to retrace her steps to meet Meghan's friend at Tulachna Celeste. By the look of the night sky, several months had passed since she had set out from the secret valley. Perhaps it would be best to strike out toward Blèssem, and so to Rhysmadill that way. Now she had Lasair again . . .

"Eat and rest for now," The cluricaun's voice was almost serious. "When ye are a wee better I will take ye into the Tower. *She* will ken what to do."

"The Tower of Dreamers?"

"Indeed, what other Tower would I be talking about? The Tower o' Warriors?" The cluricaun was vastly amused at his own joke, clutching his stomach with laughter. Isabeau was not amused, for no one from the western lands had been near the Tower of Warriors since the warrior-maids had closed their borders four hundred years earlier. Tirsoilleir had been a land of mystery ever since.

"Who is *she*?"

Immediately the cluricaun sobered, sitting up with straw sticking in his hair. "She is my friend. She will ken what to do."

After the cluricaun had trotted off to gather berries and nuts for their evening meal, Isabeau carefully began to unwind the makeshift bandages which Brun had wrapped around her injured hand, biting her lip against the pain. When she saw her swollen, infected fingers, roughly splinted, tears filled her eyes. Isabeau knew her healing. There was little chance she would regain much use of the broken hand—the bones had been crushed close to the joint and the weeks that passed between the torture and the cluricaun's rough treatment had seen infection set in. If she did not get expert help soon, she would lose her hand altogether. Isabeau did what she could to clean the wounds; the pain was excruciating but at last she bound the hand up again, and made herself a tight sling that would cradle it against her body.

Brun took Isabeau into the Tower of Dreamers the next night. They waited until it was fully dark before wrapping up well against the chilly night air and sneaking round the outside of the Tower to its great entrance in the western wall. Brun insisted on absolute quiet. "No' want the Horned Ones to ken," he said, his triangular face anxious.

When Isabeau asked him who or what the Horned Ones were, Brun only made a frightened face, and ran around the clearing with two fingers poking up through his curly mop like horns. He finished with a forward tumble, grinning at her with his sharp little fangs shining.

It was a beautiful night, and Isabeau was happy to be away from the cluricaun's quarters. The massive trees soared up into starry distances, and overhead the two moons leaned against each other, the smudges of darkness, like hand prints, on Magnysson's flank, easily seen.

Isabeau had no clothes left but her torn and muddied dress and plaid, but Brun had cleaned them for her and stitched up the worst of the tears, so she at least was dressed again. The talisman was in its pouch and hung on the inside of her skirt, with her rings tucked inside as well. It had taken her a long time to get her rings back from the cluricaun, who thought them pretty and had "borrowed" them. She had teased and cajoled him without effect, only getting her rings back when she recognized them on his chain and grew angry.

Lasair trotted along behind her, and she wondered again how he could have found her. The thought frightened her a little, for if he could track her down, so could others. She must have left a hefty trail. She pondered how he could have got free, but all Lasair did was toss his head and give a few jittery bucks when she asked him. She hoped with all her heart the Grand-Seeker Glynelda was not hot on his trail as she had been the last time. Isabeau did not think she would survive another encounter with the Grand-Seeker.

Isabeau had been told stories of the Towers since she was a babe in arms and had always longed to see one. As they walked slowly beside the walls, drenched in moonlight, her excitement grew. The Towers were said to be the most beautiful and mysterious of places, built by the greatest witch architects at locations of magical significance. She was bitterly disappointed when they came round the corner and saw the great entrance to the Tower of Dreamers broken and blackened. Overlooking the small loch, where two burns flowed together, the Tower was made of white stone. Once it would have been topped with delicate spires and a crystal dome. Now only two spires remained, and the entire west wall was tumbled down, littering the hill with blocks of marble. In the silence and darkness of the forest, it looked an eerie place, seemingly filled with ghosts. Both Isabeau and Brun came naturally to a halt, and she turned to him to ask him a question.

He put his thick, hairy finger against his mouth. "We mun be quiet," he whispered. "We do no' want the Horned Ones to hear us."

"What are the Horned Ones?" Isabeau whispered back, bending over so her mouth was closer to the cluricaun's ear.

"I do no' ken where they bided afore, but the forests here are thick with them now, and we do no' want to meet them."

As Isabeau was about to ask again, he put his tiny, rough hand on her arm. Across the clearing was movement. A woman was bounding forward, heading down to the stream. That is if she was a woman, for Isabeau had never seen anything like her. At least seven feet tall, with muscular legs and arms, her head was crowned with seven goatlike horns. Isabeau opened her mouth to ask another question, but Brun shook his head at her furiously and laid his finger over his mouth again.

"They have ears like a deer. Ye mun be quiet. If they

catch us they kill us," he said, long moments later when all sounds of the horned woman had gone.

"Why?"

"They are the Horned Ones. They fain hunt."

Isabeau was obediently silent. They waited in the shelter of the wall for what seemed like hours before Brun finally put his hands to his mouth and hooted like a horned owl. Three times he called, then was silent, then called three times again. Faintly on the evening breeze the reply came—three long hoots, silence, then the sound again.

"Come," he said. "It be safe, we can go inside."

Like thieves they flitted from shadow to shadow, at last slipping inside the great arched doorway. Once there would have been a massive oaken door here, with strong bolts and hinges. Now there was only the space where it had been. Inside the Tower was a long hall with a staircase winding up at the other end. The walls were painted with figures of people and fairies, only just visible in the gloom and giving Isabeau a little scare when she first made them out. Cobwebs hung in great loops from the vaulted ceiling, and there was broken furniture lying here and there. She began to feel afraid, and even looked at the cluricaun askance, wondering why he had lured her here. Again he knew just what she was thinking, and slipped his hairy hand into hers.

They climbed the stairs to the very top level, Isabeau peering anxiously down the four corridors that branched off from each landing. She was a little reassured that the talisman did not burn and tingle as it had done previously each time she'd been in danger, but she was still unnerved by the ruined beauty all about her. Enough of the original grandeur remained to move her—delicate columns holding up arched ceilings, walls carved in intricate patterns, with here and there the design of a flowering tree. The staircase was wide enough for seven men to walk up it abreast, and the ceiling so far away the apprentice witch felt dwarfed. Beside her, the cluricaun seemed more like a toy than a living being, a wood and cloth doll she might have owned in her childhood.

The top floor was all one great room, and Isabeau saw it was the central dome of the Tower. Once it must have been crystal, perhaps stained with brilliant colors. She could see the jagged edges of what was now a gaping hole, revealing the entire night sky. The spiral staircase had come out in the middle of the floor, and she was standing directly under the center of the glowing disc, the stars spread out in brilliant patterns above her. Isabeau stared entranced.

There was a movement, and a figure came toward her from one corner of the round room. She was tall and very slender, and dressed all in white. Her eyes were hidden by the darkness, but when she turned slightly and the faint moonlight struck the edge of her eye, Isabeau saw it was translucent, like a bubble. Her forehead was heavily corrugated, the moonlight falling upon the lines and casting them into deep shadow that seemed to gather in the center, while her hair fell in vigorous pale waves down her back.

Isabeau NicFaghan, greetings.

Greetings, Isabeau responded, wondering at the name the stranger had called her, and feeling a sense of fear and wonder mingled. What this creature was she had no idea, except that it was by no means human. *Do ye ken me?*

Indeed. I have been watching you for a very long time. As she spoke, the shimmery figure moved closer and Isabeau backed away nervously. *There is no need to be afraid. I mean you no harm.*

I'm sorry, but I do no' ken who ye are. I mean, what are ye doing here? Do ye live here? Are ye one o' the Dream-Walkers?

The Dream-Walkers are all lost or gone, Isabeau. Can you not guess what I am?

Isabeau shook her head. The tall, faintly shimmering figure before her bowed her narrow head, the long pale hair swaying, and from deep in her throat came a strange humming sound that swelled and broke like the sound of the wind in pine trees. Only then did Isabeau realize that all their conversation had been in mind-speech and this deep hum was the first sound the stranger had uttered.

Do ye understand?

Again Isabeau shook her head, and like a fresh spring breeze came the word *Celestine* in her mind. Isabeau felt a certain awe. The Celestine were the original inhabitants of these forests and mountains, thought to have disappeared many years ago. A peaceful people who studied the movements of stars and seasons, they had been swamped by the quickly growing population of humans who cut down the forests for farmland and quarried the mountains for stone for their cities and towers. Meghan had a profound reverence for the Celestines, who loved the beasts of field and forest as she did. Whenever she spoke of them, which was often, her voice grew hushed and sometimes her eyes filled with tears. Meghan had always loved the hunted creature, the small and weak and defenseless.

All Isabeau's fear and distrust melted away. She started forward with a cry, saying, *Celestine! But ye canna be . . . they're gone. I have always heard . . .*

The Celestines, as your people decided to call us, are indeed gone, the Celestine spoke in her stilted, sorrowful mind-accent. *Here and there one still sits in the ruins of what we knew and grieves, but soon they too shall pass, and then there shall be none.*

But why? Can ye no' save them? Is there nothing ye can do? My guardian weeps sometimes when she thinks the Celestines are no more.

Meghan of the Beasts is indeed our friend.

Ye ken her?

I remember her as a lass. I have not seen her for many years, not since Aedan Whitelock died. I have often observed her, though, and you.

And me? How?

I see many things . . .

Are ye a seer?

In a way. I cannot see the future, the way the dragons and some among your kind do. I can see what is invisible or concealed. I can see what is in the heart. I can see you have been hurt, and that you are unused to pain. I can see you have a fierce spirit that shall grow fiercer yet. I can also see that lying comes naturally to you.

Isabeau was taken aback, her first impulse to refute the accusation heatedly. Then she blushed, for it was true.

Isabeau, I know you are tired and your body still weak. Why do we not sit down and look at the stars together and talk? I can see questions taut in your mouth, and I can see that you fear me. You are wise, Isabeau Apprentice-Witch.

We of this land are not like you. Even Aedan made this mistake. He thought we were alike under the skin. This is not true.

She lead the way to a stone-carved bench against the stairwell balustrade, and sat there, leaving most of the bench for Isabeau. She stared up at the stars and said, *When Magnysson shall at last hold Gladrielle in his arms, all will be healed or broken, saved or surrendered . . .*

I've heard that somewhere before, Isabeau thought dreamily, resting her head back and nestling her throbbing hand against her side.

There is to be a conjunction of forces at Samhain, night of the dead, that has not been seen since Aedan Whitelock first wrought the Lodestar, four hundred and eighteen years ago. The power in the Lodestar is dying—it needs to be touched and held, its power nurtured and used, not to lie in darkness and hollowness.

The Lodestar . . . is that no' the Inheritance o' Aedan? It was destroyed, in the battle between the witches and the Red Guards.

It was not destroyed. Destroy the Lodestar so easily? No, it was hidden. This I know. It may soon flicker out, though, if it is not found and given to the hand of a MacCuinn. And if it is found and used at Samhain, then indeed all shall be saved or surrendered . . . I know you have part of the Key with you.

Pardon?

The bag of nyx hair you have hidden it in cannot hide it from my eyes . . .

Involuntarily Isabeau touched her hand to the pouch at her waist. Fear sent cold tendrils twisting through her stomach. The talisman was cool though, and still.

It is possible you do not know what you carry. It does not matter. The Key must be united. I know this was the task Meghan of the Beasts set you, and I know you must fulfill it. The year is creeping away and there are many threads yet to be spun.

What is it? Isabeau asked, and clutched the pouch through the material of her dress.

It is the third part of the Key of the Coven of Witches. Meghan locked the Inheritance o' Aedan away with the

Key and it cannot be freed without it. Have you not felt its magic? It is a powerful talisman.

I think so, Isabeau said, remembering how, when she had been thrown into the loch, her bonds had broken with a great surge of power that she had never experienced before.

You have an interesting history, Isabeau. As much fairy as human, if the people of the Spine of the World are included in your classifications. Your face is wrapped in a veil, and it is not a veil of your making. I hope soon you will be free of it, for indeed your other eye could be of use to you in these times. It is shaking loose, though, that blow to your head has freed it . . . Do not look so puzzled, Isabeau, just listen to what I say and what you cannot understand now, remember later. I have a gift for you.

Really? Thank ye . . . What is it?

Brun had been most uncharacteristically silent since they had arrived in the observatory, sitting at the Celestine's feet while she ran her fingers through his curly mop. At her words, he jumped to his feet and went to rummage in one corner of the room. When he returned he was staggering under the weight of a saddle and bridle, the tack jingling with every step.

What is it? Isabeau asked, although she could see it quite clearly in the mingled light of the two moons.

It is the saddle of Ahearn Horse Tamer. He made it himself and rode it all his life. His magic has soaked in deep, and it is a good magic. I see you have a horse.

He's no' exactly mine.

I think you will find he is more yours than you expect. Besides, he has chosen to be with you, and that is his right. You knew he threw and killed the woman who said she was his owner?

The Grand-Seeker? Lady Glynelda?

A woman with a cruel face and a red dress. The day after you were given to the loch serpent, she took him out onto the moors and rode him cruelly with whip and spur. He fought her, and she spurred him on until at last he threw her as she tried to make him jump a burn. She fell and hit her head, and drowned in the water, and the stallion bolted. Although her companions chased him, he was fleet of foot and they could not catch him. How he found you I do not know, though I see a strong link between you. He was clever enough to find the Old Way and so brought you straight to me. I want you to have the saddle.

But why? If it is really Ahearn's, does it no' belong to someone now? His descendants?

Yes, it does, and they miss it sorely. But now is not the time. I found it green and decaying in a disused carriage house many miles from here, and though it is heavy and not a relic of my people's, I brought it here for you.

Why?

You are not safe here. These forests are infested with Horned Ones and the Fairge queen still casts her eye here at times to see the Tower remains in ruin. While you carry the Key you cannot be safe enough. You should not have the Key. You do not understand its power and it is not your right. The saddle will help you make it to the blue palace safely.

How? A saddle would be welcome, I agree, Lasair's spine is bony, but—

Things of magic are always unpredictable. Ahearn rode it, and he rode as if he were the horse's own flesh. I think you will find it will help you, for the journey from here to Dùn Gorm is still a long one, and the road is dangerous.

But I must return to Tulachna Celeste! Meghan told me I must wait there for a friend of hers . . .

I am that friend, Isabeau. Had you not guessed? I watched and waited for you, knowing Meghan had sent you to me. I saw you had wandered astray and so I walked the Old Way to find you. The Celestines may not walk the forests and hills freely anymore, as you know, so I had to take a great chance . . . Shadows darken the Old Way, as they have always done, and I am weak without my kin and afraid . . .

What is your name?

Again the Celestine made the low humming noise in her throat, and Isabeau saw in her mind's eyes the shadows of clouds racing over fields of wild wheat. *Cloudshadow.*

Yes, ye can call me that, since you cannot speak our language. That is what Meghan always called me . . . Take the saddle, Isabeau NicFaghan, and ride for Dùn Gorm.

Then thank ye, I will guard it well, Isabeau replied formally, and received into her arms the saddle and bridle from the cluricaun, who had been staggering comically under its weight as he waited.

If you make it safely to Rhyssmadill, send Meghan this message. Cloudshadow of the Celestine sends greetings and warnings. Tell her to remember the dark constellations, for it is they that bear the message she seeks in the skies. Tell her Samhain, the first day of winter, is the time, and she must make ready.

Isabeau nodded.

You are tired and your injuries pain you. I will see if I can heal you. At the stroke of midnight, it shall be the beginning of the spring equinox, when day at last reaches the same length as night. It is a time when the energies run strongly, and I will try and tap them to find the strength I will need. The infection has dug its claws in deep, I am afraid. It will not be an easy healing.

Turning to the Celestine, Isabeau felt a shudder go through her as she suddenly realized the strange folds of skin in the center of her forehead had rolled back and a bright eye was glaring at her from between the wrinkled lids. Isabeau was transfixed, unable to look away. The Celestine regarded her with her third eye for a long time, then slowly the folds of skin closed and the eye was gone.

Isabeau, your injuries worsen. I see great pain washing around you. Come let me touch you, Isabeau. It is midnight, and the tide of the seasons is turning.

For some reason, Isabeau was reluctant, perhaps because the Celestine's third eye was so unnerving. Cloudshadow held out her long-fingered hands and slowly Isabeau moved forward until she was only a foot away. The Celestine smiled and the clear eyes regarded her kindly. *Do not be afraid. If I do not heal you, you shall die, Isabeau. I do not wish that to happen. It shall hurt, but better a clean hurt now than the slow agony of that poisoned blood. Trust me.*

Isabeau nodded slowly, and felt the Celestine reach out and lay her hands on her forehead. There were several sharp flashes of agony, a strange roaring noise that filled her ears, then slowly, a sweet pain that filled her blood, rose like a flood, then gently receded. Then all pain was gone, although she was left light-headed and her hand felt strange.

I could do nothing else, the Celestine said, in her usual cryptic way. *I am not a powerful healer and you have a long journey ahead. I had to remove the infection . . .*

Isabeau nodded, wishing she could lie down for a while. Her body felt odd, too light and too thin, though the consistent, throbbing pain in her hand was gone, replaced by an odd sense of nothingness.

Fare you well, Isabeau NicFaghan, was all the Celestine said then, but she touched her palm gently to Isabeau's cheek and smiled in her grave way.

Isabeau nodded, and repeated the words. *Fare ye well, Cloudshadow.*

The Celestine then rose and glided down the staircase, the room growing dark as she left. Isabeau rose to follow, trying to heft the saddle without jarring her hand. She found carrying the saddle with only one hand very difficult, and though the cluricaun attempted to help her, he was so excited and boisterous that he hurt her quite badly in the attempt. He had been so silent and still during the entire episode with the Celestine that Isabeau had almost forgotten he was there. Now her restraining presence was lifted, he chortled and capered about, the chain of bright objects around his neck jangling loudly. He lead Isabeau back to her bed of cushions and carpets in the old kitchen, gave her water and nut bread with soft cheese to eat, and left her there to sleep. Isabeau thought the many mysteries she had been given to ponder would keep her awake, but so exhausted was she that she slipped into sleep as soon as her body relaxed into the bed.

When she woke, in the dim grayness that comes just before dawn, she peeled back the blood-stained bandages to examine her hand and only then did she understand the Celestine's last cryptic words. With sorrow she saw she had lost two fingers of her left hand, the fingers which had been most badly infected. She had only two fingers and a thumb remaining, and these were stiff and crooked, and badly scarred. Although the scars were fully healed, they were an angry red and very itchy. She stared at her ruined hand for a long time, then slipped it back inside her sling.

Feeling only a cold shakiness, she gathered her things together, then pulled the saddle toward her so she could examine it more closely. Of simple make, with no decorations or embroidery, the saddle was a shabby, worn affair. Apart from crimson-dyed reins, the bridle was unprepossessing, and quite unlike the magnificent harness Isabeau had expected. On reflection, however, she thought this was probably for the better. It was going to be difficult enough not to draw attention to herself riding a stallion like Lasair through the fields of Blèssem. A kingly saddle and bridle would have drawn eyes, and aroused suspicions. And the saddle was finely made and surprisingly light given its bulk.

During the night Brun had packed her up a bundle in one of his coarse-woven blankets. Investigating, Isabeau found cotton pouches filled with salt, oats, flour and tea, potatoes, a rather moldy hank of corn, and a great wedge of hard cheese. Neatly folded on the floor was a pile of rough clothing and, turning it over in her hands, Isabeau realized Brun must have sat up all night unpicking some of his own clothes for her. There was a pair of brown knee-length breeches, a pair of leather gaiters, a boy's coarse linen shirt, a little small, and a leather jerkin. Isabeau had been rather concerned about having to ride in her dress and was sick of its confining layers, so she seized upon the clothes with relish, though dressing was very difficult with only one hand.

As soon as she felt herself ready, Brun was there and Isabeau wondered again if he could really read minds as easily as he seemed to. He carried the saddle and bridle outside for her, grunting with the exertion and staggering exaggeratedly under the weight.

The stallion's reaction to the saddle and bridle was Isabeau's first indication of the magic in Ahern's saddle. At first sight, Lasair's eyes rolled back and he danced away, telling Isabeau clearly he wanted no more of these instruments of control. She held out the bridle to him and let him sniff it, and immediately his ear pricked forward and he nuzzled her arm. When she slipped the straps over his nose, he took the bit between his teeth with no head-tossing or jibing, and he stood patiently for her when she heaved the saddle onto his back.

Isabeau had never saddled a horse before and she thought it would take her some time to work out what straps went where. However, in moments it was done and with a sense of achievement she tied her bundle behind it and lead Lasair to a tree stump so she could mount.

At first the saddle felt odd beneath her and strangely precarious, and she had no idea what to do with the reins. In the end she settled for holding them in her one good hand and twining the fingers of the same hand in Lasair's mane, as she was used to.

The goodbyes were said awkwardly, and she was touched when Brun held her foot in the stirrup, and said, "I have a riddle for ye, Is'beau . . . There are two splendid horses, one as black as pitch, t'other o' shining crystal. Each runs ahead o' t'other but they never catch each other. Wha' are they?"

Isabeau had begun to work out some of the cluricaun's strange riddles, and hesitantly, after several minutes' thought, she answered, "Night and day?"

Brun was delighted that she had at last consented to play with him, and he danced a high-stepping jig, before clinging to her boot again. "Ride as fast as they, Is'beau! Ride fast and canny!" As she began to move he ran with her, holding on to her boot, shouting instructions and directions that Isabeau did her best to remember. Soon he fell behind, and Lasair broke into a smooth canter.

Isabeau was still easily tired from her fever and she expected to need many breaks and rests, at least in the first day's journey. To her surprise, she felt quite fresh by the time the sun was directly overhead and Lasair was only slightly damp beneath the saddle. She decided to push on as long as she could before stopping to rest and eat, but by late afternoon was still feeling only slightly fatigued. She must have been hardened up by the riding before Caeryla, she decided, pulling Lasair to a halt.

However, when she dismounted, a wave of giddiness overcame her and she had to sit in the shade of a tree a while before she could gain the energy to open her pack and eat. She had intended to remove the saddle and bridle so Lasair could crop the grass in comfort, but so great was her exhaustion, she decided to leave it on until they stopped for the night. She ate and drank, and was just deciding to sleep for a while in the comfort of the sweet-scented turf, when the talisman began to burn and tingle against her side. At once Isabeau was tense and looked about her, but the clearing seemed deserted. There was a rustle of leaves and a crack of a stick, and immediately Isabeau got to her feet and shoved everything back into her bundle before strapping it behind the saddle.

Just as she put her foot in the stirrup to heave herself into the saddle, there was a rush of motion and a pack of horned women ran from the shelter of the trees toward her. Naked, their muscular bodies gleamed with sweat and she saw that a spine of stiff hair ran down their backbones, finishing in a short tail with a tuft of hair at the end. The horns of each were different. There was one with a single horn, long as Isabeau's arm and rapier-sharp. Another had the spreading antlers of a *geal'teas;* another, four short stumpy horns like a goat's. Each had a wild, gloating expression on their faces and as they ran they yelled and shouted in blood-curdling tones.

Isabeau was in the saddle and her heels hard in Lasair's sides in a flash. Lasair bolted gladly, his ears flat against his skull, his powerful hindquarters heaving beneath her. The Horned Ones were close behind, however, running swiftly as deer. The one with the rapier horn came close enough to graze Lasair's rump, bringing blood swelling; and another grasped Isabeau's stirrup so she had to smash her face with her boot to shake her. As the five-horned woman tumbled down, Isabeau urged Lasair toward a gap in the trees, leaning as close to his neck as she could. The stallion lengthened his stride and soared through the gap, so that the Horned One waiting in the tree branches misjudged her leap. Instead of knocking Isabeau from the saddle, she slammed into her, unbalancing her but falling backward herself so she landed heavily on the ground. Isabeau clung to the saddle and wondered how she had ever managed to stay on.

It was only when they left the shelter of the forests and struck across open ground that the horned woman fell back, and by that time Lasair was badly winded and flecked with gray foam. It was sunset, and the rolling fields were lit with a glorious light, vivid against a backdrop of storm clouds. Lasair slowed into an easy canter, and a fresh, green-scented breeze cooled their sweaty faces. Isabeau felt a great sense of freedom and salvation pour over her. Already she was free of the mysterious forests of Aslinn and into Blèssem—she could not believe how far they had traveled in just one day.

It was fully dark before they at last stopped and rested. Lasair buried his face contentedly into a field of fresh, young oats, and Isabeau made herself a cheese and herb omelette from some eggs she found in a nest in the hedge. She built the fire in the shelter of a stone wall so the flames could not be seen, and banked it low after she had cooked her meal. Already there were clear signs of the crofters of Blèssem. A red road ran decorously between stone walls, a patchwork of lush pastures spreading out on either side. Here and there small crofts broke the uniformity of hill and field, lamplight sparkling from the windows. Overhead a canopy of stars spread, and Isabeau, lying on her back in sweet meadow grass, pondered their mysteries, wondering what Cloudshadow had meant by the dark constellations.

Isabeau slept for only a few hours before rising and again saddling and mounting the stallion, an awkward job with only one hand. She had decided Blèssem was too populated for her to risk riding much by day, and she knew the crofters had a reputation for mistrusting strangers, especially strangers with an air of witchery about them. When the Rìgh had first passed the proclamation against *uilebheistean* in the months before the Day of Betrayal, the people of Blèssem had rejoiced and had been the most assiduous in enforcing it. They had been a little troubled by the secret raids on the Towers and the Decree Against Witches which followed, but since they had never trusted the magic powers of the witches, they muttered it was probably for the best. In the sixteen years since the overthrow of the witches, the people of Blèssem had easily come to believe they had always thought magic and witchcraft evil, and were proud that their country was clean of any sorcery. It would definitely be far safer for Isabeau to travel at night and spend the days resting.

It rained before dawn, and Isabeau had trouble finding a safe place to stop. Here the land had been cultivated for centuries, and there were few woods in which to conceal herself and the horse. It was fully light and she had already seen the silhouette of workers trudging along the horizon before she at last found a copse of trees thick enough to hide in. Even so, children playing hide and seek woke her a few hours later, and she had to hide in a tree, her heart thumping. She found she was terrified of meeting anyone, and thought grimly that her experience at the hands of the Grand-Questioner had given her a legacy of nightmares and starting at shadows, as well as a ruined hand.

The beauty of the cornfields under moonlight soothed her, so she rode without thinking about very much at all. She found she and the stallion had grown so attuned to each other she barely had a thought before the stallion reacted. Many times she was so tired she barely realized they had stopped until she looked up and saw the safety of overhanging branches around them and knew Lasair had chosen them a place to rest. Other times vague anxieties troubled her and the horse would lengthen his stride so the moment of unease was left far behind. Soon the clear weather broke, and day after day of chilly rain followed. Isabeau was hungry, for her supplies had soon run out, and so the need to forage slowed her down. Several times she crept into some crofter's cottage and stole bread or a pie left cooling on the table, or pulled vegetables from a neat little garden. She had lost all guilt over her thieving ways, knowing only that she had to survive, to make it to Rhyssmadill.

Unable to keep herself dry, fever often swelled up and overtook her, so that her journey was broken by periods of inertia when she lay in someone's barn and stared out at the rain, unable to find the energy to search for food. On one such night she had taken shelter in a stable, hiding Lasair in a back stall and feeding him handfuls of the farmer's good grain. Hunger and exhaustion warred against each other in her body so that she drifted in and out of sleep, dreaming of feasts with tables groaning with food. Suddenly she woke with a jerk and huddled deeper into the scratchy straw as a shadow passed in front of the stable door.

Feeling uneasy and vulnerable, Isabeau wrapped her filthy plaid about her and cautiously knelt and peered out into the yard. Across the cobblestones crouched the old farmhouse, light spilling from the kitchen door. She saw a shape flitter against the light. Nerves jangled everywhere in her body. She had seen a shape like that before.

Shaking with trepidation but drawn forward by an irresistible curiosity, Isabeau climbed up into the loft so that she could see across the stable yard. Through the kitchen window she saw two small children playing with sheep's knuckles while their mother stirred a pot on the fire. From a chair that had its back to the window she saw two long legs protruding, a pink toe peeping out from a hole in a woolly sock. The mother turned to say something but, instead, her mouth fell open and she screamed. Isabeau could see her eyes protruding and her mouth as wide as a mine shaft, but could hear nothing. As the father leaped out of the chair, a piece of wood he was whittling falling out of his lap and rolling across the floor, Isabeau saw the shadow detach itself from the door and step smoothly inside.

Isabeau felt like screaming herself. Seven feet tall and ghostly gray, the creature had wings like a dragonfly's—stiff and iridescent gray—and a calm, beautiful face. Remembering all too well the last time she had seen a Mesmerd, Isabeau wanted to cry out and warn the crofters, but it was too late, both mother and father were gazing at the winged ghost with a fascinated smile, and the Mesmerd had bent and scooped up both children, one in each pair of arms. Smoothly and silently the Mesmerd turned and left the cottage, with the parents still standing in the middle of the floor, idiotic smiles fixed to their faces, and the children equally as still and hypnotized in the fairy's arms.

As the Mesmerd crossed the stable yard, it turned and looked up at the opening into the loft straight at Isabeau, who immediately ducked her head down, trembling. For five agonizing minutes she lay as still as a stone, waiting for the moment when the Mesmerd's clawlike hand would touch her. At last she realized it was gone, and sat up, seeing the farmer and his wife still standing in the same positions. As she watched, the farmer stirred and the smile faded from his face, to be replaced by horror and fear. She watched him slap his wife across the cheek to rouse her, and then the wailing and crying began. Quickly as possible, Isabeau gathered together her things and saddled

Lasair, knowing a search would be mounted. She had to be gone.

That night, as she rode through the endlessly driving rain, fearful questions hammered at her. Why had the Mesmerd stolen the children? Why had it not killed the parents as it had so lovingly killed Seychella? Most of all, why had she been spared? She was sure the Mesmerd had been aware of her presence—why else had it turned and stared up at her as she crouched in the straw? Was it waiting for her out in the wild night, the howling storm? In a panic, she kicked Lasair in the ribs and he shot forward, racing over the fields, careless of stones or coney holes or ditches.

After seeing the Mesmerd, Isabeau again began to fear pursuit, and her nightmares returned with frightening force. She took to riding through most of the day as well as the night, hidden behind veils of rain, her plaid drawn up to cover her face. Small villages huddled in every fold of the land, and it was now rare to ride more than a few miles without passing a croft or farmhouse, smoke rising from their chimneys into the damp air.

Most of the time, she existed in a daze, clinging to Lasair's saddle as he cantered through the streaming rain. They barely stopped, either to sleep or eat, for the magic of the saddle meant both felt reasonably fresh while riding, but pulverized with exhaustion once they stopped. As soon as she lifted the saddle off Lasair's back, he would begin to tremble with exhaustion, and soon she never removed it at all, riding day and night, sleeping in the saddle and only dismounting to search for food or to find a bush to squat behind.

One night they cantered up a steep incline to find a blaze of light and movement on the other side. A procession of torches was winding its way along the road toward her and, in a panic, Isabeau urged Lasair off the road and behind a wall, admonishing him to be quiet. In the darkness she crouched, sure the procession was angry villagers or soldiers come to capture her again. Then the cavalcade came closer and she heard laughter and jesting, and saw men and women dancing together and holding hands, crowned with leaves and flowers.

Beltane, she thought with a pang. *It is Beltane already, the first of May.* She had been riding for over a month.

At the head of the parade danced a tall, thin man, dressed in leafy branches from head to toe. Isabeau peered over the wall in delight. *The Green Man . . . I have always wanted to see the Green Man . . .*

She would have liked to follow the laughing, dancing figures and seen the end of the May Day celebrations, but with a sigh she mounted as soon as they had passed, and set her face to the south again. Later that night she saw another village in the distance and could not resist sidling close to the village square to watch the bonfire and the dancing. They had just crowned the May Queen and were tying up the maypole in honor of her. A feast was spread out on tables in the square and, overcome by a temptation she could not resist, Isabeau crept from tree to tree until the tables were tantalizingly close. She waited until all attention was on the acrobatics being performed in the center, then dived under the cover of the white cloth. There she lay all night, putting out a dirty hand and pulling whatever her fingers encountered back into her shelter. For the first time in weeks she was able to eat to her heart's satisfaction, watching the show from under her cover and wishing she could dance and laugh like the other girls, but feeling a chasm between them like the Great Divide.

Isabeau watched until the flames were beginning to die down, then slipped away again to resume her silent journey. This time though her pack was crammed with remnants of bread and roasted vegetables and baked cheese and mushroom pies, and waves of dizziness no longer washed over her.

Two days later Isabeau and Lasair came within sight of the river, winding down the valley in silver loops that once almost met itself before twisting away again. To the south lay the flatlands of Clachan, which had once been flooded with the winter tides every year. The Clachans had built retaining walls and causeways and canals with locks to control the wildly swinging tides, and nurtured the soil with seaweed and manure until it was almost as rich as the fields of Blèssem.

Far in the distance she could see great rocky crags thrusting up through the soil to tower above the flat plains around, and it was here the villages and towns were built, far above the threat of the king tide that every winter rushed in and threatened to drown the land again. Although the walls and canals controlled the tide better than any other measure, the tide was still an unpredictable thing, and the people of Clachan had learned the hard lessons of living near the terrible power of the sea. It was on their shores that most of the great battles with the Fairgean had taken place, and here that generation after generation of Clachans had struggled to make a living. It was only since Aedan's Pact and the defeat of the Fairgean that they had succeeded. The people Clachan were hard-working, dour and suspicious, and Isabeau would have to be even more careful.

The road she had been following eventually joined the royal highway, and Isabeau joined the hordes of workers, merchants, mercenaries, beggars and footsore travelers heading toward Dùn Gorm, the blue city. Keeping her tam-o'-shanter pulled low over her hair, Isabeau wished the rain would return to help conceal her as she tried to work out a plan of action. She had to cross the river to get to the palace and this posed a problem, for the ferry would be guarded and the river was too swift and wide for her to attempt a crossing. On a sudden inspiration, Isabeau brewed up an evil-smelling potion and washed her hair in it. The dye, made from elder and bay leaves, did not cover the ruddiness of her hair as well as she had hoped, but the dirty brown that resulted was still far more inconspicuous than her original color.

She then covered Lasair with old sacks and tried to make him walk more like a broken-down workhorse than a proud stallion. Since she had traveled the distance from Aslinn to the Rhyllster in less than half the time it should have taken her, and both she and Lasair were greatly travel stained, this was an easier task than it might otherwise have been. Their dirtiness and their exhaustion made it much easier for them to pass, through one guard scrutinized Isabeau's face carefully, making her heart thump so hard she was sure he would hear it.

The ferry rolled alarmingly as it crossed the rushing river, and Isabeau hid her face against Lasair's shoulder, triumph and gladness welling up in her.

Gently, gently, she admonished herself. *We're no' there yet.*

Then they rounded the curve of the river and there was

the Berhtfane, crowded with ship masts like toothpicks in a jar. Only the stretch of water before the palace was clear and the water shone a heavenly blue, the delicate spires of Rhyssmadill rising behind. Built on one of the rocky crags which reared like fingers out of the plain, Rhyssmadill seemed to float in the haze above the waters, its sharp towers shining. Despite herself, joy shot through her and she touched the pouch at her belt.

She removed Ahearn Horse-Tamer's bridle and saddle in the forests behind Rhyssmadill, having to fight the weakness that came over her as soon as she put foot to ground. The moment the saddle was removed, Lasair stumbled to his knees, his eyes glazing with exhaustion. Isabeau rubbed him down with a damp cloth, and brought him armfuls of sweet-smelling grass. He lipped at the grass, too tired even to eat, and she rubbed his ears and promised him oats, tears of remorse stinging her eyes. She was shocked at the effects of their journey and was beginning to understand the effects of the magic saddle. When Isabeau had first met Lasair, he had been a full-chested stallion, glossy and well-fleshed, still in the prime of his life. Now he was so thin his ribs stuck through his rough, bedraggled coat, and his mane was tangled with burrs.

Despite her own weakness, and her fear of being caught, Isabeau risked a journey into Dùn Gorm to steal him oats and strengthening medicine, and these she mixed into a warm mash and fed him by hand till his strength returned. The saddle and bridle she hid in the trunk of a hollow tree, and with what little strength still remained to her, protected it with a magical ward. For three days she stayed with Lasair, caring for him, whispering endearments, covering him with her plaid and bringing him sweet herbs and water. Then, when he was well enough, she made her way toward Rhyssmadill, leaning on the stallion, the talisman hidden in her clothing.

At the edge of the forest, they parted company, tears wet on Isabeau's cheek. "I'll come soon, to check on ye," she promised. "Be careful . . ."

Lasair shook himself, snorting loudly, and she hugged him fiercely before letting him canter away.

He'll be safe in the forests, she thought. *No one will go so near the sea, and he's too canny to let himself be seen.*

Then, taking her courage in both hands, Isabeau went to breach the Rìgh's palace. *Latifa is the name, Latifa.*

She approached the slender stone bridge guarded by a full contingent of guards in plumed helmets and with long spears. At first they thought she was a beggar and tried to drive her away, but she whispered Latifa's name and it worked like a charm, winning her a smile and kind instructions toward the kitchen.

Weariness was pressing down on her like a giant hand but she managed slowly to make her way, leaning against the wall for support and stopping every few steps to allow her dizziness to pass. She made her way down a narrow stone walkway between the palace wall and the outer ring, and then she was in a garden, planted with herbs and vegetables, fruit trees espaliered against the walls. A kitchen maid in a blue dress and a mobcap, digging up carrots from the garden, looked at her curiously and tried to shoo her away but, on hearing Latifa's name, smiled and pointed toward the courtyard at the other end. A great arched door stood open, and delicious smells wafted out, along with a babble of laughter and gossip. Cautiously Isabeau looked inside, and there was the kitchen, a huge bright room with four fires burning along its sides. A tiny fat old woman, with twinkling black eyes like currants and a squashed brown face, saw her and came toward her, beaming.

"At last! I'd given up on ye, Is'beau! My sister's grand-bairn, come to stay wi' me at last! Come in, come in. Are ye hungry? Here, have one o' my gingerbread men, they're famous in these parts . . ."

Isabeau took it gratefully, warm from the oven and delicious as it was. Latifa fussed about her kindly, exclaiming over the travel-stained sling and the dark shadows under her eyes. "Come up to my room, lassie," she said, and feeling unaccustomedly shy, Isabeau followed her obediently. Halfway up the stairs such a wave of dizziness came over that she almost fell, and the old cook came back, and half carried her up the remaining steps.

Once in the privacy of her room, a remarkable change came over Latifa. The cheerful bustling cook was replaced by a keen-eyed hard-mouthed woman who fired questions at Isabeau while swiftly unravelling the sling with accustomed fingers.

"In Eà's name, where have ye been? Meghan has been fretting herself sick about ye, no' to mention the talisman. Do ye have it?"

Isabeau nodded, and rather reluctantly slipped her hand under her shirt to find the black pouch. Contrary to her expectations, Latifa did not open the bag, but merely felt through its material anxiously. Her face cleared and she smiled, her whole face changing. "Thank Eà! Now we have all three parts, that is if Meghan can travel safely through to meet us wi' the last third! The Banrìgh has put the MacRuraich on her trail, and Eà knows they never give up once they catch the scent. I have been guarding my third wi' great anxiety all these years and very relieved I will be to be free o' it."

"I do no' understand," Isabeau said wearily but just then Latifa undid the last bandage and drew in her breath sharply.

"By the Beard o' the Centaur, what have ye done to yourself?"

"I was tortured," Isabeau said and to her surprise, began to cry. Once the tears began she could not stop, and an intense longing for Meghan rose in her throat, almost suffocating her.

Latifa sat beside her, and put her plump arms around her, murmuring and comforting, but still Isabeau sobbed for her guardian. "Sshh, sshh, my dear, Meghan will be with us soon enough. So ye fell into the hands o' the Awl? Silly silly lass. However did ye escape? No, no, time enough for storytelling later. Let's get ye into bed."

Being the head cook and housekeeper at the palace had its advantages. Within moments Latifa had maids scurrying about, bringing pails of hot water to pour into the hipbath hidden behind a screen, hot strengthening tea for Isabeau to drink, and bottles of ointments and medicine. Isabeau sat in the bath, her eyes closed, as Latifa washed her hair for the first time in three months, the dark stain of the dye dissolving in the warm water. When she was clean, Latifa rubbed sweet-scented ointment into the livid scars and carefully strapped up the crippled hand again. Then Isabeau was tucked up in Latifa's own bed, luxuriantly stretching and turning her cheek into the softness of the pillow. For three months, since the Red Guards had driven them from their tree house, Isabeau had slept on the ground, in hedge-rows and tree-roots, haystacks and ditches. She thought drowsily that she was going to enjoy living at Rhyssmadill, at least for a while.

Sani the Seer

Four stories above Isabeau's head, the old servant Sani stared into the magic mirror, a strange smile tugging the corners of her mouth.

So, Latifa, she thought, *ye are in league with the Arch-Sorceress. I always thought so, though Maya would never believe me, the foolish bairn. Well, well, so Meghan's own apprentice has joined us. There canna be another with that color hair.*

She looked down at the mirror again at the reflection of the sleeping girl, her damp hair spread over the pillow like tongues of flame. She smiled again. *I wonder . . . what's in that pouch o' nyx hair? What did the girl carry? It has to be strong magic else the nyx magic would no' be needed. Latifa did not dare remove it from concealment . . .*

Wrapping the mirror back in its fraying silk, Sani locked it away in its box. *Soon, my liege, soon . . . soon we will hold the land in our fist. The tidal wave o' Jor's wrath is rising, and to sand these rebels shall be ground!*

The Black Jewels Trilogy

by Anne Bishop

"Darkly mesmerizing...fascinatingly different."
—Locus

This is the story of the heir to a dark throne, a magic more powerful than that of the High Lord of Hell, and an ancient prophecy. These three books tell of a ruthless game of politics and intrigue, magic and betrayal, love and sacrifice, destiny and fulfillment, as the Princess Jaenelle struggles to become that which she was meant to be.

Daughter of the Blood
Book One

Heir to the Shadows
Book Two

Queen of the Darkness
Book Three